Dark Hero

Reluctant Heroes Series
Book One

Lily Silver

Lily Silver

Dark Hero

Reluctant Heroes Series
Book One

By Lily Silver

Copyright: Lily Silver 2012

This is a work of historical fiction. All characters are a product of the author's imagination. Any resemblance to actual persons in history is coincidental and not intentional.

Cover Design by John Stuttgen, Graphic Designer

Cover Photos: Dreamstime & IStock Photos

Dedication

Thank you to the following people:

To Daniel, my love, my companion and my best friend;
my reclusive Dark Hero.

To Denise Wittman, Mary Grace Murphy and
Christine Olson-Mader; Thank you for your hard work
& patience in proofing the final manuscript.

A *Special Thank You* to Holly, Mary and Barb
for reading a very rough draft of this book several years ago.
These wonderful, intelligent women offered the first sparks
of enthusiasm, encouraging my writing from the beginning.

Thank You Barb Raffin & Bob Rogers of WisRWA
for reviewing and giving critiques of the first chapter.

"Out of suffering have emerged the strongest souls;
The most massive characters are seamed with scars."
Edwin Hubbell Chapin

Chapter One

The Wealthy Mayfair District, London, 1795
The thumping scrape of unsteady boots on the stairs pierced the tranquil summer night.

Startled awake, Elizabeth sat bolt upright in bed as the forbidden book hit the floor with an incriminating thud. The familiar gnawing grew in her belly. This time Mrs. Radcliffe's deliciously horrid Gothic novel was not to blame. The heavy boots paused outside her door. Her eyes flew to the brass knob gilded by orange firelight as she waited breathlessly for it to turn. She watched the slight twist of the knob and heard the protective click.

It was locked. She released her captive breath.

As danger moved past her door with an unsteady gait, singing an old army ditty hopelessly out of tune, Elizabeth slipped from her bed to retrieve her treasure. She caressed the raised leather spine of the book, wishing she could disappear inside it. With fourteen years to her credit and quite sensible in all other matters, Elizabeth had lost her heart to her dark hero, a fantasy figure she created and nourished by devouring the Gothic tales her mother forbade.

Oh, her gothic hero might be off-putting at first. Once the heroine understood him, she realized he was not such a bad sort after all, despite his tormented past and dark secrets. Hidden beneath that sinister exterior was a kind and lonely man, desperate for love and the right woman to understand him. More to the point, her dark hero could be depended upon to step in when his beloved was in a difficult patch. He always appeared just when the heroine needed . . .

A cry of pain came from mama's room, the cruel reality shattering her beloved daydream.

The captain was home. He was drunk and in a nasty mood. That was about all that was dependable about her stepfather, Elizabeth thought, with no little resentment.

Stuffing *The Mysteries of Udolpho* beneath her mattress, Elizabeth listened to the noise beyond her refuge. Papa always came home late, in his cups and belligerent toward any who dared cross his path. He bellowed threats at Mama, usually from the outside of her locked bedroom door. Tonight, something was different. Tonight, Mama was yelling back.

Elizabeth tiptoed to the door, unlocked it and opened it a crack. "--I won't allow it!" Her elegant mother, who never raised her voice for it was unladylike to do so, screamed at her stepfather. "Sheila stays—she's Elizabeth's grandmother, her only O'Flaherty kin."

"—and no kin of mine." The captain interrupted. "We can't waste money on servants we don't need." Something went crashing in Mama's room to punctuate the captain's words. "And the tutors go, Angela. We can't afford them." He insisted.

"It is an investment, William." Mother spoke in a calmer tone, attempting to appease the beast. "Elizabeth has every expectation of marrying well, bringing us affluent connections. Her father was a Viscount—"

"Aye, an Irishman." Her stepfather spat. "Hanged for treason."

A floorboard squeaked beneath her bare foot. Elizabeth paused, offering a silent prayer that the noise didn't give her away as she lingered outside her mother's open door.

"No one knows, unless you intend to advertise it. When she makes her come out in society, she'll be known as the granddaughter of the Earl of Greystowe."

"And a grand good piece of *shite* that gets us, woman. Your high and mighty father hasn't darkened our door for well over a year."

"He still provides our support. The future of the Wentworth line rests in his grandchildren."

"On Michael, my son, not that Irishman's leavings you saddled me with."

It shouldn't hurt anymore, but it did hurt, dreadfully. As the only father she knew, Elizabeth craved a few crumbs of affection from the captain. She was the flaw in their perfect English family, the Irish taint in the bloodlines. The captain never let her forget it.

"Papa set up the trust to support *my* children, not your gambling habits!" Mother rallied in rare defiance to the tyrant who ruled their home. "Sheila O'Flaherty stays. I will not toss her to the streets like unwanted baggage."

"Damn it, woman, this is my house!"

"No, it is *mine*! Papa bought it for me, not you. I could petition the courts for a divorce. With Papa's connections it shouldn't be any trouble. He'd still send the quarterly support to me while you would be out on the streets, begging like the other soldiers--umphh!"

There was the terrible sound of fist against flesh that never failed to make Elizabeth cringe. Heeding her grandmother's warning about not interfering when Captain and Mrs. Fletcher fought, Elizabeth took cover behind the heavy curtains framing the open hall windows.

"Divorce me? We'll see about that." Her stepfather marched past the curtains, pulling her mother along behind him with his fist wrapped in her long, dark hair. Mama had no choice but to follow as his fist in her hair and his arm braced about her neck made escape impossible. And Mama's rare bravado had waned.

Elizabeth cautiously peered out from the thick hangings. Fletcher stood behind her mother at the top of the stairs. "Useless bitch, you can't divorce me if you're dead." He shoved her.

"Mama!" Elizabeth ran down the hallway that didn't seem half as long before.

It was too late. Mama was lying still at the bottom of the stairs.

Before she could go to her mother, large hands seized her and slammed her hard against the wall. Elizabeth stiffened and clenched her jaw, determined to put on a bold face and not betray her fear before her enemy, as her grandmother O'Flaherty had taught her. Granny Sheila was right, if you cried and whimpered

7

before him, it gave him pleasure. If you held your ground and refused to show your pain, he lost interest and sought weaker prey. Elizabeth eyed him with defiance even as her eyes stung and her throat tightened from terror.

"Spying on me again, eh?"

"You pushed her—I saw it!" Elizabeth accused, determined not to succumb to tears.

"You saw nothing." A flurry of slaps assaulted her face. "You hear me—*nothing!*"

Captain Fletcher held her by the throat as he talked in that quiet, calculated voice. "Your Mother tripped and fell down the stairs." His hot, sour breath assaulted her nose as he leaned close. "She gets woozy sometimes, what with all the Laudanum she indulges in.

"Mama doesn't take Laudanum."

"But that's what you're going to tell the constable. Tell him you awoke to a noise and found your Mama at the bottom of the stairs. Wait twenty minutes after I leave, then summon the constable. Ask him to send the runners to my club to notify me that there was an accident--"

"I'll tell them I saw you push her."

His grip tightened, squeezing slowly about Elizabeth's neck, cutting off her air. "Who would believe the daughter of a traitor over a loyal servant of his Majesties Regiment? No one, I tell you, *no one!* Talk and they'll hang you at Tyburn; both you and your crazy old granny. I'll tell them she's a witch. I'll tell them she made you murder your mother."

Elizabeth crumpled at his words. She was growing lightheaded. She nodded.

At last, he released his grip about her throat. "Go ahead. Tell them girl. We'll just see who ends up hanging at the end of a rope!"

Time dissolved. Elizabeth was sitting at the foot of the stairs, hugging herself in an effort to recover her wits. Her mother's body was lying before her. The captain left--left her to clean up his mess. Her limbs were quaking so she feared they would never be still. Mama was dead. Murdered by her husband. And now

Elizabeth must lie to the authorities, lest she and her dear grandmother pay the price for Captain Fletcher's sins.

"Mama--I'm sorry." She choked out the words as she sat staring at the crumpled body of her mother, a raven haired china doll with empty blue eyes that gazed up, seeing nothing. Blood pooled from behind Mama's head. As she studied her mother's corpse, the air was suddenly sucked out of Elizabeth's lungs. She whimpered. Her body would not be satisfied with that weak noise. The sound transformed into a deep, guttural cry that cut through her soul like shards of glass. Agonizing sobs rocked her frame.

A hand gripping her shoulder sent screams through her as Elizabeth released the pent up horror.

"My poor lass." It was Granny Sheila's gnarled hand. Granny Sheila was Elizabeth's paternal grandmother. The thin, frail form surrounded her and drew her close.

"He killed her. I saw it. He pushed her." Elizabeth sobbed against the sagging bosom and hunched shoulders that had given her comfort throughout her life. She told her grandmother O'Flaherty what had taken place, and of her stepfather's looming threat.

"Best do as he says for now, child." The old woman cautioned. "He'll not go unpunished, I promise. For now, we must bide our time while we're in the enemy's camp."

"I'll send Lucy out to the constable."

"Lucy left this evening." Granny Sheila informed her. "Susan went with her."

Elizabeth clung to her grandmother and silently absorbed the knowledge. She knew why the newest maids resigned their post, like so many others before them. Papa frightened them with his drunken tirades and unlike the family they served, the hired help had the option to leave this house. Aside from Granny Sheila, only Cook, a stout woman in her fifties, had remained over the years. Cook slept in the cellar off the kitchen and kept a cleaver ever at the ready in case thieves broke in during the night, or so she told the children. Elizabeth knew better.

"Kenny can go for the constable." Sheila whispered. She soothed the hair from Elizabeth's wet face in that old, familiar way. Kenny was a chore boy, an orphan who had nowhere to go,

9

save the workhouse so he stayed, ignoring the madness behind his attic door. Old Sheila rose to go rouse the boy.

Kenny left and later returned with the constable. Elizabeth reported exactly what her stepfather told her to and that was it. They accepted the lie without question. Mama's body had been moved upstairs to be prepared for burial.

Elizabeth sat alone on the bottom stair. It was quiet, deadly quiet. Pink streams illuminated the fan window above the front door. Papa was home, in his study, snoring loudly. Sleep came easy for someone who lacked a conscience. Elizabeth nibbled her lower lip and stared at the deep red stain on the parquet flooring in front of her bare feet. She'd scrubbed and scrubbed after the men l Mama's body was taken upstairs. The wood remained stained.

She looked at her hands in the red light of dawn. A sob broke the awful silence. *If only Kieran were here. He'd know what to do.*

Kieran was her elder brother. He disappeared mysteriously before she was born. She grew up imagining him as her savior. *Her hero.* Elizabeth often imagined how different her life would be if Kieran were here. He'd been born in Ireland years before their father died and Mama had moved back to London after marrying Captain Fletcher. Kieran was her elder by nine years. He'd be a man now—able to march in and confront the captain, able to take her away from the Captain and his cruel ways forever.

Ah, but it wouldn't answer to cling to childish fantasies any longer. Kieran was dead, just like her parents. She was an orphan now. Kieran couldn't save her. No one could.

Two nights later, Sheila O'Flaherty crept silently down the servant's stairs to make a quick reckoning of the house before she went about her work. It wouldn't do to have Captain Fletcher catch her creeping about the Mayfair townhouse in the night with a knife in her hand.

Alas, her investigation showed that the captain was out for the evening, gambling and drinking, no doubt, on the eve before his wife's burial. Sheila glided out to the kitchen garden to collect rose petals and rosemary under the waxing moon. The cool June earth felt good beneath her bare feet. The warm breeze caressed her loosened white hair like a patient lover.

Stuffing the herbs into her apron pocket, she entered the house and moved silently into the parlor. Elizabeth was asleep in the chair next to the open coffin, keeping watch over the dead in the Irish way as Sheila instructed. The blood of chieftains and Druids flowed through Elizabeth's veins, and one day she would take her place as seer and priestess of Clan O'Flaherty. Sheila took great care to raise her granddaughter to be strong and brave like her Celtic ancestors, not weak like her English mother.

Sheila made the sign to ward off the evil eye. It wasn't right to think ill of the dead, but Elizabeth's mother had the mettle of jelly. The silly woman could have petitioned the courts after her first husband died in order to keep the castle and land for their son, Kieran. Angela Wentworth O'Flaherty was English, after all, and the daughter of an earl! It would have been no trouble for her to swear fealty to the crown and promise to raise her son as a loyal English subject. The English would have liked replacing the rebel father with a son loyal to the crown.

Alas, the woman simply wilted and waited for another man to rescue her.

And so, the beautiful widow had fallen prey to the devious Captain Fletcher. She succumbed to his oily lies with no more sense than a goose being fattened for Sunday dinner. Angela had enough loyalty after remarrying, bless her, to insist Sheila have a place in the Fletcher household as the nanny. Sheila didn't resent being relegated to the role of servant in her daughter-in-law's new household. Nine year old Kieran and the babe Angela carried were both O'Flahertys. They would need someone to teach them the ways of their Celtic ancestors during their exile in London. And who better to train the wee ones then the household nanny?

A bitter ache rose in her chest. *Poor little Kieran, lost forever.*

As the eldest grandson of Lord Greystowe, Kieran would have inherited the title of earl and the Wentworth fortunes. T'was little wonder the lad went missing after the newly married Captain and Mrs. Fletcher arrived in London. Fletcher claimed he'd lost his stepson in the crowds on the wharf and made a show of looking for the boy for weeks afterward.

Sheila knew better. The lad was dead. There could be no other explanation. He'd been efficiently removed to make room for the captain's child to become the legal heir. Sheila couldn't prove it, and Angela, the boy's mother, refused to believe it.

Careful not to awaken her grandchild, Sheila reached into the casket and cut away a raven tendril from Angela's corpse. She hid the pouch she'd prepared beneath Angela's skirts.

Once back in her attic room, Sheila placed the dark lock of Angela's hair next to her son Shawn's length of burnished copper she had set out on the table. Reverently, she removed a curly red lock from its yellowed tissue wrapping; a snippet of Kieran's hair she'd saved from his first haircut. With moisture glazing her eyes, she pressed the soft tendril to her lips, saying a final goodbye to her eldest grandchild. She began plaiting the three tendrils together; father, mother and son into a tight braid. She used Elizabeth's silk hair ribbon to secure the plait and to bind the living with the dead in the quest for justice.

Placing a pinch of saltpeter in the bowl of burning herbs, the old woman chanted her curse as the flames shot up; "Angela Wentworth-O'Flaherty-Fletcher, may your soul never rest, may your grave lack peace, until justice is accomplished, until the wrongs done to my family are avenged. You kept silent as a grave, unwilling to speak for those without a voice, your own children. You denied them justice through cowardice; let justice be denied your murdered soul."

Sheila picked up the knife and sliced her palm open. She made a fist and let the blood drip over the twisted braid. "By the power of three, bound by blood; my blood, Shawn's blood, and Kieran's blood—O'Flaherty blood--you'll wander this earth a restless spirit until those who know the truth are willing to speak for you and set the wheel of justice turning to avenge your murdered soul." The blood soaked braid was placed in a leather pouch. All that was needed to seal the spell was fresh dirt from Angela's grave. She would have that tomorrow, at the burial.

Next, Sheila considered her charges, Elizabeth and Michael. Orphans, they were. They needed someone to claim them, take them away from Fletcher, but who would come for them?

Not the Earl of Greystowe, their maternal grandfather. The haughty ass hadn't come to visit his grandchildren for over a year. As for the O'Flahertys, none were left to come to their aid. Sheila's three sons had died together on the same day, the Fighting O'Flaherty's as they were known far and wide.

Elizabeth and her younger brother, Michael needed a protector, yet lacking family to provide for them, Sheila was going to have to conjure a guardian. The old woman nibbled on her lower lip, considering the situation from all angles before she worked her magic. Elizabeth would be fifteen in two months time. That was still too young to wed.

Sheila drummed her fingertips on the small table. Girls were married young in her day, often at fifteen; even fourteen wasn't unheard of among the cottagers. But that was an Ireland fifty years past. In England today, a lass typically didn't marry until she was at least seventeen, with the preference being eighteen in polite society, after a girl had made her proper come out. Ach, there was no hope for it. She'd just have to cast the spell and leave it to the ancients to bring the bridegroom to them at the proper time.

The man would have to be noble in spirit. Heaven knew there were plenty of jackasses out there claiming noble birth who hadn't a thimble full of integrity between them. He must possess a strong sense of honor like a knight in one of Michael's storybooks. He should be sensitive so as not to crush to her grand-daughter's tender spirit, yet possess a will that outmatched Elizabeth's in order to master the headstrong girl and prevent her from rushing headlong to her own ruin. More to the point, he would have to be someone Elizabeth could fall in love with or the stubborn lass wouldn't accept her knight when he came forth as summoned.

The old woman stroked her chin. T'was no easy enchantment to fashion together, it was as complex as an apothecary's formula. What would Elizabeth find appealing in a man?

Ach, the girl talked incessantly about the dark heroes from those cryptic romances she devoured. *A Dark Hero*? Yes, a dark and mysterious man would be just the thing to capture her grand-daughter's fancy; a man tested by life's trials, mature beyond his years, responsible, honest--and yet cunning as the devil in order to surmount Fletcher's trickery.

Sheila placed one of Elizabeth's baby teeth and a lock of her hair in a pouch, along with the fresh rosemary and rose petals from the garden. Remembering Michael, an innocent lamb caught in his father's web of intrigue, same as them all, she added one of his tin knight figures to the bag. She held the pouch in her hands and began chanting;

> "Bring a Dark Hero, faithful and true,
> With hair black as midnight, and eyes bonny blue.
> Send a Dark Hero, one we can trust;
> With a will forged in iron, yet, tempered and just.
> Send Elizabeth a champion with the soul of a Celt,
> With a heart full of love, a sword on his belt.
> Bring a Dark Knight to fulfill all her desires.
> With a soul that's been purified;
> *Through blood and through fire.*"

Chapter Two

The Island of St. Kitts, The West Indies 1795

The jolt moved through him as swift and sure as a lightning strike.

Kieran O'Flaherty sat up in bed, panting, uncertain of his perceptions. The boundaries he put in place should have kept the spirits away. A body could go mad listening to all the spirits roaming these islands. The cruel slave trade ground out a steady supply of confused, angry ghosts needing help crossing to the otherworld.

It wasn't a ghost, he decided after carefully evaluating the atmosphere about him. It was an ancient Fetch sent out by someone with a keen mastery of the occult arts. Powerful magic had been wrought this night. It knew him by name and it called to him from beyond the moonlit harbor of Basseterre on the island of St. Kitts. It had called to him from across the sea.

There came a familiar scratching noise at his door, and then Nickolas Barnaby, the man who had purchased his indenture years ago, poked his head inside Kieran's small room. "Do we have a visitor, lad? I sensed something odd creeping about the house."

"Just a misguided element from an ancient spell, nothing to worry about."

"Have a care, boy. Old magic is the most powerful." With that dour warning, the ancient apothecary left Kieran alone in the darkened chamber.

A faint ringing disturbed his thoughts. Kieran slipped into his shoes and headed for the stairs. Once in Barnaby's service, he learned quickly to sleep with his clothes on, as a goodly portion of their business was conducted after midnight. The face at the back door was pale with fear. "It's my first wife; she won't stay away from the new one. I need you folks to do something about it."

Kieran let the man into the back of the shop. "How long has she been deceased?"

"Six months." The man looked about him nervously as he spoke. "You got to do something to make her go away. Money isn't a problem."

Jeremiah Townsend was frightened. His first wife died suddenly and the second one was in her bed before she was cold in the ground. Kieran's gift didn't tell him that, local gossip was the culprit. What Kieran did pick up was a strong feeling of guilt. "Before your first wife died, was there any reason to suspect that you were having an affair?"

How dare you! The words were in his eyes, but Townsend didn't give them voice. "I've plenty of money, I need you to make her stop scaring Mary; it ain't her fault Prudence died."

"Are you certain?" Kieran asked.

Townsend opened his mouth to speak, and then smashed his lips together as he gazed anxiously about the room. "Mary was my mistress, true. Begged me to leave Pru. I couldn't do it. I told Mary that. I said the only way we could be together as man and wife was if--"

Kieran remained silent, allowing Townsend to turn the idea over in his mind.

"If Prudence died--but I didn't mean it like you think. I didn't tell her to do nothing', I was just stating facts, nothing more."

"We understand." Barnaby oozed with sympathy behind Kieran. "It's a job, banishing an angry spirit, it's difficult, but it can be done."

"Name your price." Townsend responded, falling easily into to the old man's snare.

After Townsend left, Barnaby rushed about the downstairs shop, collecting the ingredients for a banishing spell they would need to assist their newest client.

"Why do you do this?" Kieran asked. "That woman was murdered. Her spirit seeks justice. Binding her with a banishing spell won't serve justice."

"Justice?" Barnaby paused in his gathering. He turned to Kieran, his bony fingers twining his snowy goatee. "Justice is not our business, lad." Realizing he still wore his red silk nightcap, the old man removed it and brushed a stray wisp of white from his

16

eyes. "We're here to help those troubled by restless spirits. Lawyers don't quibble over whether a client is guilty; they just worry about him paying the bill. Justice, my boy? Leave that sorry business to God."

Snow swirled outside the windows as Elizabeth gazed about their home for the last time. It took six months for Papa to lose the townhouse. He wagered it against his debts and lost. He had a place for them, so he said. He'd won a deed to a cottage in the country months ago and had been holding it for such a time as this. The cottage was twenty miles from London, a day's ride by horseback. They were allowed one saddlebag each and told to put their belongings in it. Elizabeth took the tattered sheet music from the old crate where Mama's beautiful piano-forte once stood. The Broadwood Grand piano-forte along with Michael's violin and most of the furniture had been sold to pay for Papa's growing debts.

She gazed at the front door. He didn't come. Elizabeth had written her grandfather to inform him of her mother's death and asked if he might take Michael and her into his keeping. James Wentworth didn't attend his daughter's funeral nor did he come to rescue his grandchildren. They heard naught from him in the past months.

It didn't matter. She'd been foolish to pin her hopes on the man, on any man stepping in to rescue her.

They were leaving London, fleeing in the night, so her stepfather might escape the hangman's noose. He'd been involved in some nefarious scheme that ended in the death of a noble's son. Elizabeth managed to glean that much from his gin besotted ramblings. That he'd stooped to drinking gin was another sign of their poverty, as his preference was whiskey.

At dusk, Fletcher brought two horses to the back of the house, one for himself and one for Michael and Elizabeth to share.

He was adamant that Mrs. O'Flaherty would not be welcome in their new home.

Standing in the empty parlor, Elizabeth cast about for any sign of her mother's spirit. Mama appeared frequently to her since her death. Mama's mouth would move, but Elizabeth couldn't hear what her mother was trying to tell her. She glanced about the room, feeling foolish for addressing a ghost. "Papa's moving us to the country. I can't leave Granny Sheila behind as he insists and I cannot allow Michael go with him alone. What am I to do, Mama?"

Only the wind outside answered as she stood waiting for guidance from a ghost who hadn't troubled herself over her children's wellbeing when she'd been alive.

"The O'Flaherty's always take care of their own!"

A chill surrounded Elizabeth. The voice was not that of her mother, as she'd hoped. It was deep, masculine voice with a pronounced Irish brogue. She turned to find room behind her empty. She frowned, trying to see even the barest hint of a shadow lingering behind her. There was nothing but emptiness and silence surrounding her.

"Come, Liz, Papa's getting nasty." Michael's thin voice called from the hall.

Smoothing the folds of her cloak, Elizabeth stepped forward. "I'm not going with you."

"Why?" Fear swallowed her brother's features. At twelve, Michael was mama's image, with pale, delicate features, jet black curls and large, soulful eyes that were a deep violet-blue.

"I cannot leave Sheila to starve in the streets. I'm all she has left in this world."

Michael was visibly frightened. His eyes pleaded for her not to abandon him.

She didn't want to let him go on without her, but Fletcher was his father. Her stepfather would try to look after his own son. She had to believe that. The Captain had Michael's future earldom tempting him to have a care for his son's welfare. Michael was to inherit grandfather's title and lands as Kieran, their older brother, had been declared legally dead years ago. Michael would be taken care of. Sheila would die if she spent the winter starving in the streets.

"Get your skinny arse out that door, you useless twit." Captain Fletcher appeared behind Elizabeth's brother. "The runners will be after me, I can't afford to linger!"

"I'm not going." Elizabeth informed him. "Not without my grandmother."

"Fine, there'll be less baggage to slow us up. Michael, get moving." Fletcher barked.

"No." Michael crossed the room to stand beside Elizabeth. "Not without my sister."

The sharp intake of breath from the captain told them he'd not been expecting mutiny from his charges, least of all from Michael, the youngest and most easily cowed.

A fitting revenge Old Sheila had on the captain, Elizabeth thought, being careful not to smile. Michael might carry the captain's name, but he'd cut his teeth on Sheila's stories of the Fighting O'Flahertys of County Galway. He had the O'Flaherty sense of honor and integrity.

Elizabeth steeled herself for her stepfather's response. It would be physical, and brutal.

In silent agreement, Michael locked his elbow with hers.

They were of one mind; they would go together or not at all.

Captain Fletcher slapped the riding crop impatiently against his boot, eyeing them for a dangerous moment. "Get the witch then, quick, before the night watch sees the horses out back."

That nagging feeling wouldn't go away. It clung to Kieran like stale tobacco smoke.

The shock he'd experienced months ago had been a summoning from his Celtic ancestors. Yet the purpose behind it remained clouded. He felt a powerful urge to return to England-- not to Ireland, where he spent most of his childhood. He resisted, but the call was getting stronger, the dreams became more insistent as time passed.

"You take this one, lad." Barnaby gestured to the window facing the street.

Kieran looked up from the mortar bowl he'd been so intent upon. A tall, dark haired man in a wide brimmed hat and a long leather coat was striding down the deserted street toward their shop, undaunted by the heavy afternoon shower. Kieran set down the mortar and pestle and wiped his hands on his apron to remove the fine dust from them. "Who is he?"

"That's what I hope you'll be able to tell me." Barnaby sat at his desk and gave his ledgers his attention.

Kieran scowled. The old man was testing him again. While Barnaby was in awe of his gift, Kieran considered his intuitive powers to be a curse. He didn't like seeing people's pain. He didn't like feeling it if they happened to touch him. And he hated having ghosts pop in on him all the time, pestering him to help them solve their problems post-mortem. He wished he could be normal, oblivious to the unseen world, like everyone else.

"Good day, Sirs." The stranger entered the shop and offered them a greeting in a lilting Irish brogue. "And soft fine day it is, too, as they say in Dublin."

"What can I do for you, sir?" Kieran responded. It wasn't that the man didn't *sound* Irish, he was convincing. The impression came to him that this man was an actor, using costumes, false accents and fictitious names as a means of protection. This man had been hurt and was hiding from the world that had caused him so much pain.

"I need three ounces of goldenseal, two ounces of comfrey leaves, and a bottle of Laudanum. What part of Erin do you hail from, lad?"

The stranger was perceptive. After living here for nearly fifteen years, few people noted Kieran's accent. "County Galway. I didn't catch your name, Sir."

"O'Rourke, Donovan O'Rourke."

"Kieran O'Flaherty." He extended his hand. O'Rourke didn't return the gesture. Kieran withdrew his outstretched hand. He sensed danger in those bonny blue eyes, a promise of death to anyone who threatened this man's fragile existence. "How long have you been in the Indies?"

"A few months. My master inherited his grandfather's cane plantation."

The tall, lean stranger appeared casual. His hands rested jauntily on his hips. And yet, those pale blue eyes kept moving from the street to Kieran and then Barnaby repeatedly, as if he expected to be set upon at any moment.

"Which plantation is it you'll be staying at? In case we get a delivery order." Kieran added quickly as the steely gaze pinioned him with malice.

"Ravencrest." The man ground out after a moment of consideration.

Ravencrest Plantation was a small island several miles off the coast of St. Kitts. The owner had recently passed on. The man's daughter had married a Frenchman years ago, and the grandson had arrived from France to take over the estate after his grandfather died.

The grandson was a count, a refugee from The Terror in France.

The Count. Kieran set the jar of comfrey leaves down on the counter with a clumsy clank. *The one everyone was talking about.* Count Rochembeau had been horribly disfigured, so they said, tortured to the point of madness. No one had actually seen the man. His estate was an island separate from St. Kitts. He sent his servants into the harbor city to attend his business. The count wore a mask, so the rumors went and spent his days in his laboratory performing grisly experiments on the unclaimed corpses the hangman delivered to his isolated island.

This dark, dangerous soul was in his lordship's employ? Heaven help the fellow who crossed Mr. O'Rourke. Their end would be swift and undoubtedly painful.

"I assume your master is Count Rochembeau?" Kieran probed as he wrapped the herbs in folded paper and tied the pouches with string.

"I look after the man." O'Rourke replied. "Let's leave it at that. How much?"

"I need to get the laudanum--just a moment." Kieran slipped behind the curtain. He picked up a slim, brown bottle of the heady substance and let the cool glass rest against his cheek. Laudanum was an opium derivative, used for pain, to calm nerves or induce sleep in heavier doses. What did the nefarious count need it for: to manage pain or forget his past?

Returning to the shop, Kieran set the bottle on the counter and tallied up the order. "Two pounds and ten shillings. Would you prefer an open account? We can bill his lordship if you--"

O'Rourke tossed a bag of coins onto the counter in answer. Kieran handed him the packets and the bottle of Laudanum. The moment O'Rourke's hand touched the bottle Kieran held, a wave of unbearable pain slammed through Kieran. He felt as if his torso were being torn to shreds, just raw flesh with no skin covering the festering wounds.

A figure moved and blurred. His face was dirty, swollen and bruised. He stood bared to the waist, arms outstretched tight, wrists shackled. It was O'Rourke and he was screaming. His tormentors were peeling away narrow strips of flesh on his chest. Time disintegrated. O'Rourke was still shackled. This time a glowing orange poker was held in front of the man's face then lowered ominously. A searing agony followed. The acrid smell of burning flesh overcame Kieran as tormented screams filled the subterranean chamber.

Kieran stepped back, away from the blinding pain of this man's past.

Unaware of what occurred, O'Rourke nodded stoically and strode through the door.

"What did you see?" Barnaby pounced upon him as soon as the door swung shut.

"They tortured him. They burned and cut his flesh."

Barnaby didn't comment. Seeing Kieran was upset by his experience, he placed a steady hand on his shoulder in fatherly concern.

"He doesn't work for the count." Kieran continued, bolstered by that hand. "He *is* the count--the one everyone's talking about. O'Rourke is one of his disguises. He's dangerous, Barnaby. He's embraced violence, become a highwayman, I believe."

Barnaby rolled his lips together. "Well done, my boy. Well done. Say nothing of this to anyone." He cautioned, turning his attention to the pouch on the counter. He lifted it and weighed it in his hand. Curious, he opened it and counted the coins. "Plenty of reasons to keep his secret, lad. There's over ten pounds here."

Money. With Barnaby, it was always about the money.

Disgusted by his mentor's greed, Kieran closed his eyes and tried to recall the fleeting impression he experienced moments ago of O'Rourke dressed in black holding a bloody sword in his hand.

He had a silk sheath tied around his head, a mask of sorts, pushed up over his brow. Hard blue eyes stared back at Kieran in the vision, daring him to give the warrior a reason to run him through. Sails furled behind the man. The smell of sulfur choked the air as black smoke billowed up ominously behind the dark clad figure.

"He wasn't a highwayman." Kieran murmured, gesturing toward the empty portal where the mysterious stranger exited moments earlier. "O'Rourke was pirate."

Chapter Three

Three years later, August 1798, Rural England

Elizabeth delivered the laundry packets, collected her fees and stopped at the mercantile to purchase a bit of sugar. It was a luxury they couldn't afford, but it would cheer Old Sheila. And at her great age Sheila deserved any indulgence they could give her before she passed into the Summerland, the Celtic place of the Dead.

Today was Elizabeth's eighteenth birthday. It was also the Festival of Lughnassa according to the Celtic calendar. Sheila always said that it was fortunate Elizabeth was born on the day honoring the Celtic god of the sun, as she was the last ray of hope for the O'Flahertys.

Elizabeth didn't believe in the old ways. She'd outgrown the fanciful stories her grandmother told of fairies and elementals long ago, when her mother died and her childhood ended. She pretended to believe, to keep her grandmother happy and give the old woman a sense of purpose as she passed on her peculiar knowledge. Elizabeth escorted the old woman out into the clearing in the woods every full moon and watched over her as she performed her mysterious rituals. Then she would guide the dear old woman home again. Fairytales no longer appealed to Elizabeth, nor did the presumption that one could change their circumstances by chanting over a handful of herbs under a full moon. She believed in hard work, in foraging for wood to light their hearth, not enchanted sprites or mysterious brownies who did favors for mortals in need.

And wasn't the proof of her conviction in her hand? She clutched the small packet in her fist, bought from her pay for laundering shirts for the bachelors in town. They couldn't afford a real feast in honor of the Celtic god Lugh but tonight Granny Sheila would have sugar in her tea!

Captain Fletcher provided them with a roof over their heads and that was all they could say about the dilapidated cottage he took them to years ago on that cold December night. It turned out that Sheila O'Flaherty provided the perfect foil for the captain's schemes. He could hide in the country without fear of the authorities ever finding him, for what connection would an old Irish woman and her two grandchildren have with a notorious gambler wanted for murdering a viscount's son?

The captain came home a sparse few days out of each month, when his luck ran out. The arrangement gave the siblings a measure of freedom that few could boast of at such a young age. Sheila taught Elizabeth how to cook. They raised a garden and kept a few chickens to sell the eggs. They took in laundry and mending. Michael acquired odd jobs with the blacksmith and the butcher. Recently, he'd been given a position as stable boy at the Hamilton Estate up the road.

Ah, life might even be called good--except Captain Fletcher was scheming again. As Elizabeth came of an age to be properly married, he was busy trying to secure a match for her from among his gaming associates in the hope of settling some of his debts.

Elizabeth was determined to evade his snare. She had it all worked out in her head. She'd run away before she'd agree to such an unsavory match. She would take Sheila and head for London, become a lady's companion or a governess. Her mathematics might be atrocious as her schooling ended when mama died, but she could play the pianoforte better than most and that one talent might secure her a position tutoring wealthy merchant's children in their homes. She could also teach the merchant's daughters comportment and manners, prepare them for entering society since her mother had been a lady.

Preoccupied with her plan of escape, Elizabeth walked right past the fine roan stallion tethered outside their cottage without caring how it got there. Michael must have taken it for a stretch of the legs, she assumed, as she opened the front door. He often did so with Lord Hamilton's stock, and then stopped at the house to brag a little. He was mad about horses, but what lad of fifteen wasn't? Elizabeth untied the strings of her bonnet and hung it on the peg.

True to form, Michael was standing next to Sheila's chair, facing the door with a pleased smirk on his thin face. "Ah, Liz, we were just discussing your tardiness!"

"I see you've stolen a horse again for the afternoon." She teased, and then scolded him. "Quit preening like a lord and go get some wood so I can warm your dinner."

"Is that any way to talk to me on your birthday?" Michael returned in a high good humor. "I shan't give you your present." He affected an adorable pout, dimples and all.

"You haven't the means to buy me a present, and even if you did, I've told you I have need of nothing, except good companionship and pleasant conversation."

"You're lack of faith in me is disheartening, Mademoiselle. I've brought home a companion to entertain us in exchange for dinner. But after hearing your acid tongue I wager he'll be making his excuses and heading for the door."

A dark haired man rose from the high-back chair he'd been sitting in that faced away from the door at Michael's nod to him. He turned to face Elizabeth with an amused smile.

"My brother doesn't steal horses, sir, it was a jest." Elizabeth's face grew hot.

"Liz!" Michael raised his hands. "Donovan is my friend. You needn't worry about him sending the sheriff after your wicked tongue."

The stranger's smile widened. He had a complexion that had been kissed by the sun. His hair was as black as midnight, secured behind his neck with a black bow. And such *blue* eyes!

"This is Mr. O'Rourke. Michael invited him to dinner." Grinning, Old Sheila made the introductions. "And this is my grandchild, sir, my darlin' lass, Miss O'Flaherty."

"A pleasure, Miss O'Flaherty." The man stepped forward to make a formal bow. The parlor echoed with a distinct crunch. His gaze dropped to the small packet lodged beneath his boot. The stranger bent to retrieve it and held the packet out to her with a beguiling smile. "Your sugar, Miss, I believe you dropped it."

"Yes, Mr.?" Elizabeth stammered, uncertain of his name.

"*O'Rourke*, Donovan O'Rourke, Miss, at your service."

"Thank you, sir." She struggled to retrieve her addled wits as she took the packet from him. "I'll not need to break the lumps now. You've done that for me." She attempted a smile.

The Irishman nodded and smiled back. Elizabeth was taken hostage by the lively interest in those dazzling blue eyes, such a pale shade, the color of the sky on a cloudless day.

Uncomfortable with his frank, open regard, she dropped her gaze to his boots, tall brown top boots. She noted the unusual color, as most men wore black ones with brown trim. His were just the opposite. Her eyes ambled up long, muscular thighs molded into buff doeskin breeches that fit him like a second skin. Brown leather gloves encased hands resting jauntily on trim hips as her vision moved steadily upward. A leather work vest protected O'Rourke's shirt from his labors. A sloppy neck linen draped about his tan neck, not truly tied and fashioned, but rather stuffed into conformity. His cotton shirt was discolored from frequent wear, a soft buttery yellow rather than white. The sleeves were rolled up to his elbows, revealing tanned, corded forearms that made her pulse jerk like a colt kicking up its heels gleefully in the pasture. As her gaze moved to his face, the smile creasing his lips conveyed the silent message that her inspection hadn't escaped his notice. He had the audacity to wink at her.

Flushing crimson, Elizabeth fled to the kitchen. She should be outraged by his forward behavior or shamed by her own. Instead she was at once giddy, nervous, uncertain and weak at the knees--all in the space of five minutes!

Oh, Bollocks. Her stepfather's favorite curse word came to mind. Elizabeth couldn't get in trouble for thinking it, could she? Not unless Sheila could read minds. She gazed guiltily at the parlor door. *How do I make it through the rest of the evening?*

Elizabeth remained silent throughout the meal, not trusting herself to speak with her wits jumbled about. Michael and Sheila kept the conversation flowing with the enchanting Irishman. She found herself continually drawn to the pale blue orbs that studied her from the face of a bronzed god. She tried to be sly about her admiration of his masculine beauty, but she was caught staring by him time and again. Each time their eyes met, she blushed and looked away.

"Am I correct in assuming your father is working away from home, Miss O'Flaherty?" O'Rourke asked when she was caught on one forbidden foray.

"Ha. He's never found work to be profitable." Michael answered for her, and set to chewing a piece of sinewy meat with extra vigor. "Good stew, Liz. Is it chicken again?"

Elizabeth nodded and smoothed an imaginary wrinkle from her skirt, keeping the truth to herself. Or so she thought until she noted the smirk on the face of their guest. O'Rourke knew it was rabbit, poached rabbit, more to the point, a crime for which she'd face serious charges if caught—and yet, her little brother had to have meat to eat.

"Our father is out seeking his fortunes. He doesn't trouble himself much over ours." Michael added pouring more milk that had come to them in exchange for Sheila watching the neighbor's babe this week so the farmer's wife could help him bring in the grain harvest.

There was a price for every morsel they ate. Elizabeth was always keenly aware of it. Tonight she felt it more than usual. Lucy, her favorite amongst the bevy of stray cats that congregated at their cottage, jumped onto Elizabeth's lap. They couldn't fall much lower, when having a guest made her worry where their next meal would come.

Michael poured a portion of his milk onto a chipped tea saucer and pushed it in front of Elizabeth. Lucy promptly stood up on her lap and lapped the milk from the saucer with her pink tongue, purring loudly. Elizabeth stroked the calico's neck as she chanced a look at Mr. O'Rourke. They wouldn't dare indulge Lucy so in Papa's presence. It would earn them both a harsh cuff alongside the head and the cat would be thrown across the room.

Mr. O'Rourke didn't arch a brow as he gazed serenely at Elizabeth. "Ah, hoping to provide coin to ease the burdens of his family, no doubt." He said, gallantly dismissing Michael's impertinence as easily as he had the cat's presence at the table.

"Easing no one's cares but his own!" Sheila's fist slammed down with such force the sugar bowl danced to the edge of the table and shattered when it met the floor. It christened the rough boards with tawny granules. Lucy ran out the door, her tail bristled. "He's out drinking and gambling away every last ha'penny, while his son here mucks out stables and my darlin' lass is reduced to taking in laundry so we can eat. And their mama was the daughter of an Earl!"

"Pray excuse her, sir. She forgets herself." Elizabeth jumped up to fetch the broom, and then knelt to brush up the mess before it attracted pests.

"Perhaps I might be able to assist you. Lack of coin isn't one of my flaws."

Elizabeth started at the sound of that lush, rich voice beside her. Mr. O'Rourke was crouched behind her. He took up the broom pan from her and angled it so she might sweep the sugar and shattered porcelain into it. It was a simple gesture, yet her heart beat a swift tattoo at not only his nearness but his eagerness to help her in such a menial chore. She had to gain control of her wild emotions and remind him that she was not an easy mark.

"I'm not in the habit of accepting money from strange men under the guise of charity." Elizabeth rose and tossed the contents of the broom pan into the pail at the kitchen door. She turned on her heel to confront the man. "If you wish to assist us you might see if your employer has need of a scullery or maid of all work. I'm not particular, as long as its *honest* employment."

Those crisp blue eyes widened. "Miss O'Flaherty, you misunderstand my intentions." He gestured broadly toward the table. "Surely you don't believe I'd make an illicit offer to you in front of your grandmother and your brother?"

Oh, wasn't he the quick and clever fox? Assuming perfect innocence while implying she was the one with improper thoughts. Well, perhaps she was, at that.

"Have you not shared this delightful stew with me?" He continued, with the veracity of a preacher warming to his sermon. "Not expecting coin or other forms of compensation? You did it out of the goodness of your heart, did you not?"

Flustered, Elizabeth crossed her arms before her and ceded his point with a terse nod.

"Well, is it wrong for me to wish to share a portion of my own bounty with such generous friends?" He replied, and his warm smile dissolved the remains of her anger.

Mr. O'Rourke dropped by frequently in the following weeks, nearly every day.

He sat and listened patiently to Old Sheila ramble on when Elizabeth was busy tending chores. Seeing the tonic the Irishman had on her grandmother's spirits, Elizabeth didn't mind sharing their meager fair with him.

His offer of assistance was never voiced again. Instead, they began finding coins in the strangest places; under the tea kettle, in the pocket of the apron left hanging on a peg in the kitchen, or in the bottom of a basket. Granny Sheila nearly broke a tooth one morning when she bit into a coin that had been cooked in their breakfast oats.

O'Rourke entertained them with tales of life in the West Indies. He spoke of hurricanes, fierce pirates and shark attacks to entertain Michael at dinner. With Elizabeth and Sheila he boasted of brilliant sunsets, exotic flowers and birds that made up the wild landscape he likened to paradise. He was attached to a French nobleman who had fled France during the Terror and owned a sugar plantation near St. Kitts. As the count's agent, O'Rourke was in England negotiating with Lord Hamilton on the purchase of some fine breeding stock for his master's stables, which is where he met Michael. He insisted on being called Donovan, and had such an easy manner he made it seem as if they had been friends for ages instead of mere weeks.

He held Elizabeth's hand as they strolled in the August twilight each evening after dinner, just the two of them. On a particularly warm night, Donovan attempted to point out the constellations. He claimed it was easier to find them in the Indies, as the skies were so cloudy here from the factories. To encourage his efforts, Elizabeth took him on a familiar path deep into the woods. They stood in the center of a small clearing ringed by oak trees Sheila called The Sacred Grove. The old woman believed that it was guarded by nature spirits, imbued with magic.

Elizabeth gazed up at the expansive sky. "The fireflies are dancing among the flowers, the crickets are singing lullabies to their little ones and the trees stand by as ancient sentinels, guarding this sacred place from the prying eyes of the outside world. Isn't it beautiful?"

"Aye." Donovan whispered in a voice that slid down her spine like warmed honey. He leaned close, his head dipped and his lips brushed her mouth in a brief, gentle caress. It happened so fast, and it was quite unexpected. Elizabeth remained still, her head inclined upward, encouraging him to kiss her again. She was not disappointed. The second time he lingered, coaxing her lips to join his in an intimate dance of lovers. His kiss brought a pleasant tingle to her lips and made her insides swell. She felt all soft and fluid inside, like jelly that hadn't set properly. Donovan was the one to pull away. He stepped back and looked up at the stars as if nothing unusual had happened while she stood reeling in amazement at the delightful and all too brief kiss she experienced for the first time.

He pointed out the North Star, the beacon for gaining one's bearings on the high seas, and then a cluster named Sirius, after the Greek dog, he told her. His rich voice trailed on as Elizabeth tried to find her bearings in this uncharted sea of sensual pleasure his kiss evoked.

One week later, Elizabeth cleared the table after the evening meal. Michael wasn't home yet, but he often worked late at the stables. She set the remains of the stew near the fire to keep it warm. That boy could eat a Christmas goose and still claim to be starving. She wiped her hands, removed her apron and helped Granny Sheila to her favorite chair in the parlor. After a short time, the old woman's snores overwhelmed Donovan's enchanting deep Irish brogue.

He smiled from his seat across the room. "Shall we go for a walk, my darlin' lass?"

Once outside, he took her hand, a familiar gesture as he led her to the wooded glen. He stopped in the center of The Sacred Grove. It wasn't yet dark. The sky was pink above them. He gazed down at her with eyes that were serious for the first time since she'd met him. "I sail in a fortnight. Come away with me, Lizzie. I want you to be my wife."

Elizabeth was struck mute by his declaration. Knowing he was leaving England soon, she'd been careful not to read more into their relationship than it was; a brief summer romance to cherish when her life returned to a struggle of survival once more.

But he just asked her to *marry* him, not to remember him after he was gone. "I can't leave Sheila." She explained. "She's suffered several episodes with her heart. We don't expect her to last through the winter, sir."

"We'll take her with us." Donovan murmured, lowering his head. Elizabeth melted beneath a kiss that was sweet yet demanding. The mild taste of tobacco teased her as his tongue expertly courted her own. The new sensation of his tongue inside her mouth was shocking but oddly pleasing. She leaned into him, her arms winding about his tall, solid form and surrendered to his masterful kiss. She longed only to lose herself in his embrace.

He drew back abruptly, as if scalded by her touch. His breathing was labored. He raised his head to the stars. "Lizzie, my sweet girl, you're in my blood. Come away with me. I'll take care of you. And Sheila and Michael, as well. I promise."

"Your employer wouldn't approve." She reasoned, trying to still her singing blood. "He wouldn't pay for our passage to the Indies. And Sheila wouldn't survive the arduous journey."

"I have plenty of coin. I'll ensure your grandmother's comfort during the passage. And you will never work another day, I promise." He lifted her chaffed hand to his lips and lightly kissed the center of her palm.

Elizabeth cooed and shivered as delicious warmth settled low in her belly. She knew now why the young women in those novels could claim to be about to swoon.

"Gretna Green is a few days journey by horse. We can leave tonight and come back for Sheila and Michael after it's done. Come away with me, darlin'. I swear you'll never regret it."

"I've known you but three weeks, Donovan."

"Long enough." He said with confidence. "Let's talk to Sheila." He began leading her down the wooded path to the house. Once there, he led her in through the kitchen door. "We've planned this. Sheila agrees with me, Lizzie. You'll see--"

"She'll see about what?" A voice snarled as they entered the kitchen holding hands.

"Papa, you're home. This is Mr. O'Rourke, he's been--"

"--home, yes, just in time to catch you carrying on like the village whore."

"Sir--" O'Rourke began, stepping toward Fletcher with his hands up in a conciliatory mien. "If you'll listen to what I have to say, I believe we might come to an agreement—"

"Get out of my house." Fletcher snatched up the knife from the carving board.

"I'll come back tomorrow, when you aren't in your cups, sir." O'Rourke reasoned, stepping back a pace. "We can talk like reasonable men."

"Come back and I'll send for the sheriff. I'll see you hanged for molesting my girl."

Donovan's gaze moved to Elizabeth. He seemed uncertain, in light of Papa's threat.

"Just go." Elizabeth whispered. "Let me talk to him. He'll calm down if you leave."

It was a lie, but her goal was to get Donovan away before Fletcher stabbed him with that knife. She knew the captain was more inclined to do that than set the sheriff after him.

Donovan turned toward the door. He paused at her side and whispered, "Meet me at dawn, in the clearing." With that, he stepped into the night. She knew what he meant. He expected her to run away with him to Scotland, come morning.

First, she had to survive the night. Instinct told her to run out the back door and hide in the woods until Papa passed out, as she had done many times before. The cottage was silent as they listened to the sound of O'Rourke's horse trotting toward the village—to safety.

"I've heard tales in town, about how that swaggering Mick comes here every night to eat and to lay out his prospects of bedroom privileges--"

"Mr. O'Rourke has not behaved improperly. He asked me to marry him tonight, Papa. He asked me to go with him to Gretna Green."

"Hah! Aren't you the ignorant little slut?" He laughed in that frightening timbre. "Gretna Green is a lie, a convenient place where men despoil stupid chits like you. Oh, promising marriage all the way, to be sure!"

"I don't believe you. Donovan is not like that."

"You don't believe your pa? Tell me, girl, have you ever met a woman who ran away to Gretna in the middle of the night? No, you haven't, because they never come back. They're ruined, coaxed into giving up their maidenhead to some conniving prick like him, and then left to rot by the man once he's had his way with 'em."

Elizabeth remained silent, having learned it was best not to provoke him further when he was in this mood. The crickets chirped beneath the steps. The soft summer breeze rustled through the trees outside the open kitchen door. The captain gulped down the last remains of his bottle and eyed her with speculation.

"So, you've been playing the little slut while I was away." He moved close and grabbed her arm with iron fingers. His foul breath choked her. "Fixing to present me with some Irishman's brat, just like your mother; spread your legs for some penniless Mick and snub the fine English gents I've brought here wanting to wed you proper." His fist rose up to punctuate his words. Elizabeth was caught off balance by the sudden blow. She pulled herself up from the floor, only to find he'd slid his belt from his waist and was wrapping it about his fist to use as a whip. "There's a stubborn streak I failed to beat out of you when you were a girl."

"Lay a hand on her and I'll blast ye straight to hell where you were spawned!"

Fletcher took one look at the old woman in the doorway, her hands trembling as she tried to hold the heavy pistol aimed at him, and laughed. A thunderous crack rent the air as the ball went whistling past Elizabeth's head and into the door jamb behind her.

Fletcher's face registered surprise, and then outrage.

Elizabeth moved to put herself between him and her grandmother. The captain spun about. Catching Elizabeth, he shoved her head first toward the stone hearth. A searing pain snatched her back from the shadowy mists. She was lying on the floor, her hand inches from glowing embers. Jerking her stinging fingers from the blistering heat, she struggled to her feet, determined to protect Sheila from Fletcher's wrath.

It was too late. Sheila lay crumpled on the floor, her eyes closed. Seconds ticked by with the beating of Elizabeth's heart.

Fletcher slowly turned his attention back to her. "I'll kill the old hag if I catch you so much as speaking to your precious Donovan again. Understand me, girl?"

"Yes, Papa."

Elizabeth hurried to the village in the grey light of dawn. She hoped to bring the parson's wife to have a look at Old Sheila as they hadn't any funds for a doctor.

Donovan emerged from a wooded copse after she rounded the bend. He held the reins of his horse in one hand. "Did your stepfather do this?" He asked, eyeing the welt on her cheek.

"Certainly not! I tripped and fell against the well handle as I was going to the privy after dark." Elizabeth forced a smile, "I should have taken a lantern, but the moon seemed light enough, and here you have it, a nasty bump."

Donovan dropped the reins and seized her hand. "Come with me, Lizzie—I'll take care of you. I promise."

"*No!*" Elizabeth jerked her burnt fingers free and glanced with uneasiness toward the cottage that was not quite hidden by the curve of the road. Papa had been asleep when she slipped out, but should he awaken and see her talking to Donovan . . .

Elizabeth straightened her spine. She was well versed in lies, in denying the truth and the pain that went with being Captain Fletcher's stepdaughter. "I cannot run away with you." She said, being careful to mask her mangled emotions. "My stepfather has expectations that I marry well, our very survival depends upon it."

"Are you implying that if I had money he'd change his tune?"

Elizabeth's heart opened, just a tiny bit. And then reality destroyed the brief illusion. "No, Donovan. He would still refuse your suit."

"Why?" His fluid body became tense and alert. He was offended by her statement.

"Because you are Irish. He hates the Irish--even more than he hates Yankees. Mostly, he'd refuse your suit because he knows I would wish for his approval. I'm forbidden to speak with you again, sir. There will be dire consequences if he finds me with you even now. If you care for me—if you care for Sheila—I must insist you make no further attempt to contact us during your stay in England, Mr. O'Rourke. Now, let me pass, sir."

Donovan glanced in the direction of the cottage and muttered a low curse. The soft blue eyes that were full of merriment had hardened to a steely gray. His features became severe, almost feral as he stared at the cottage in the distance. He appeared at once dangerous as he hovered over her on the lonely road, his clothing wrinkled, his hair askew and his face unshaven from spending the night in the woods like a highwayman waiting to rob an unsuspecting traveler.

"As you wish, Miss O'Flaherty." He muttered coolly as he stepped aside, allowing her to continue on her way.

Donovan watched Elizabeth march away from him with her back stiff. He turned his gaze back to the cottage barely visible at the turn nearly a quarter mile away. Lizzie wouldn't let him help her. She was afraid to be seen talking to him, was she?

That drunken sot was likely the cause of her fear, and the bruise on her cheek.

Well then, perhaps it was time to let The Count step in and take control of the situation.

Chapter Four

At the elegant hotel, Captain William Fletcher was welcomed into the well appointed suite by his host's solicitor, Mr. Jamison. Their previous meeting had been at the law office during the day. Tonight, Fletcher was meeting the reclusive count face to face to finalize the arrangement between them for Elizabeth's hand in marriage.

"His lordship will be with us shortly." Jamison assured him. "Don't let the dim lights alarm you. His lordship's eyes are sensitive to light and he prefers the shadows, given his unfortunate appearance."

Fletcher took a seat near the hearth. A goblet of fine claret was handed to him with silent deference by the white gloved footman. Ah, the good life. He had it, until that senseless twit he married made him lose his temper. With his name connected to the murder of a viscount's son, he couldn't go to the bank to collect the quarterly allowance for the children's keeping. He couldn't go anywhere in London these days, lest someone recognize him and turn him in to the law.

This Frenchie didn't know his reputation was mired in horse droppings. The count was one of many nobles turned refugee due to the upset in France. The man was rich, disfigured and looking to purchase a bride with which to produce an heir. He owned a plantation across the sea and planned to leave England as soon as he acquired said female.

Ah, yes, fortune was definitely on the upswing!

The door opened, and the count emerged. The lawyer rose and Fletcher followed suit.

"My Lord, this is Captain William Fletcher, the stepfather of the young lady you had me inquire about. Captain Fletcher, may I present Le Comte de Rochembeau."

Fletcher stared at the apparition dominating the chamber, rendering it even darker by his mere presence. His host's mutilated face was covered by black silk scarf. Only his lips and chin were visible beneath the dark silk. The skin just beneath the fabric appeared angry and swollen. Tiny holes had been cut into the cloth, yet all one could make out in the dim light was the eerie shifting of light behind the eyeholes of the dark sheath.

"My lord." He made a bow, recalling his manners. The mute specter nodded and gestured to the chair. Fletcher sank into it quickly, the better to hide his knocking knees.

The count sat in a chair next to the door he just emerged from--a dark corner devoid of illumination--and gestured with a wave of his hand for his solicitor to begin.

"His lordship wishes to know if you've had sufficient time to consider the agreement." Jamison asked, unaffected by the veiled creature staring at them from the gloom.

"Aye, its fine, I'll sign." He had been warned not to stare, but couldn't restrain himself. The dark sheath hiding the man's face made him uneasy. It reminded him of an executioner's mask. The count was a sizeable man, with inky black hair that swirled about his broad shoulders in wild disarray. Unable to hold that disturbing silvery gaze, Fletcher focused on his host's attire; gleaming black Top boots, black breeches, and a silk dressing gown of blood red. The gown was opened to reveal a mass of scars riddling his chest that were long and precise. Compliments of the revolution, along with his ruined face, Fletcher guessed.

"You realize the offer includes your son, Captain." The solicitor's voice jarred him, reminding him that he was gaping at his host. "He's to be educated and brought out as a gentleman. You do understand that this contract rescinds any future claim you have to the boy?"

That part stung, but there was naught to be done for it. He couldn't make Michael into a gentleman, not without Angela's money and society connections. He'd made a mistake when he pushed her down those stairs years ago; he hadn't thought things through properly. He was the son of a butcher who clawed his way up the ranks as a soldier to become a captain and then tricked a widowed heiress into marrying him while he was stationed in Ireland. Now, his son would inherit the Wentworth fortunes when the old earl popped off, and he had no means to polish the boy for the title, save this queer fish he had dangling on his hook.

"I understand." Fletcher replied, sneaking a rueful glance at his sinister benefactor.

"The magistrate has granted us a special license. His lordship signed the papers before the official today. As soon as you sign them, Miss O'Flaherty becomes the count's legal wife. The ceremony will be merely a formality to satisfy the inherent female need for pageantry, as is the case with most arranged marriages. Any further questions, Captain?"

"How did you know I had a stepdaughter of marriageable age, my lord?"

"You may be surprised to learn that his lordship moves in the same circles as you." The lawyer answered for the count. "There has been much talk in them regarding the girl and your attempts to auction her off indiscriminately--for a hefty sum."

True, he'd talked to many in the past months who he thought might be in the market for fresh breeding stock. Angela's ugly duckling had grown into a beautiful swan. If not for that Irish witch sleeping next to the girl with a loaded gun, he'd have sampled her wares long ago.

"We will collect her Friday." The Frenchman spoke at last in a harsh, grating tone. "I will attend the ceremony and then escort her to London. Jamison will take over for me there and see my lady is settled on *The Pegasus* before it sails with the evening tide. I must head north as I have pressing business to conclude before leaving England's shores. I will rendezvous with my ship and my lady outside the channel, within two to three days. By then, she will have had time to recover her nerves and accept her circumstances, *Oui, Monsieur?*"

"Aye, my lord." That was good thinking. One look at him and the chit would try to bolt as soon as she left the church if she stayed on land for even one night. Once she was at sea there would be no escape from the dark lord and his passions. "And you've paid off all of my debts?"

"My Lord purchased all of the notes you specified. Your only debt now is to him."

Fletcher signed the documents giving Count Rochembeau his stepdaughter's hand in marriage and also the one making Michael the count's legal ward until he reached his majority.

Jamison took the documents. "We will destroy the notes we purchased on your behalf and deposit two thousand pounds in your name into the bank of your choice as soon as the girl is transferred into his lordship's keeping."

"I thought you'd give me my settlement tonight. I need coin to provide a wedding feast."

"The ceremony will be simple with only your family in attendance." Jamison countered. "Afterward, the countess will be settled onto his lordship's ship. So, you see, there will be no need for a feast."

He'd been outfoxed. Sure, his debts were paid, but they promised him two thousand pounds, free and clear. He couldn't walk into a bank to collect it. He might be arrested.

Ah, so the count was leaving his bride unattended while he concluded his business, was he? Well, perhaps he could line his pockets before all was said and done. Fletcher smiled. He knew a few scoundrels on the docks who owed him since their military days, men without a conscience who wouldn't quibble about how evenly the purse was cut between them.

Chapter Five

On Friday morning, a foggy, damp day by all accounts, Elizabeth delivered her laundry packets in the village. She trudged through the muddy ruts on the way back to the cottage, her skirts soaked to the knees. She didn't care. Sheila wasn't there to chide her for her carelessness. Sheila was dead. She died three days after Fletcher drove Donovan away, having never awakened again. Elizabeth kept her eyes on the road as she walked, not the beautiful countryside she'd come to love during their exile.

Oh, Bollocks.! A coach and four was parked at the cottage. It meant only one thing; Papa cheated another noble at cards. They had undoubtedly tracked him here and now she would have to endure the victim's crude insults along with her stepfather. Having been an unwilling participant in that scenario more than once, she pondered the wisdom of going home or going off into the woods until the arrogant fellow took himself off. The choice wasn't difficult.

She entered the sacred grove, the place where Granny Sheila held her strange rituals, and where Donovan kissed her under the stars and asked her to come away with him.

It was all ashes now, just like the nursery rhyme. She was alone.

Sheila was dead and Donovan had sailed to the Indies without her.

Elizabeth sank down in the wet grass, uncaring of its effect on her gown. Her life couldn't get any more damp or muddied at present. She still had Michael, but Michael was no longer a child needing her to take care of him. Their roles had changed. Without her to support, he wouldn't need to muck out stables. He could go off on a grand adventure by himself.

The wind caressed her hair, brushing a stray wisp from her brow as Old Sheila so often had. *"Not alone."* It whispered. Elizabeth grew still, desperate now to believe in the nature spirits and elementals her grandmother spoke of when she was alive.

41

"Time to go, time to break free--free--free!" She glanced up at the branch above her. A chickadee gazed down at her with snappy black eyes. *"Time to go, time to break free--free--free!"* A queer foreboding came over her as she listened to the wisdom of the bird. Sheila was gone. There was no need to stay at the cottage. She could leave. It was time to leave, time to break free of Fletcher's influence. In doing so, she'd also be freeing her brother.

A trampling of brush came from behind. She turned to find Michael glaring at her. "Liz, are you daft? We've been waiting for you to return from the village for over an hour."

"I'm waiting for whoever Papa fleeced this time to leave. Why aren't you at the stables?"

"I was retrieved by the coachmen in that fancy rig out front." Michael informed her with an exuberance that puzzled her. "No more mucking out stables for me. I'm going to be a gentleman, and you, Liz, you're to become a countess!"

Elizabeth stood in the foyer of the church, her knees shaking and her chest tight, clutching the bouquet of white roses her bridegroom generously provided. Her heart was numb.

She had no idea whom she was marrying at the church. An exiled count. A nobleman with a scarred body and a disfigured face. It didn't matter whose name she would bear.

What mattered was Michael. By accepting the Frenchman's offer Elizabeth knew she was saving her little brother. As her husband's legal ward, Michael would have all the advantages wealth could provide. He'd be away from Fletcher and his scheming. He'd finally be safe.

The organ was drowning out all thought and feeling as the minister's wife did her best to hide the missed notes. Elizabeth stood frozen in the entry arch, gazing at the bizarre scene as if watching a play. The minister was waiting. So was the mysterious French nobleman who paid her stepfather's debts in exchange for her hand. Fletcher stood beside Michael.

They were waiting for her to join them at the altar.

Elizabeth stood still, rooted to the floor at edge of the aisle, clutching the flowers in her gloved hands, staring at the men waiting for her to step toward them in pace with the music.

The captain's face grew mottled and strained. He took a step into the aisle. He was coming for her—coming to drag her to take her place beside the hideous creature they'd summoned from Hades to be her bridegroom.

Elizabeth could barely contain the razor sharp panic slicing through her, and the urge to run screaming from the church. The captain's eyes narrowed with unspoken threat and he moved as if to come after her.

The slender foreigner in the white tunic and turban left the count's side and caught the captain's arm. The Indian raised a hand to Fletcher, and then came gliding elegantly toward her.

"Miss?" He spoke in a soft, conciliatory mien as he took her arm and laid it gently on his crisp white cotton sleeve. "My master bade me to give you a message if you began to falter. He said please forgive the disguise, t'was necessary to fool the dog Sirius and put him off the scent. He said to trust him just as a sailor trusts the North Star to steer him through the turbulent seas."

Elizabeth gasped aloud. Donovan had talked about the constellations, of sailors using them to guide their ships home using the North Star and Sirius while they were courting.

The air tasted a little less thick and oppressive as she joined the dark figure at the altar. He was dressed in unrelenting black, except the white linen shirt beneath his velvet vest and frock coat. Elizabeth studied the profile beside her, anxious to see some semblance of the man she loved. She'd been too distraught at the cottage to truly look at the ghoul her stepfather presented to her as her imminent bridegroom. Black hair hung wild and loose about his shoulders. It seemed thicker than Donovan's, and it lacked his smooth sheen.

Oh, but that face. The cheeks beneath the leather mask were deep red. Angry blotches of raised, rough skin were visible beneath the shroud. And his mouth was not curled upward in a teasing smile as Donovan's would be. Rather, it was set in a grim line.

"Miss O'Flaherty." The minister prompted, and she started at the reminder of her surname, realizing she was supposed to be repeating her vows after the minister. Elizabeth cleared her throat and repeated the words being leveled at her from the dour faced preacher.

Before she was prepared for it, the ceremony was over. Someone had removed her glove and there was now a ring on her finger, a huge emerald. She couldn't remember having it placed there. She stood staring at the gem, perplexed, commiserating with the Greek Goddess Persephone at being tricked into marrying Hades. Too soon, she must take her place as his bride in the underworld.

"Elizabeth." The gravel edged, commanding voice of the man beside her was not the kind Irish burr of the man she adored. "I have a schedule to keep. The tide waits for no man."

She glanced up at him, unable to connect this brusque, frightening creature with the jovial Mr. O'Rourke who had courted her so sweetly. The man before her was rigid with impatience and although his face was concealed, she could feel his displeasure.

Captain Fletcher came to her side, his eyes gleaming as he observed her trying to regain her composure before the creature beside her: the bridegroom he had chosen for her. The dark, masked apparition dominated the atmosphere like a suffocating cloud of black smoke.

"There now, you be the brave girl I know you can be." Fletcher said as he leaned in to give her a noisy peck on the cheek. "Take heart, I hear he's only half mad."

Elizabeth gasped. The floor shifted beneath her feet and she stumbled, searching for purchase as the ancient stone chamber seemed to close in upon her.

She welcomed the darkness clouding her surroundings.

"Lizzie, sweet Lizzie, wake up." Donovan's rich, soothing voice rumbled pleasantly down her spine, sending comforting warmth through her.

The bed swayed rhythmically beneath her. The jangle of harnesses and the sound of steady hoof beats echoed around her as her world slowly came into focus. She was reclining at an awkward angle against something warm yet hard.

"Elizabeth. Open your eyes, Sweetheart."

She obeyed, beholding a beautiful yet ghastly sight. "Donovan? It is you. Oh, but what happened to your face?" She was cradled across his lap, her legs curled against his hip on the seat beside him. They were in a carriage, a very costly one with red velvet squabs.

And yet, his face was all red blotches and appeared to be cracked and peeling.

"It's the whites of eggs, oatmeal, and a little stage rouge thrown in for color." He replied, grinning. His hair was wild and full, an untamed black halo about his mottled face. He lifted the leather mask from the seat and allowed her to take it and examine it. "Convincing, wouldn't you say? As was your swoon, although that wasn't an act, was it, darlin'?"

"I never swoon." She stated, irritated with herself for such a weak display.

"It's your wedding day." He teased, his eyes alight with amusement. "It's expected."

"You—" She gasped, shaking the mask at him. "Oh, no—you shouldn't have done this. It's against the law to impersonate a noble—if they find out--"

"Shhh, love." He extracted the leather mask from her. "I rightfully possess the title of Count Rochembeau. It may not be worth much in France due to the revolution these days, but I assure you, it still holds a great deal of power and respect in the rest of the world."

"Why didn't you warn me?" Elizabeth wanted to smack his hideously lovely face. She wanted to hug him and cry into his neck like a ninny. Instead, she glowered at him, refusing to give in to her jangled emotions. "Do you have any idea how terrified I was?"

"Your fear helped convince Fletcher you were marrying someone you didn't know. Had he the slightest inclination that it was me beneath the disguise, he could have made trouble for us." The lightness left Donovan's eyes as he reflected on his words. "As it is, we must get you aboard my ship before he discovers my signature on the marriage contract and cries foul."

"Where is Michael? I was told 'the count' would be Michael's legal guardian. Surely he's coming with us . . .?" She paused, confused by all that had happened since she left the Sacred Grove this morning. "We are still going to the Indies, aren't we?"

Donovan sighed. "Yes, we are going to the Indies. I own a plantation near St. Kitts, as Count Rochembeau. And yes, Michael is under my protection, but he's staying in London. I've set him up in a suite at the Carlton Hotel and hired a tutor to help him prepare to enter St. Paul's Academy after Christmas. He has a great deal of catching up to do before then, years of schooling to make up for if he's to enter in January. Mr. Jamison, my lawyer here in London, will look in on him regularly to make certain that Michael has everything he needs."

"I didn't get to say goodbye." She stated, tears stinging her eyes at this sudden parting.

"We'll visit him in the spring. There are no schools in the Indies. All of the planters send their sons to England to be educated at St. Paul's and then on to Eton."

The reality of not seeing her little brother for months brought panic. Michael had been her responsibility, for so many years. Protecting Michael had been like breathing. What would she do without him?

"What's this?" Donovan's voice was gentle as he cupped her cheek with his palm. "Lizzie, don't cry. I've hired a tutor to look after him."

"A stranger." She retorted in a thick voice. "The captain won't leave him alone. He'll come after Michael. He'll bully him into giving him money. Michael has to be protected."

Donovan's hideous oatmeal, egg and rouged face crinkled when he frowned. Intelligent sapphire eyes studied her. "Trust me, *Cherie*." He whispered, brushing the moisture from her cheek with light fingertips. "Michael will be fine, I promise."

The intensity burning in his eyes made her want to believe him.

He leaned closer and she closed her eyes, knowing what was to come, surrendering to it. Donovan's lips brushed over hers in a gentle caress. She reached up and cradled her hands on either side of his face, kissing him back, daring him to set caution aside and kiss her like a proper bridegroom.

He didn't back down from the challenge.

Chapter Six

At sunset that same evening, Elizabeth stood before tall windows in a richly appointed cabin watching the city of her birth diminish as Donovan's ship left the harbor.

She turned from the window and gazed around the main room. The master cabin boasted two rooms and a privy closet that emptied into the sea--a convenience the first mate pointed out to her with pride earlier. A gold brocade settee faced tall galleon windows festooned with red velvet curtains. A Turkish carpet in deep red and gold hues covered the plank floor. Elizabeth wandered about the luxurious room, pausing to caress a bronze tiger statue on the desk, admire an oriental vase and study the watercolors depicting oriental landscapes on the wall.

She glanced at a paneled door leading to an adjoining room. Opening it, she discovered it was little more than a closet housing an enormous bed with a silk coverlet and stacks of lush pillows instead of the crude sailor's bunk she expected to find there.

Six weeks. *A honeymoon voyage with Donovan.* Remembering the potent promises of passion inherent within his kisses in the coach, she blushed and then smiled. She was a little uncertain about the mysteries of the marriage bed, being a virgin, but she trusted Donovan. He loved her. He proved it with this wild scheme, riding in like a knight in a fairytale to rescue both her and her little brother from the evil dragon. She had nothing to fear from his love.

Ah, but he wouldn't be here tonight. He promised to meet her beyond the English Channel, once his business affairs were settled. *Three days.* It might as well be a lifetime.

Exhaustion pulled at her. Elizabeth removed the pins from her hair and busied herself by brushing it and then plaiting it. Finished with the chore moments later, Elizabeth slipped out of the elegant coral silk gown and into a bed gown that had been laid out earlier in anticipation of her needs. She didn't have a maid. Donovan had been smug as he explained that he would serve her in that capacity during the voyage.

He seemed convinced that helping her dress and brushing out her long hair every day would be a treat--for both of them. She'd give it two days, and then he'd be letting her attend those chores herself. Sheila often cursed as she tried to rake the tangles out of Elizabeth's hair, and had threatened to take a scissors to the mess if she didn't hold still.

Dismissing the notion of her husband's assistance in the dressing room, Elizabeth held out her arms, admiring the billowy sleeves of her bed gown that gathered at her wrists with an elegant flourish of lace covering her hands. She caressed the crisp cotton fabric, pleased by the feel of it beneath her fingers. There hadn't been any new gowns, for sleeping in or otherwise, not since Mama died and they'd been plunged into poverty. Mindful of the expense of new clothing, she bent to retrieve the silk dress from the floor. She folded it carefully and placed it on the chair in the corner, and then crawled into the feather bed and snuffed out the candle.

A gut wrenching pain brought Elizabeth awake in the darkness. That invisible swordsman had just paid her an unwelcome visit while she slept. That damnable villain, and in her mind it had to be a male phantom responsible for such pain, was thrusting his sharp blade into her lower belly and out through her back. She was relieved that Donovan was not here, as she'd be mortified to have to explain her painful courses to a man. She cradled her belly and tried to ride out the fresh wave of agony. She should get up and find some toweling, but it was difficult to leave the cozy bed. She curled into a ball and hugged a pillow as the cramping intensified.

A sharp cry came from out on the deck, followed by agitated shouts and loud thumping noises. Heavy boots echoed on the planks outside her cabin. Donovan wasn't supposed to return for at least two days.

What on earth were those men doing out there, yelling and making such a terrible racket?

It sounded like they were fighting. She sat up, confused and frightened by the sounds.

The outer door burst open. Light moved and wobbled about the murky darkness beyond her closet door. Several men with torches filed into the small chamber and surrounded the bed.

Elizabeth screamed. She was roughly seized by two men. She kept on screaming, writhing, squirming, and fighting them--to no avail as her wrists were bound in front of her and she was dragged from the bed and out into the dark night.

Once on deck, she was hefted over the rail and into the waiting hands of other men on a smaller craft that was tied alongside the count's ship. As her eyes adjusted to the dim lantern light, she saw she was surrounded by a tight circle of men. They groped at her bottom and her breasts, and laughed at her outraged cries. They pushed her back and forth between them, like a toy. She screamed with every fiber of her being. She scratched at them with her tethered hands and shrank away from those rough, pinching hands, hoping to awaken from this nightmare.

The crack of a pistol rent the air. The men stopped tormenting her. One of their comrades slipped to the deck with his chest blooming crimson. She looked about for her rescuer, hoping Donovan had returned during the melee. A portly, unkempt fellow waved his pistol in the air. "Stand away from the Countess." He bellowed. Stepping closer, he grabbed her forearm and pulled Elizabeth toward the hole in the deck, while placing himself in front of her with his pistol leveled at the crowd who had tormented her moments ago. He pointed to the ladder and gestured for her to descend into bowels of the ship. Frightened, confused, and grateful for his interference, she did as he instructed, climbing down the ladder. He jumped down behind her, rather than climbing as she had done. Once there, he took her wrist and pulled her along by behind him until they came to a small cell with iron bars. He shoved her inside. "There, now. You'll be safe here. My apologies, Miss." He said, freeing her bound wrists with a knife. "My men don't know how to treat a fine lady."

Her first thought was to thank him. She caught herself. This man might have prevented her from being ravished, but he wasn't helping her escape, he was locking her up. Elizabeth rubbed her chaffed wrists and concentrated on summoning the courage to demand her release, and manage not to sound frightened into the bargain.

Before she could form the words to chastise his actions, she was abruptly flattened beneath him on the dirty floor as he attempted to take over where his comrades left off. With her arms free of the bonds, Elizabeth fought hard, determined to wriggle from beneath his considerable bulk. She hit him with her fist and then clawed at his face, aiming for his eyes, but succeeding only in scratching his cheek. A fist slammed against her temple, stunning her with an explosion of bone shattering pain. As she tried to recover her senses, her assailant grabbed her ankles and pried open her legs. She kicked and twisted, to no avail. His hands were iron shackles. Crawling upwards, he pinned her legs beneath his knees, unbuckled his belt and yanked up her bed gown.

"God's tooth--what's this!" the dirty sailor swore, drawing his crimson hand from between her thighs. "No wonder that spook left you alone. You're a disgusting mess!" He sidled away from her and stood, wiping his bloody fingers on his yellowed shirt.

Thankful for the first time for something she'd considered a curse, Elizabeth scrambled back into the shadows, away from him. "Who are you? Why have you abducted me?"

"Cap'n Sully's the name. I could have left you up there to deal with my men." He cocked his head at her like an old dog. "I'm thinkin' you ought to be more accommodatin'. Oh, but you'll warm to me, won't ye, girl? After you've spent some time down here; with the rats."

The apothecary shop was bustling with activity. Six customers waited for assistance and Barnaby was in a conference with a client for the Midnight Bell. A searing pain in the back of his skull made Kieran O'Flaherty drop the jar in his hand. The sound of shattering glass echoed in his ears as the shop faded from his perceptions.

He was backed into a corner in a dark, dirty place, curled into a tight ball. His knees were instinctively drawn up to protect his abdomen. Someone was trying to kick him to death. The attack waned. The owner of that lethal boot huffed and wheezed in the semi-darkness. Kieran braced himself for another onslaught. None came.

Gazing about, Kieran surmised he was in the bowels of a ship, in a dirty cell lit by a single tinned lantern. He was seized by the hair---it seemed he had handfuls of the stuff—and was roughly dragged from the corner he'd been huddled in. The stench of unwashed flesh assaulted his nostrils as something vile was pushed at his face. He clamped his mouth shut, refusing to cooperate, only to have his head slammed against the bulkhead.

Waves of blinding pain made him too weak to resist any longer.

He must have blacked out. He was alone in the cell, huddled in the corner on moldy straw. He was linked to a young woman, seeing through her eyes, feeling her pain, tasting the bitterness of her fear. He was inside her mind. Fetid water wicked up the material of her thin gown, and the cold seeped through to her very bones. Kieran felt sick and disorientated from the oppressive pain in his skull. Bursts of light flashed in front of his eyes and the taste of dirty pennies was in the back of his throat. He heard the sound of labored breathing as the girl struggled to contain her horror at what had been done to her. There was a furry sensation on the back of his neck. Kieran jerked convulsively, his gut seizing with revulsion. Every nerve along his spine tightened. He reached up to slap it off. Another creature ran across his bare foot. The girl, whose mind he had been linked with, slapped at the vermin and screamed.

She kept right on screaming long after the rats had scurried into the darkness . . .

"Kieran!" Barnaby's face slowly formed in front of him. "You had another vision." His mentor clarified, for the benefit of the patrons surrounding them with concern.

"Aye, a vision." Kieran muttered, feeling sick and exhausted from the experience. The shop was silent. A burly footman offered him a hand. Kieran was pulled up from the floor. He nodded his thanks, limped to the back room and sagged against the wall. He'd never experienced anything like this in all his life. He'd just been inside the mind of a young woman while she was being attacked.

"Go upstairs, lie down." Barnaby insisted with the voice that brooked no refusal. "You look like you've just escaped the lower regions of hell!"

"I did." Kieran mumbled. "But that poor girl is still trapped there."

To the bewildered smuggler crew, the dark, cloaked figure leading the charge over the rail appeared to be a giant black bird swooping down on its prey. Hence, he'd come to be known as The Raven, a bird associated with dark omens and death in ancient myth, a name he made synonymous with death to any who dared cross his path on the Indian Ocean.

He tracked the small fishing vessel along the southwestern coast of Wales since dawn. When they ignored his signal, he fired a warning shot over the prow. The sloop responded by widening the sails in an effort to flee. They could not outrun his schooner, it was lightest, fastest craft of the times. As he was flying the Union Jack, not pirate colors, he took their unwillingness to communicate as a sign they had something to hide.

Through the cover of cannon fire from his larger Merchantman, The Raven maneuvered his schooner alongside the smuggler's sloop. He didn't wait for the grappling hooks to be secured as he dropped to the deck and began hacking a wide path through the befuddled crew. A portly man emerged from the hold. Raised, angry red scratches marred one cheek, confirming The Raven's suspicions; an unwilling female was on board and had attempted to fend off this filthy cur. The man wobbled with inebriated shock as he took in the stream of armed men flooding his vessel. "Who are you?"

The Raven slipped his blade beneath the captain's ribs, disarming him with the sure promise of disembowelment if he so much as moved. "Did our employer neglect to inform you I was coming? T'was made clear to me, a split by three."

"Fletcher didn't say nothin' bout splitting the cut by three! The deal was him and me."

"He sent me to make sure you were following orders. Where's the girl?"

"I follow captain's orders, always have, since Ireland. A body'd be a fool to cross him. Ruthless prick, even when he was under military orders."

"Where is she?" The Raven pressed his blade into his victim's gelatinous paunch.

"In the hold, and there she stays, 'til that rich cove what owns her delivers the coin!"

The Raven gestured to the opening in the deck. His Indian servant and several men took his cue and disappeared down the hole.

"Sent you to steal her from me, did he!" The captain was fairly frothing at the mouth, furious but unable to lunge without impaling himself on his adversary's blade.

"Perhaps." The Raven shrugged. "How much did he offer you to steal the wench?"

The captain remained silent. With one steady pull of his blade The Raven sliced through layers of flesh. Not deep enough to do any real damage, just enough to make his victim bleed; make him panic. He stopped at the throat, holding the captain like a fish on a hook.

"Five hundred pounds." The captain offered in a hoarse whisper, aware that a careless movement of his Adam's apple could cause the sword to pierce his windpipe. "Three hundred to be split between the crew and two hundred for me--for services rendered."

"What *services*?"

The seaman remained tight-lipped.

The Raven was not going to play this game. He withdrew a pistol from his belt and pulled the trigger. The captain howled and slumped to the deck cradling his shattered foot. "Answer, if you want to keep the rest of your toes."

"Wanted her ruined—broken and scared when we returned her to her husband—them be his words, mate, not mine. Wanted me to rough her up, make certain there'd not be another heir popping up later on to compete with his son's claim to the family fortune."

53

"Did you? He said you couldn't do it! Said you were weak, limp, *his words, not mine!*"

"Oh, I shagged the bitch, make no mistake, scared her real good, just like he wanted. I earned my cut and I ain't sharing it with the likes of you. Who the hell are you?"

"We have her, sir!" His Indian servant called out as they carried the unconscious woman's battered form to the waiting vessel.

Dr. Linton approached him as he stood over his prey. "I'll need to examine her to determine if she's been *damaged* by these brutes--"

"Don't touch her." The Raven warned, blood pulsing dangerously in his temples at the thought of any man touching his prize.

"She needs tending, my lord, there is a great deal of blood."

He removed the second pistol from his belt and cocked it. "I said don't touch her. I'll kill you if you do. Is that understood, doctor?"

"Yes, sir." The surgeon backed away with raised hands.

The Raven crouched over a dead body. He snatched a scarf from the limp neck and began wiping the blood from his steel. He lifted it and turned it about to inspect the blade under the glare of the noonday sun. The razor edge winked at him. Cold, hard steel; there was nothing like it for settling scores. It could be as precise as a surgeon's blade; sever tendons, penetrate organs, or remove a man's most offensive part. A devious smile burst forth from his lips as his eyes moved to the man crouched at the rail.

He pushed the black scarf that hid his face onto his brow and returned to his captive.

"Who are you?" The captain asked a third time in a voice weak from loss of blood. The man squinted against the glare of the sun as he gazed up at the unmasked face of his executioner.

The Raven poked the captain in the throat with the tip of his blade, forcing the swine to look him in the eyes before he killed him. "I'm the rich husband."

Chapter Seven

Donovan gazed at his bride now safely bundled in his bed. Her head was wreathed in bandages instead of a lace veil. Her eyes were ringed in purple. She had two cracked ribs and her shins were a mass of bruises that pained him to look at. Rat bites marred her hands and feet. He applied a paste of golden seal to them and clean linens to stave off an infection.

The most worrisome injury was the contusion on the back of her head. Five days had passed, yet his sleeping angel refused to wake up. As a physician he knew the longer she remained in this unnatural slumber, the less likely it was she would recover. She might awaken as a beautiful, living doll, incapable of cognizant thought---or she might never awaken at all.

A cough echoed in the small room. He jerked his head up. It was that idiot doctor again. Damn it, if the old fool wasn't pestering him about bleeding Elizabeth, he nattered on about the need to examine her to determine if she'd been molested by her captors. The dried blood on her inner thighs, coupled with her captor's confession, seemed quite conclusive in his mind.

"I didn't mean to startle you, my lord." Linton moved noiselessly around the bed, reminding him of an alligator gliding silently in the Carolina swamps. The doctor was a thin, nervous man sporting a full head of gray hair, wire spectacles and a neatly groomed goatee. "I'm going to have to insist that we try the bleeding, sir."

Donovan stood. At six foot and then some, he towered over the doctor. "She's lost a great deal of blood already, you idiot. The last thing she needs is another man to cause her pain."

"The pain might bring her about." Linton argued. "Come now, trained in the Far East as you were, you're not familiar with modern medical practices. Why, even a medical student understands the benefits of a good bleeding."

"Put that lancet away, doctor, unless you want me to sink it in your throat."

Dr. Linton stared blandly up at him, deluded in the belief that a younger physician would give way to age and experience if pressed. So, no one bothered to warn the new ship's surgeon about crossing him. Apparently no one cared enough about Linton to do so. Few men could comprehend that a consequence of surviving torture was the peeling away of that thin veneer of a civilized gentleman, exposing the primitive beast beneath.

Donovan no longer feared that beast; he learned long ago to embrace it.

Without further warning, he snatched the lancet from his opponent and pressed the sharp point beneath Linton's jugular. Linton sidled back with alarm and quickly exited the cabin.

"Imbecile." He muttered, closing the door with a defining thud. He knelt beside the bed, lifted a limp, bandaged hand and pressed it against his cheek. Tears breached the barricade of his tightly closed eyes before he could stop them.

After depositing Elizabeth on his Galleon at the London docks, Donovan journeyed to Lord Greystowe's estate to confront the cold English lord and inform him that in spite of his callous neglect, his grandchildren would be well provided for from this point on. The meeting didn't go as he anticipated. The old earl broke into tears at the news that his grandchildren were alive. He'd been out of the country when his daughter died. The note Elizabeth sent to his estate was set aside unopened until his return, a year later. The earl hurried to London only to find the townhouse belonging to his daughter had been sold. He hired investigators to find his grandchildren, but Fletcher had gone aground like fox, taking the children with him. The old Earl was relieved to find they were safe, and demanded Michael be placed in his keeping immediately. Donovan couldn't refuse the old man. Michael was his heir and would . . .

A soft moan brought him back to the present. He rose and sat on the edge of the bed. "Elizabeth, wake up." He shook her gently. "Come now, you have to wake up, dearest!"

Those enchanting turquoise pools fluttered open. Elizabeth stared up at his face for a few brief seconds, and then she started screaming.

His valet burst through the door from the outer suite with Dr. Linton following. The invasion of men sent Elizabeth fleeing into the corner. She braced her bandaged hands against the walls and regarded them all with the eyes of a cornered doe.

"You shouldn't be out of bed, you're too weak." He held his hand up to warn the others back. "Come, Lizzie, bed rest is what you need."

"M-m-my n-name is . . . E-liz-a-beth!" She insisted, in slow, halting speech. "M-mother doesn't allow anyone t—t--to call me Lizzie. She says its w-what you call a sc-scullery maid."

"Well, Elizabeth, are you hungry?" He coaxed, relieved that she could speak at all after what she'd come through. "I can have the cook warm some milk and put in a pinch of nutmeg. Or perhaps hot chocolate would be more to your liking?"

"H-h-how is it t-that you have s-such things h-here? W-we're at s-s-sea."

Cognitive reasoning. The tightness lessened about his chest a little more. "I'm a wealthy man. We have goats in the hold, chickens, apples, cheeses, hams, all manner of delightful things. I can have the cook prepare you whatever you desire." He rose and extended his hand to her. "First, let's get you back into bed, Sweetheart."

Her eyes scanned his black attire. "H-he sold me, didn't he? Papa sold me to you!" Moisture welled up in her purple ringed eyes. Pressed into the corner, barefoot, wearing a bed-gown, she gave the heart-wrenching impression of little girl ready to burst into terrified tears.

"No, lass, it wasn't like that." With careful movements so as not to startle her, he edged close. She froze. He inclined his head to examine her eyes. Her pupils were unequal, a sign of disorientation. "Don't you remember me? I bought up all Fletcher's notes in exchange for your hand in marriage. I'm your husband--"

"No—it isn't true!" Elizabeth shrieked. She darted from him as if he were the very devil sent to claim her soul. His valet and Dr. Linton blocked the doorway, so she scurried around the bed and crouched in the opposite corner, her breath reduced to quick, short gasps as she cast panicked eyes at the three men hemming her in.

Donovan realized the sooner the other men left, the better his chances were of calming her. "Pearl, bring warmed milk and buttered toast. Dr. Linton, there is no need for you to be lurking about my suite. I'll summon you if I need you."

She continued to stare at the open door after the men retreated. The quaking of her limbs continued, but rather than over-breathing Lizzie didn't appear to be breathing at all.

He rounded the bed and crouched beside her, attempting to put himself at the same level so as not to appear so intimidating to the poor girl. "It's all right, Sweet Lizzie." He held out his hand. She didn't take it. He didn't expect her to. He was just trying to get her past her terror.

She turned her gaze to him. The fragile look in her eyes burned like acid in his chest. He couldn't stand the inches between them. He sat down on the floor, stretched out his long legs and gently but firmly pulled her out of the corner and settled her on his lap.

He cupped her bandaged head, guiding the weaving orb to rest against his shoulder and continued to talk to her in a reassuring timbre. Elizabeth melted against him, too weak to resist. She was soft and warm in his arms. The thought nibbled at him that he really should put her back in the bed. He was loath to relinquish this sacred moment after days of watching her linger between this world and the next.

Elizabeth shivered, from fear rather than cold, he surmised, but she didn't fight his careful embrace. "My Sweet Girl." He whispered, battling the urge to plant fevered kisses across her dear face. "I won't let anyone harm you. They'd have to come through me to get to you. They'd have to kill me, and I'm not so easy to kill." He inclined his head to gauge her reaction.

She seemed bewildered. "Y-you rescued me?"

"I did." He affirmed, offering a tender smile. "You are safe, Elizabeth. I promise."

She licked her cracked lips as relief softened her tense features. "C-could you t-t-take me home, sir? I-I'm sorry. I don't remember your name."

"Yes." He whispered, stroking the cheek that wasn't marred by cruel bruises, anxious to banish her tears. Never mind if it was a different home than the one she meant. He just wanted her to feel safe in his keeping. "I'm taking you home, lass."

Lizzie sighed, weariness evident in the sound. She placed her small, bandaged hand on his chest. Nestling against him, she closed her eyes, content to sleep in his arms. It was a simple gesture, yet priceless, revealing a trust he didn't deserve. His eyes stung. His throat closed up as he fought the desire to crush her against him in a painful mixture of grief and gratitude that she was alive, warm and safe in his arms.

"Don't argue with me, just drink it." Captain Jack Rawlings, Donovan's friend and ally from their pirating days, set the whiskey bottle on the table and shoved the glass in his hand. They were cloistered in Jack's quarters, in the outer suite where the captain held card games to entertain his officers during the long passages between England and the Caribbean.

"She doesn't know me." Donovan sat forward on the chair, elbows on his splayed knees, cradling the drink between his palms. "It's been a week, Jack."

"Her memory is affected." The blond captain sat across from him, a bright grin breaking the bronzed terrain of his face. "Shouldn't that be a good thing?"

Donovan studied the carpet between his splayed knees. He set his glass on the table untouched. "She remembers her captivity—rather—she vaguely recalls being held captive by men intent on harming her, but she doesn't remember me--at all."

"A little confusion is normal after a knock on the head, even I know that."

This was more than a little confusion. Elizabeth believed she was sixteen years old, not eighteen. She couldn't remember him because in her mind she'd never met him before she'd awakened in his bed last week. She slept most of the time since then. Each time she awakened she asked him who he was. When he told her, she responded with shock and outraged denials. He tried not to let it bother him too much, as she forgot everything he told her in a short time.

Jack picked up the untouched drink and shoved it at him. "Here, one drink won't muddle your reasoning."

Donovan swirled the amber liquid in his hand. As Jack continued to eye him, he downed the glass in one gulp and exhaled sharply as the fiery libation spread warmth through his insides.

Nodding with satisfaction, Jack poured himself another portion, took a sip and murmured, "I'd give my soul to be in your place, to have Amelia here with me. And if she were a mite confused I'd count myself fortunate and start wooing her all over again."

Jack's fiancée, a merchant's daughter from Boston, had accompanied her father to the east to purchase silks years ago. Their ship was taken by Barbary pirates. Her father escaped and sent word to Jack that Amelia had been sold to an Arab prince. He authorized Jack to empty his bank account for a ransom. Jack arrived with the funds for her release, only to learn that his beloved had been executed one week earlier for defying her captor.

Half mad with grief, Jack turned to piracy. They crossed swords on the Indian Ocean as rival corsairs. Donovan shot Jack in the leg during their skirmish. Jack kept fighting with the spirit of a Viking berserker, propping himself up on a barrel and artfully deflecting his opponent's blade, all the while assaulting Donovan with that wide, brilliant grin--until he passed out from loss of blood. Donovan removed the bullet and weaned the sailor from his opium addiction. They formed an alliance, becoming The Raven and Black Jack, and made their fortune terrorizing ships in the East Indies.

Donovan turned his empty glass about in his hands. He wished he could be like Jack and toss back a bottle now and then to forget. There were risks for those seeking forgetfulness at the bottom of a bottle. His body would forever bear the marks of such carelessness. He could have stayed home and studied medicine at Harvard College, in America. But no, as a lad of seventeen he wanted to be free of his overprotective mother and her smothering, so he felt it necessary to put a sea between them. If he hadn't been perpetually drunk during his time in Paris, he might have noticed his uncle's seditious bent and distanced himself from the man before the King's Guard came to his uncle's chateau to arrest them both.

What a sorry pair they made, Jack and himself. They often debated who had saved whom from madness in the East. The truth was they had somehow managed to save each other.

Chapter Eight

That strange man was sitting in the chair beside her bed again. He was reading, unaware Elizabeth was awake and studying him. Shoulder length black hair was secured in a neat queue. He wore a clean linen shirt with the sleeves rolled up at the elbows. A neatly tied stock hung from his neck, secured by a ruby pin. A black silk vest shot with gold and green threads remained unbuttoned. Black breeches hugged muscular thighs, disappearing beneath gleaming Top boots. His hands were neatly manicured. A signet ring circled one finger but she could not make out the crest in the dim light. It was obvious the man was a gentleman, not a sailor.

She tried to remember who he was and why she was here with him. There was the vague impression that he had rescued her, yet how she came to be in that dark hold in the first place and needed his rescuing was a mystery to her. "Excuse me, Sir?"

Pale blue eyes gazed up from the book. Hair as dark and shiny as a raven's wing swirled in elegant swathes about a face that had been lightly kissed by the sun. What mischievous pooka had enchanted this handsome man to make him take an interest in her affairs?

"Do you need to use the privy closet?" He set the book aside and started to rise.

"No!" Elizabeth flushed scarlet, all the romance of the previous moment effectively doused as she recalled he'd been carrying her to that small closet frequently during her illness. "I-I just needed to ask you a question, sir, that's all."

He sat down, hunching forward slightly, elbows resting upon splayed knees, his large hands laced together before him. "Go ahead." He sighed with an air of resignation.

"You've been very kind to look after me, sir. I'm afraid I don't recall your name."

"Dr. Donovan O'Rourke Beaumont, Count Rochembeau, at your service, my lady."

"You're a doctor and a nobleman? How can that be?"

"My father was the younger son of a French Count. Being the younger son and not the heir, he went off to make his fortunes in the American colonies. He bought a plantation in the Carolinas and married the feisty Irish lass who stole his heart. My mother christened me with both her parent's surnames so I might never forget I'm half Irish." He spoke in a languid colonial drawl with just the hint of an Irish burr in it, a mixture she found alluring.

Elizabeth couldn't help but smile. He smiled back, and her insides did a peculiar little twist to be the recipient of such bounty.

"I went to France to study medicine, and lived with my uncle, the former count. My uncle died without heirs, bestowing upon me the ancient title of Count Rochembeau. So, I'm American by birth, a count by default, and a physician by choice."

She nodded at his explanation. "I owe you a great debt for rescuing me, my lord. My grandmother will be very worried. She's quite old and frail. We must send word to her."

Her caretaker reached forward, took her hand and cradled it between his own. "Your grandmother passed on some weeks ago."

"*No!*" She protested as her throat closed around a hard stone that suddenly lodged there. She squeezed her eyes shut to contain the moisture gathering before it spilled out onto her cheeks. The large hand encompassing her own tightened slightly, not enough to hurt, but enough to convey his compassion, enough to say he understood her grief. She opened her eyes. Releasing a strangled sob, she swiped at the tears escaping down her cheeks with the lace sleeve of her gown. "Sheila loved me, more than my own mother."

"Yes." Something flickered in her caretaker's eyes. "Sheila loved you very much. That's why she made me promise to take care of you after she died."

"Well, I do have a brother, sir. Michael Fletcher. Have you attempted to contact him?"

"Ah, Michael's a good lad." He patted the hand he had firm possession of, and took to stroking her captured limb in a manner that seemed far too intimate. "He's in London, preparing to enter St. Paul's Academy in the spring."

"And just w-who is p-paying f-for that?" She huffed, enraged by his strange claim and frustrated by her inability to speak clearly.

"Your grandfather. I was planning to, but the earl insisted upon it in the end."

Elizabeth sat bolt upright in the bed and jerked her hand from his grasp. "Lord Greystowe? The Earl wouldn't care if Michael and I were d-drowned in the Th-thames as infants! H-he disowned my m-mother—h-h-he-he-"

"Easy, lass!" He rose to stand over her. "You're getting upset and there's no need. Michael is fine, and I'm going to take good care of you, just as I promised Old Sheila."

"I want to go home." She tossed back the covers and swung her legs over the bed.

Strong hands circled her shoulders, preventing her from rising. "You're not leaving this bed. You suffered a severe blow to the head that nearly killed you. That's why you can't remember the past two years of your life."

Two years? What a queer world she'd awakened to; Sheila was dead and Michael was at a school for rich boys? And she was in the keeping of a stranger. "Where are you taking me?"

"To the West Indies."

"But I don't know anyone in the Indies!" She whispered above the load roar in her ears. The room seemed hot and confining, like a prison cell.

"That's where I live, darlin', on a beautiful island." He sat down on the bed, facing her, his arm resting along her thigh. She could feel the weight of his hand on her leg, the heat of him even with the blanket between them. "We can go riding in mornings and picnic on the beach in the afternoons. You can collect sea shells and swim in the ocean."

"I don't know how to swim." She managed in a voice that sounded high and tight to her ears. Fisting the blanket in her hands, she gazed about the room for some portal, some magical means of escape that would take her back to Sheila, Michael, and all that was familiar to her.

"It's all right. I'll teach you." The count caressed her cheek with a light forefinger.

Elizabeth grew still. His caress, his nearness, his manner were too familiar. "Are you—are you my legal guardian, s-sir?"

He studied her for a torturous moment, as if debating the answer in his mind. "I suppose in a manner of speaking, I am." He confided, then paused before adding, "I'm your husband."

She gasped in outrage. "That's impossible—"

"It's the truth." He countered, his intense blue eyes softening in commiseration. "I would never trifle with you on such an important matter, my dear."

Elizabeth stared at the man, unable to think as the frightening absurdity of it washed over her. Married—it was so permanent. "I'm too young to be married, I'm only sixteen."

"You are eighteen, Elizabeth. The year is seventeen ninety-eight, not ninety-six."

Elizabeth nibbled her lower lip, her mind working furiously for a way out of this mess. *Married, yet tainted*—there was the rub. "You don't have to keep me, sir." She spoke rapidly, desperate to barter her release. "You can have the marriage annulled. No one would blame you after what happened—I can take care of myself, I've been doing it for most of my life. I'm strong--I can find work, and-and, you could remarry—someone who isn't tainted—"

Two long, lean fingers pressed against her lips to stop her impulsive rambling. She shivered, recognizing the steely resolve in those bonny blue eyes.

"There will be no annulment." The voice that had been velvet became stone. He removed his hand from her lips. "You are my wife, not a horse to be traded at the market. And you insult my integrity by suggesting I should cast you aside for what someone did to you. What happened is not your fault. You must never believe for a moment that it is. I should be the one begging your forgiveness. It's pointless when I'll never be able to forgive myself."

An awkward silence stretched on after his emotional outburst. Elizabeth didn't understand why he should feel her abduction reflected badly upon him.

Recovering quickly, he rose from the bed and took to tugging the covers up about her with jerky movements. "Lie back and rest." He commanded in a clogged timbre, as if his throat ached and he found it painful to speak. He turned away from her and stalked to the door.

"Wait, might I ask one question, sir?"

Turning on his heels to face her, an ebony brow sliced upward at a dangerous angle.

"How long have we been married?"

"Not quite a month."

"And, how long have I been ill?"

"That's two questions." He warned, taking a step nearer the bed. "You were abducted after the wedding ceremony, while I was detained elsewhere on business. So, the answer to both questions is the same; we've been married and you've been ill for over three weeks."

Elizabeth blinked. What seemed a sparse few days in her mind had been nearly a month?

She rose up on an elbow as more questions rose to the forefront. "But how—"

The count's eyes narrowed. "I told you to lie down and rest quietly, and that is precisely what you are going to do." With that, he left the room.

Elizabeth experienced a pang at his retreat. She felt safe when he was near. She felt an inexplicable panic whenever she awakened and found herself alone in this strange place. Deep down, she knew he would not hurt her; he'd protect her if need be, with his very life.

Perhaps that was significant; she felt safe with him, trusted him on a purely instinctual level. He had been kind to her. He was wickedly handsome. And young--she was fortunate in that respect. She could have awakened to find herself married to some ancient, foul smelling . . .

The count strode into the room with a purposeful mien. He held out a parchment.

Elizabeth took the sheet from him. It was a certificate of marriage—dated two years into the future. Dr. D. O. Beaumont, Count Rochembeau is joined in the bonds of holy matrimony to Elizabeth Grace O'Flaherty, on September the fifth, Seventeen Hundred and Ninety Eight.

There it was, in permanent black ink. She belonged to this man, like his horse or his cane plantation. He could do with her as he pleased and none could interfere, the law was on his side. She dropped the parchment and shrank back, into the corner of the bed.

"There is no need to be frightened, Elizabeth." The count soothed as he sat down on the bed and gently took her hand in his. "I know you've been hurt. You needn't fear me. I'm not like those men who hurt you. I'm a gentleman, and a gentleman does not abuse those in his keeping. I'll not expect more of you than you're able to give. I'll give you time . . . to heal."

Elizabeth quelled the rising panic as she listened to his persuasive timbre. He spoke on, of separate rooms at his estate if she wished, of taking things at a leisurely pace and allowing her to come to know him as her friend before they pursued the intimacy of lovers. She felt herself relax by degrees. His voice, his words were compelling as he spoke in that soft, deliberate tone.

As she listened, her mind latched onto a detail that might be her salvation in all of this: he didn't know she was still a maid. He said she'd been abducted after the wedding, which meant it was *before* the wedding night. That being the case, he couldn't know her heavy courses prevented her from being abused by her captors. He assumed she'd been molested and he was offering her a celibate marriage based on his assumption.

Good Heavens! She'd be a fool to set him straight now.

Elizabeth mumbled her gratitude for his kindness to her. She slumped onto the pillows, feeling as if she'd escaped a harrowing fate--and that by inches. Her limbs were shuddering. Her insides felt like a great, looming cavern infested by gnawing fear.

"Just rest, my sweet. All this agitation isn't good for you."

Elizabeth closed her eyes. She was surprised at the weariness pulling at her. The count continued to sit on the bed, his hand stroking her forearm in slow, patient circles. The gesture was comforting as she lay quietly as he bade, closed her eyes, and let the world go by.

Chapter Nine

The waters were murky and turbulent beneath the moonless October sky.

Donovan leaned against the rail on the forecastle deck nursing his tobacco and watching smoke rings float into the night. The melody of an overworked fiddle carried up from the main deck as the men laughed and bantered while sharing their rum rations.

Ignorance had its benefits. His medical texts described a plethora of symptoms in patients with head injuries, everything from mild dizziness, disorientation and impaired coordination, the abrupt loss of vision or hearing and speech impediments to limb paralysis and full blown grand mal seizures. Lizzie's speech difficulties manifested only when she was fatigued or agitated. They diminished with enforced rest, so he attributed that symptom to anxiety, not brain damage.

He ran a hand along the tense muscles of his neck and gazed into the dark horizon.

So far, there had been no presentation of grand mals, but he was noticing petit seizures occurring with alarming frequency now that she was awake for longer periods. Lizzie took to staring into space, as if in a trance. She wasn't aware of their occurrence and she emerged from the odd spells with verbal prompting, so he was trying to not worry overmuch.

Donovan exhaled a wreath of smoke and studied the fluid reflections of light dancing upon the surface of the water from the ship's lanterns. Lizzie seemed more alert than usual this afternoon. She kept asking him questions, her mind voracious for answers after weeks of lethargy. That was a good sign, a ray of sunlight amid the shadows of uncertainty.

He tossed the stub of his cheroot into the sea and gazed out at the dark horizon.

A movement from behind caught him off guard. Instinctively, he reached for his pistol.

It was Jack, coming to join him at the rail. Donovan dropped his hand from his belt. He turned his back to the sea, stretched his arms out along the railing, and enjoyed the crisp breeze blowing through his hair. Since their retirement from piracy Rawlings lost his wealth to gambling, including his ship. Donovan asked his friend to captain of *The Pegasus*. The position benefited them both. Jack would have a ship to sail and Donovan could rest easy knowing his cargo would reach the markets unhindered. Who better to guard a treasure than a former pirate?

Jack looked surreptitiously about them. "We need to talk, in private."

"Come to my cabin." Donovan replied, fiercely aware of the passage of time. Lizzie was asleep, and his valet was looking after her, but it pained him to be away from her for too long.

At the arched entrance to the officer's deck, just outside his cabin door, a figure leaned against the wall. Donovan stopped. Jack cannoned into him from behind.

A glint of steel in the lantern light made Donovan reach for his pistol a second time.

"What are you doing lurking outside his lordship's suite, sailor?" Jack demanded.

Donovan recognized the slim figure of Ambrose Duchamp beneath the dim circle of light next to his door. "It's all right, Jack, its Duchamp." He holstered his weapon. Duchamp had been Donovan's first mate in the east. Jack brought his first mate with him to his new position. Duchamp was barely tolerated by Rawlings. It didn't help that the Frenchman liked to sit alone in the shadows, paring ripe fruit with his enormous dagger.

"I know who it is!" Jack barked, resenting Donovan's intrusion in matters of discipline. "I asked you a question, sailor. Answer it."

"I was sitting under the stairs when the Indian went below." Duchamp explained. He waved his dagger at the portal. The door was left slightly ajar. "Damned careless, my lord. A man might be tempted to sneak in and visit *la petite belle* while she sleeps."

Donovan nodded. Duchamp sauntered past them. Jack scowled after the man.

The smell tipped him off as soon as Donovan entered his cabin, the pungent aroma of his valet's intoxicating tobacco. The hookah was on the carpet near the open window, as was the valet's sitar. Pearl had been on one of his wool-gathering expeditions again, forgetting he was supposed to be minding Elizabeth as he wandered off to the galley for something to eat.

Jack sat at the small table and reached into his coat to remove an envelope.

Donovan lifted the curtain and peered into the smaller room. Elizabeth was asleep, as he expected. He opened the cabinet to retrieve two goblets and an unopened bottle of whiskey, Jack's sedative of preference. He poured a measure in each glass, pushing one toward his friend.

Jack cradled the crystal goblet in one hand, holding the stem between splayed fingers. "What did that angry mob want with Duchamp in France? You tossed him a rope and hauled him onto your ship as you were leaving the quay. Suppose he was guilty of some heinous crime?"

"Ambrose has proven his loyalty to me a thousand times over." Donovan replied, dismissing Jack's insinuation. Taking the seat across from his friend, he gestured to the envelope. "What is it you wanted to discuss?"

Jack opened the packet and spread the two letters from the abduction before them. "I've interviewed my officers and the crew. No one remembers who delivered the kegs of ale before they set sail from the London docks. Jinks said this letter accompanied the delivery."

"We've been over this. The crew accepted the ale as a gift from me with the forged note encouraging them to celebrate my good fortune in taking a bride. We know Fletcher was behind the abduction. He probably pried the seal from the letter I sent him a week earlier and reused it."

A lock of red hair also lay between them. It had been tied about the handle of the dagger pinning the ransom note to the main mast. The note demanded two thousand pounds for the safe return of the Countess de Rochembeau.

Fletcher is going to die, he thought as he caressed his wife's hair. After learning the gambler orchestrated Elizabeth's

70

abduction, Donovan sent his own couriers of death to London to ferret out the man and exact revenge. Duchamp volunteered, but he preferred to keep his most vicious dog close to heel in case they suffered further hazard during the voyage.

"Damn," Jack's fist hit the table. "If I'd been here that night, I'd have known this note was a forgery. It doesn't sound like something you'd say." Jack had accompanied him to Lord Greystowe's estate, at his request.

"My wife is sleeping." Donovan chastened sharply.

Jack gave him a pained look. They sipped their drinks silently, tensed like two old nursemaids waiting for a whimper to come from the smaller room.

"I'm thinking someone was planted here." Jack whispered after a few moments, hunching forward slightly. "One of their own could have been hiding below, waiting to give signal when our crew was knocked out by the drugged ale. How else would they know it was safe to attack?"

"Does it matter? They're all dead."

"Yes, but, how else could aging sailors overcome seasoned fighters who took down Barbary Pirates--" Jack's eyes widened as he looked behind Donovan. He rose. "*My lady!*"

Donovan followed Jack's startled gaze. Elizabeth was standing pale and silent as a wraith behind him. Sleepwalking, he guessed, due to the decrease in her nightly Laudanum.

Rising, he blessed Duchamp for his heightened vigilance that seemed to annoy everyone else. Unguarded, Elizabeth might have wandered out on deck and fallen overboard. At the moment, her womanly curves were visible through the thin gown with the lantern light behind her. He stepped forward and hugged her to him to shield his wife from Jack's hungry gaze.

Lizzie leaned into his embrace, all softness and compliance. Lavender scented hair he'd washed for her earlier this evening wafted deliciously beneath his nose. He nuzzled the top of her head with kisses, savoring the feel of her in his arms as she sagged trustingly into his embrace.

A discreet cough made him remember his guest. He shook off the stupor. "Sit, Jack."

"Jack?" Lizzie asked in a sleep thickened voice. Her head lifted from its haven beneath his chin. She turned to face Jack. "Are you Captain Jack Rawlings, from Boston?"

"I am." Jack made a gallant bow. "A pleasure, Madame Beaumont."

"Amelia asked me to give you a message, sir."

Jack went rigid. Donovan could feel the man's heart seizing in his chest.

"It's just the Laudanum." Donovan said. "Pay it no mind, Jack, sit down, and pour yourself another drink. Let me get her settled." He swept Lizzie up in his arms, determined to remove her before things turned nasty. He deposited his wife on the bed and took his time tucking her in, giving Jack time to compose himself. "There, my sweet, go back to sl—"

"What did she say?" Jack's voice boomed like cannon fire behind him.

Donovan turned about, incensed that the man would follow him into the bed chamber.

"What did my Amelia say to you?" Jack demanded, eyeing Lizzie with determination.

Elizabeth sprang out of bed and backed into the corner behind Donovan. The fleeting thought came that despite her confusion, his wife seemed to grasp the idea that the safest place for her was behind him when she was being threatened by another man.

"What the hell is wrong with you?" Donovan growled, stepping forward to block any advance toward his already traumatized bride. "I told you, it's just the opiates."

"It's not the opium! Christ, Donovan, for someone who's a damned genius, you sure as hell miss the simple shit! Your wife is a seer; she can talk with the dead!"

The flagrant flood of vulgarities hung in the air like smoke from cannon fire.

Donovan stepped forward with menace. "Mind that foul tongue, sailor, you aren't in a brothel, you are in the presence of a lady—*my lady*." He seized Jack by the shoulders and pushed him into the outer suite. Drawing the man close, he whispered, "You've frightened my wife with your crude behavior. I suggest you remove yourself from my cabin straight away."

Sanity returned to Jack's eyes. Well he knew that few men would receive a warning before Donovan reacted. "My apologies." He held up his hands. "I lost my head. Just let me speak to her. For the sake of our friendship, please, Donovan. Amelia was my whole life."

"And Elizabeth is mine." He returned, releasing his hold upon the man and stepping back. "She may be very ill but she does not have conversations with dead people."

"Pearl told me about her gift. He says she's given him messages from his mother."

"Superstitious twaddle embraced by an uneducated man. Pearl would believe anything when he smokes his hookah, even the confused ramblings of a feverish girl."

"It's not confused ramblings! She tells him things about his mother she couldn't possibly know. Ask her how Amelia died. I'll bet a month's pay; she knows!"

Donovan was well aware that his wife had been changed by her injury. He didn't understand how she could have moments of startling clarity about others lives when she was barely cognizant of the circumstances of her own. He'd rather ignore these odd incidents, chalk them up to another bad symptom and hope they went away as she recovered.

"Let me get her calm." He said, intending to sedate her and that would be the end of it.

Returning to the small chamber, he restrained the urge to rush in and gather the fragile waif in his arms. She was still backed in the corner, her face ashen, eyes staring ahead, seeing nothing. He expected any moment her eyes would roll back as she slipped into convulsions. At that thought, he reached for her. Elizabeth slid to the floor to escape his embrace. Her knees were drawn up to shield her torso. At last, he divined the mystery of why her shins had been a mass of bruises weeks ago. The bastard kicked her while she'd been huddled into a corner like this.

"Lizzie?" He crouched before her, careful not to touch her and frighten her further. "It's me, Donovan." Her memory was like morning dew, transient, evaporating quickly when she was distressed. "I'm not going to hurt you. Let's get you back into bed, darlin'."

"No, go away." Tremors shook her tender body. She covered her head with her arms. "*Pirates?*" Her shrill voice echoed in the small chamber. She lifted her head, seeming to just become aware of him beside her. "She said the pirates came in the night—they took her away from her father—No--leave me alone!" Elizabeth shrank into the corner. She covered her ears with her hands. "I don't want to talk to you anymore Amelia! Go away, you're scaring me."

Donovan placed a light hand on her forearm, measuring her response to his touch.

"Oh God!" She whimpered, making him withdraw his hand. "Why would they do that? Why cut off your breasts and pull out your tongue if they were going to kill you afterward!"

A plunge into an icy sea could not be more chilling. A moan from the doorway distracted Donovan. Jack was there, his face grim as he listened to Lizzie's part of this odd conversation.

The air became thick and close as before a heavy thunderstorm. A tingling moved along his forearm, from elbow to wrist. He looked at his arm. He'd swear he'd just been touched by someone. There was no one in the room besides the two of them and Lizzie was curled in a tight ball on the opposite side of him. The queer sensations continued as someone tugged at his queue. Donovan jerked back, flattening himself against the wall to avoid that eerie contact.

The table on the opposite side of the bed started shaking and rocking. The sheets lifted in the air and hung there. This was no parlor trick. *Something* was in this room, and it was hurting his lass. Anger spurred him to shake off his stunned stupor. "*Stop it!*" He shouted. "She asked you to leave her alone. Stop frightening her!"

"Amelia, don't do this." Jack added his plea to the mix. "You can't force her to speak for you if she doesn't want to. Stop it, I say. She's just a frightened little girl!"

The table stopped clattering. The sheets dropped. The air became still. Elizabeth exhaled sharply and slumped forward like a marionette released from its strings. Donovan put a light hand on her forearm. Lizzie threw herself against him, wrapping her arms about his neck, nearly choking him in her terror.

"I'm here." He cradled her head in one hand and whispered against her ear. "I have you, I have you, Lizzie." He rose and sat on the bed with Elizabeth cradled in his arms. She buried her face in his neck, shivering. He rocked her and whispered assurances.

Jack watched from the door, white, grim, as badly shaken as he. "Is she all right?"

Donovan nodded. Elizabeth was frightened, but she would be all right.

He intended to make damn sure of it.

Chapter Ten

Morning sunlight bathed the master suite. Elizabeth held out her hands, luxuriating in the warm, healing light as it caressed her skin. She was reclining on the sofa in the outer suite, content as a cat as she alternately reflected and dozed. This was the first time she'd been allowed out of bed since her illness. She was still in her bed gown, but a lavender silk dressing robe had been bestowed upon her for the occasion, along with matching slippers.

The count was out on deck enjoying his tobacco. He did not leave her unattended, as he seemed to understand her fear of being alone in the cabin. His Indian servant sat on the floor before the large windows surrounded by a perfect grid of sunlit squares on the rich oriental carpet. He leisurely strummed an instrument that lent an exotic air to their repose. Pungent incense drifted about the room. Elizabeth watched the smoke winding about the valet like a transparent snake.

The valet intrigued her. He had a peaceful, serene demeanor that put her at ease. His manner of dress was always eccentric. Today, he reminded her of a parrot in his yellow silk vest with no shirt beneath, and baggy white breeches that gathered below his knees. A green silk sash was tied about his waist and a red turban covered his head. A thin ebony braid was draped over one shoulder, swaying with the movement of his head as he kept time with his music. Fastened at the end of the braid was a pearl nearly the size of a cherry, hence the nickname given him by the count's crew: *Pearl*.

Pearl absently strummed his sitar while Elizabeth basked in the glowing rays of the sun and reflected on the week's event's.

The week had progressed in a casual repetition of domestic rituals, making her new circumstances seem less bizarre. The count brushed out her hair each morning and braided it each evening. Sheila had tended her hair for most of her life so Elizabeth found the nightly ritual soothing as it reminded her of her grandmother's tender care.

The domestic companionship of the past week had filled the long days for Elizabeth as they shared their meals in the small bedchamber. The count sat in the chair with a tray balanced on his lap across from Elizabeth, who remained confined to the bed. He ate gracefully with the manners of a nobleman while attempting to draw her into polite conversation. As he was a physician and a scholar, Elizabeth found it difficult to make small talk with him. She would undoubtedly sound tedious, as she possessed little education or experience with the world beyond her home.

The count talked about his childhood in the colonies. He was an only child. His father fought in the militia during the revolt in the American colonies. Elizabeth relished that tidbit of information, as her own father had fought the English in his homeland as well. Her husband's voice thickened as he spoke of his father, Major Gaston Beaumont, dying slowly in a dirty surgical tent from a botched amputation, mere weeks before the British surrendered at Yorktown. As a boy of eleven, he vowed never to allow another loved one to succumb to the effects of bad medicine, and grew determined to study medicine. He had paused in his tale to gaze rather sweetly at Elizabeth, making her blush. *Another loved one?* With no memory of a courtship--not even a stolen kiss to cherish--she was uncertain as to his feelings toward her.

Elizabeth realized the music had stopped. The valet's eyes were closed, his fingers were still poised on the strings, as if he were concentrating or just nodding off in mid-song. He was such a peculiar man, kind, loyal to her husband, but odd, to say the least.

Elizabeth stretched and sat upright to ease the aches from her body as she continued to ponder her peculiar circumstances; married to a perfect stranger with no memory of him or their courtship before she'd awakened in his bed two weeks past.

She was distantly aware the count was sharing the bed with her. And yet, she never seemed to encounter him there. She fell asleep before he retired and each morning he was up and dressed by the time she awakened.

Last night, she'd been forced to acknowledge the awkward truth when she awakened screaming. The count was gradually decreasing the Laudanum he'd been giving her at night, claiming she would form a dependency to it with prolonged use. And so, the nightmares rose up as the barrier to their advancement was eased.

He quickly rose from the bed and went into the next room, returning with a small lantern from the outer suite as he assured her there were no rats in her bed. An insistent knock was heard at the outer door and a voice calling from the room beyond asked if they needed assistance. The count replied in a terse growl that his lady had a nightmare and commanded the intruder to leave. Realizing she'd awakened not only her spouse but the crew with her night terrors was mortifying.

The count hung the lantern on a hook and lay down beside her, quickly pulling the sheets over his legs. She was on her side, staring at him with unease. He watched her watch him, gauging her reaction, as was his habit. After a moment he rolled onto his side with his head propped in his palm. He placed his other hand on the pillow between them, open in invitation. Meekly, she took that hand, surprised by the gesture, and by his unfailing patience.

"Close your eyes, my love. I'm here, you're safe."

Elizabeth had fallen asleep clutching that hand. When she awakened today he was out on deck, as usual. Neither of them spoke of the incident this morning when he joined her at breakfast.

Am I truly his love? Elizabeth wondered as she basked in the sunlit chamber and reflected upon the events of the past days. She didn't have the nerve to ask him. She was in awe of him. And the count had a confident, predatory air about him, like a wolf you'd encounter in the woods. You could admire it at a distance but you didn't want to provoke it or draw its attention to you by being too curious. She sensed violence lurking in him, tightly restrained, ready to come to the fore if provoked.

All men were dangerous to some degree, but he was more so than those she encountered during her abduction.

Elizabeth squirmed on the settee as fear lingered low in her belly, a relentless gnawing that never fully went away. She crossed her arms over her belly to prevent her tender flesh from tearing beneath the cruel memory of a terror more horrifying than the rats could ever have been.

The sunlit cabin faded. She was plunged back into the suffocating dark prison cell.

Captain Sully loomed over her, a fat gargoyle grinning from ear to ear as he stroked his obscene member, making it grow longer and harder before her eyes. Elizabeth had never beheld such a disturbing sight before. Sickened with paralyzing fear and shame, she shrank into the shadows to escape his lewd display. The captain stopped fondling himself. He seized her by her hair and dragged her from her refuge . . .

"My lady?" A familiar, high, nasal voice spoke nearby and the revolting image faded.

She was snatched back from the frightening abyss, returned to the luxurious cabin suite. Her husband's valet was crouched near her, studying her with worried eyes.

Elizabeth was panting. Her short, quick breaths reverberated in the chamber. She was shivering yet sweat misted her skin, beading above her lips and along her brow. She feared she was about to be sick from the foul memory of what happened after her captor dragged her from her hiding place. She closed her eyes and placed a shaking hand over her mouth as if to ward off the perverse invasion yet again. "It didn't happen!" She whispered.

It didn't happen-- it was just a dream, a very bad dream. It didn't happen. If she kept repeating it, she might just believe it.

A slender hand rested on her shoulder. Startled, she opened her eyes. The valet mumbled an apology and dropped his hand. "Do you wish for me to find his lordship?"

"No." She said quickly. "No, I'm fine, please, just stay with m-me."

Pearl nodded. He seemed to be considering fleeing to find his master and sending the man to deal with his wife's bout of panic in his stead. He cleared his throat and rolled his shoulder in an uncertain shrug. "You have no need to be afraid, mistress. My lord killed them that hurt you. No man will be given the opportunity hurt you again, he'll see to that, I promise." He smiled slightly at her, offering encouragement. Suddenly the soulful brown eyes lit up. "Why, you're safe as a chick nestled beneath its mother's wing in The Raven's keeping!"

"The Raven?" She repeated, unable to follow his odd implication.

"Aye, The Raven, that was his lordship's pirating name."

Pirate? The word froze in her throat and cooled her skin. *No.* The count was a gentleman, a nobleman not a lawless scoundrel who preyed on the weak and ravaged innocents.

"Do not fear him." Pearl assured her as he took in her stricken features. "My lord has retired from his pirating days. He is a respectable planter now." His expression changed from pride to apprehension. "I was forbidden to speak of it with you. I beg you, do not mention it to him, Mistress. He'll be very angry if you do."

Nodding, Elizabeth promised to not betray the valet.

Pearl resumed his position on the floor without another word. He seemed to be trying to ignore her as he picked up his instrument and began strumming again.

Watching him, Elizabeth digested the verification of her husband's violent past. So, her intuition was correct. Elizabeth believed she didn't possess the gift of second sight, but Sheila was dead and the old woman insisted her gifts would pass to Elizabeth when she was gone. Was that why she suddenly possessed odd insights and knowledge about people around her, namely the count and Pearl, that she hadn't been able to 'see' before? She trusted her husband because she could sense a deep, genuine concern for her radiating from him. And she knew, despite his gentleness toward her, that he was a very dangerous man if provoked. Now she had proof.

"Have you been with his lordship for a long time?" She asked the distracted valet.

"Nearly six years." Pearl murmured as he concentrated on his finger movements and continued to play the enchanting music of his homeland.

"Did he acquire the scars on his chest during his exploits in the east?"

"No, Madame, it was done to him before then, when he was in the Bastille."

"The Bastille—he was in the Bastille?" Elizabeth nearly choked on the words. Her husband spent time in a French prison? He'd neglected to mention it when he spoke of studying medicine in Paris. Nor had he mentioned pirating in the east. "What was his crime?"

"There was no crime" Pearl replied calmly. "My lord lived with his uncle, the former count, during his university days. His uncle was arrested for conspiring to assassinate the king. My lord was taken to prison with him, suspected of being his accomplice. They tortured my lord, but he knew nothing, he was an innocent, a youth caught in circumstances beyond his understanding or control."

Pearl's words made Elizabeth think of Michael. He yearned to go to Italy and study with the masters so he might become a famous painter one day. Elizabeth imagined her brother, a naïve adolescent, staying with people he did not know in a foreign land. He could easily become a victim of circumstances, just as her husband must have been. "How did he escape?"

"His lordship was to be executed in the public square with the other conspirators. A few days before the execution the peasants rose up, they seized the Bastille and set all the prisoners free. His uncle died not long after, leaving him all his earthly wealth. After burying his uncle, my lord traveled east, to Greece, Arabia, India, and Ceylon. After a few years of adventure, he returned to the west and settled into life as a cane planter."

A few years of adventure, indeed. That was a neat and tidy version of the tale. Elizabeth grew quiet as she pondered the mysterious and intimidating man she now belonged to.

The count returned half an hour later. He removed his coat and draped it over the desk chair. He withdrew a pair of pistols from his belt and placed them on the desk. Elizabeth watched him disarm himself with a horrid fascination. A sheathed dagger remained strapped to his right thigh as he strode to the sofa and leaned over the back of it to plant a kiss on her brow.

Oh dear, this was new. He'd never kissed her before, not that she remembered. And he didn't ask her first. He just took—well, it was in his nature, wasn't it-- being a pirate?

"What's wrong, my sweet?"

"Nothing, my lord."

"My name is Donovan." He insisted yet again in a wearied tone. He leaned so close she could smell the tobacco on his breath. "As my wife you've no need to address me so formally."

"Yes, Donovan, sir." She parroted, anxious to keep this pirate turned planter appeased.

Lean fingers lifted her chin, forcing her to meet startling blue eyes that seemed sharp enough to tear into her very soul. "*Donovan.*" He corrected as he had often in recent days.

"Donovan." She repeated, her heart wilting beneath his scorching gaze.

The master's hand dropped to cup her shoulder. "Why are you so distressed?"

"Forgive me, my lord!" The valet stood suddenly and clumsily. "She was asking questions, sir. I beg a thousand pardons- -it just slipped out!" He hung his head dutifully.

Elizabeth glanced up at the austere man beside her to gauge his response. He was looking at her, not his servant. And his expression was no longer pleasant. "What did you tell her?"

"He didn't tell me anything!" She lied quickly. She didn't want the poor man to be punished, even if he was dumb enough to confess his indiscretion without it being suspected. "I asked him how we met— that's all—he wasn't sure—"

"I see." Sharp blue eyes pinioned the servant. "Pearl, what did you tell Elizabeth that has so obviously distressed her?"

"About the Bastille, O Great One, and that you were once a pirate known as The Raven."

The hand on her shoulder tightened, and then it lifted and coiled into a fist. "Get out." He hissed. "I'll deal with you later!" The door slammed behind the valet's retreating form.

The count stalked to the window, his hands tight fists at his sides. He took in the valet's elaborate incense burner on the floor, scowled his fury at it and opened the window. He made a wide sweeping gesture with one hand in an effort to wave the noxious smoke out of the cabin.

A pirate, it made sense now. The strong undercurrent of danger simmering beneath his skin now had a purpose, a name. A cut-throat pirate had taken her to wife. Had he killed? Surely. What kind of pirate would be unwilling to shed blood? A weak one, an unsuccessful one, and this man was not weak. Power emanated from his aura. He had only to walk into a room to gain command of it. Others deferred his command, recognizing that invisible force of will.

Elizabeth cradled her hand over her stomach. She pressed the palm flat in a futile attempt to calm the twisting serpent as it coiled beneath her fingers. Why was he angry? Did he think she'd betray him? Did her knowing he had been a pirate make her a liability to the man in his new life? Oh, dear---she hadn't thought of that. Would he maroon her on an island so none could learn his secret? No. The madhouse was a more civilized solution.

"You'll disappear forever, and no one would ever be able to find you . . ."

The serpent coiled beneath her hand, and her head started to churn and buzz.

God, not that. . . . The West Garden Madhouse.

The count paced before the window and then stood for several moments with his back to the room. He turned abruptly. His eyes were twin blue flames of fury. "Why do you look at me like that?" He accused. "I've not sprouted horns or a tail in the past five minutes!"

She understood now why Pearl confessed his offense so easily. It was horrible being the object of that unnerving blue glare. "Don't send me away. Please. I'll be good, I promise."

The count's anger melted into turbulent confusion. "What are you talking about?"

"I won't tell anyone you're a pirate. Your secret is safe, I swear it!" She pleaded like a street urchin caught picking pockets groveling before a powerful magistrate. She didn't care how she sounded, as long as it stayed his hand. "You've no need to send me to the madhouse!"

The madhouse incident. How could she have forgotten it?

"No one will find you." The cruel voice taunted. *"You'll disappear forever."*

Elizabeth's vision blurred. She choked as a bitter taste rose in her throat. She fought the rising swell of nausea as the room shifted and changed. *Fletcher kept her subdued in a painful grip*

83

while they waited in the outer foyer for an audience with the superintendent of the West Garden Madhouse. "You'll disappear, just like that other Irishman's brat. They'll wonder what happened to you, but no one will ever find you."

The front door opened. Fletcher's grip loosened for a mere second. Elizabeth slipped out of her stepfather's restraining grasp, determined to gain the door and run all the way home. She ran headlong into the skirts of Lady Beverly, her mother's friend from the Methodist Society.

"Elizabeth?" Lady Beverly gasped. "Your mother was to meet us here to minister to the poor unfortunates. Is she ill?"

"Yes!" Elizabeth lied. Mama was hiding in her room until the bruise on her porcelain face faded. "She's sick. She had Papa bring me here to minister in her stead."

"Such a brave little girl. The Good Lord will reward you." Lady Beverly smiled down at her with kindness. "Thank you for bringing her, Captain. We'll see that she gets home safely."

Papa had no recourse but to relinquish her into Lady Beverly's care. He couldn't proceed with his plans to leave Elizabeth there, for mama would surely hear of this from Lady Beverly. With a brusque nod to the woman, he strode, red-faced, towards the street door.

The skirts of her angelic redeemer disappeared. Elizabeth was caught in the perturbed gaze of the dangerous man who now controlled her life. He had crossed the room during her odd mental lapse and was standing over her. He glanced at the outer door as if it, too, had offended him, and then his calculating eyes returned to her. "Where did you get the outrageous idea that I would send you to a madhouse!" He demanded rather than asked. Before she could answer, he fired another question. "Has that idiot surgeon been here prattling nonsense while I was out? I instructed Pearl not to allow him to see you, and by God, if he's neglected his duties due to his hashish indulgences I'll have the skin flogged from his useless hide."

"No! Pearl didn't admit anyone while you were out. I had questions--and I was afraid to ask *you*." She hated the panicked wobble in her voice. Her chest ached as if she wore a corset that had been laced too tightly and she feared she was about to disgrace herself by crying into the bargain.

Elizabeth sucked in her breath and closed her eyes. She drew her knees up to her chest and hugged them. It was too much. She was trapped between two nightmares, the present one colliding with a long forgotten incident from the past. Papa had actually said he'd get rid of her, "*Just like the other Irishman's brat.*" He'd been behind Kieran's disappearance, Sheila knew that, and she believed her grandmother when no one else did. Fletcher made her older brother disappear forever. *Had he killed Kieran or did he hire someone else to do it for him?*

Lost in the tormented memory, she was distantly aware of the count sitting beside her and pulling her onto his lap. "Lizzie, look at me, let me see your eyes. Tell me what's happening. Can you hear me, Darlin'?"

Elizabeth opened her eyes. The count's face was grim. "It was a bad memory, from childhood. It just came—so suddenly." She explained, not liking the fear she saw in his features when up until now he had always been her source of calm.

"Tell me." He insisted. "Tell me what frightened you just now."

"It was my ninth birthday," She began in a shaking voice, explaining the incident to him as best she could remember it. "Fletcher told my mother he was taking me to the zoo. He took me to the madhouse instead. He intended to leave me there under a false name. One of mother's friends came, and he was forced to let me go with her to help hand out blankets to the insane, as he couldn't explain why else he would be there with me."

"That is reprehensible." He admitted. "You must have been terrified."

"I forgot about it." She admitted in a thin voice. "Until, just now."

"Because you thought I might do the same. But listen to me now, sweet girl." He said in a firm, insistent tone. "Even if my behavior in the past month is all you have to go on, you should know I would never treat you so cruelly."

"But I don't *know* you!" She retorted, anger and frustration rising to the fore. "You say I've been with you for a month—I can barely recall the last two days. And a few days is not enough to determine a person's true character, not when he goes about threatening to flog anyone who crosses him!"

That was it, the final unraveling of her thinly held self-possession. Elizabeth was overcome by frantic, frightened, throat-shredding sobs.

Chapter Eleven

Elizabeth didn't remember falling asleep, or being carried into the small bedchamber. She'd been weeping bitterly and then everything went black. She touched her cheeks, unaccustomed to the sensation of dried tears making the skin feel tight over her bones.

It was evening. The lanterns had been lit in the outer suite. She sat up in bed. A rectangle of light fell across the mattress from the larger room. It was quiet in the suite; too quiet.

The count had been indulgent regarding her fear of being alone in his cabin, but she learned at an early age that indulgences were rare where men were concerned and like promises, they were not enduring. Eventually, he would consider her an annoyance and his kind indulgences would cease. He seemed to be nearing that point this afternoon.

She rubbed her eyes, feeling stupid for her irrational bout of weeping. She didn't want him to think she was a spineless twit who was easily cowed. That had been her mother's mistake. She'd just have to show this count she did indeed possess a backbone.

She rose from the bed to peer cautiously into the larger suite. Relief filled her. The count sat at his desk, calm, strong and so wickedly handsome, like a dark hero in a gothic romance.

His eyes lifted from the ledger. "You're awake. I was just about to check on you again." He was at her side before she could blink. His arm went about her waist, and she had the distinct feeling of being herded toward the sofa. Once there, he urged her to sit. He took a seat on the opposite end, leaving a discrete space between them.

Elizabeth turned about to face him. She drew her knees to her chest, adjusted her gown for modesty, crossed her ankles, and then hugged her knees. Satisfied with her barrier against probing eyes, she regarded her opponent with a mask of wide eyed innocence.

"I'm sorry about this afternoon. I didn't mean to frighten you, Elizabeth."

Rule number one in any engagement was to not let the enemy know he'd succeeded in his efforts to unnerve you. "May I have a drink of water? I'm terribly thirsty, *my lord.*"

His lordship seemed taken aback by her request in the midst of his apology. He didn't even correct her deliberate formal address. "Of course, you must be parched."

When the count returned with a goblet of sparkling water, Elizabeth fairly inhaled it. Holding the empty glass out to him, she asked for another just as he started to sit down. He took the glass from her, stalked to the sideboard, and returned with her refilled glass. This time, he sat close and pulled her bare foot onto his lap. He took to alternately stroking and massaging it, running light fingers over her toes and across the top of her foot.

She sipped her water, quelling the urge to retract the limb, which would be taken by her opponent as a sign of surrender or unease.

Yet, Elizabeth had never experienced the singular sensation of a man fondling her bare foot before. She squirmed against the pleasure of his finger lightly tracing her arch. His free hand cradled her heel, retaining firm possession as he continued to explore its contours with his fingertips. He gazed at her sweetly, as if men played with their wives toes every evening.

Elizabeth studied her glass, intent on weathering the storm.

He gently unfolded her bent leg, extending it across his lap. He did the same to her other leg, adjusted her gown, and let his arm drape lightly across her knees, his palm flat on her outer thigh. Elizabeth was astonished at how easily he uncoiled her from her defensive posture.

Looking at his face was a mistake. His pale eyes had become pools of regret. "Will you forgive me for upsetting you earlier, dearest?"

She wanted to forget this afternoon. "That depends. Does Pearl still have skin on his back?"

A brief irritation marred his countenance. Well, if the man thought she'd melt into a gooey puddle at his feet if he played the romantic swain, he had another thing coming.

"It was a figure of speech, nothing more. I was concerned Pearl may have allowed a bad element into the cabin in my absence."

Elizabeth remained silent. She clutched her glass with both hands.

Lean fingers lifted her chin to meet his gaze. She was unprepared for the soulful expression therein. "I behaved badly. I frightened you and I'm sorry. Forgive me?"

As a nobleman, the fact that he would apologize at all was remarkable. "Yes, my lord."

"My name is Donovan." He whispered, his breath caressing her cheek.

Elizabeth released her stilted breath, unsettled by his nearness. Muscular arms surrounded her, drawing her close. The fragrance of spices greeted her, and the faint scent of tobacco. Beneath the familiar, the faint musky smell of his skin was alluring. Her eyes wandered to his lips. She wondered how they might taste if he kissed her.

"*Donovan*." They whispered and his rich lyrical voice added to the seduction. "Say my name, Elizabeth."

Apology or not, he was still very much in control, while she was swiftly becoming the aforementioned puddle melting in his arms. "I like calling you 'my lord'."

"Everyone calls me 'my lord'." Hovering an inch from her face, his lips tantalized her as his warm breath caressed her mouth.

"Well, you are my lord, are you not?" Too late, she realized her mistake.

"I am. Say my name."

"Donovan." She whispered, lifting her gaze from his lips to those mesmerizing eyes. Elizabeth knew in that instant she'd been neatly cornered by the wolf. All she could think of was that he might kiss her. She hoped he would.

The water glass was pried from her hands. He set it on the floor. A firm hand slid between the cushion and her bare bottom as he lifted her onto his lap. He removed his hand from her bum as soon as he had her settled and wrapped both his arms about her waist.

"'And slowly, Beauty came to realize the Beast would not devour her before the evening meal, perhaps not at all'." A shiver ran down her spine as she recognized the quote from *Beauty and the Beast*. "At least not in one night. Such a delicious morsel should be savored slowly."

"Where is your big knife?" She asked, her face growing hot. She hoped to steer the conversation to a safer subject.

A deep rumbling laugh was his answer. Elizabeth started, and stared at him with amazed pleasure. She'd never heard him laugh before. It was a pleasant sound, but she failed to see what he found amusing. He'd had that nasty dagger strapped to his thigh this afternoon. The sharp buckle should be biting her bottom as it had when he held her like this earlier, but it was not.

"I put it away." He said, grinning. "I noticed you had a mark on your bottom when I put you to bed earlier."

Elizabeth gasped her outrage and looked away as the color rose fast and furious to her cheeks. "You've no business poking about down there!"

"I beg to differ. As you pointed out, I am your lord."

She'd never live down that stupid remark! "Stop it." She demanded. It came out as a plea.

His lips curled into a wicked smirk. "Your nightgown was twisted about your hips when I put you to bed. As your delightful derriere is typically flawless ivory, I couldn't miss a nasty red welt glaring up at me, now could I?"

Averting her gaze, she groaned at his casual description of her undignified state, fearing her complexion could not turn a deeper shade of crimson if she were standing naked before him now with her backside openly displayed for his perusal. Did he have to be so bloody honest?

He rubbed her arm affectionately. "You should have said something earlier, my sweet."

She hadn't noticed earlier. She'd been crying so hard nothing else compared to the raw ache in her chest. It was only being on his lap again that made her recall the small buckle hasp was not poking painfully into her bottom as before.

"You blush so easily, my love. I'll just have to find another way to bring color to your cheeks." He laughed as his palm cupped her face. "I meant these cheeks, of course."

Elizabeth didn't reply to his saucy remark. Her hot cheeks said quite enough. She was starting to feel weak and spent, not up to the task of sparring verbally with him any longer.

Noting her weariness, he shifted beneath her and arranged her so she was reclining across his lap with her head cradled in the crook of his elbow as it rested against the sofa arm. "Would you like to hear the story again of how we met?"

Again? She didn't remember him telling her before this. Elizabeth nodded and settled into a comfortable repose as he explained their first meeting. Michael brought him home for dinner one night. Not just any night, it was her birthday, and Donovan was her 'present'.

Elizabeth nibbled her lower lip and concentrated, very hard. Nothing. He may as well have been telling her the events of another person's life. She couldn't recall any of it. Apparently the man had gone to great lengths to make her his wife—but it didn't mean that he loved her. He wouldn't be the first to marry the descendent of a cast off heiress with the hope that all would be mended within the family one day and a sizeable portion of the inheritance might come to him.

"I see a question." He prompted, watching her. "Share it with me."

"Well," She began, fearing it was entirely too cheeky to question the man's motive for marrying her. "I can't remember any of it. And you didn't actually say--" *That you love me!* She sucked in her breath. Oh, Bollocks., *there was no going forward and no going back.* "I-I was wondering—sir--if you ever . . . kissed me?"

"Yes, many times." He replied with amusement. "It must be terrible to not remember one's first kiss or the man who gave it to you beneath a canopy of summer stars."

He made it sound so poetic. "Could you do it again, sir--so I might have a sense of what it must have been like?"

Before she knew what he was about, he bent and his lips brushed hers in a brief caress. "There, a typical first kiss from a devoted suitor." He said, smiling as he drew away.

"Is that how you kissed me before?" Elizabeth felt oddly disappointed by the brief exchange. She sensed there was more to this kissing business then he was letting on.

"I was holding back a little. I didn't want to overwhelm you. Would you like me to do it again, properly this time?"

She nodded. His face lowered and his lips caressed her with more enthusiasm. Not merely his lips, but his whole body suddenly became dedicated to the single purpose of kissing her. Powerful thighs tensed beneath her bottom, strong arms tightened about her, enfolding her and cradling her against his solid form as his sensual mouth teased and tantalized her lips.

A knowing thumb on the depression of her chin parted her lips. Their lips formed a tight seal as his kiss deepened. She mimicked his movements, and was rewarded as the pleasure intensified. His lips were soft, yet insistent, his mouth warm and inviting as it melted into hers. It was an exhilarating, deeply satisfying, and very intimate gesture.

He drew away, his smoky pale eyes measuring her response. "Does that please my lady?"

"Yes." She whispered through tingling, swollen lips. Demented butterflies seemed intent on creating an exit through her abdomen. Elizabeth took a deep, steadying breath in a futile effort to calm her shuddering heart.

The count's satisfied smirk told her she'd just given him the advantage in the war of wills between them. If this was the pleasant reward of surrendering, then perhaps surrender was not as distasteful as she'd been led to believe.

Donovan gazed at the sleeping angel in his arms. These incidents of narcolepsy were disconcerting. Ah, but she looked peaceful, his own sweet Aphrodite fallen from Mt. Olympus, straight into his open arms.

He was content to sit with his goddess draped across his lap, watch her sleep and savor the victory of engaging her in her very first kiss--for the *second time*. It was a pleasant end to a harrowing day. In the midst of her frantic weeping this afternoon, her eyes had rolled back and she succumbed to the effects of a full blow grand mal seizure. When the convulsions ceased he carried her to the bed, dreading the moment her eyes would open and he'd have to explain what just occurred. But Elizabeth did not wake up. She slept like the dead for six hours.

Tonight, she didn't seem to recall the seizure.

He wasn't about to tell her, it would frighten her needlessly.

As for himself, he was not going to panic.

One seizure did not constitute epilepsy.

Chapter Twelve

Another week passed with inescapable languor. After days of coaxing, Donovan finally led his anxious bride into the invigorating world of brilliant sunshine and crisp sea breezes snapping at full sails.

He'd taken the precaution of sending most of the crew below, save the handful it took to mind the rigging. Still, Elizabeth scanned her surroundings continually, keeping track of each man's movements in proximity to her own. Donovan ground his teeth to restrain the urge to comfort her. There was nothing to be done except face her fear of strangers—of male strangers in groups. His chest burned. It was his fault, this pervading fear haunting his darling's eyes.

He was well acquainted with that species of fear. He killed because of it. That first year after his release from the Bastille all it took was an unexpected hand on his shoulder. He didn't think. He reacted, like the cornered animal he'd been reduced to in the torturer's den. His crew learned quickly that it was not healthy to touch him without permission. He still didn't like being around people who he didn't know well. He preferred to live as a recluse. Lizzie would carry her aversion to men for a long time, perhaps forever. It wasn't her fault. It was his. He failed to protect her, and he would never make that mistake again as long as he lived.

"Look down, darlin'." He coaxed to distract her. "Sometimes dolphins swim alongside." Lizzie did as he asked, forgetting the men minding the rigging above their heads.

"Oh, did you see that!" She rose on her tiptoes and leaned over the rail.

"Don't lean out so far." He chastened, suffering a pang at her quick movements. He placed a hand around her waist and pulled her back from the dangerous precipice. "Two more." He pointed out a pair surfacing beyond the ship's prow and hugged her securely about the waist with both arms, from behind her.

94

They watched for half an hour before their aquatic escort disappeared beneath the rolling seas. Elizabeth turned in his arms to look up at him, her cheeks flushed, her eyes vivacious with excitement for the first time in many weeks. Donovan couldn't resist. He lowered his face and captured her lush pink lips in an exhilarating kiss. Elizabeth merely endured his caress but did not return it. He drew back, deeply aware she was intimidated by her new surroundings.

"What do you think of my winged horse?" He waved a hand about the deck expansively. "*The Pegasus* glides through the winds and the rolling waves. She bears us home, lass."

"It's a grand ship, my lord." Elizabeth forced herself to smile. She could see that her husband was as proud of his ship as any boy might be with an expensive toy. He talked about his 'winged horse' a little more and held her hand on his arm as they strolled the main deck.

"My lord?" She ventured after several moments of silence between them. "You said if I had concerns regarding my past you wished me to share them with you."

"I have also asked you to address me informally, my dear. Is that so much to ask?"

"No sir." She mumbled. Addressing him by his Christian name was a form of intimacy, one she wasn't certain she was willing to embrace. She hadn't the benefit of a long courtship to become as familiar with him as he seemed to be with her. She'd awakened in his bed and was told they were married. She was still trying to reconcile herself to the abruptness of it. Thus corrected again, she retreated into silence.

"What troubles you, my sweet?" The count asked after a few prickly moments.

"When did you start calling me Lizzie?"

"Since the day we met or shortly thereafter. Do you dislike it?"

"No, sir—*Donovan*." She tested the name with her tongue. "I was just curious."

She liked his pet name for her. She liked the way he said it, with a happy inflection that was full of warmth and affection as if they were old chums.

"You mean, that night, when Michael brought you home." She clarified, mentally feeling about for the security of a stone wall as amnesia had left her groping about in the darkness.

"Yes, my love." He replied in his usual patient tone when she quizzed him about their courtship. He seemed to understand her need to review what he had told her from time to time to help solidify the events in her mind. "It was your birthday. Michael asked me to dinner. He didn't tell me that I was to be your present." He gave her a charming smile.

Thus fortified by the familiar conversational pattern, she pushed herself to ask the unpleasant question nibbling away at her. "So then, how did Sheila die?"

The count regarded her with arched brows and parted lips, shocked by her odd inquiry. He quickly mastered his surprise and trained his features into a practiced calm. "I'm not certain. I was in London arranging things with Fletcher. It was probably her heart."

"Yet, you aren't certain." Elizabeth pointed out. She let go of his arm and walked slowly along the deck with her hand skimming the rail as she tried to summon a memory that would validate the strong suspicion in her mind. "I fear she may have been murdered."

Silence punctuated her statement. She turned to face the count, wondering if he'd heard her or if the wind had carried away her confession. He hadn't followed her. He stood several feet away, leaning forward with his forearms braced on the rail. He looked at her as if she'd said something outrageous, which was often the case these days due to her head injury.

"That's enough sun for one day." He held out his hand, waiting for her to come to him.

Elizabeth ignored him. She gazed out at the sea, concentrating, trying to force a spark of memory to burst forth. Thoughts of Fletcher and his constant threats against the old woman brought a gloom to the otherwise sunny day. She shivered and wrapped her arms about herself as a sick, suffocating dread crept closer. A wave of inexplicable terror claimed her as a long shadow inserted itself across the plank decks between the count and herself--the shadow of a man.

"Good afternoon, my lady." An elderly man in a stark black suit stood close enough to touch Elizabeth if he wanted. *Oh, he wanted to, very much.* Elizabeth could feel the hunger.

Instinct overtook reason. She ran the sparse few feet separating her from her husband.

The count's arm wrapped quickly about her, drawing her tight against his solid frame. She heard a click and looked down. Her husband had a pistol leveled at the intruder. "That's close enough, old man. What the hell are you doing, sneaking up on us?"

A sailor swooped down from the rigging and landed on the deck with a thud beside the count. He unsheathed an enormous dagger. "Trouble, *mon ami?*"

"Only a little." The count said, holstering his weapon. "I see you still have my back."

"Always." The Frenchman's grin widened. "Say the word, my lord, and he's fish bait."

A third man was fast approaching from the deck above. Elizabeth moaned and pressed tighter into her husband's powerful, muscular body. It was happening again, she thought with desperation as her heart squeezed into her throat and she quelled the urge to scream.

"I have you." The count whispered, wrapping both arms around her once more.

"Linton, Duchamp!" The blond man bellowed. His face was mottled with fury. "Did you misunderstand my orders about staying below? They were inclusive of the entire crew."

"I was in the crow's nest, Cap'n. My lord drew his pistol, I sensed trouble."

"You were looking for a fight, Mr. Duchamp, as usual. Put the weapon away, you are upsetting the lady. What is your excuse?" The captain rounded on the old man.

"Blame an old fool's curiosity, sir. When I heard she was coming out on deck, I just had to have a peek at our little countess." Mr. Linton's eyes darted to Elizabeth. "My prayers have been answered. The Good Lord has granted you a miraculous recovery, my dear."

The captain frowned into the distance, grim faced, attempting to contain his rage.

The count cradled Elizabeth firmly against him. Every muscle in him seemed taut as a cat preparing to pounce. She looked up into his face, searching for reassurance. There was none. His expression was impassive, like chiseled stone. His eyes had transmuted from pale blue to a stark wintry grey as he glared at the old man who dared to approach them.

Mr. Duchamp sheathed his weapon as ordered, but he continued to glower at the intruder.

The old man edged closer. "There's no need to be frightened, child." His voice oozed over her like sweet, thick poison. "I wanted to tell you I'm here for you, my dear. If there is anything troubling your tender spirit, anything at all, I'm at your service, my lady."

"Thank you, Reverend." She responded.

"Reverend?" He attempted a blush, and failed in pretending humility. "I'm the ship's surgeon, my lady. T'was I who nurtured you through the worst of your illness—"

"You've seen her, now take yourself off." The count interjected.

The physician bowed in deference. As he rose, he extended his hand toward her.

Elizabeth did not want to touch that hand. It was gnarled, resembling a claw. The others were watching and the thought came that she must be shaming her husband with all this cowering and shivering in front of his men. She swallowed, determined to be gracious as she'd been taught by her mother, as was expected of her as the wife of a count. She reached out.

The moment Dr. Linton's hand touched Elizabeth's skin, an onslaught of unspeakable images washed over her mind, and then darkness smothered the scream rising in her throat.

Kieran opened his eyes. He was in his bed, upstairs. He'd been in the shop, packing orders to be delivered about town. A wave of inexplicable terror had claimed him and then horrifying visions slammed into his mind with rapid succession.

It was that girl again. She'd formed a mental bond with him when she was trapped in that dark cell. Confronted by appalling perversity again, she transferred the disturbing images to him as her mind simply shut down. He sat up and rubbed his forehead. "How long was I out?"

"An hour." Barnaby leaned forward in the chair nearby. "What did you see, lad?"

"Sails, the mast of a ship." Kieran said evasively. He wanted to go take a hot bath, scrub his skin with a brush. Hell--he wanted to scrub the sickening images from his mind. "I was looking up, someone was holding me and then everything went black."

"I don't like this." The old magician muttered. "This is a linking spell. It's gaining more power over you each time this happens. I'll get the cards."

Barnaby returned moments later and handed Kieran the tarot deck. Kieran shuffled the deck and began laying the cards out on the bed in the proper order.

"A predominance of swords." Barnaby remarked. "The two—things hidden; the three--a broken heart; the nine--night terrors. Oh dear, all of that, plus the eight?"

Kieran stared at the eight of swords. He hated that card; the dark haired woman reminded him of his mother. She was bound and blindfolded, encircled by eight swords stuck upright in the ground about her.

"Who was that man holding our little lady when she passed out?"

"You saw it, too?" Kieran asked, realizing he wouldn't be able to fool the old man.

"Just a fragment, when I touched you. That man looked familiar."

"Mr. O'Rourke, her husband, I think." He rubbed his brow. "It came and went so fast."

"He's grown more powerful, I see." Barnaby said, studying the tarot spread.

Kieran's gaze dropped to the King of Swords; it signified a man of keen intellect, he could be a powerful ally or a daunting opponent. "I fail to understand what all this has to do with me?

Why am I being assaulted by his wife's nightmares? I've never even met the woman!"

Barnaby tapped the last card in the spread, the six of cups.

"It's not possible!" Kieran protested. A boy was passing a cup to a younger girl. It was obvious the pair were brother and sister.

"The cards do not lie." Barnaby reminded him. "O'Rourke's bride is a relative, perhaps distantly removed, but a blood relation nonetheless, one who shares your Druidic ancestry. She formed a metaphysical link with you while in great distress and as the ship they are on draws near, that link is becoming stronger. This is why you've been having visions and dreams lately."

Kieran wasn't having dreams. He was having nightmares, because of that girl on the ship. "You have to do something, Barnaby. You have to make it stop. I'll go mad."

"Don't you think I've tried?" The old man's words left him cold.

It took a moment to reconcile herself to her surroundings. Elizabeth was in her husband's cabin, lying on the bed. The last thing she remembered was looking up to see billowing, white sails flapping against a brilliant blue sky. She'd been on deck with his lordship and then . . .

No, I don't want to remember that horrible man! She didn't think it possible to feel any dirtier, but the memory of his touch made her skin crawl. Her hand flew to her mouth. She made a mad dash for the necessary closet and emptied the remains of her lunch into the sea. She crumpled to the floor in the tiny closet, her brow beaded with moisture and her limbs quivering sporadically. She hugged her knees to still her limbs, and tried to make sense of the jangled images that assaulted her mind before she passed out.

"Lizzie, my sweet, what are you doing on the floor?" The count peeked into the closet. "Ah, casting up your accounts, I see. Are you finished?" She nodded and took his outstretched hand. He pulled her to her feet. With an arm about her waist, he walked her back to the small bedchamber and guided her to sit on the bed.

"Do you remember what happened?" His manner was casual as he stood beside the bed and dipped the cloth into a basin on the nightstand, and then wrung it out.

"I swooned." She bristled at the confession. Silly, weak women swooned. She did not. "I assure you, my lord, I've never fainted before in my entire life."

"A swoon lasts a few moments. You've been unconscious for over an hour." Donovan sat on the bed and brushed her face with the cool cloth. "Was it heat sickness? We are in warmer climes." Elizabeth made a face at his assessment. "Oh, I've seen it take down grown men among the new indentures, so it's not a sign of weakness, my pet."

"It wasn't the heat; it was that disgusting old man! He's not a doctor. He's running from the law—I saw it all when he touched me—he's trying to--" The storm clouds gathering in her husband's eyes silenced her attempt to explain her disturbing vision.

Elizabeth closed her eyes and leaned back against the wall, desperate to calm her trembling limbs. *Oh, God, he'll never believe me!* No one would. They would think her mad.

"He's trying to do what, Lizzie?" Donovan asked.

"Nothing." She gasped, finding her lungs starved for air. "I was confused, sir."

Chapter Thirteen

"Lady Beaumont, you do me a great honor." The captain of *The Pegasus* made a gallant leg before Elizabeth as they entered his suite. It was a mirror copy of Donovan's.

"Captain Rawlings." Elizabeth gave him a demure smile. "It was kind of you invite us to dine with you. And who is this gentleman?" She fixed her gaze on the towheaded boy at the captain's side, feeling less intimidated by the lad while in the forced company of two men this evening. She didn't want to come but Donovan was adamant that the invitation to dine with the captain could not be refused without appearing rude as the man was his friend and partner.

"This is my nephew, Peter MacCafferty, Madame." The boy bowed awkwardly before her as prompted. "That was very well executed." The captain noted. "But mind you don't stare so. Forgive him, Ma'am." Placing his hand on the boy's shoulder, Rawlings confessed, "Living the life of a sailor, he's a bit rough around the edges."

Elizabeth couldn't stifle a giggle as the captain's nephew rolled his eyes and made a face that betrayed his thoughts about such stiff formality among the adult set. "It's a pleasure to meet you Mr. MacCafferty." She smiled at the lad. "Would you mind terribly if I called you Peter?"

"Everyone calls me Peter. I don't think I'd remember to answer otherwise, ma'am."

"Yes, I know what you mean." She agreed, unaccustomed to being addressed as Madame Beaumont after being Miss O'Flaherty all of her life. "You may call me Elizabeth. If the Queen stops by for tea, we'll make every effort to impress her, of course. Until then, we'll do fine without all that stiff formality, don't you agree?"

"I like her!" Peter informed the count. "Want to see my kittens, Elizabeth—"

"*Lady Elizabeth.*" Rawlings gave the lad a quelling look. "Remember our discussion about manners--"

"You have kittens? I'd love to see them." Elizabeth put in quickly, hoping to deflect his ire from the boy. "After dinner, of course. I'm famished." She gave the captain a sweet smile.

"Yes, yes, quite." The blond captain murmured, giving her a generous grin as he gestured to the table glittering with crystal, silver and fine china in the candlelight.

The captain possessed a sunny personality, putting her at ease quickly with his kind eyes and his penchant for spinning a good yarn. Donovan remained silent and pensive. She didn't understand his sullen mood when he insisted they must dine with the captain in the first place.

Rawlings confided to her that they had been adventurers in their youth. The word pirate never came up. In fact, the word was carefully avoided as the man insisted they earned their fortunes as merchant sailors in the East. As the captain spoke, the impression rose before her of a pair of masked buccaneers dressed in black, terrorizing all they encountered on the seas.

Perhaps it was that second glass of wine. Perhaps it was the curious gleam in the captain's eyes as he embellished his tale. Whatever the cause, Elizabeth couldn't control her tongue. "And you wore black scarves over your faces. Was it to protect your delicate complexions from the harsh sun, Captain?" She asked sweetly, dimpling at the man.

The captain's fork stilled in mid-air, he regarded Donovan with uncertainty.

"I'm afraid she has you, *Black Jack.*" Donovan quipped, smiling for the first time that evening. "Lizzie has the extraordinary ability of being able to see beyond the masks people wear. She gets it from her grandmother O'Flaherty, isn't that right, my love?"

Elizabeth couldn't tell if he were bragging or mocking her abilities. Perhaps he was merely covering for her impertinence. It was borne on her yet again in the strained moment that she spoke her mind too easily since her illness. She often spoke her thoughts aloud without realizing it until it was too late. Donovan was patient with her odd mental lapses, but society would not be. "I beg your pardon, Captain. It was rude of me to contradict you."

"Don't apologize!" The captain said with a wave of his hand. "I appreciate plain speaking. It's a rare gift, in a woman." Leaning back in his chair, Captain Rawlings picked up the sagging conversation. "My great aunt had that gift, *the knowing*, she called it. Have you had the knowing all your life, my lady, if you don't mind my asking?"

"I've only recently acquired the ability, and I consider it a curse, not a gift, captain."

"Oh, but you get to talk to ghosts!" Peter exclaimed. "That must be great fun. Do they only come out after dark---can you make them appear? Can you look into a person's eyes and tell their future like a gypsy? Can you see if they be good or evil, Lady Elizabeth?"

Elizabeth blanched at Peter's questions. How did he know she saw spirits? How did any of them, she wondered, when Donovan and the captain didn't discount the boy's wild claim?

"I'm not a gypsy, Peter." She began, looking at the boy so as not to have to deal with the men. "My family descended from an ancient warrior-priest class that ruled Ireland before the English conquest. My ancestors were the guardians of the Old Religion of the Celts. They communed with nature spirits. Merlin was a priest of the old ways."

"Merlin's my favorite in King Arthur." Peter's brown eyes grew hopeful. "Can you teach me to bring forth the dragon's breath?"

"I'm afraid not." Elizabeth smiled at the boy's enthusiasm. "Merlin's abilities were greatly exaggerated in those stories. According to my grandmother O'Flaherty," she continued, "The gifts of second sight and the ability to walk the veil between the worlds were passed down through the bloodlines of the Chieftain's family. My grandmother was the last seer, she claimed when she died I would inherit her gifts. Of course, I never believed her." Elizabeth added with apologetic tone in front of the men. "I always considered her tales of visits from dead ancestors to be just an old woman's fancy."

"But then she died and now you have them!" The boy concluded, slapping the table decisively. "What is the veil between the worlds? Is it a place in Ireland? Can anyone go--"

The captain put up a hand. "Enough." He gave Elizabeth a harried look. "Never runs out of questions, that one. If *I* might ask, Madame, do you see the future in these visions?"

Elizabeth studied her wine glass that had been conveniently refilled by their host, making it her third for the evening, if she drank it. Something was afoot, she could sense it. The men were on a hunting expedition, searching for hidden treasure like the pirates they were. "It's still so new. I see bits and pieces of a person's life if they happen to touch me."

"What about him?" The captain nodded toward her husband. "Can you see through his many masks of deceit?"

"I don't experience visions with his lordship."

"Why?" Captain Rawlings leaned forward to peer at Donovan speculatively. "Does he have a black soul that defies reading, by even God himself?"

"Jack." Donovan warned. "I'll thank you to stop scaring my lass."

Elizabeth smiled at their host. She knew he was poking fun of his lordship because Donovan was always so perpetually grave. The impressions she received from the count were rare and difficult to read, like brief flashes of lightening illuminating a dark sky. The captain, and her spouse, didn't need to know that. "His lordship's touch is familiar to me." She evaded.

Rawlings extended his hand. "Here, tell me what you see."

"No." After her encounter with Linton, she didn't want to see the dark secrets in another man's soul. "Please, I cannot." She was torn by his request. She didn't wish to offend her husband's friend, either.

"It's all right. I promise." The captain persisted in a playful tone.

"She said no." Donovan intervened in a brusque tone, reaching across the table to offer her his hand. She clutched that big hand, relieved to have him settle the matter for her. "Peter, tell us about those kittens." He effectively took charge, changing the subject.

"Would you like to see them, my lady?" Peter asked.

Elizabeth was all too happy to escape the men. She rose and followed Peter to the crate in the corner and knelt down with her back to the men. She couldn't help sighing over the delightful, furry, little bundles.

"I'm keeping the big red one." Peter informed her. He reached in to snag the plump fellow by the scruff. "The rest are yours to choose from, my lady."

The creak and scrape of chairs made Elizabeth start. The count crossed the room and hunkered down on beside her. "So, which one will be sharing our bed tonight, my love?"

The suggestiveness of his words was not lost on her. "You'd let me have one?"

"I'll give you anything if it makes you smile like that."

The man could charm the scales from a snake, she thought, blushing and averting her gaze to the kittens. "They still have blue eyes. I adore blue eyes."

Captain Rawlings seemed to be choking. She glanced up. He was grinning from ear to ear after spraying brandy all over his sleeve. The count was smiling as well. When she found herself caught in his adoring blue gaze, she knew why the men were so amused.

"Cats are good hunters." Peter put in, ignoring the men and their snickering grins. "They'll cut back on the smaller lizards on the estate, and the spiders, too."

"Spiders?" Elizabeth repeated, looking at the boy with alarm.

"Aye, big ones, mum, hairy and big as a tea saucer with their legs extended—least wise if they grow to full size." Peter grinned with all the wonder that only a boy could possess at such a ghastly fact, "A good fat Tom or two will keep 'em out of your bed chamber."

"They don't come in the house." Donovan countered. "Not unless there's an unusually heavy rainy season. And even then, it's just the first floor."

"The spiders or the lizards?" She demanded, not liking the news one bit. What else did this man forget to mention when he talked in glowing terms about his island paradise?

"The spiders, of course. The lizards and snakes prefer the jungle brush." He put an arm about Elizabeth. "And the manor house is up on a hill, away from—"

"Snakes!" This place was sounding worse by the minute. "What kind of snakes?"

"Big ones." Peter stretched out his arms as wide as he could. "Big as—"

"That's enough horse crap from you!" Donovan snapped at the boy.

"Peter!" Captain Rawlings intervened. "It's time you left and let the grownups talk for a while. Off with you now, and none of your sulkiness." With a hurt expression, the boy sprang up, his favorite kitten slung over his shoulder as he rushed to the door.

Donovan gazed into the box of wriggling fur. "How about the red tiger? I have a fondness for red heads." He scooped the kitten up in one hand and lifted its tail. The kitten meowed indignantly at his inspection. "A tom." He offered her the kitten. "A sturdy little fellow to guard milady's bedchamber."

"It's not my choice. Cats choose people." She said, holding the kitten up to her face. "What do you say? Would you like come home with me and be my mischievous little Puck?" The poppet placed a tiny paw on her cheek and began licking her face with that sandpaper tongue. She giggled, delighted by his acceptance.

The men were staring at her, and both had ridiculous grins on their faces.

Her husband stood and offered her his hand. Elizabeth hoped that meant their evening was drawing to a close as he pulled her to her feet. Instead, Donovan led her to the cushioned window seat and gestured for her to sit down.

Feeling uncommonly light and free, Elizabeth slipped off her shoes and sat down. Her gown covered her ankles, so she wasn't making an untoward display. Donovan sat beside her. His arm snaked about her waist, drawing her against him and the world suddenly seemed a much sturdier place. She was feeling more than a little wobbly, she realized. She gazed up at her husband, wishing they were alone so Donovan might kiss her. An ebony brow lifted in censure but as he was smiling the look lost much of its power. He directed his gaze in front of them.

The captain was standing before them, holding a tray of drinks, a brandy for Donovan and a goblet of wine for Elizabeth, which she declined. Any more wine and she'd be taking her dress off because of the heat next, convinced there was nothing improper with that, either.

Rawlings seated himself in the chair opposite them. Steepling his fingers in front of him, he directed his gaze at her instead of his friend. "I confess to inviting you here because I have a great curiosity about you, my lady. You possess the ability to see into a man's soul and glean insights about his character. I could use your gift to discern the character of one of my crew."

"I've had no dealings with your men." Elizabeth blurted. "I've kept to my lord's cabin the entire voyage."

"No one is accusing you of any wrongdoing, my lady. Please, hear me out." The captain countered, lifting a hand to still further protest. "Our surgeon fell ill a couple of days before we set sail. Linton offered to fill the position in exchange for free passage to the Indies. My first mate took him on. Normally, I trust Mr. Jenkins' judgment, but I don't care for Linton, my lady. My gut tells me something's not right about the fellow, and your husband has had similar misgivings regarding him and his persistent interest in you."

Interest? She gazed from the floor to the captain's face, and then her husband's. How did they know about his 'interest' in her. "I don't know what you mean." She said as innocently as she could manage. All the giddiness of intoxication was gone. It was replaced by a sobering fear.

"I won't lie to you. We're men of action, your husband and I. Over the years, we've learned to trust our instincts as lives have depended upon them. Yesterday, you crossed paths with Linton. I couldn't help noticing the man frightened you. Considering your intuitive abilities, I'm curious to know if you experienced any disturbing impressions about the man during your brief encounter."

"No, sir." Elizabeth sat up straight, edging away from Donovan. His arm remained about her waist. She tried to appear distracted by playing absently with the kitten in her lap.

"Lizzie." Donovan said in serious tone, setting his brandy aside. "Tell Jack what you started to tell me yesterday. You said he isn't a doctor, and that he was trying to do something. You didn't say what, and I have the distinct feeling it involved you in some way."

"I can't!" She wailed. "He's a doctor. I know I forget things, but I'm not all about in the head---and that's what he'll make you think if I say anything about those poor women---" She clamped a hand over her mouth. Once again her tongue was far ahead of her mind.

"I don't doubt your reasoning in the slightest." Donovan took her hand and lifted it to his lips. He kissed her fingers while gazing at her with tender, pleading eyes that seemed impossible to deny. "Nothing that idiot can say will change my opinion of you. Now, no more hedging about, my sweet, tell us what you saw or experienced when Linton touched you."

"We all sense something's up with the man." Rawlings coaxed. "You're the only one with a spyglass. Please, my lady, tell us what you see. The safety of others may rest upon you."

Oh, what a pair they made, Black Jack and The Raven. Together, they were inescapable.

More than Donovan's pleading, the captain's words struck a deep chord within Elizabeth. Linton would go on hurting women when he reached the Indies—it was a hunger, a need. He wouldn't stop—he couldn't. What if more women were brutalized because she didn't speak out when given the opportunity?

"He's not a real doctor." She whispered. "He was an attendant at an asylum many years ago. He stole a doctor's case and he's passed himself off as a physician ever since." She paused to recover her breath, feeling small and dirty for having to confess such vile things.

Donovan released her hand and placed his arm about her waist. "Go on, Love."

Elizabeth looked down at her lap. The kitten had escaped her grasp and jumped to the floor. "He preys upon the women in those places, using drugs and restraints to keep them in his power. And he's adept at convincing his associates the women are suffering delusions if they tell anyone what he did to them. He was found out recently. He's running away, hoping to start a new life in the Indies where no one knows about his evil."

"Has he hurt *you*, Madame?" The captain asked. "Has he threatened you in any way?"

"No." Her face grew hot with humiliation. "But he's marked me as his next victim."

There was a harsh intake of breath from the man seated beside her.

"What do you mean?" Rawlings prodded, leaning forward in his chair. "Don't be afraid, my dear. He'll never be able to get near you. Tell us, how has he has marked you?"

Elizabeth groaned. It was horrible. She didn't know the words for such perversion.

"I have you." Donovan whispered, "I have you, Lizzie." His hand cradled her cheek, urging her to settle her head in the hollow beneath his chin. She closed her eyes, wishing she could melt inside his vest and escape the vile images in her mind.

She inhaled the crisp, clean scent of his skin and tried to absorb some of his strength. She kept her eyes downcast, focusing on the silver threads adorning his waistcoat, unable to meet his gaze. She touched an embroidered flourish and traced it with her finger. "H-he takes mementoes from each of his victims--two locks of hair. The first lock is taken from the back of the woman's head to mark her as his intended prey. Once he's *had* them —h-he takes a lock from between--" She couldn't say the rest, but with these two, she didn't think she needed to.

"Bleedin' Christ!" The captain swore. He rose from his chair and began to pace about. "I told you, Donovan. The lock of hair; the evidence was in front of us the whole time!"

The captain kept right on venting his spleen. Donovan's arms surrounded her. He held her firmly against him. Elizabeth buried her face in her husband's neck. She squeezed her eyes shut to block out the perverse imagery assaulting her soul. She was so cold. Her limbs were shaking. Bile rose up in her throat. She feared she might be ill and then she couldn't draw a breath against the tightness in her chest.

"Brandy, Jack, now!" Her husband barked, bringing the captain out of his monologue.

The captain was beside them in trice, holding out a glass of amber liquid. Donovan took the glass and pressed it to her lips. She drank it at his insistence. It burned all the way down.

"Misogynist prick." Donovan muttered. "I'm going to kill him."

Chapter Fourteen

Getting Elizabeth settled for the night was foremost in his mind as Donovan led her down the hall to their cabin. He carried her shoes in one hand and his free arm was wrapped firmly about her waist to steady her. She was tipsy after wine and a shot of brandy to steady her nerves.

"I'll see you tucked in before I leave." He said as they entered the cabin. As soon as the words left his mouth, he wanted to retract them.

"You're leaving me alone after what I told you?"

"I have to write a statement for Jack to deliver to the governor of Basseterre when he hands Linton over to the authorities. He'll hang for sure, for aiding the abduction of a noblewoman, if not for the rest."

Still pale, she nodded, accepting his lie.

If they were on land, it might work out that way. They were at sea. The punishment for betraying one's crew was death. Linton would be forced to walk between two rows of men armed and thirsting for his blood. Donovan intended to be waiting at the end of that line. If Linton survived the trial by his fellows he'd be hung or keel-hauled; either way, he'd be dead.

"How do you know he helped the smugglers?" She asked.

"He showed up offering to take the place of our ship's physician, who suddenly became too ill to sail. That's too much of a coincidence, Lizzie. And, there is the lock of hair we found attached to the main mast with the ransom note. My guess is, he cut your hair, and kept a piece of it for himself. Jack will be searching his quarters as we speak. And, someone had to be here to signal the smuggler crew when my men succumbed to the drugged ale. Turn around." He directed, and began unfastening the ties of her gown when she did as he bade.

He pulled the gown over her head and slung it over the sofa. Lizzie turned to face him. His height gave him an unhindered view

112

of her breasts beneath the opening of her shift. Perfect ambrosial spheres. Pink nipples matched the shade of her lush, sensual lips. He hardened to granite, unable to pull his gaze from the delightful creamy swells.

". . . *Donovan?*" Her impatient tone slapped his conscience.

He swallowed, forcing himself to listen and look at her face, not her breasts.

"I said, what if someone comes in here while you're out?"

"No one will come through that door." He assured her, tracing the outline of her arm with a light forefinger. That finger moved across her collarbone, yearning to circle a delicate orb. He yearned to taste those tender buds and tease them with his tongue. Instead, he pulled her against him, mindful not to press against her and intimidate her with his molten male need.

Elizabeth pushed tight against him, not noticing the rock formation at the apex of his thighs. She was distracted by a greater threat, he realized, as she wore out the subject.

"How can you be sure? Why can't you do this with the captain tomorrow? I could come with you. I promise not to be a--"

Donovan captured those enticing pink lips, silencing her. He slipped his tongue into that warm, moist cavern. *What was this?* Damn if she didn't appear to mind the intrusion. She remained pliant in his arms; pouring oil on the fire heating his blood instead of wriggling away from him as she should be if she knew what was good for her. He cupped her curvaceous bottom and drew her hard against him in spite of his bulging erection. Perhaps if she knew the danger, she'd cease her pleading and let him go kill Linton.

He devoured her mouth with his kiss. Damn it, why wasn't she retreating?

The brandy--chasing two glasses of wine. She was intoxicated. She didn't understand what was happening between them. Holding her by her shoulders, he set her away from him and lowered his head so he could look her full in the eyes. "Listen to me, Elizabeth. Every man on this ship sailed under me when I was the Raven, every man, save one. You could dance naked in front of them and they wouldn't touch you. They wouldn't dare because they know me."

A frown crumpled her adorable features. "Then, why did you make your men go below when I was out on deck the other day?"

"That was for your comfort, my sweet."

Lizzie quickly found the chink in the wall of protection he was trying to build around her. "You said every man but one sailed with you in the east, you meant Linton, didn't you? He could come in here while you're away."

Donovan was grateful Lizzie's reasoning was sound, despite the annoyance it was giving him at the moment with her worrying and supposing. It wasn't long ago he feared she might not be capable of reasoning deeply at all. Taking her sweet face between his hands, he held her worried gaze. "And that one man will be with me."

Lizzie kept looking at him with those big, worried eyes. "I'll let you do whatever you want if you stay with me."

The words should have thrilled him. They did give him pause. He studied her, noting the apprehension in her eyes. Her invitation was borne of desperation, not desire. She was trading her body in exchange for protection from a greater threat than the one straining his breeches.

"No, Lizzie." He turned away while he still could and busied himself by removing his silk vest and untying the annoying neck linens required for formal dinners. He shrugged off his dress shirt and replaced it with one more suitable for bloodshed. He moved to his weapons cabinet and unlocked it to select a blade that would cause the most damage without actually killing the man. He examined the blade of one dagger and set it aside in favor of another.

"You don't want me?" The hurt in her voice was unmistakable.

He turned and stalked back to her, took her hand and pressed it against his granite cock. "Oh, I want you. I'm in pain from wanting you so desperately, Madame."

She jerked her hand from him and retreated into the bedchamber, intimidated at last.

He studied the beamed ceiling for several seconds with his hands on his hips, released an exasperated sigh, and then surveyed the room with venom. He cursed himself for his callow behavior. It wasn't Lizzie's fault that he was hot and horny, ready to explode from the heady combination of pent up lust and the primitive desire to kill something.

He knew he should march in there and apologize for being so crude.

Donovan groaned, his rage defying his conscience. The gentleman in him was appalled by his savage behavior. And yet, he was in no mood to have to explain himself to a naïve miss. And having an erection *was* painful—sort of--it was bloody uncomfortable.

Shoving aside the guilt for intimidating his bride, he returned to his weapons cabinet.

Elizabeth listened to the angry shouts coming from the outer deck. Donovan left several minutes ago. She heard the door slam and the lock turned with a key. She should be grateful the man remembered to lock the door, given his foul mood and his desire to be well shot of her.

The arrogant, self-absorbed cad. He had no idea how difficult it had been to offer herself to him in the first place. And then to be callously set aside like a meal that was unappetizing!

A shrill cry of pain brought Elizabeth up short. She remained still. A sudden cacophony of shouts overwhelmed that single wail of anguish. The angry sounds brought a sharp, jarring memory of the night she was abducted. There had been shouts outside her door that night, the clanging of swords, and finally those filthy creatures swarmed in with their torches and dragged her out into the night.

Elizabeth shrank against the headboard and clutched the covers up to her neck as the memory invaded her mind. She released a tortured breath, tossed back the covers and jumped to her feet, anxious to distance herself from the memory of being groped by cruel hands.

She returned to the larger suite. It was silent out on the deck, deathly silent. What was happening, a mutiny? Donovan left with haste, before arming himself heavily. And he never locked the door when he left before.

The sharp rat-a-tat-tat of drums broke the tense silence that descended beyond the cabin door. She sighed as understanding came. This wasn't a mutiny; it was an execution. There would be no trial for Linton in St. Kitts, her husband was making certain of that.

"Miserable prick, I'm going to kill him" He vowed in the captain's cabin earlier.

Elizabeth returned to the small room and sat down on the bed. A morbid part of her longed to go out on deck to witness Linton's execution, on behalf of the poor women he abused at the asylum. The sensible part of her overruled such lunacy. She couldn't endure being surrounded by rough seaman again, even those under her husband's command. Following his assurance to its rational conclusion, what he was actually telling her was that she was a female on ship full of ruthless pirates but she was safe only because she belonged to the head pirate, a man far more dangerous than the rest of the crew.

An eternity passed before she heard the key grating in the lock. A resonant clang of metal echoed as something was deposited on the desk. She rose and peeked into the larger room. Donovan stood at the desk, a pile of weapons being loaded onto it from his body. His shirt was saturated with blood. He didn't seem injured. He stood calmly at his desk cleaning the curved dagger he'd taken out on deck with him, unaware she was watching from the doorway.

He replaced the weapon in the case and locked it. The keys were deposited in the desk drawer. He removed the pistols from his belt along with his sword and set them on the desk. He unbuckled the leather holster strapped to his thigh and placed the dagger holster on the desk next to his pistols and sword. He lifted his foot, braced it on the desk, and removed another long dagger from the shaft of his boot and set it with the others. He dropped his foot and peeled the bloody shirt over his head, tossed the soiled garment to the floor and then stalked to the washstand. Elizabeth watched his elegant profile as he poured water into the basin, lathered his hands and rinsed them. Wet skin shimmered like burnished bronze as he dipped a cloth into the basin, rung it out and washed all trace of blood from his torso with practiced movements. His taut muscles rippled in the golden light, making her insides reel with admiration and wonder.

The man was lean, graceful and dangerous--a beguiling combination for any woman.

"Why are you not asleep?" His voice jarred her out of her strange enchantment with his physical form. He did not turn to face her as he waited for her reply.

"You lied to me." Elizabeth replied, recalling the reason for his blood spattered shirt. "You said Linton would be handed over to the magistrate in St. Kitts. I'm not a simpering miss with tender sensibilities that need minding. I've been forced to deal with the ugly realities of life since my mother died. I assure you I can endure them without sinking into hysterics, my lord."

That magnificent torso swung about and advanced. Elizabeth was confronted by a wall of naked male flesh. Always the gentleman, he remained clothed in her presence except when he came to bed. When she awakened from night terrors, she felt rather than saw his damaged flesh in the darkness as he drew her close to comfort her. Now she could see them clearly for the first time. Long, narrow ruts of pale purple lined his chest. The marks were vertical and precise.

"They tortured my lord." Pearl confided not long ago.

Elizabeth stiffened. She would not disappoint this man by cringing at his disfigurement. She stared at his mutilated flesh, her heart cracking while outwardly she maintained the mask of calm perfected during her years with Fletcher. The damage was akin to surface scratches on a fine Greek statue. The vandals failed miserably in their attempt to ruin a masterpiece.

Fascinated by the power and grace of his male form, she placed her palm against the contours of that muscular chest. His skin was firm and slightly moist from his labor. Dark whorls of hair curled about her fingers. Fearing her action was too brazen she tried to retract her hand.

Donovan captured her wrist. His free hand covered hers, flattening it against his chest, as if savoring the intimate contact. "I don't want you to *endure* the ugly realities of life." His brusque tone made Elizabeth glance up at his face. "As my wife, you will never be forced to deal with them again. From this point on, if a man offends you, if he looks at you inappropriately, you will tell me so I can deal with it. Is that understood, *Mrs. Beaumont?*"

Elizabeth jerked her hand from his grasp. "I should take comfort in the fact that you intend to go bludgeon every man who looks at me? Good God, this isn't the Dark Ages!"

"I can't kill a man for looking at you, but I can make damn sure it goes no farther." He replied in that high-handed tone she was coming to loathe. "You belong to me."

Oh, the arrogant coxcomb! Biting back a saucy retort, Elizabeth gave him her back, determined not to argue with his archaic reasoning. "And you killed Linton, I suppose?"

"No, I merely wounded him. Linton still lives." Firm hands circled her shoulders from behind. "Jack found the box of *trophies* from his victims, just as you described, along with a cache of Laudanum. Jack revealed only Linton's treachery in helping the smugglers take the ship to the crew. What happened with you will remain between us. Linton was forced to walk the gauntlet between the men and endure their wrath for betraying them. He'd been clubbed and stabbed several times when I met him at the end of the line."

"I was afraid—I thought it was a mu-mutiny." She whispered.

"No, darlin'." He squeezed her shoulders. "Linton begged me to save him. I informed him that his hunting days were over and his fate was sealed the moment he cut your hair and marked you as his victim. He seemed surprised that I knew his secret. And then, I gave him a gut wound that would kill him slowly and painfully over several weeks as it turns septic."

Elizabeth's hand flew to cover her mouth. She was appalled by his grisly admission.

"Don't worry, Jack won't let him linger. He'll hang before dawn for betraying the crew.

Linton cannot harm another woman. Elizabeth reminded herself as the chilling report sliced through her. Donovan was being honest instead of sugaring the truth to protect her tender sensibilities as he had earlier. She wasn't sure she liked his brutal honesty after all.

Donovan's arms enveloped her from behind. Elizabeth leaned into his embrace. She tipped her head back against his shoulder and placed her arms over his as he cradled her against his solid form. She traced the ropy contours of his forearms and his big hands, marveling at the masculine strength surrounding her like a fortress of stone.

"You're safe in my keeping." He whispered against her ear. Elizabeth swayed with him as his body moved behind her in a timeless gesture of comfort. "You'll always be safe with me."

What was happening to her? She prided herself on her ability to face the dragon without wilting like a fragile flower. Yet, she was trembling in this man's arms as the events of the past days and weeks pressed upon her.

"You've had a very distressing evening, haven't you, my sweet."

Elizabeth nodded, voiceless and close to exhaustion as he lifted her in his arms and carried her into the bedchamber. A tinned lantern on the wall above the bed made a pool of light on the sheets, casting a warm, buttery circle on the bed beneath it. Donovan lowered her to the bed and turned as if to go.

"Donovan, don't leave me. Please." Even as she said them, she cringed at pathetic timbre of her words. "I don't want to be alone." She pleaded, unable to contain the wave of panic rolling through her. It seemed as if a dam were bursting inside her, the walls of her self-control crackling and rippling beneath the constant fear pressing against them, demanding release.

"Hush, my sweet girl." Donovan eased down beside her on the bed. He gathered her in his embrace. They lay quietly entwined in the circle of pale golden light. He reclined with his back propped against the wall. Elizabeth was lying curled on her side between his splayed thighs as she leaned against his rugged chest. She huddled against him, well aware that she was behaving like the weak, insipid females her grandmother despised.

She didn't care. She'd hate herself later, when she no longer trembled and started at every noise and shadow. Right now, she just wanted to feel safe in this world of violent men.

As Donovan held her the frantic churning in her ears receded. She breathed in the clean scent of his skin and surrendered to the urge to caress the soft whorls of hair curling beneath her cheek. She traced the path of a scar with her finger and pressed a light kiss against it.

The man holding her flinched, and then inhaled sharply. He became a statue.

Had she given offense by her naïve caress? Perhaps she should not be so curious about his body, or at the very least, his scars.

In the stilted silence, she glanced up at his face, searching for clues as to his mood. He was gazing down at her. His face was bathed in shadows, being just outside the circle of light.

"*Ma Cherie.*" He whispered, as a long, lean finger moved along her arm. It edged along her shoulder and then her neck in leisurely pattern. His hand cupped her cheek, traced it with light fingers and smoothed a stray tendril behind her ear. Donovan's finger glided across her jaw, circled her chin and nestled beneath it as his thumb outlined her lips in a patient exploration. Each new pass of his thumb along her lips raised fresh trails of desire. Her lips parted under the sensual caress. The tip of his thumb brushed inside of her mouth and then emerged to spread a moist trail along her tingling lips.

Elizabeth reached up to caress his cheek. It was rough, shadowed with stubble in the late hour, accentuating the sharp planes of his handsome face. It made him look wicked, dangerous, but at this moment, he was neither. Her hand traveled from his rough cheek to settle on the back of his neck. She pulled slightly, urging him to lean in to kiss her.

His lips quickly descended to take possession of her mouth. In that moment nothing existed beyond the sweet persuasion of his lips as his mouth merged with hers. Taking, giving. Possessing, fulfilling.

His tongue slid across her upper lip, curling, teasing, and silently pleading for her to open to him. She surrendered her mouth to his intimate caress. It wasn't the first time he'd been so bold with her in recent days. Elizabeth was entranced by the silken feel of their tongues blending together like musical notes, forming a rich sonata of unrivaled pleasure.

As he persisted, gently wooing her tongue and enticing it to dance with his, Elizabeth experienced an anxious, needy feeling that was very different from the usual gnawing fear that clawed her insides. This was a pleasant, buoyant urge to be closer—ever closer--to him. She followed her instincts, pressing against him, seeking solace in the warmth of his masculine form.

Practiced fingers unfastened the lacings of her gown. Elizabeth started as the cool air invaded her tender skin. She stiffened, no longer confident regarding the sensual path he was guiding them down. Without a thought, she clutched the edges of her gown with her fist, blocking his advance.

Donovan stopped kissing her. He inclined his head, leaning into the circle of light so she could see his eyes. He wanted her, badly. He said as much earlier and she could feel his rigid desire protruding into her backside. It felt as if a rock were lodged between them. Elizabeth swallowed nervously. She'd offered herself to him earlier in a desperate bid to keep him near.

She shouldn't have been so rash, but she couldn't withdraw the invitation now. Still, her hand held the gown closed.

"Don't be frightened." His voice, so soft, so pleading, was like a verbal caress. "You kissed me so sweetly. Allow me kiss you in the same place. It's all I'll ask this night, I swear."

Shackled with uncertainty, Elizabeth was unable to pull her eyes from his potent gaze.

She gave a slight nod, her jaw having become so tight it wouldn't allow speech. She dropped her hand to her lap, resigned to endure the proceedings as best she could.

"I would never hurt you, Elizabeth. You know that, don't you? You trust me, don't you Sweetheart? After all this time together, nearly six weeks . . . come, my love."

Oh, God! Was this how women fell at men's urging throughout the ages? His words were as powerful as a magician's spell when spoken so seductively. Elizabeth found herself nodding agreement as he gazed intently into her eyes and whispered his sweet incantation. "Trust me, Sweet Lizzie. Let me kiss your breasts."

At her nod of acquiescence his hand slipped inside her gown. He cupped her breast with gentleness that robbed the gesture of offense. His palm was warm and firm as it cradled and then stroked her tender flesh. She released her captured breath, intrigued by his sensual caress. He wasn't pinching or squeezing with cruel glee as the smuggler crew had when they cornered her.

He was gentle, so gentle, as he promised he would be. Somehow, he guided her to lie on her back. She was unaware of it happening, but now he was lying on his side next to her, his face hovering above hers. His face descended, he engaged her in a long, leisurely kiss, a gentle reminder of many such kisses they'd shared in recent days.

His head dipped and his hair tickled her skin as he placed a light kiss on the tip of one breast. Elizabeth was shocked by the delightful sensation of his warm, moist lips enveloping her nipple. He suckled briefly, sending odd shivers through her breast that resonated deep within her.

Donovan's head turned and he gave the same attention to her other breast, once more gently taking the tip into his mouth, suckling and rolling it between his lips until it tingled and budded with desire. She sighed as he teased and suckled the sensitive bud and rolled over it with his tongue. He released it and then blew on it, intensifying her pleasure as his breath caressed the hardened bud he'd moistened by his tongue.

Elizabeth opened her eyes to find his pale gaze upon her face, not her breasts. She knew that look. He was studying her, measuring her reaction to his touch. Satisfied that he had guided her successfully through what she expected to be an unpleasant experience, he pulled the gaping fabric over her exposed flesh and tied the top lacing with quick fingers.

She was confused by his gallant retreat. It would be so easy for him to keep kissing her and coaxing her until he had her pressed beneath him, forced to accommodate to his desire.

Instead, he was keeping his promise?

"Go to sleep, Lizzie." He whispered sweetly, as she continued to stare at him with disbelief. He lay on his side, curled about her. His arm circled her waist, and his head nestled near hers on the pillow. "I'll be here to chase away the monsters."

Chapter Fifteen

Birds? Surely she was dreaming. Entranced by the sound of birdsong after weeks of silence, Elizabeth sprang from bed and crossed the outer room to kneel on the window seat with her hands palmed against the glass. Tall, green mountains were gliding rapidly past her line of view. A white gull glided past the glass pane, followed by two others.

"Good morning, my sweet." Donovan was seated at the table. Pearl stood behind him, brushing out his dark hair. Elizabeth blinked and looked again. Yes, the servant was combing his hair backwards, making it appear thick and unruly where normally it was sleek and neat.

She studied Donovan's abrupt transformation. Dressed in stark, unrelenting black, he gave the appearance of the fierce pirate he had once been. His black shirt was left open, displaying the scars he usually kept hidden beneath a fine lawn shirt. The scars added to his frightening persona, as did the tousled mane of jet black hair hanging wildly about his shoulders. Dark stubble peppered his jaw, emphasizing those pale, penetrating blue eyes.

Pearl set the comb aside and picked up a black scarf. He tied it about his master's brow. The empty eyeholes on Donovan's forehead left no question as to the purpose of that sheath.

"This is Ambrose Duchamp." Donovan gestured behind her.

She turned with a gasp. A tall, lanky fellow with a swarthy complexion leaned against the wall beside the door. Elizabeth crossed her arms about her chest, keenly aware of her state of undress. She wore only a thin night rail. Her hair was in disarray, and she was barefoot, a severe disadvantage when being presented to a frightful scoundrel.

"Mr. Duchamp and I escaped France together." Donovan explained.

Duchamp made a bow. His dark eyes revealed a tendency toward sulkiness. She sensed he, too, had suffered untold horrors in France. Unlike Donovan, Duchamp had yet to emerge from his malevolent cocoon and rejoin the human race.

A discreet cough behind her caught her attention. Pearl held open her lavender silk robe. Elizabeth slipped into it and looked about her with unease as she stood between the dangerous stranger before her and the imposing pirate inhabiting the body of her husband behind her.

"Lizzie." Donovan intoned. She turned. He held out his arm. She went to him quickly. He wrapped his arm about her in a protective gesture, pulling her close to his seated form. "I'll find you a position on the estate." He addressed his guest. "Assisting me in my scientific studies is not feasible. I prefer to work alone, and the opportunity for acquiring specimens is rare."

"I could provide you with plenty of specimens, *mon ami*."

"No." Donovan's voice deepened to a warning timbre. "Coming across a fresh corpse is one thing, but deliberate killing for scientific--" Elizabeth gasped at his words. Donovan's arm tightened about her, as if fearing she might flee his grip. "Ambrose is rendering the remains of shark for me, dearest." He stared hard at his henchmen as he spoke to her. "I use the cartilage for medicinal purposes. Ambrose procures them for me from time to time."

"*Aye, a shark.*" The Frenchman's eyes gleamed with amusement as he gazed at her.

"You will be paid handsomely for your services, as usual. But make no mistake; you will not take it upon yourself to provide future specimens for me without my request. Do we understand each other, Mr. Duchamp?"

The lanky Frenchman nodded, pushed himself away from the wall, and left the cabin.

"Ambrose tires of life at sea." Donovan explained, stating the obvious and shoving aside the ambiguous as if it were of little consequence. He gazed up at her. "You're frowning, my sweet. Did you awaken with a headache again?"

It was a valid question, as sometimes she awakened with a punishing migraine.

"No, I did not, thank you. Why are you wearing this. . . this costume?" She gestured to his odd attire. "I was led to believe that you were no longer a pirate, my lord."

"It's true. The Raven is long retired. May I present *Le Comte de Rochembeau*, one of the identities I maintain on my estate."

"One--one of your--" She stammered, taken aback by his statement.

"Count Rochembeau is the owner of Ravencrest Plantation. Mr. O'Rourke, my other persona, is his servant, or to be more precise, the steward of the estate." He stood and placed his arms about her. "No one knows we are the same man."

"Why?" Elizabeth asked in a high voice, tamping down the rising panic.

"Servants blend into the background." He replied with confidence. "As O'Rourke, I can gain people's trust, learn their secrets, and discern potential plots against me as the count."

Oh Dear! A man would have to be greatly unsettled in his mind to fear others were plotting against him continually. She released her hand from her throat, hardly aware she'd been clutching it as the full import of Pearl's words swept over her anew. *"They tortured my lord."*

"I must insist that you play along with the ruse for a short time."

"But why? Why the need for such an elaborate disguise?"

"The count adds a dramatic element. His face is rumored to be disfigured, making him a recluse, hence the silk sheath." He touched the scarf. "It keeps people at a respectful distance. Ach, don't worry, my bonny lass." Donovan switched to a convincing Irish brogue. "When you see my face I am Mr. O'Rourke." He pulled the mask down to conceal his features. "When you do not, *ma cherie*, I am Count Rochembeau." He added in a flawless French accent.

The ease with which he switched from one personality to the other was frightening,

"Does the captain know?" As soon as she asked, she knew it was futile to expect aid from another man. Donovan was her spouse. Legally, she was required to obey him despite his eccentricities. Captain Rawlings couldn't help her. She was alone in this.

"Of course he knows." Donovan replied, seeming perturbed by her question.

"What about when we're alone? How should I address you, sir?"

"By my name." He pushed the mask up and gave her a dazzling smile.

She studied his eyes for a hint of madness, but saw none. "And your name is Donovan?"

"Yes." He studied her, appearing perplexed. "Interesting point. I use Donovan with my O'Rourke disguise. You must not address me by my Christian name when I'm the count."

Elizabeth nodded, stunned by this strange turn of events.

"You'll see me as Mr. O'Rourke most of the time. Don't worry, you'll be fine, Lizzie."

It wasn't herself she worried about!

"I'll be ending the ruse soon, a week at most." He added, caressing her brow thoughtfully with a forefinger. "Do you think you can manage?"

Did she have a choice? "I will try not to disappoint you, my lord."

"Lizzie, you're taking this too seriously!" He said, laughing and hugging her. "Just think of it as my way of keeping you safe."

How does pretending to be two different people keep me safe? She wanted to ask, but did not. The question might upset him, and more than anything, Elizabeth did not want this man to become upset. "Are you afraid your slaves may have planned an uprising?" She asked, endeavoring to see things from his perspective, and perhaps help him.

"Slavery is a vile business, Elizabeth." His tone became severe. "You have no idea the horrors that met my eyes when I took over the estate. I came to hate Richard O'Donovan and everything he stood for. I released his slaves. I buy prison indentures to use as a labor source."

"What became of the slaves your grandfather owned?" Elizabeth asked, intrigued by his confession. "Surely you didn't evict them? If they left your estate, wouldn't they risk being subjected to slavery again by others?"

"You are very perceptive." He admitted. "A few left. Those with families still reside on the estate. They run the saw mill and a smithy. Some men oversee the cane operations during the harvest. It is an exacting process, and they've done it for many years so I trust their judgment and pay them accordingly for their expertise."

He pulled the chair out and gestured for her to sit at the small table.

She hadn't noticed Pearl returned with her breakfast. Elizabeth sat down and gave in to her hunger. Donovan sat next to her and continued to converse with her as if nothing were amiss. "Aside from cane production, I breed horses to sell in the local markets. I added a small coffee grove and planted a hundred nutmeg saplings since taking over the estate. It will be years before they bear fruit, but once established the spices will bring a steady profit for years to come." He took a sip from the steaming cup of coffee before him. The alluring aroma filled the cabin.

Elizabeth had never tasted the exotic brew. "May I?" She asked. Donovan held his cup out to her. She took a sip and grimaced at the bitter taste. She'd stick to good English tea.

"It's an acquired taste." He mused, lifting the cup to his lips.

The vast expanse of turquoise sea gave way to lush emerald foliage. Stark volcanic peaks towered against the brilliant blue sky as the ship passed the small islands of the West Indies. After close to seven weeks at sea, with silence surrounding them and the endless expanse of ocean, it was invigorating to see land again, to hear birds and breathe in the the rich scent of foliage. The wind caressed Elizabeth's face with moist, warm kisses. The aroma of Earth, spices and flowers permeated the sultry air. Birds called to one another from the lush greenery.

She cast a furtive glance at the 'Dark Count' as they stood at the rail. He looked like a highwayman with the black sheath concealing his features. Just before coming on deck he rubbed cream on his cheeks, a rouge containing stinging nettles, he said, as he tucked the small tin in his pocket. The skin beneath the fabric was angry red, giving the illusion of disfigurement.

As they drew near his island she could see a small village hugging the wharf. Fishing boats dotted the pale, sandy beach. In the distant horizon she could make out the hazy outline of another island; St. Christopher's, or St. Kitts as the locals called it. The harbor was a town called Basseterre. St Kitts and Ravencrest Estates, a smaller island, fell under British jurisdiction.

A mount was waiting for him near the wharf, a sleek black stallion that could only belong to the dark count. Donovan lifted Elizabeth up into the saddle and swung up behind her. "It's not far, just up the hill." He explained. "They didn't know to send the carriage. It will take too long to have it brought down now."

Wrapping his arms about her, he took up the reins and urged his mount to a bracing trot.

Lush jungle vines and brilliant tropical blooms lined the road as they traveled up the hill to the plantation house. Vibrant red and brilliant pink blooms abounded among the brush. A cluster of birds called to each other from the thick jungle on either side of the road and were answered with sharp trills and deep, screeching caws in the hot, sultry air.

They crested the hill. Elizabeth drew in her breath at the stately beauty of the white baroque manor house in the distance. It was enclosed by iron fencing. Beyond the gate, palm trees lined the wide drive. A pillared porch embraced the second story.

Donovan dismounted at the gate, unlocked a heavy chain, led his mount through, then wound the chain through the iron fencing once more and locked the paddock. A pair of mastiffs came bounding down the drive from behind the manse, snapping and snarling. The horse reared. Elizabeth lurched forward to clutch its neck, bracing herself to hit the ground in a painful thud.

Her husband snatched the bridle and secured the anxious beast. "Halt." He commanded the approaching dogs in a harsh, guttural snarl. The dogs stopped in their tracks several feet ahead. He snapped his finger and pointed at the ground. They sat down. "That's better. Come," he instructed, holding out a hand to them, while keeping a tight grip on the bridle. The beasts approached him with wagging tails and pressed against him, vying for their master's attention.

Donovan pushed the sheath over his brow and smiled up at Elizabeth. She didn't smile back. The estate seemed far from welcoming as she took in the neglect of the grounds that weren't noticeable at a distance. There were weeds where flower beds should be and iron fencing with razor sharp spikes preventing anyone from entering or leaving. An empty fountain in the courtyard had moss and weeds in it. The house had most of the shutters drawn on all the first floor windows.

"It needs work." Donovan admitted, seeing her apprehension. "It's lacked a woman's touch for many years. Just think of all the fun you'll have redecorating, my sweet." He led the stallion past the fountain to the front steps, his guard dogs flanking his tall form. The front lawn had been cut recently, she noted, trying to find sunshine among the clouds.

Donovan helped her dismount and led her up the stone stairs to the front door.

Just as she feared, he placed a key in the lock.

Was there no one here to welcome him?

Chapter Sixteen

The large entry hall had parquet flooring and furniture from earlier in the century. Hunting scenes were painted as frescoes in the white plaster walls.

"Stay here, I'll be right back." He admonished, leaving her to gaze up at the winding marble stairs that lead to the second story. The mahogany banister had been polished not too long ago, she noted, feeling hopeful that the interior was not as neglected as the exterior grounds.

Double doors to the right of the stairs piqued her interest. She decided to peek beyond them. She was relieved to find this door unlocked, only to have hope crushed as she gazed inside. The room was dark, the shutters were drawn to block out the sunlight. The furniture was covered with white sheets, resembling ghosts in the darkened room. She crept in a few feet and waited for her eyes to adjust to the gloom. Slats in the shutters allowed jagged shafts of light to diffuse through the shadows. Something dark and furry scuttled across the floor in front of her. Elizabeth stifled a scream and stepped back, remembering Peter's tale about hairy spiders the size of tea saucers.

Who lives here? She wondered, eyeing the room with disappointment. The house had an empty, desolate feel to it, as if no one occupied it for a very long time, at least, no one who cared.

"Lizzie." Elizabeth turned at the sound of her husband's voice, his normal voice, not an affected one. He stood in the foyer, seeming perturbed that she wasn't standing precisely where he'd left her. "Come." He held out his hand. "I've ordered a bath for you. Tabby will see to your comfort while I'm out."

"Where are you going?" She grimaced as she left the dark room for the sunlit foyer. "We've only just arrived."

"I want to take a ride about the place while I'm still dressed as the count. Enjoy your bath and a nice nap. You look all in, darlin'." His lips brushed hers, teasing lightly, reminding her of the tender, caring man on the voyage. He smiled down at her, and then straightened as a lone figure stepped from the shadows of the hall. "This is Tabitha Wilkes, my grandfather's--" He paused. "*Housekeeper*. I kept her on after he died, and the cook."

Mrs. Wilkes was clad in an informal muslin gown rather than the starched black uniform that housekeepers wore in the wealthy homes in England. She was barefoot. Her white hair was unbound, cascading down her back in gentle waves. She was thin, graceful, her complexion golden from time spent in the sun instead of indoors, cleaning her master's home.

She did not resemble any servant Elizabeth encountered in England. Nevertheless, she smiled at the older woman. This was Donovan's home. She was going to have to accept his odd ways and get along with the people in his employ. "It's a pleasure to meet you, Mrs. Wilkes." Elizabeth responded, knowing her mother would scold her for being familiar with a servant. Alas, putting on airs would not win her acceptance from the count's household staff.

"It's Tabby, Ma'am. I'm not married." The woman archly corrected Elizabeth, looking her up and down as if she were a dead rodent the cat carried in from the woodpile.

"Don't be impertinent, Tabby." Donovan interjected before Elizabeth could form a response. "My wife is the grand-daughter of the ninth Earl of Greystowe. She'll put you through your paces, old girl. You might wish to put some thought into retiring. I'm certain my lady will be more particular than I am regarding the household routines."

The woman bristled at his words, looking for a brief second as if she might curse out loud at them. She managed a limp smile from taut lips. "Welcome to Ravencrest, your ladyship." She made a polite curtsy to Elizabeth.

"Take care of my lass, and mind your tongue, Tabby. I'll tolerate none of your cheek with her!" Donovan directed as he made his exit, effectively abandoning Elizabeth.

Elizabeth followed the woman up the stairs and down the hall to the master's chamber. She sensed resentment within Tabby. She dismissed the impression, reasoning that she'd be cranky, too, if she was in this woman's place and the master dropped a new mistress on the doorstep without warning and then left again. It was an awkward situation all around.

Donovan's bedchamber was furnished in a deep forest green that complimented the oak paneling. Very masculine, indeed, befitting a bachelor lord.

"Rest Madame, your bath water will take a while to warm." Tabby said, and left her.

Elizabeth stepped over to the louvered doors and peered through the slats. They gave access to a veranda winding about the second story. And they were locked. She was suddenly seized by a rush of sheer panic.

"*Watch out!*" A thin, frightened voice from beyond the grave warned in the empty room. "*He'll lock you away for his pleasure. He'll never let you feel the sunlight on your face or the wind in your hair again.*"

"Who are you?" Elizabeth glanced about. No one appeared or answered her query.

This was just too much; an isolated estate, a house with chained gates and locked doors, a cranky, resentful housekeeper and now a spirit whispering cryptic warnings to her in the middle of the afternoon. Elizabeth whirled about to the double doors adjacent to the veranda doors. Those, too, were locked. She hurried to the hall door as a frightening presentiment of being kept a prisoner in this dismal place washed over her.

To her relief, the door to the hall opened. "Tabby, bring me the keys." Elizabeth insisted, hoping her warbled voice carried enough authority to garner the precious items.

"I have only this one set, Madame." Tabby called from the far end of the hall. "Why do you need them?"

"I wish to unlock the doors to the veranda and the next room."

The woman padded down the hall on bare feet. She unlocked the balcony doors and then the doors to the adjoining suite.

"This was Maureen's room." Tabby informed her. "She died young, leaving her husband to raise their daughter alone. He let the girl run free, without discipline. 'Tis little wonder the girl got herself with child and ran off with her French lover at sixteen." The housekeeper paused and twisted the doorknob beneath her hand in an odd gesture. Apparently she liked doors to be locked. "Alicia broke his heart."

"Who is Alicia? And Maureen?" *Good God, had Donovan had another wife before her and a child, too?* No, he couldn't have a child of sixteen, he wasn't yet thirty. Still, she couldn't comprehend what the housekeeper's murky tale of undisciplined young ladies running off with foreign lovers had to do with her.

"Maureen O'Donovan was the old lord's wife, your husband's grandmother. Alicia O'Donovan is his mother; a selfish, spoiled, difficult woman. You'll meet her soon enough. She comes from Charleston to spend Christmas with his lordship each year. Why, I can't imagine. He keeps the place about as welcoming as a tomb. Fired all the servants here, he did, sent them all packing four years past when he took over. Just Fritz and myself was kept on, so don't be expecting too much *service*, my lady."

"I'm sure his lordship will not be averse to hiring a few maids to help about the place."

"Oh, there's little hope of that, Madame." The woman scoffed, giving her another measuring look that clearly questioned Elizabeth's reasoning. "Your husband don't like people mum. Keeps to himself, he does. I'm giving you fair warning, because I know how men sprinkle sugar all over a girl when they're trying to win her favor, but once those favors are won, they show their real colors and we're left to deal with the mess."

Such a bitter soul this woman had become. It was obvious someone broke Tabby's heart long ago and left her to fend for herself. She deserved kindness, and that was probably why Donovan kept her on after letting all the other servants go.

Elizabeth walked past the housekeeper and into the adjoining suite. The smell of dust assaulted her senses. She coughed. Tabby moved from the door to open the shutters at the nearest window. The black curtains became royal blue velvet when the sun hit them. The housekeeper tugged up the sash to allow in fresh air. Golden sunlight illuminated the chamber. Elizabeth stood in the center of the room, awed by the revealed opulence as the shadows retreated. The oak paneling had been painted white. The moldings were gilded to create sparkling accents.

"It's beautiful." Elizabeth said, gazing wistfully about her. "I'll take this room as my own. The two of us should be able to have it tidied by nightfall, don't you think?"

"His lordship told me you were to rest, he was adamant about that. He said you've been ill. I can't allow you to overexert yourself. He'll be angry, Madame."

"He promised I could have my own room."

"You'll have to take it up with him." Tabby paced to the door, head held high as she waited for Elizabeth to follow her back to the master suite. Once Elizabeth returned to Donovan's room, the housekeeper locked the doors to the room she'd just vacated, preventing any further exploration. "I'll leave you to rest, Madame. The bell pull is near the bed. Don't be alarmed if no one answers right away. The cook is deaf as a stone and I have to go out to the stables to fetch the lads to carry up the water up for your bath. Just keep ringing. I'll come as soon as I can."

After the housekeeper left, Elizabeth wore a path on the carpet trying to convince herself her world wasn't falling apart around her; that she wasn't married to a madman; that she wouldn't be locked in a shuttered room in the attic if she displeased him. This place was so sinister, just like Mrs. Radcliffe's Gothic stories she used to devour years ago.

Within an hour, the lads from the stables delivered her hot bath water. Tabby lingered to assist Elizabeth with her gown. She accepted the help and then dismissed the older woman once she stood in her chemise.

"I'm supposed to stay, Madame."

"I prefer my privacy."

"He said you weren't to bathe alone. He instructed me to stay with you in case--" The woman smashed her lips together, and looked away.

"He said *what*?"

"You'll have to take it up with him, Madame." The housekeeper replied.

Elizabeth removed her chemise and petticoat and stepped into the luxuriant tub, determined to not allow anyone to spoil the long awaited treat. She closed her eyes and leaned against the tub back, relishing the feel of the warm wetness as it enveloped her body . . .

"Madame?" A hand settled on her shoulder, startling Elizabeth out of a contented doze.

She sat up suddenly, disorientated and groggy. The housekeeper helped her wash her long hair and then hefted the pail of rinse water and let it drizzle over Elizabeth's head and back. Oh, it was pure heaven after six weeks without a proper bath. There was the basin of wash water rationed out every other day, but Elizabeth never truly felt clean with that arrangement.

A nap would be just the thing, she decided as she emerged from the tub.

"Let's get you into one of his shirts." Tabby suggested, seeing where her mind was taking her. "Your trunks are downstairs. Pearl said your bed gowns need washing. Oh, he brought your cat, do you want it up here?"

Pearl was here! She'd forgotten about the gentle servant. Having him around would make all the difference. "Yes, his name is Puck, after Shakespeare's play, the one with the fairies. Can you have a box of dirt brought up—or I could do it if it's too much trouble."

"You'll not be doing any such thing. I'll see to it." The housekeeper huffed, and then her features softened. "Puck, you say? Gareth will be pleased, he adores Shakespeare."

"Who is he?" Elizabeth asked with exasperation. She'd had her fill of surprises for one day.

"Oh." Tabby's eyes darkened. "My lord didn't tell you about Gareth?"

Elizabeth shook her head.

"Oh, isn't that just like a man!" Tabby exclaimed, the sourness returning to her features. "Master Gareth is the natural son of your husband's grandfather by one of his mistresses." The older woman stopped plaiting Elizabeth's hair and pursed her lips. "There's no polite way to put this. Gareth O'Donovan is of mixed blood, his mother was a slave. He lives in the manor, has his father's name and an allowance, but the property belongs to your husband as the legitimate heir. And as his lordship married so suddenly, Gareth is concerned about how the new mistress will receive him---if she'll allow him to continue to live here."

So, that was why the housekeeper was on edge; as Donovan's wife, her presence here was a portend change and change was not always welcomed with open arms. Smiling at the woman's reflection, Elizabeth said, "Please tell to Mr. O'Donovan I look forward to meeting him and I hope that he and I shall become very good friends."

Elizabeth awoke to candlelight and the fragrant aroma of earth and foliage coming in from the opened balcony doors. She rose and walked out on to the balcony. The stunning hues of the sunset took her breath away. She leaned against the balustrade and watched the red orange sun melt into the golden sea. Crickets chirped in the darkness. An owl hooted from a nearby tree.

"A perfect end to a new day, *oui, ma petite*?"

She whirled about to find Donovan lurking behind her outside the door, still in that awful black costume. The glow of a cheroot was in his hand. He lifted his cigar to his lips. The red glow revealed that his face was unsheathed.

The stench of ale and more potent beverages wafted about her as he stood. He tossed his cheroot over the side of the veranda and ran an unsteady hand through his wild hair. "I was just about to join you in that great bed." As he advanced she noted his gait was unsteady. His arms wound about her possessively as he bent to capture her mouth. He'd been drinking. She could taste it on his lips. She turned her head away.

"You smell so sweet, and you taste so damned good, Lizzie." His mouth left wet, clumsy kisses across her cheek as it searched for her lips.

"You smell like an alehouse." Elizabeth replied, as she tried, unsuccessfully, to push him away. "I want separate rooms, Donovan, just as you promised."

"Oh, I intend to keep you much closer than that, my sweet. I've come to enjoy crawling into a bed warmed by your succulent flesh." Large hands moved over her hips to cup her bottom and pull her against his hardened manhood.

"So all of that rot about waiting for me, not pushing me beyond what I was able to give was a lie?" She argued, trying to reach the kind man inside this groping oaf as she pushed and wriggled and tried to escape his cloying arms. "I believed you. I trusted you. And now I know you're no different than those disgusting men who kidnapped me!"

"I'm not like them! But I am your husband and I have a right to touch you, damn it."

His words chilled her. Elizabeth slapped him hard across the face. The sound of her stinging blow echoed in the night air. "Stop groping me like a piece of meat. Let me go!"

His hands circled her shoulders roughly, as if he intended to shake her. "You didn't mind my attention last night. In fact, you gave me an open ended invitation, as I recall."

Oh, he would have to bring that up, wouldn't he? Damn the man. Last night, she'd been frightened out of her wits, desperate to keep him with her. Last night, he turned her down. He was tender and considerate, gallant to a fault. Tonight he was drunk and demanding his rights like a vulgar sailor expecting service from a strumpet in a back alley he'd paid to mount.

And yet, he was her husband. No matter how she justified her refusal, she could not escape that fact.

"I'll endure your pawing and rutting if I must, but I'll not give you the pleasure of my screams. And just so we're straight, Mr. O'Rourke, The Lord of Darkness or whoever you are, I'll hate you forever if you force yourself on me. I'll hate you! You promised—you promised!" She stopped, aware she was near hysterics as she heard the shrill edge to her voice.

His hands dropped from her shoulders. "I do not require screams from you or endurance, for that matter. I am a gentle—"

"--Stay away from me, you arrogant coxcomb!" She threatened. Her fist raised and coiled, ready to clout him if he persisted.

"Oh, I'll stay well away, Madame. I'll have nothing more to do with you until you come to your senses." The count stalked through the room to the hall door. He made his exit with a defining thud, leaving her standing on the veranda in his shirt to savor this hollow victory.

Chapter Seventeen

When Elizabeth came downstairs the next morning she was greeted by the housekeeper and even given the ghost of a smile. "We didn't expect you up and about so early, Madame. Fritz wishes to know what time and where you wish breakfast served."

"Where is his lordship?" She asked, feeling it be best to consult Donovan's wishes, since he'd undoubtedly have an opinion in the matter.

"He left *hours* ago to inspect the cane fields. He's sent word to the port city with Captain Rawlings yesterday that you will be hiring a full staff. He wants you to be prepared to interview them after luncheon today. And he's decided I'm to stay on as the housekeeper." There was no mistaking the triumphant gleam in Tabby's eye. "What is my lady's wish regarding breakfast?"

So, the old woman talked to Donovan before she could address the issue with him. "I'll eat in the dining room today, but send breakfast to my room from now on, when I ring for it." Elizabeth said, embracing her role as mistress of her new home with vigor. "Tell the cook I will discuss the menus with him at a later time. Today I want tea, toast and fresh fruit."

The housekeeper nodded and left her at the entry to the dining room.

Elizabeth surveyed the room. The shutters were opened and the sashes pushed up to evict the stale air. The curtains were faded and moth eaten, they would need replacing. The dust covers had been removed from the chairs and folded in a stack near the door. She stroked the bare wood of the table, a rich, dark cherry that would gleam with an enthusiastic application of polish. Cobwebs clung to the chandelier above her head. The walls needed fresh paint. Dreary paintings graced them, masculine hunting scenes she did not care for. She wondered if her husband would mind if she swapped them for more appealing florals from another room.

The thought of Donovan brought a hot flush to her face. How was she to face him after last night's nasty exchange? In the light of day she realized she insulted him by comparing him to the smugglers. Well, he'd been boorish and demanding, so he deserved it.

Tabby appeared with her breakfast. "You need to drink plenty of water, my lady." She remarked, noting the color in Elizabeth's cheeks. "You'll become ill in the heat if you don't."

After breakfast, Tabby gave her a tour of the house. They inspected the first floor rooms and discussed which ones should be cleaned and aired first based on their practical use. The second floor was composed of bedrooms for family and guests. There were six bedchambers aside from the adjoining suites for the master and mistress, making a total of eight. One was occupied by her husband's uncle. Another was set aside for Donovan's mother, leaving four empty guest bedrooms. Elizabeth made a mental note to assign one for Michael's use.

The third floor made up the servant's quarters, the nursery and a suite for the governess.

Elizabeth felt an invisible hand tug her toward a room at the end of the hall.

Tabby thinned her lips into a disapproving line when Elizabeth asked for the key to the room. "I don't think this is a room you're supposed to see, mum."

"I am the mistress of this house." Elizabeth reminded her archly.

"Suit yourself." The older woman muttered. Elizabeth didn't miss the amusement twisting the woman's thin lips as she unlocked the door. "This was Gareth's mother's room."

Elizabeth stepped inside. Faded coral pink silk curtains hung from windows that were not shuttered as the rest of the household had been. The curtains were parted, revealing bars on the outside; a curious arrangement as the room was three stories from the ground. A matching rose bedspread covered the four poster bed. There was a small white marble fireplace, a blue chaise lounge beside it and dried flowers in a vase on the mantle, skeletal remains of ancient blooms that would dissolve to dust if touched by a human hand.

It was a luxurious suite, not a plain room intended for a servant. It was also a gilded cage.

A wicker cradle stood in one corner. Elizabeth walked to it and peeked inside. A silver rattle lay in the dusty lace coverlet. She stepped away from the cradle and considered the barred windows. An oppressive hopelessness whirled about her, the desire to be free to walk outside, to feel the sunlight on her skin and the wind in her hair. Free of bondage to a man she did not love.

"*Run away, hide! He'll keep you locked in here forever, awaiting his pleasure.*"

Elizabeth stood very still, listening to that frightened whisper. It was the same voice that warned her yesterday in the count's room. Vowing to return alone so she might discern why the poor woman's spirit remained trapped in this house, even in death, Elizabeth turned to the older woman. "How did Gareth's mother die?"

"I wasn't here at the time. They say it was complications of childbirth, the fever. Gareth was two months old. The O'Donovan cleaned up the body himself and forbade any to come up here after she died. He loved her. He told me that, many times."

"She was his prisoner." Elizabeth countered with disbelief. "That isn't love, Tabby."

"She was a Darkie." The housekeeper said, as if that made all the difference. "I don't know what they teach delicate girls like you in England about these things, but here a black man cuts the master's cane in the fields and the Negro girls, the pretty ones, end up in his bed."

Elizabeth flushed scarlet, appalled by the woman's coarse remark. No housekeeper in England would dare speak to her mistress in an abrasive manner, not if she wished to retain her position. Alas, since arriving here she was constantly being reminded that she was no longer in that polite, civilized country, despite her husband's assertion that these islands were ruled by King George.

"In England, in polite society, slavery is considered a barbaric and outdated institution that needs to be abolished. It allows evil men to prey upon the less fortunate." She replied in a condescending tone, wearied by the housekeeper's insulting mien.

The housekeeper's lips tightened into a thin, puckered line. "Richard O'Donovan was a good man. He bought Marissa from a brothel in Martinique and brought her here to be his mistress. She was better off here, the darling of one man instead of a whore to all." Tabby's features softened. "He could be so charming, a girl could hardly resist him."

"Being locked in here would make it rather difficult." Elizabeth countered.

"He had no choice, she'd run off otherwise." Tabby defended the man. "Marissa was a fool. Richard was everything a girl could wish for in a protector; rich, handsome and uncommonly tender. Oh, he liked his games of dominance and submission. If she'd have just played along, why, he'd have given her the world." Tabby looked like a lovesick girl ready to swoon as she gazed longingly at the bed.

Elizabeth scoffed aloud, mortified by Tabby's eagerness to defend the man's perfidy against a member of their sex. *Marissa was a fool for not wanting to be someone's private whore? For wanting to be free?* She marched out of the disturbing room, past the impertinent housekeeper, too flustered to reprimand the cheeky woman as she ought. She returned to first floor via the servant's stairs, with Tabby trailing behind her.

As she marched down the long hall of the east wing, toward the center of the house, Elizabeth paused, realizing there was a room she had not been shown earlier, by design.

"That's his lordship's laboratory." Tabby informed her dismissively.

"I wish to see it." Elizabeth insisted.

"His lordship doesn't allow anyone in there, Madame." When Elizabeth held her impervious gaze, Tabby added, "I suppose you're the exception. But mark, me, you must never to go into the surgery, Madame."

"Why?" The housekeeper's forbidding tone made Elizabeth ask.

"Sometimes there's a corpse there, awaiting dissection."

Elizabeth gasped and then recovered her shock. The woman was obviously making sport of her. "I'm sure my husband does nothing of the sort."

"Well, I'm not making it up." Tabby insisted, challenging Elizabeth to say otherwise with her insolent gaze. "After a hanging in the port city, if no one claims the body, the count has a standing arrangement with the hangman to send it here. I know, as I'm the one who pays the delivery men. I'm only warning you so you don't go in there and give yourself a fright, mum."

Elizabeth sat in a chair in housekeeper's parlor just off the kitchens after nearly swooning at the news that her spouse hacked up corpses as a hobby. She sipped a glass of lime water.

The count was an *anatomist*, Tabby had been quick to explain as she escorted her wilting mistress down the hall with a steadying arm about Elizabeth's waist. As a scientist, he studied the organs of the human body to order to understand disease and to thus preserve life.

The distinction did little to improve Elizabeth's opinion of the man at present.

She patted her neck with a handkerchief for the third time in mere minutes. Noting her discomfort, Tabby refilled her glass and glowered at her until she sipped it. Pearl appeared briefly and handed her a folded note. Elizabeth opened it. It was not an apology but rather a command for her to come to the laboratory at four o'clock today. She stared at the signature, a large letter D, and feared her world was shifting too quickly beneath her feet.

After luncheon the applicants began to arrive. Elizabeth made her selections for maids and footmen quickly, based on her impression of each candidate. She spent more time interviewing those applying to be her personal maid and settled upon a Spanish woman named Miss Chloe Ramirez whose father had been the steward here years ago. Those laughing brown eyes and her warm smile promised Elizabeth she would be great fun, while the other women vying for the position seemed to have taken vinegar in their tea instead of sugar.

The housekeeper gestured to Elizabeth for a private word. "You must not hire her. She passes herself off as Spanish with her light skin but she's a quadroon, she has darkie blood."

Elizabeth knew what it was like to be the subject of open disdain. Her stepfather frequently disparaged her for her Irish heritage, calling it a taint in the blood as if she were diseased and inferior to those of pure English descent. "Her parentage is not my concern."

"Madame, her grandmother was a voodoo priestess." Tabby argued. "Old Suki used to shake a dried chicken's foot at your husband's grandfather, cursing her master. Choose one of the others. They're good English girls. Please, for your children, mum. The girl might poison them, or you."

"Well, then, we should get on famously." Elizabeth had had enough of the housekeeper's opinions. "My grandmother was a witch." It was the housekeeper's turn to appear scandalized.

Elizabeth left Tabby to deal with her new staff. She meandered down the long corridor to the west wing of the manor house to explore her new home unhindered by the older woman's dour presence.

"Madame Beaumont?"

Elizabeth turned to find a tall fellow with a dark complexion deliberately tracking her. She looked about the empty corridor with unease, wondering if he had followed her from the servant's hall without her being aware of it. "I'm sorry. The interviews are over."

Too late, she noted his gentlemanly attire. "Mr. O'Donovan—I beg your pardon!" She said, fearing she'd offended her husband's uncle by mistaking him for a hireling. "I meant no offense."

He held up a gloved hand. "It is you who must forgive me. My nephew cautioned me that you are reticent where men are concerned. I should have waited for a proper introduction."

"My lord exaggerates the issue, sir." *How dare Donovan imply she was a shrinking mouse afraid of her own shadow!*

Like Donovan, his uncle had a high brow, chiseled cheekbones, an elegant nose and a firm jaw. Mr. O'Donovan's eyes were slate gray, not pale blue. His dark complexion was tempered by a subtle golden hue that complimented the aura of warmth surrounding him.

"Nevertheless, I am a stranger to you, my lady." He said in a pleasing baritone and made an elegant leg before her. As he did so, thick serpentine twists of hair moved about his shoulders as if they were alive. "Gareth O'Donovan at your service, Lady Elizabeth."

"Please call me Elizabeth." She smiled warmly at the man. She didn't know what to expect regarding her husband's uncle after being presented with this sorry, neglected estate and even sorrier excuse for a housekeeper. She didn't expect to find such a charming, engaging gentleman.

"Elizabeth it shall be. I was just about to take a ride about the island. Care to join me?"

The offer was a burst of sunshine in an otherwise dismal day. "I don't ride. My lord has promised to tutor me. Perhaps at a later date, sir?"

"I look forward to it." Gareth O'Donovan bowed and took his leave.

She wandered along the west wing, determined to find a room to establish as her own. She passed over the opened pristine 'pink' room with its fussy ivory satin furnishings, dainty rose tea setting and fragile glass figurines. Elizabeth assumed it was a room the count's mother favored and was loathe to take it over and cause resentment from her new mother-in-law. She moved past room after gloomy, shuttered room along the corridor, finding none to fit her taste.

The room she finally settled upon was the library. The rows of books and oak paneling reminded Elizabeth of her grandfather's study at his estate in Devonshire, in her beloved England. She'd spent many a happy hour there as a girl during the summer months, when her mother took Elizabeth and Michael to the country and left Fletcher in London to pursue his vices. That had been years ago, before Mama and Grandfather Wentworth had quarrelled.

She would add a serene landscape to replace the portrait of that nasty old bloke with bushy eyebrows glaring down at her. A vase of fresh flowers from the gardens would do nicely on the mantel . . . and then she remembered the sad state of the gardens.

Elizabeth sank into a chair with a compelling urge to cry. *Crying won't mend a leaky roof,* her grandmother would be quick to say. She took a deep, steadying breath and gathered her resolve. Nor would crying make this mess she'd been presented with into a proper home. Hard work was the answer, not useless tears.

With that thought she returned to the task of designing her private retreat. The blue floral chaise in a room down the hall could be moved here and situated next to the fireplace. Add a few novels, and this could become a cozy sanctuary.

Tabby intruded to remind Elizabeth that she had an appointment with her "lord and master" and she was keeping him waiting. Elizabeth rolled her eyes at the woman's odd phrasing. Tabby seemed to relish the idea of female subordination to a male master too much for her liking. Elizabeth valued her independence. She had planned to ignore Donovan's summons and claim forgetfulness.

Elizabeth followed the housekeeper to the east wing. Tabby stopped at a door, indicating that Elizabeth should venture into the laboratory alone. She sucked in her breath, feeling like an errant child being summoned to Papa's study for a taste of his leather belt.

As she contemplated fleeing to her room, the housekeeper gave her a verbal prod. "He's waiting, Madame, and his mood isn't improving with the passage of time."

Chapter Eighteen

Elizabeth gathered her courage and stepped through the open portal. As soon as she did so, the door was shut by the housekeeper, as if to further unsettle her.

She focused on the books lining the oak shelves to the right of the entrance. Medical tomes in English, French and other languages she couldn't discern. She stepped around a pile of wooden crates near the door and walked toward the windows. Sunlight reflected on the array of glass vials and metal instruments crowding a massive, rough hewn table near the tall windows. As she went deeper into the room, the pungent smell of chemicals and compounds became more pronounced.

The silence of the chamber was unnerving. She turned to face the master of Ravencrest.

Donovan sat behind a mahogany desk calmly puffing on a cheroot, watching her move about his lair. Dusty brown riding boots were propped upon the desk. Muscular thighs were encased in buff riding breeches that appeared shabby from frequent use. A cotton shirt marked him as a commoner, and a brown leather work vest completed his costume. He appeared the master of the stable yards, not the master of the estate.

"*Mr. O'Rourke.*" She acknowledged tersely. They were alone, but she favored the distance of the formal address.

"Sit down, my sweet." He gestured to the chair in front of his desk as he remained seated.

Elizabeth looked away from the handsome wretch as she sat down. A stuffed owl perched with wings outstretched on top of the cabinet looked down at her with fierce eyes. A raven and various reptiles filled a display case to his left

A sheet of canvas hung over the open shelves directly behind him, concealing the contents from her view. She could see a few delft blue apothecary jars at the edge of the canvas. Avoiding his steady gaze, she next took to studying the desk between them. The surface was cluttered with open ledgers and parchment sheets. A tray with cigar stubs smashed into it sat next to a crystal decanter. And grinning at her on the desk between them was a stark white skull.

"Is that---is it *human?*" She gestured to the hollow-eyed skull.

"Yes." He picked it up and stared at it with puzzlement. "Why? Is it talking to you? I can shut it in my desk drawer if it's being impertinent."

"How dare you mock me, sir."

"Mock you? Christ woman, it was a joke!" He set the grisly head aside with a scowl.

She turned away, allowing the tension to thicken as she continued her inspection of the room. Her eyes wandered to the door leading to the next room, the surgery. Did he truly cut up corpses and examine their insides, as the housekeeper claimed?

"I believe I owe you an apology." His words drew her gaze back on him. "I didn't mean to frighten you last night. I was at the alehouse on the wharf and everyone kept shoving drinks in my face, toasting my good fortune in finding such a *rare jewel* in a wife."

Elizabeth couldn't tell if the last was meant as compliment or a sarcastic barb. The look in his eyes was less than generous. "You promised you wouldn't pressure me. You unsettled me with your odd disguise yesterday, and then you bring me to *this*—" She waved a hand about her in emphasis, "—dismal place and abandon me half an hour after we've arrived. While I'm trying to gain my bearings you come in drunk and start groping me just like those revolting smugglers."

"I was inebriated." He insisted, dropping his feet to the floor with a resounding thud. "I've apologized for upsetting you. It won't happen again."

Elizabeth felt herself shrinking inwardly at his furious tone. His parting taunt last night came back to her. *"I'll have nothing more to do with you until you come to your senses!"*

"Since you insist on having your own room, you may take the room next to mine." He stubbed out his cheroot with a vengeance, grinding it into the silver plate beneath his fingers.

"For the present. Once we cease this celibate arrangement you'll sleep in my bed. My parents slept in the same bed and they were deliriously happy, a tradition I intend to continue."

She nodded, relieved by the concession.

"I make one condition. Do not lock the doors between us, Madame. This is my house and it is my right to enter your room as I please." His voice sliced through her with the precision of a surgeon's blade. "If you lock them I'll have them removed. Do you understand?"

"Yes." She replied in a tight voice, but managed to keep her chin high.

"Excellent, now as to the rules I expect you to abide by. First, you are not to leave the house alone, not even to walk in the gardens. You'll have Uncle Gareth's escort outdoors."

It was past believing! "If you are afraid I'll run away, why don't you just lock me in that room on the third floor?"

"How do you know about that?" He retorted, visibly shaken by her words, as she intended. She'd had enough shocks from the rude inhabitants here. It was time to start returning the favor.

"Tabby." He said, decisively. "I'll deal with her later. I told you before we arrived that I had many reasons to despise the man whose name I bear. I have no wish to imprison you here. I told you this before, I use indentures from the prisons as my labor force. I discovered three indentures have gone missing as of last week. Until they are found, I will not have you set foot outdoors alone for your own safety. I will also caution the maids not to wander the grounds alone until those men are caught. In that light, does my demand still seem unreasonable?"

"No, sir." She mumbled, averting her eyes and winding her finger through a satin bow on her skirt. His concern for her might seem more convincing if he weren't snarling so.

"Rule number two," He continued in that commanding tone, "You do not leave the estate grounds without my permission."

"How could I? The estate is surrounded by ten foot fencing and the gates are locked."

"My grandfather had the fencing erected to keep intruders out after the slave uprisings on another island. The master and his family were murdered in their beds, even the children. I've maintained the habit. Now that I have a family, I appreciate the virtues of such precautions."

Elizabeth remained silent. She had heard of slave uprisings in the Indies, as had most of England. It was one of the arguments for abolishing slavery.

"As to the subject of locks," He continued, "Tabby informed me that you asked her to relinquish the household keys. There is only one set. Since you are the rightful mistress here, I will have a second set of keys made for you. Does that satisfy you, my lady?"

"Yes." At last, a concession amid the rules and strictures. She pressed for another one. "I insist you to lift this ridiculous edict that I cannot bathe unattended by the housekeeper."

"No." He said coldly.

Her eyes glazed with moisture. "I suppose that is for my safety as well, or is it some sick need to humiliate me?"

"I'm not the monster you make me out to be. You have the propensity to drop off into a heavy doze without warning. You just drift away without even realizing--"

"I do not!" Elizabeth insisted. "I'd remember it if I did."

"Would you?" He countered. The implication struck deep.

Elizabeth smashed her lips together. "I—I—wasn't aware of it." She said, shamed by her inability to notice the weakness. This was appalling, she was trying not to succumb to his bullying, and now she was afraid she might start crying into the bargain.

"If you find Tabby too grating, then have your new maid present in the room when you bathe. Please, for your own well being." Donovan's voice softened as he came around the desk. He offered her his handkerchief and watched her dab her eyes with it.

Why wouldn't he take her in his arms as he had when she was upset on the ship?

"I'm not a tyrant." He sat down on the edge of the desk and crossed his arms about his chest. "I'm just trying to look after you. It appears no one has done that, not for a very long time. Your grandmother allowed you to wander about the countryside alone. You could have been set upon by bandits or a nobleman determined to have his way with you. Mark me, you'll not be wandering about free as the gypsies anymore, not in my keeping."

Elizabeth glared at him, resenting his remark.

"Whether you remember is irrelevant, it's true." He persisted. "Sheila let you go traipsing off to the woods alone with me every night. *I* could have taken advantage of you."

"Who's to say you didn't? My memory eludes me, sir."

The look on his face told her the arrow had met its mark. "An honorable man does not take advantage of a girl he wishes to make his wife." He insisted with exasperation. "Aren't you the stubborn mare who has been given her head far too often. You don't want to accept the bridle, but you'll have to, it's for your own good."

Damn that man, comparing her to one of his horses. Elizabeth made no effort to hide her contempt at the allusion. No doubt he thought himself quite clever for it.

They stared at one another, a battle of wills, with neither of them looking away.

A knock sounded at the door.

"One moment." He called out, not breaking eye contact. Those pale blue eyes were as impenetrable as the sky above her.

Elizabeth was not going to back down. She was not going to become a timid mouse like her mother, afraid of her shadow, apologizing for simply taking up space in her husband's home.

"That's my accountant." Donovan informed her in a pleased tone. *He was enjoying this!*

"One more rule and then you're free to go. Make certain the new staff understands no one comes in here, on pain of dismissal. Pearl will tidy up when needed. Do as you wish with the rest of the house. Order wallpaper, paint, anything that pleases you. Mix the furnishings as you will or burn everything. I don't care. Just leave this room alone. It is my sanctuary."

Had she heard right—he didn't care if she spent money on fixing up the place? He was being generous. Or perhaps he truly didn't care. The house was sadly neglected, even for a reclusive bachelor who didn't entertain.

"Yes, you may re-feather the nest as you see fit. I'll inform my accountant that you are authorized to purchase whatever you need to update the house." He said, unsettling her with his uncanny ability to discern her thoughts. "That's all—you may go. Oh, yes, don't expect me at dinner. I've gathered men. We'll be searching for the runaways until sunset."

Elizabeth tossed the handkerchief at him as she rose from the chair. So, she was being dismissed like naughty child summoned to Papa's study for a scolding. Oh, if he dared to pat her on the head as she passed him she would kick him soundly in the shin.

"I'll try not to be too late." He commented, as she made her retreat.

"Don't rush home on my account." She returned saucily after gaining the safety of the door. "I'll follow the rules, I promise, *Papa*." She said the last with relish. She gained a wicked pleasure in reminding him of their age difference; she was but sixteen as she remembered it, and he was a grown man nearing thirty. "But I'm too old to be spanked."

"Don't tempt me." He replied, his pale eyes glacial with resolve. "It would be a pleasure to take you over my knee and slap that adorable bottom with my bare hand."

Elizabeth blanched at such a lewd suggestion. Baiting the wolf was no longer amusing. "Lay a hand on me, sir, and I'll never forgive you."

"As you wish." Donovan quipped, giving her a bemused smile. "But do remember it was you who brought up the subject of spanking, darlin', not I."

Chapter Nineteen

The Forgotten Bride of Count Rochembeau.

It was a title worthy of one of Mrs. Radcliff's Gothic novels. Much as Elizabeth enjoyed reading them, she didn't relish the thought of becoming the heroine in one. Her husband vanished in the week that followed, becoming a ghost in his own home.

She bumped into *Mr. O'Rourke*, Donovan's servant persona, several times during the long week. He nodded as he passed her in the hall, behaving as if they were strangers. She happened upon him in the servant's hall one afternoon entertaining the footmen with some coarse story that had them chortling with glee. One of them spotted her in the doorway and they became red faced and sober, each one but him. Donovan smirked and started telling another one, not even waiting until she was out of earshot.

She stepped into the kitchen one morning to speak to Cook and found *O'Rourke* sitting on a wooden barrel outside the open kitchen door. His knees were parted and his boots were planted firmly on the ground as he leaned forward and held tightly to a stick. He was playing tug of war with one of his dogs. She stood silently, admiring every inch of him; that handsome profile, his tanned, corded, forearms and long, muscular legs. Those powerful thighs flexed when the mastiff growled and tugged at the other end of the stick, trying to pull his master from his perch on the barrel. Donovan was smiling, appearing care free as he played with the dog.

He looked up, sensing he had an audience in the doorway.

"Be there somethin' you need from me, milady?" He asked in a feigned Irish brogue.

A hug, a kind word—some small acknowledgement that I matter to you!

Elizabeth swallowed the ache rising in her throat. He didn't need to pretend. They were alone in the courtyard off the kitchen.

"No, Mr. O'Rourke." She replied, turning quickly about and exiting the kitchen with her eyes stinging.

She could overlook his bizarre masquerade if he'd come to her at the end of the day, at least to check on her and acknowledge her existence in his world. She left the doors between them unlocked as instructed so he might visit her if he wished. He did not. The fact that he did not seek her company, even in private, brought home to her that she was in disgrace.

In response to his rejection, Elizabeth attacked the house with a vengeance. She was determined to open all the first floor rooms by Christmas, when his mother was scheduled to arrive. She worked herself to exhaustion every day alongside the maids, polishing and scrubbing everything she could find. She welcomed the distraction from the agonizing crack that was slowly rending in her heart.

Gareth O'Donovan was the one bright spot in her bleak existence. Donovan's uncle had an easy smile and a singsong Caribbean accent that intrigued her. He strove to maintain conversation with her instead of subjecting her to long, pensive silences as her husband had been wont to do. His favorite author was Shakespeare, and he tended to sprinkle his conversations with quotes from the bard like a preacher reciting verses from the Bible.

She dined with Gareth in the formal dining room each evening and discussed literature and music with him in the refurbished salon afterward. Each night, she secretly hoped Donovan would appear at dinner or join them in the salon. He did not. Elizabeth played the small harpsichord at Gareth's insistence while he turned the music pages for her. He humbly admitted to playing the cello, being self-taught as he'd never left the island and asked if she might teach him to read musical notations. She was grateful for Gareth's easy companionship; without him she'd be truly alone as Donovan seemed to have abandoned her.

As the dinner hour approached one evening, Elizabeth brought her kitten to the dining room and set him on the chair beside her. Dinner was enlivened by Puck's antics. The little imp climbed up on the table and sat very somberly next to her plate, watching her eat every spoonful without trying to intrude. Gareth teased him by making shadows on the tablecloth with his hand.

The chubby little tom was confused and then fascinated by the shadows, attacking them and tipping over a water goblet in his attempts to capture the moving shadow. The floral arrangement captured Puck's attentions next. He took to nibbling the flowers. Puck pulled one from the vase without tipping it over by some miracle, and then rolled on his back on the table to shred the bloom while they laughed at his antics.

They left the ruin of the table to take an evening stroll in the gardens. Elizabeth caught sight of Donovan in the stable courtyard. Dressed as O'Rourke, he mounted a chestnut bay. The groom handed him his musket, which he balanced across his lap before spurring his mount to gallop. The dogs barked a noisy farewell as the groom locked the gate behind him.

Elizabeth clutched her shawl about her and watched her husband leave. Gareth put an arm about her consolingly. "'Our count is neither sad nor sick, nor merry nor well; but a civil count, civil as an orange, and something of that jealous complexion.' So says Beatrice in *Much Ado About Nothing*, and upon her sage advice we shall take no notice of his foul mood nor allow it to poison our evening."

Elizabeth sighed. "He despises me."

"No, dear one. Tis not you who makes him ride hard away, but Duty, a demanding mistress, and a cruel one." Uncle Gareth took her hand, settled it upon his arm, and guided her down the garden path to watch the golden sunset melt into the molten sea.

Once Elizabeth retired she paced about her room. The stillness in the next room screamed accusation at her for the rift between them. Seeking distraction from her treacherous thoughts, she began sorting through her wardrobe. She removed a box from the bottom drawer and spread Sheila's belongings on the bed. Paper packages contained dried herbs. She examined cloth pouches the old woman had fashioned as charms that held mysterious scents.

A bound leather book was wrapped in a plaid shawl. It was a history of the O'Flaherty Clan dating back to the thirteenth century, containing notes of marriages, births and deaths. Elizabeth unwrapped it with reverence. It passed down through the Chieftain's family, and it was difficult to read as it was written in old English at the beginning with passages digressing into Gaelic. She found Gaelic easier as Sheila taught her the forbidden language with her letters as a child.

She turned the pages containing recipes for healing potions, instructions for conjuring earth spirits and performing sacred rituals. She read notes on where to find wild plants with detailed sketches to aid in identification. Druid secrets were recorded within the yellowed pages; spells for healing, protection, fertility, love and revenge. As she studied the pages her fascination grew regarding the rich heritage she disregarded when her grandmother was alive.

The clock chimed eleven by the time she wrapped the book in Sheila's plaid shawl and placed it back in her wardrobe. She sorted through the box of cloth pouches and settled on one that smelled of earth, imagining it to be soil from O'Flaherty lands in Ireland. It would be a protection against nightmares, she told herself as she put the box away. She placed the pouch beneath her pillow and settled into the bed, careful to avoid the lumps in the old mattress.

"Elizabeth--wake up, you must help me!"

Elizabeth jerked awake at the sound of her mother's voice.

Mama was beautiful, as always, a porcelain doll, fragile yet cold. Long ebony hair cascaded in waves to her waist. Her eyes were not violet-blue as they had been in life. They were dark and soulless. *"I cannot endure this. You must tell that man what happened to me."*

Just as in life, her mother was too absorbed with her own worries to care that her daughter's heart was breaking. Liquid dripped down Elizabeth's chin. She wiped the annoying tears away with the sleeve of her bed gown. Clutching Puck against her, Elizabeth slipped out of the bed on the opposite side. Mama didn't appear pleased to see her, she seemed menacing.

"You have to speak for me! You are the only one, Elizabeth. You know what he did to me. You must release me. You have to tell them what truly happened to me."

"No one will believe me."

"You must help me." Mama insisted, drawing close. The smell of sulfur wreathed about her, noxious and vile. The air surrounding Elizabeth became ice. *"And you will!"*

"Leave the child alone." A woman's smoky Irish burr chided from behind Elizabeth. She whirled about and nearly dropped her cat at the sight of another spirit. It was the former occupant of this very room, Maureen O'Donovan. Elizabeth recognized her from the portrait in the salon.

Puck hissed and arched his back. His claws were like needles in her skin, assuring her she was awake as he struggled to be let free. He dropped to the floor and scurried under the bed.

"Go away. This is my house. You have no right to be here." Maureen's ghost drifted forward to challenge Elizabeth's mother.

Mama's face contorted into something ugly and then she disappeared.

"It's all right, little one." Maureen glided to Elizabeth's side. She extended a pale, luminous hand and Elizabeth felt a light breeze caressing her hair.

Gareth had warned Elizabeth about their resident spirit. He told her not to be afraid if Donovan's grandmother visited her one night. It was said she watched over Gareth in the night when he was a babe and had been seen lingering over her grandson's cradle as well. It made sense. The woman left behind a small child. That daughter was grown and so was the daughter's son, yet Maureen still yearned to comfort the frightened child she left behind.

"You're safe, darlin'. I won't let her hurt you."

"Mama wouldn't hurt me!" Elizabeth replied, edging around the apparition. She crossed the room and touched the cool knob leading to her husband's suite. Light flickered beneath the door, illuminating the floorboards and her pale toes. She heard Donovan pacing. She wanted to go to him, to seek the comfort and protection he offered without reservation on the ship.

Remembering his cool detachment of recent days, she let go of the handle.

There was no comfort to be found behind that door.

******

156

The sweat ran off of him in rivulets. Still, he pressed his opponent, determined to work the tension from his body with a punishing session of swordplay. Donovan feinted, and just as he moved in to deliver a deadly thrust, his uncle blocked him with the move he had taught the man before sailing to England. "You've been practicing." He said, pleased as he dropped his defensive stance. "Whose hide have you been scratching while I was away?"

"O'Reilly's." Gareth grinned. "I let him win a few times so he wouldn't become discouraged, as you've done with me." Gareth mopped his brow with his discarded shirt.

"Oh, you think I let you have that?" Donovan taunted, knowing it was so. "*En Garde*, old man. I'll send you back to Johnny in the stables with your tail dragging!"

Gareth held up a hand, his chest heaved as he bent forward with hands on his knees. "You've too much energy for a man who has recently taken a bride." He huffed.

Gareth's golden torso gleamed with moisture, although it was early morning. Donovan's shirt stuck to his back, but he would not remove it and reveal the scars of the count when he was dressed as O'Rourke. His uncle's face broke into a feral grin as he positioned himself to accept the challenge. They parried across the cobbled garden, intent only upon the clash of steel.

"Do you think Winslow speaks the truth?" Donovan asked after a break in the action as they circled one another with wariness. "The men escaped the compound in the night?"

"Winslow has a brutal streak, one he hides well."

"A man's true nature emerges when he believes his master isn't there to see it."

"Winslow displayed his temper frequently in your absence. I warned him, but the color of my skin negates any authority he thinks I have as your representative."

"My apologies." Donovan deliberately turned his back on his opponent.

"It's is not your fault the world does not accept me as I am."

As anticipated, Gareth made a bold lunge. Donovan twisted on his heels and swung his blade to the right to meet Gareth's sword, blocking his attack from behind. "Don't attempt that move unless you are certain your opponent is unprepared to block you."

With Gareth behind him, their blades crossed to his right, Donovan stomped his opponent's left instep. Using the sparse second's distraction of pain and surprise in his adversary, he captured Gareth's wrist and applied pressure on the nerve until Gareth was forced to drop his blade.

"Ooow! That is unfair!" Gareth exclaimed as his sword clattered to the cobblestones.

"Only a novice keeps to D'Anver's philosophies about honor when the fight is to the death. Never allow an enemy to draw you close. Your sword should keep him at arm's length at all times." Donovan lowered his weapon. "Perhaps it's time you moved on to my Italian texts."

"I welcome the challenge." Gareth bowed to him as the master swordsman.

He's eyes caught the figure observing them from the veranda as he looked beyond and above Gareth. Elizabeth's unbound hair cascaded in radiant waves about her shoulders like a cloak of fire, giving her the appearance of a Byzantine icon as she stood in the sunlight.

Donovan stood, clutching his sword like a knight of old beholding a surreal vision. The allusion was not lost on him; she was the goddess who haunted his dreams, the object of his desire, and she was so high above him. *Beautiful, divine, and unattainable. His Aphrodite.*

Gareth turned to see what captured him so. "Ah, your shy hummingbird is awake. That reminds me, as your elder it is my duty to call you to account for your ill behavior."

Donovan grimaced. Gareth was his elder by not quite two years, yet the man delighted in exchanging affectionate parries as uncle and nephew almost as much he enjoyed their fencing exercises or trying to best Donovan at chess.

At the moment the man's eyes held no affection for him. "How long are you going to keep playing this ridiculous charade? It's not fair to the girl, Donovan."

"That's none of your concern."

"You made it my concern when you asked me to keep your wife company during your ruse as O'Rourke. You're bride yearns for your companionship, not mine."

"She has yet to inform me of any *yearning* for my company. Until she does, I will continue as I have."

"Your dark Count frightens her."

Donovan bent to retrieve Gareth's weapon. He straightened and handed it to him. "The count is a fictional character created to keep people at a polite distance. I told her that. If she does not understand, then perhaps you might remind her of that."

"It is you who fail to understand." Gareth shot back. "When you put on that costume it transforms you. The mask makes you vicious and cold. Your voice hardens. Your body becomes a tightly coiled serpent ready to strike at those about you without provocation." Gareth advanced and stood so they were eye to eye. "I realize it has served you well over the years, but if you wish for the woman you love to trust you, then you must put away the dark count. You must seek her company and assure her that you are not like those animals that hurt her."

"She told me to stay away from her."

"No." Gareth chided. "It was that dark creature she told to stay away, not you."

"How do you know?"

"I was on the veranda, outside my room. I heard her cry out and beg you to let her be. I heard you demand your rights like a spoiled child with a servant who will not let him have his way."

Donovan looked away, ashamed. "I was drunk. I apologized the next day."

"Yet, you remain distant. You play childish games of hide and seek with her. The girl is frightened and confused. *You* informed *me* of these facts when you arrived. She needs solid ground beneath her feet." Gareth's boot crunched the cobblestones for emphasis. "She needs you to be the rock beneath her that remains steady and enduring as she struggles to overcome her fear and recover her balance. How can she trust you when you are constantly changing?"

"Did she tell you this?" Anger filled him at the thought of Elizabeth complaining of her lot to his uncle. She was the one who demanded separate rooms and separate beds.

"She says *nothing*!" Gareth insisted. "I watch and observe people, you know this. Every time you cross paths with her as

O'Rourke, I see her heart crying out for a kind word from you, for some small acknowledgement, for love and acceptance. For *forgiveness*--for what she perceives as her failing in your eyes." Gareth's voice roughened, "And you just walk away, oblivious to the fragile flower you've crushed beneath your boots, day after day. Every day, she wilts a little more. You shame the girl with your behavior, and you shame me!" His uncle slapped his chest. "For I must lie to make her think it is business that keeps you away and not your schoolboy sulking!"

With that, his uncle left him standing in the garden to consider his unwarranted advice.

Elizabeth stood at the window overlooking the small kitchen garden. She was observing a maid flirting with her husband. She couldn't hear the exchange, but she could see Sally trying to look coy as she giggled over something he said. Donovan stood with his hands on his hips and a detached smile, playing the affable Mr. O'Rourke—a bachelor—in front of the woman.

With quick wrist action, Sally made it appear as if she'd accidentally dropped the bundle of herbs. She bent to retrieve them, giving him a view of her ample bosom. Donovan smiled and then laughed at something the vixen said, behaving as if he hadn't a care in the world.

Elizabeth held her breath, waiting for her worst fears to be realized.

To his credit, her husband did not step forward to embrace the maid in a clandestine tryst. He turned away from blonde Sally with her overflowing bosom and strode down the cobbled path to the stables. The maid gazed after him with a yearning Elizabeth knew well.

She turned away from the window. Her time was better spent taking inventory of the linen closet. A short time later, she entered the second floor closet and set the candle on the shelf. Just as she suspected, the sheets were showing their years. Lace edges were unraveling and small holes appeared as the fabric showed signs of disintegration due to age.

The door closed with a whoosh, snuffing out the candle. She spun about to open it only to find that the door was locked. *Nobody locked linen closets, for pity's sake!*

Elizabeth tried the ring of keys her husband gave her. The lock was jammed, it wouldn't respond to any of the keys, and she was on her second round of trying before she realized it wasn't an accident, something was keeping her imprisoned in the dark closet.

"Tell him!" Mama's desperate voice cut through her in the darkness. *"Tell that man what your stepfather did to me. I can't rest until you do."*

"What good would that do? Can't you see I'm nothing but an annoyance to the man?" She retorted, weary of Mama's dramatic petulance. "Why are you never concerned about me?"

Mama didn't answer. She left to go sulk somewhere else. Elizabeth pounded on the door and called out. The idea that no one might notice she was missing brought a rush of terror as she went from patient calls to panicked cries. No one came. No one heard her cries for help.

She tried to remain calm. It was difficult as she imagined dying alone here, trapped in the dark, no one even noticing she was missing until she'd joined her mother in the hereafter.

"Don't be frightened." A soft, husky voice like rustling silks whispered to Elizabeth in the cloying darkness. Maureen's radiant form materialized and it was then Elizabeth realized she was crying, just like the other night when Maureen appeared. Ghostly fingers moved over her hair and her wet cheeks. *"I won't let her hurt you, darlin'."*

"Mama would never hurt me." Elizabeth asserted. "Would she?"

Without a reply, Maureen disappeared.

The door popped open, just like that, setting Elizabeth free.

Chapter Twenty

Donovan sauntered into the room behind the kitchen that served as the servant's dining area. He plopped down on the wooden bench beside the footmen playing cards at the end of the long trestle table.

Elias Jones set his tin mug on the table and belched. Donovan could understand why Elizabeth had hired him. Elias had a neat, clean shaven appearance and knew how to behave in a respectful manner in the presence of a lady. What she didn't know was that Elias fancied himself a rake and had already boasted of having tupped one of the maids more than once since his arrival here. The conversation among cards each night this week had been dominated by Elias's bragging about his secret trysts and his companion eating his every word as if it were toasted cheese and not a pile of horse shit.

Henry Chilton was a small, unremarkable man with mud brown hair and mutton chops that met beneath his chin. He possessed wide brown eyes and a ready smile, traits that might seem appealing in a footman. By himself, he was no more threatening than an overgrown puppy. Unfortunately, Henry seemed to be under the thrall of Elias, the more conniving one of the pair.

"You in, O'Rourke?" Henry asked, offering him a toothy welcome.

"Aye." Donovan rubbed his nose with the back of his hand.

Henry dealt him in. Donovan picked up the cards and arranged them in his hand. The footmen had invited him to join their nightly game the on second day they were here. They complained to him that Giles, the middle aged footman, was a starched shirt determined to get into her ladyship's good graces and thus shunned their manly pursuits after hours, and the fourth footman, a lad of nineteen, was too close to a Methodist to warrant an invitation to their circle.

As O'Rourke, Donovan had been taking his meals with the new staff. He bantered with them in the back rooms whenever possible and tucked away tidbits of information about each one as they spoke openly among themselves. He didn't like having his home crowded with strangers as a rule when he was a bachelor. Having a wife who experienced petit seizures made him doubly anxious regarding the integrity of said strangers residing under his roof. A dishonest maid could pocket milady's necklace and make her mistress believe she had misplaced the item herself. A footman might swoop in with more dangerous intentions while Lizzie was caught in an episode of confusion. Donovan had to make certain his darling was safe in her own home.

Elizabeth's maid of chambers, Miss Ramirez, had only good to say of her mistress. She seemed to have developed a fondness for her lady in the short time of her employment. She exhibited a loyalty that became apparent when another maid uttered a complaint about hauling water due to milady's penchant for bathing so frequently in her hearing. Chloe Ramirez was an effusive, chatty sort, the type of female Donovan found vastly annoying. As long she proved loyal to his wife he didn't care about her other flaws.

"Why the grim face?" Elias asked, watching Donovan study the cards he'd been dealt. "Horse kick you in the bollocks?"

Henry guffawed loudly, acting as if Elias' remark was clever instead of crude.

"Not me." Donovan grinned disarmingly as he spoke, determined to ride out the uncouth jesting until he completed his mission. "The Count's Arabian damn near gelded poor Johnny. And I doubt the lad's even gained his spurs."

"Aw!" Elias howled. "I know a chit or two who'd be pleased to 'educate' the boy. We'll take him with us to the alehouse, next time, eh, Henry?"

"Spades." Henry replied, turning the top card over on the table. "Your bid, Eli."

Elias opened the bid. Donovan bid higher. Henry passed. And so went the evening.

After losing to Donovan, Elias complained that he was out of quid until next quarter day. "I have a different wager in mind." He looked behind him to assure they were alone and then leaned forward to let them on in his plan.

"What is it, dice?" Henry bubbled forth while Donovan remained silent.

"Not dice." Elias smirked. "The countess. That spook she's married to acts as if she doesn't exist. Makes a fellow wonder if he ain't crazy like they say, ignoring a sweet young thing like that. Spending all day locked up in his lab pulling the wings off of flies."

"He is a queer one." Henry chimed in. "She deserves better, aye, O'Rourke?"

He grunted his assent, placing a finger on his brow. "But what does Madame Beaumont have to do with this wager?"

Elias sat up a little straighter with a smug smile on his face. "It's like this; a young woman married to a lunatic. She's bound to get lonely, being ignored by her man, stuck on an isolated island estate halfway around the world from her kinfolk."

Donovan didn't move. He didn't breathe. He remained still, so as not to startle his prey. "Go on." He muttered, keeping his balled fist locked on his thigh beneath the table.

"Oh, you want to bet how long before she leaves the count?" Henry put in. "Good one, that way we don't have to pay up 'til it happens—if it happens."

"No, stupid." Elias cuffed Henry's shoulder. "I never had a noblewoman beneath me." He went on, looking and speaking to O'Rourke as if only he were man enough to understand. "And that one's mighty fine. It's a shame to let a good pussy go to waste, don't you think?"

"Ah, Elias, you aren't suggesting we hurt her, now, are you?" Henry whined.

"I'm proposing seduction, you twit. Been watching her, I have. She's lonely. Why, she fairly lights up every time that bastard uncle gives her the time of day. What I propose, my lads, is a wager between the three of us, with the countess as the prize. Which one of us can charm her into giving him a place in her bed? That one gets 10 quid from the other two."

Elias paused, letting his words settle before asking, "What do you say, lads? Are you in? You up to hunting peacock instead of pea hens?"

Henry nodded, agreeing to the scheme. "Aye, she is a pretty little thing."

"O'Rourke, are you in?"

Donovan stood, his fists clenched. "I'm in. Deeper than you care to know."

Without warning, he kicked the stool out from under Henry, who was seated at the end of the table between Eli and himself. As the footman fell on his ass, Donovan lurched across the wooden table and dragged Elias over it. The wily footman raised his fist, attempting a right hook in his defense. Donovan blocked the attack with his forearm and twisted the man's hand behind his back. Elias tried to wiggle out of his grip. Donovan pounced on the man, wrestling him to the floor with ease. He knelt over the man, pinning him with his knees.

"Mr. O'Rourke?" Pearl appeared in the doorway. "What goes on here?"

"Debauchery, Mayhem." Donovan answered through clenched teeth. "And it ends, here." He turned his eyes to the man in the doorway while keeping his hand on his victim's throat. "These two are out of the game. I want them trussed up and delivered on the docks of Basseterre before dawn. Get me some rope."

Chapter Twenty One

Elizabeth was perched on a ladder in the freshly painted salon just off the stairs. She was attempting to hang the newly washed curtains herself as the maid below was afraid of heights, the other two were outside hanging the rest of the laundry, and the fourth was helping the cook prepare lunch in the kitchen.

"You shouldn't be up there, mum." Sally informed her. "I'll catch hell from his lordship if anything was to happen to you!"

"Stuff and nonsense." Elizabeth replied, attempting to maintain a good humor. "My lord wouldn't notice I was missing. He'd keep working, trying valiantly to cure the diseases plaguing mankind until someone screwed up the courage to inform him that I was buried last week."

"Oh, mum!" Sally trilled. "That's funny. You be a rare one, working alongside the rest of us, mopping and scrubbing and polishing all day as if you weren't a countess, why I have never heard the like, have you Mr. O'Rourke?"

Oh, Bollocks.! Elizabeth braced herself for some lewd remark about her backside to be expressed by the man. He was nothing if not brash when in his swaggering O'Rourke persona.

"What the hell are you doing up there?" A languid colonial drawl barked from the vicinity of her ankles. Elizabeth looked down at him and then at the maid, wondering if Sally noted the abrupt change in his speech. As Elizabeth hesitated, he placed a boot on the lower rung and clasped the ladder firmly with both hands. "Get down, before you fall and break your neck. I should paddle your bottom until you can't sit down, just for being so damned foolish."

"Mr. O'Rourke, you've no right to be talking to the mistress like that!" Sally cautioned.

Elizabeth smiled. *The woman raised a valid point.* Mr. O'Rourke was a servant. She let the heavy curtain drop to the floor and then carefully descended the ladder.

"What's your excuse, Alice? You're gaping up at the ceiling, laughing while your mistress is doing work I'm paying you to do." Donovan reached up and grabbed Elizabeth about the waist to pull her from the last few rungs when she didn't move fast enough to satisfy him.

"This is Sally, *Mr. O'Rourke*, and she's afraid of heights." She informed him.

"I don't give a damn about her." Donovan returned, glaring daggers at Elizabeth.

She couldn't help but smile. He couldn't tell buxom, blonde Sally from plump Alice, the scullery maid? That was encouraging since Sally had been flirting with him shamelessly all week.

"You are not to be climbing ladders, young lady." Towering over her with a dangerous forefinger stabbing the air between them, Donovan seemed to forget the gruff Irish tone he used as O'Rourke. He was scolding her in the cultured colonial drawl that was his natural speech. He looked from her to Sally, then her again. "What's this about scrubbing and mopping? You're not strong enough to be doing menial chores and the moment my back is turned I find you risking your neck hanging heavy curtains. That's a man's job. Where is a footman?"

"I don't know. I seem to be short two this morning. Some pompous ass took it in his head to fire them without so much as a by your leave directed at me." Elizabeth replied.

"My lady!" Giles came rushing in from the hall, his face flushed as if he had run a great distance. "Is everything under control, Madame?"

"No, it isn't!" Donovan turned on the middle aged footman. "*My* lady was perched on that ladder, hanging curtains because *you* where nowhere to be found."

"Stop it!" Elizabeth stepped around Donovan to stand beside the footman. She wished she could make Giles the butler. It was a sticky situation as rum sodden Tabby had been installed here for some years, and raising Giles in rank would place him in charge of all the servants, Tabby included. Elizabeth couldn't make such a sweeping change without Donovan's approval, and finding the man, let alone finding him in a mood to grant the concession, proved impossible.

"I was unloading the supply wagon." Giles replied after regaining his breath. "Cook came out to warn me that some very foul language was being directed at the lady of the house. Now I suggest you return to the stables, O'Rourke, unless you care to go a round or two with me. I've had a few boxing triumphs in London in my younger days." As he spoke, the stout Englishman was rolling up his shirt sleeves as if he meant to make good on his offer.

"Yes, O'Rourke." Elizabeth chimed in. She was enjoying this. If Donovan insisted upon acting like a servant, she'd treat him like one! "Giles is here, and he's a *gentleman*. I'm sure he'd be happy to hang the curtains for me instead snarling threats at me, as you were doing."

"He threatened you?" Giles' face took on the snarl of a bulldog as he jerked his thumb toward the door. "Out, O'Rourke now. The master shall hear about this. Depend upon it."

Donovan moved in like a mad dog, his face full of color. "Oh, let's go meet him, then, just you and me, old boy! Let's go find the master."

"No!" Elizabeth stepped between the two men. "You've no right to be badgering this man, Mr. O'Rourke. If I know my husband at all I would expect him to be pleased Giles is quick to defend me when another man is behaving boorishly toward me." She waited, hoping her words would penetrate his thick skull.

Her husband's eyes remained hard as he pulled his gaze from the footman to pinion hers. "You haunt my dreams and posses my thoughts every waking moment. Beautiful little witch. What sorcery is at work to make me mad with wanting you, ready to kill any man you favor?"

"*Mr. O'Rourke!*" Giles gasped. "My lady's well being is not your concern."

"I would that it were so." Donovan muttered as he stalked out the door.

Elizabeth retreated to the library. She hugged her kitten and gained comfort in his rumbling purr. His words were like shards of glass piercing her heart. He regretted marrying her, just as she feared. How could he say such hurtful things to her; calling her a witch, accusing her of casting a spell to make him lust after her—blaming *her* for his ill behavior!

A discrete scratching sounded at the library door. The footman entered. "A letter arrived for you, milady, from Basseterre." Giles held out the missive on a silver tray.

"I don't know anyone in Basseterre."

"Shall I destroy it, Madame? Since you do not know this person?"

"Oh, no!" She sat forward from her recline on the chaise and snatched it from the tray. "It's from Peter! He gave me Puck." She smiled at the footman. "Would you see that Puck has something to eat and then put him upstairs in my room?" She handed him the kitten.

"Yes, Madame. Cook has prepared a dish of chopped liver for Master Puck." There was a brief collapse of that stolid English reserve as Giles placed a light hand on her shoulder. "Say the word, my lady, and I shall brave the lion's den to inform his lordship of this most unfortunate incident with that ill mannered brute from the stables."

Elizabeth was touched by his concern. "His lordship's work is important." She said in a pain thickened voice. "Don't disturb him. I'll tell him tonight, when he comes to bed."

The servant made a tactful retreat. Elizabeth was bolstered by the footman's quiet, efficient presence. He treated her pet as if the cat were a member of the family and referred to Old Fritz as *Cook*, as was traditional in England. They were small things, but she was finding comfort in the familiar customs. Her unconventional American spouse would likely grind his teeth at the servant's adherence to English tradition. Too bad. She had put up with a great deal of change in becoming Mrs. Beaumont.

Mr. Beaumont could do with some improvement, she fumed, opening the letter.

Peter's note warmed her considerably and afforded a rare opportunity. She composed a short reply, inviting Peter to visit her soon. She puzzled over the closing for a long time, choosing her words carefully so they couldn't come back to haunt her if she were questioned about it later. Finally, she scribed out;

Please be so kind as to convey my best regards to your Uncle Jack. Tell him I am in urgent need of his assistance in a matter of Grave Import—one that requires the strictest of confidences.

There, that should suffice. If Jack ratted her out and she were pressed by her husband, she'd claim she wished for the captain's input regarding a Christmas gift for Donovan. Hopefully, it would amuse his lordship rather than anger him. She hoped to confide in Rawlings regarding Donovan's odd behavior, but she had to be careful.

After giving the missive to Giles, Elizabeth inspected the breakfast room. It was the latest advance in her war against dirt and neglect. Muted tones of butter yellow warmed the walls, giving it a fresh, inviting look. She had the heavy curtains removed that shrouded the glass doors leading into the gardens. Richard O'Donovan wasn't fond of sunshine. Gareth confided his father preferred dark hangings to shield his rum saturated eyes from the harsh morning light.

Today, the clean, exposed panes glittered in the brilliant light and the sheer lace curtains allowed the room to capture the golden sunbeams, not block them out. Elizabeth was enjoying the task of bringing the old plantation house back to life. Donovan might choose to ignore her, but he had to notice the improvements to his home and realize she was responsible for them.

She stood between the French doors that opened into the gardens. The fresh sea breeze wafted around her. She wanted to sit in the garden and enjoy the comforting warmth of the sun, but Uncle Gareth was out riding and she didn't know if Donovan were home or not. Ares and Hades, the guard dogs, ambled down the path from the kitchen door, their tails wagging as they approached her with wide grins. Ares nudged at Elizabeth's hand, urging her to stroke his tawny head while black Hades sniffed at her skirt to decide if she belonged here.

She knelt and ruffled the black mastiff's ear. "Did Cook give you your treats? I saved toast crusts and a piece of bacon for each of you this morning." Hades tilted his head and gave a mournful groan, as if to say that he'd been deprived of his treat. "Oh, you big silly, I don't believe a word of it!" She chastened, amused by his antics.

It was a beautiful day. It was really outside of enough, this stricture that she was not to leave the house without an escort. Sturdy fencing lined the property, ten foot iron spikes with razor sharp points and the gates were always locked. Even if someone were able to get in, the dogs would keep him cornered. When the supply cart arrived every few days, Tabby or Mr. O'Reilly had to call the dogs off so the deliverymen could step down without risking a limb.

Elizabeth glanced about her. She'd slipped outside before alone, but only when she knew of a certainty that Donovan was out on the plantation. She wasn't sure of his whereabouts, but a few moments couldn't hurt. She hurried down the path before anyone from the house could see her escape.

Butterflies and insects fluttered about as her passing disturbed their resting places. The dogs kept pace on either side of Elizabeth. The stone path became carved steps. As she ascended them, she admired the gazebo concealed by a canopy of luxuriant foliage. So much stifled beauty, so much potential and yet this place had been left to fend for itself as the brutal jungle encroached upon the cultivated blooms. If the vines were cut away, if the statues were freed from their twining bonds, and the weeds were pulled so that the neglected floral beds were offered a bit of love and encouragement, this could become a wondrous, enchanted place.

Beyond the gazebo the stone balcony continued. During her walks with Uncle Gareth, she discovered an alcove with a stone bench hidden from view of the main gardens and the house. A gnarled tree clung to the outcroppings of the steep cliff. The profusion of flowered branches provided protection from the sun. She liked this solitary place. One could enjoy the view of the small harbor village at the foot of the hill or gaze at the serene seas ahead. She approached the wall of stones that came to her waist and leaned over the edge to gaze down.

It was a sheer drop to the jagged rocks below.

Turning from the stone balcony, Elizabeth moved to the cornerstone where a small portion of the wall had crumbled away. *A breach in the fencing*, she thought, feeling like the rebellious filly her husband was wont to call her. A grassy incline was just beyond the crumbled stone, forming a small, tilted ledge before descending sharply to the ocean swells. A large tree was bent with emerald foliage, forming a canopy over the grassy outcropping. It beckoned to her like a fairy bower, a secret retreat where she could dream away a sultry afternoon.

Elizabeth slipped through the crumbled opening and sank down on the grass. She removed her slippers and stockings. It was delicious to feel grass tickling her bare feet and the warm caress of sunshine on her skin as she sat beneath the bright azure sky. The salt tang of the sea mingled with the pungent earth. The dogs wiggled through the wall to lie beside her.

She sat for a time enjoying the feel of the wind in her hair, the soothing chatter of the birds and insects and the steady surf far below. The woods and meadow had been her refuge in England. Sheila understood her desire to be close to nature. It was so like Donovan to turn it into something shameful, to see only the danger and none of the beauty.

Time passed too quickly. Elizabeth was loath to leave her secluded sanctuary, but she knew she must return to the house before she was missed. She picked up her discarded shoes and stockings, and meandered back down the path to the house with reluctance. As soon as she came around the foliage bound statue outside the sunny breakfast room, she was confronted by a black spot of gloom whose presence chilled the tropical air. Two weeks had passed since she'd been confronted by the dark side of her husband's personality and the absence did nothing to improve the creature in her mind. She kept an arm's length away, bolstered by the presence of Giles and two men she recognized from the voyage.

The Count, her husband's darker persona, stood outside the opened doors of the breakfast room with that disturbing sheath covering features she knew to be flawless. His lips were set into a grim line. "What are you doing wandering out here alone?" he asked in a French accent.

Elizabeth lifted her chin and looked him in the eye. "I was inspecting the gardens and I am appalled, sir. Can we not afford a gardener?"

"I asked you not to wander the grounds unescorted, *ma cherie*."

She resisted the urge to laugh. He was playing the polite gentleman for the benefit of the others. They both knew he didn't ask any such thing of her, he demanded it. The dogs circled her and Ares chose that moment to nudge her hand. "I wasn't alone." She stroked the large tawny head with affection, "As you can see I had a very capable escort."

"Nevertheless, you will no longer be inconvenienced by my schedule or Gareth's whims when you wish to enjoy the grounds." The count informed her. "I have appointed these men as your guards. They will accompany you throughout the day and assist you in any task you require. You recall Mr. Duchamp, and this is Gus O'Leary."

The men stepped forward and bowed. Neither smiled. Both were armed, she noted, feeling invisible reins tugging at her, limiting her freedom. "So, confining me like prisoner under house arrest wasn't enough, now you appoint spies to report my every movement to you?"

"Nonsense, *Cherie*." Donovan replied smoothly. "Your routine is hardly worth noting, much less justifying the salaries of two capable men to observe and recount to me. You rise at nine, take breakfast in your room and then spend the day in a whirl of domestic tedium that is inconsequential compared to the complexities of managing a large plantation."

Elizabeth gasped aloud at his belittlement of her place here.

"Your safety weighs heavily upon me while the criminals roam free." He added.

"I hope these men will show more respect to my lady than Mr. O'Rourke has, my lord." Giles put in bravely. "She should not be subjected to rudeness by anyone in your employ."

"*Oui*, you've ground that point fine enough. These men will not trouble my lady. And Mr. O'Rourke will be admonished." The man himself said in that phony French accent.

Elizabeth snorted at his comment.

"Giles sought me out in my laboratory a short time ago, *ma petite*. He said O'Rourke's callow behavior made you cry." He stepped closer. Elizabeth stiffened. A lean forefinger lifted her chin, and caressed her cheek with a display of tenderness. "Is this true, Elizabeth?"

"Does it matter?" She returned. "I'm hardly worth your notice, my lord. Isn't that what you just said?"

"No, I did not." Crisp, silvery blue eyes pinioned her from behind the mask. "I said you are not being scrutinized as you so fancifully imagine."

"Excuse me, my lord. I have more tedious domestic concerns to attend to."

The master would not let her slip away so easily. His hand circled her arm. At a nod from him, the three men disappeared. "You create a villain where there is none. I apologize. I should not have yelled at you earlier but I seem to lose all sense of reason or judgment around you."

She didn't want to hear any more. So, it was all her fault. Wasn't it always?

"I'm only doing what's best for you, and you continually damn me for it."

"You're doing what's best for yourself, none other!"

"If that were the case I would do *this* more often and hang the consequences." His arms surrounded her and those hard lips descended to capture her mouth in a scorching kiss that left no doubt as to where his true interest was concerning her.

Elizabeth was shocked by his swift possession.

She didn't react as she should, with outrage. She leaned into his solid frame, hungry for the feel of his arms about her, starved for some crumb of affection from him as she shamelessly kissed him back.

The count broke away and stepped back. "Your response, my dear, is hardly in keeping with a woman who desires to be left alone."

The ultimate cruelty came when he set her aside and walked calmly away.

Chapter Twenty Two

Elizabeth was awakened by an angry male voice. She gazed about her. She'd left the home of her childhood years ago, but she seemed to be trapped in the London townhouse again.

She was in her old room, huddled under the covers, trying to shut out the noises coming from the room down the hall. Fletcher was drunk. He was hurting Mama. Mama was crying, pleading with him to stop. He wouldn't. He seemed to enjoy her tearful pleas.

Why am I here? Elizabeth sat up. She shoved the covers away and looked about her. Banked coals glowed in the hearth, bathing her old room in a familiar, orange-red glow. She gazed at her hand. Her wedding ring circled her finger. How could she be married, and still be in the room she'd inhabited as a girl?

Where is Donovan? Surely he would not allow me to be here, so far from his home.

"Stop it, William!" Mama shrieked. "Let go of me, you're drunk—"

The sound of Papa's hand colliding with her mother's flesh made Elizabeth cringe.

I must leave here. I need to go home. Home--to Donovan, and the peace of Ravencrest. Donovan didn't return drunk in the night and start tossing furniture--or people--about in a drunken rage!

She slipped from bed and opened the door just a crack, determined to make a run for it while the pair were distracted by their old battle. Suddenly Fletcher was in the hall, dragging Mama toward the stairs. He positioned Mama in front of him and then Mama disappeared.

Elizabeth tried to scream. Her effort brought only strangled sound from her throat.

The scene melted away, into another one. Now, she was the one standing at the top of the stairs, looking down at her mother's broken body. Huge hands seized her and slammed her against the wall. "Spying on me again, eh?" Her stepfather's eyes gleamed with malice. "Useless bitch, you can't turn me in if you're dead!"

Elizabeth went rushing forward. She tried to catch herself, clutching at air, only to land at the bottom of the stairs with a bone crushing thud.

The house was plunged into an inky darkness. Elizabeth placed a stunned hand against the throbbing pain in her side. Her body was slick with sweat, making her bed gown cling to her skin as she struggled to recover her wits.

The ragged sound of her breath catching and rasping in the darkness further emphasized the stark loneliness. Reality surfaced. She wasn't in the London townhouse, lying at the bottom of the stairs next to her mother's dead body. She was in her room at Ravencrest, sprawled on the floor where the angry spirit had tossed her while she slept. It was the fourth time this week she'd awakened on the hard floor after dreaming about Mama's death.

"Stop it." She protested, fear melting into anger as she sat up and rubbed her bruising side. Her body was collecting mysterious bruises with each passing day—or rather, the night. This was ridiculous, being bullied by a ghost; *one who had been so timid in life.*

The pale specter materialized before her. Mama had always been a beauty. Now, her beauty was distorted by bitterness. *"Tell him!"* Mama insisted. *"I can't stand this any longer, I shall run mad. You have to tell someone what happened to me!"*

The doors to the master's suite burst open. Donovan stood in the doorway holding a candle in one hand and pistol in the other. He came quickly to crouch beside her.

Elizabeth started at his nearness. The man was stark naked. Heat flooded her cheeks as she shifted her eyes to focus on the wavering candle instead of the dark patch nestled beneath a taut abdomen. After determining she was unharmed Donovan handed her the candle, palmed her shoulder in reassurance and stood to confront the shadows hemming them in.

He turned about slowly, surveying the room. Elizabeth was presented with the sight of his trim, bare backside. Her eyes traveled upward to the peculiar marks on his back.

Scars confronted her. Hard, inflexible knots. Weals of flesh distorted by torture.

Oh, my God! How easy it was to forget. This man had good reason to question everything and trust no one, to put up barriers to keep the world out. He wanted the world to leave him be so he could live his life in peace and solitude. It made sense now, his anger at her rejection of him that first night here. He must think she found him repulsive because of his scars. Not so, not at all. Quite the contrary; he was beautiful, majestic, regal as a tiger as he stood before her, ready to pounce on a perceived intruder he believed to be threatening his mate.

Stunned by this abrupt, awkward intimacy, Elizabeth sat in a golden circle of light provided by the candle in her hand and attempted to distract her eyes from the admiration of her husband's bum. The flame wavered in her unsteady hand.

"Who is here? Reveal yourself." Donovan crept noiselessly about the room on bare feet, stalking slowly, pausing to inspect possible hiding places with the gun held before him. He assessed the heavy curtains at the windows and the ones hanging from her bed for an intruder. He stepped to the louvered doors leading to the balcony and tested the lock. Usually she left the doors open to allow in the cooling night breeze, but Mr. Duchamp had been adamant about locking them earlier tonight, when he and Mr. O'Leary escorted her to her room.

"No one is here." Elizabeth whispered as she rose from the floor with difficulty due to a fluid sensation in her legs. "I had a nightmare, sir, that's all. I didn't mean to disturb you."

"I was awake." Donovan emerged from the shadows to stand beside her. Naked, and clearly unashamed for it, the man exuded confidence in his raw masculinity that she found unsettling as he gazed into her eyes. "I heard a loud noise and then you cried out."

"I stumbled and tripped in the darkness. Could I sleep with you, just this once?" She focused on his face to avoid the urge to gape at his dangling parts. *Sleep, yes. And take her rightful place in his bed.* Yes, she would do it without protest if he asked her. Elizabeth hadn't the courage to tell him. She could only hope he would allow her into his bed again so they might work past this disturbing estrangement of recent weeks.

"No." He crushed her tentative hope for reconciliation. "You are safe here. I won't get any sleep with you beside me." It was the last response she expected, given his reluctance to allow her to have a room of her own in the first place.

Two weeks ago he made it clear he wanted her in his bed.

Apparently, he didn't want her there anymore.

He turned and walked back to his room. He closed the doors, leaving her holding the flickering candle against the surrounding gloom.

Two days passed. The only difference in Elizabeth's routine was the presence of her guards. They followed her everywhere but remained silent and unobtrusive, like the mastiffs who followed her about the grounds when she snuck out alone. She tried to resent the guards, but gave up quickly. They were respectful and patient, even when she took advantage of them by going on a meandering walk in the neglected gardens to assess it—just because she could, without fear of her husband's reprisals. Yesterday, she'd sat defiantly in her fairy bower beneath the gnarled old tree near the gazebo and studied her grandmother's spell book for three hours in the heat of the afternoon. The guards had nothing to do except stand and watch her. It amused her to see them fidget with boredom and brush the sweat from their brows due to the heat, but cruelty was not in her nature, so she soon gave up punishing them and sent one up to the house to have lemonade brought for them all.

Today, she had set upon a plan that would make use of their strength. After lunch, she took up her household keys and led them up to the third floor, to Marissa's old room.

Despite her best intentions, Elizabeth had been reluctant to return to Gareth's mother's room. It was an eerie place, fraught with mystery and tragedy. Part of her feared being trapped in the room by an unknowing servant seeing the door open and closing it without realizing it was occupied, or by deliberate malice from the spirit realm. With two burly men to watch over her, there was little fear of that.

Elizabeth unlocked the door and stepped inside. O'Leary and Duchamp followed her.

"Ach, a queer place." O'Leary said, noting the barred windows and locked door.

"Yes, a sad place." Elizabeth responded, surprised by Gus O'Leary's confession.

The men didn't talk much, even to each other. Mostly they answered her inquiries with monosyllables, particularly Mr. Duchamp, who had a sullen nature.

"I intend to make it a more welcoming place. And you are going to help me."

The pair gazed at her as if she spoke in language they didn't understand.

"Mr. O'Leary." She instructed, "I want you to go downstairs and fetch whatever tools you'll need to remove those bars from the windows and to remove the outer lock on the door."

The sailor stared at her with disbelief. "We ain't footmen, me lady—"

"Do it." Duchamp said brusquely.

Mr. O'Leary gave an indignant huff and shuffled from the room.

Elizabeth held the Frenchman's gaze, uncertain if thanking him for taking her part was the right tact. Duchamp didn't smile, nor did his dark eyes offer a flicker of emotion as he regarded her. He nodded, and then his lanky body melted effortlessly into a courtly bow. In that brief exchange, she understood; she had his unswerving allegiance, the same as her husband.

O'Leary returned with the tools. She set the men to work on the window, directing them to try to loosen the bars on the outside from within the opened window. Their clattering echoed about the chamber. Elizabeth surveyed the room, wondering if she should box up the personal items for Gareth, as they were his mother's.

The room could be turned into a private sitting room for a governess or a nurse. The unbidden thought brought a peculiar yearning within. A governess—that meant children, her children. Would they have Donovan's crystal blue eyes and dark hair? Elizabeth never considered the idea before. She would like to have

179

his children one day. She yearned for his acceptance and his love. But she lied to him. And that lie could not easily be forgiven.

The awareness of a presence nearby slowly curled about her. It wasn't malicious. It was a frightened, transparent blur edging about the chamber like a hesitant mouse. "It's all right. Let me help you." She whispered, confident the men would not hear with their pounding.

Marissa became a faint, wavering golden light dancing about the room. She circled Elizabeth, almost playfully, save for the room's foreboding overtone. The weaving orb floated ahead of her. Following it, Elizabeth stepped toward the full length mirror, noting the spider webbing of cracks on the silvered glass. A shard was missing from the bottom of the mirror. She gazed at her distorted reflection, unsure what the spirit wanted. "What happened here?"

Amid the clanking and hammering of the men, she waited for an explanation. None came. Instead, the wavering sphere of light guided her to the bathing area beyond the privacy screen. Elizabeth studied the small ornate dressing table. The mirror above was coated with heavy dust, as were the beautiful bottles of perfumes and lotions lined up along the table. She glanced at the copper tub in the corner and clutched the chair as she squelched a rising scream.

A lovely dark woman was lying naked in the steaming bath, her head tipped back, as if she'd fallen asleep. The water was crimson with her blood. A baby was crying loudly from the bassinette in the opposite corner of the room. She heard the sound of a lock turning at the door, and hurried footsteps. A tall, blond man, his face a mirror image of Donovan's, save a moustache and goatee of burnished gold, stepped past Elizabeth and sank to his knees next to the tub. He spoke to the dead woman with a heavy Irish brogue. He clutched her wrist in both hands. His white shirt became smeared with blood as he cradled the scored wrist against his heart and sobbed out his anguish while the babe shrieked frantically in the background.

Elizabeth gasped aloud. Her head felt light, and she thought for a moment she might do something stupid, like swoon. The feeling faded. "Why do you remain?" She asked Marissa, "You aren't a prisoner anymore. You're free now, you can move on."

"*I can't.*" Marissa responded. "*I can't leave him. Not until I know he's well and truly cared for.*"

"Gareth?" Elizabeth asked, surmising the woman was concerned for the child she left behind. "He's a grown man, Marissa. He's here. He's well, and he's loved by the family."

"*But what of his birthright? Richard promised me he would have a bright future, a share in the estate income.*"

Elizabeth didn't know how to respond. What could she say? Without a written document, there was no proof of Marissa's claim regarding Gareth's share in the estate profits. It was something she might take up with Donovan---someday--if they were ever on speaking terms again.

Marissa's spirit looked so broken and full of despair. She wanted Elizabeth to help her. The spirit moved to the shattered mirror. She gestured to it insistently, as if there were some hidden meaning there. Elizabeth watched, feeling sorrow for the poor woman.

"*It's here!*" Marissa whispered. "*It's right here.*"

Elizabeth was about to question the spirit further, not comprehending her meaning as she kept gesturing to the spider webbing of broken glass held in place by the gilt mirror frame.

"My lady!" Chloe's hectic voice intruded and Marissa's spirit melted into the wall. Chloe came trudging past the hammering men, breathless with excitement. "Madame, we've been searching all over for you. You have visitors. Captain Rawlings and his nephew are awaiting you in the salon."

Half an hour later, Elizabeth was alone with Captain Rawlings. He dismissed her guards easily, citing his wish to speak to the countess alone. As he was their captain, the men didn't dare question him. He sent Peter to the kitchens for a snack, took Elizabeth's arm and led her outside and down the cobbled path toward the stone terrace at the edge of the gardens.

After looking about to see if they were alone, he asked, "What can I do for you, my lady?"

There it was; her chance to share her fears, her chance to escape. Did she dare take it?

"I won't betray your confidence. What's wrong? Is it Donovan?"

She nodded. And then she was weeping, unable to prevent the onslaught of tears at finding someone who cared about her and had come to help her.

"Don't cry, my lady." The captain crooned, pulling her into his arms. "Tell me what's happened so we can make it right."

Oh, Bollocks., this could go very badly if someone came upon them so.

She made a little noise in her throat and pushed at him. He released her immediately.

Once the proprieties were back in place Elizabeth confessed her husband's peculiar behavior in the past weeks. She ended with "Is he mad, Captain? I must know."

The captain scrunched up his face and gazed at the sea. "Troubled, yes, eccentric, undoubtedly, but mad, no! Has he spent any time with you? What about dinner?"

"He eats with the servants." Elizabeth confided. "As Mr. O'Rourke. The maids are all silly over him. They talk about trying to capture his fancy, right in front of me! It's humiliating."

He touched her arm and looked as if he might embrace her again. "I'll talk to him."

"No." Elizabeth protested, looking about with alarm. "I've been trying to make the best of it---but then, Peter sent me that note and I knew I had to risk confiding in someone in case something awful happens."

Rawlings swore and turned away. One hand fistcd at his side. "You shouldn't have to make the best of it." He sighed and turned back to her. "Do you wish to leave him, is that it?"

"Oh--I-I--" She shook head and turned away before completing her denial, afraid the captain might see the truth in her eyes. "If I were in England, sir, I would have sought sanctuary with my grandfather. How am I to live with a man who hides and behaves as if I do not exist?"

"You shouldn't have to put up with that. I'll talk to him---"

"No—please--he'll be angry. I'll have to face his wrath after you leave. I'm frightened, Captain. I don't know what to do, but I *cannot* go on like this any longer!"

Jack took her hand. "I'll see you through this, my lady, I promise; one way or another."

There was a crunching of gravel and voices approaching, Peter's voice answered by a languid colonial drawl with just the hint of an Irish burr in it.

"There they are." Peter came running up to Elizabeth. "You weren't funning me, my lady. He's bigger than Corky. I'd like to know what you're feeding Puck."

"Jack!" Donovan slapped his friend on the back, smiling.

"How are you two *love birds* getting along?" Rawlings responded without a smile.

Elizabeth waited with Jack, curious to hear Donovan's reply.

"Every man should have a wife as fine as my Lizzie. The house smells of lemon oil instead of dust and mildew." Donovan placed a possessive arm about Elizabeth.

Flustered, Elizabeth turned to the boy. "Peter, we've strawberries from the hothouse that have ripened. Would you like some? I've been longing for someone to share them with."

At the boy's acceptance, she extracted herself from her husband's cloying embrace and hurried up the path. After gaining several feet away from the men, she turned and shot the captain a pleading look. *Please don't say anything--please don't betray me!*

The captain's grim sidelong glance told her he would make no promises on that account.

"Damned fine woman." Donovan sighed, watching his delightful bride move gracefully down the garden path and up to the house with Peter in tow.

"Yeah." Jack agreed, "Tell me, are you hoping to *keep* her?"

As expected, those pale eyes swung about to meet him. "What is that supposed to mean?"

"Do you *wish* to stay married to the girl? Because let me tell you, she's ready to bolt. She's talking about going back to England to live with her grandfather and after hearing how badly you've treated her I'm inclined to help her do just that." Jack spat out, knowing he'd not planned it out carefully as he probably should have. He couldn't think of how to put it down tactful and clever, not when he wanted very much to hurt this man.

"What did she tell you? I haven't touched her. Damn it, I've kept away from her--"

"Shut up." Jack held up his free hand, distracting his adversary. He had a pistol in his jacket pocket and he had it leveled at the notorious pirate known as The Raven. If Donovan started swinging Jack knew his only chance was to shoot him in the knee so he couldn't stand. "I know you can take me down with those fancy fighting moves you learned in India. But if I don't return to Basseterre come sunset, there will be people coming here to find out why."

"Why would I wish to harm you?"

"Because, old friend, I might be taking Mrs. Beaumont to Basseterre with me."

"Like hell you are! She's not going anywhere with you."

"If she still wants to leave here after you and I finish this conversation, I am taking her with me. When you married that girl you entered the world outside your laboratory. She's not a specimen you can keep trapped under a bell jar awaiting your whims. She's a young lady with feelings and fears. Fears about your sanity, thanks to your masquerade, fears about what you'll do to her after I leave here today because I'm telling you this when she begged me not to."

"I would never hurt her. You know that, Jack."

"I'm not the one you have to convince. Like I said, if I don't get back by sunset, more people will be coming here to find out why the tortured, reclusive count is keeping a young woman here against her will. And before they come, they've been instructed to pass along what they know to others, in case they don't return." The tension in Jack's body made him feel brittle.

"Do I look mad to you?" Donovan asked as he held out his hands. "Do you think I'd deliberately terrify the woman I love?"

"Does *she* know that you love her?" Jack countered. His question was met with rolled eyes, as if it were bloody well obvious she knew the man cared for her. "Have you told her you love her? *No?* Trust me; women are particular about those trifling little details."

"I don't have time for this." Donovan looked about with impatience. "I need to ride over to the mill and check the progress on the new windmill blades I've had to replace after the storm last month so they're ready for the cane harvest and then I have to go over the--"

"And you asked me a question I haven't yet answered." Jack interrupted. "You asked me if I thought you were mad, if I thought you'd deliberately terrify your wife. It doesn't matter what I think, Donovan; *I'm* not married to you. You're not scaring me one minute as the ferocious count and then scolding me the next as Mr. O'Rourke, coldly laying out rules for me to follow here as if I were one of your indentures instead of your bride."

"We had a misunderstanding. I was drunk. I apologized, that was weeks ago."

"Yes, that was weeks ago. But let's keep going. Let's examine the evidence from her perspective." Jack countered. "How would *you* feel if you were brought to an isolated estate and ignored? How long would you be able to tolerate your maids talking openly in front of you about capturing your husband's fancy because they think Mr. O'Rourke is a bachelor? How long would you endure your husband pretending he's a fucking servant in his own house? Tell me, old friend, if you were eighteen years old would you feel safe living with the man I described? Would you feel loved by him?"

"Wait." Donovan thrust up a hand. "I don't give a damn about those wenches in the kitchen. I've been eating with the servants to wheedle out the bad seed. She has these spells, Jack." He made a motion with his hand near his head. "Bouts of confusion. Petite Seizures. She's disorientated and vulnerable when she emerges from one. I have to make certain the new servants won't take advantage of her during those times. I fired two footmen already. They were gambling over her, Jack, laying out bets as to which one of them would succeed in bedding her in the coming months. Do you think I want that trash in my house, near my darling?"

"The darling you've not spent an hour with in the past two weeks? The darling who wrote to me because she's scared out of her wits after living here alone with *you*?"

The fountain water was *refreshing* as it sluiced down Elizabeth's body in the stifling mid-afternoon heat. She'd been pleased to learn that it was just a matter of turning on the pump mechanism to get this lovely tile pool with the fountain running again. She was standing with Peter in the bottom pool of the three tiered fountain in the front drive, letting the cool spray of water from the second tier wash over her. The strawberries were a sweet memory. Their empty bowls sat on the edge of their impromptu bathing pool as they laughed and splashed one another.

Peter kicked a spray of water at her. Elizabeth bent and cupped her hands, returning his assault with a sharp skiff of water, right in his face. He gasped and kicked at her again.

"Oh, look!" She squinted into the water as little squiggly creatures swum around her ankles. "Some kind of fish is in here."

"Those are tadpoles." Peter cupped his hands and caught one. He stepped close and held it up for her inspection. "See, they've got little legs growing out their backsides."

Elizabeth shivered. "Oh, this water is starting to feel cold."

"We could swim in the ocean, and then lie in the sun and bake ourselves like clams."

"I don't know how to swim." Donovan had promised to teach her. He promised many things during the voyage and she believed him.

The sound of boots on the cobblestones made her look up from the pool. The men were coming around from the back of the house, approaching them with determined strides. Elizabeth looked down at her muslin gown. The fabric was wet, nearly transparent and clinging to her body. *Oh, Bollocks.!* She'd been caught breaking his rules again, wandering outside alone. Judging by the grim look on her husband's face, she'd be paying for her folly as soon as the captain left.

"Uncle Jack!" The boy sprinted out of the pool and rushed up to the captain.

"Let's let these two have a moment." Rawlings grabbed his nephew by his neck to guide him to the front steps. "Oh, your skin feels like ice. Go inside and get out of those wet clothes."

Elizabeth stood in the knee deep pool, her arms crossed about her to hide the nipples poking out from her now transparent bodice. She kept her gaze down to avoid the somber man on the edge of the pool who was watching her with pale, penetrating blue orbs.

"Elizabeth." Donovan held out his hand, directing her to step out of the pool.

She shook her head, unable to take that hand. The tightness in her chest made her feel as if she might break into a thousand pieces if she moved or breathed.

The water sloshed about her calves. Donovan had stepped into the fountain. She focused on his boots, unable to meet his austere eyes.

"I didn't mean to frighten you." He said in the velvet tone. "I'm sorry."

Elizabeth nodded, uncertain, as he stood before her with his friend looking on. Was he trying to appear contrite now that Rawlings was involved? Was he sincere? She didn't dare look at him for fear she'd find not love in his eyes, but contempt.

The silence was making her ill. She felt nauseous, light headed and cold.

"Don't leave me. I'll change. I swear it." He whispered.

Bewildered, Elizabeth looked up at him. She was unprepared for pleading from a man she believed had come to despise her. "I don't wish to leave, sir."

"Tell me what I need to do to make you happy here."

"I can't go on like this." She pushed the words out. Sharp as they were, they sliced raw trails of pain inside her throat. She was determined to speak her heart no matter the cost. "I cannot endure your contempt any longer. Don't you understand? I spent my childhood being unwanted baggage in one man's house. Afraid of his temper, afraid of being beaten—afraid of breaking his damn rules—I will not spend my life being unwanted baggage in another--"

"I would never hurt you." Donovan interjected, grasping her by the shoulders. "And I want you, Elizabeth, I *want* you; more than you can imagine."

"You've a strange way of showing it. You've been avoiding me for weeks."

"I thought that's what you wanted."

"*What I wanted*? Then why do I feel as if I'm being punished? All you ever do is snarl at me. You act as if you can't stand me—as if you regret marrying me—"

"No!" His grasp tightened on her arms. "I love you, Elizabeth. I would do anything for you, anything you ask. I'll do whatever I must to make things right between us."

Only the water from the fountain could be heard behind them in the agonizing seconds that passed. Elizabeth stood still, weighing his words.

His eyes were wide, pleading, never wavering from her regard as he waited for her response.

"I cannot live in fear of your dark count anymore." She went on in a rush of pent up emotion. "I'll have no more of your disguises. No more games of intrigue, no more watching you pretend to be a bachelor with the maids, or wondering which one will become your mistress!"

"—Lizzie--it's not like that—I'm trying to protect--"

"O'Rourke, unhand the lady at once." Giles was standing on the other side of the fountain, a blanket in his hand and dangerous look on his face. "Come, Madame, the boy said you were chilled." He held out the blanket, waiting for her to step out of the fountain.

"Its fine, Giles, back off!" Donovan said dismissively.

"No! It is not *fine*." The Englishman scolded. "You are bullying my mistress again and we will not tolerate such behavior. Come, Madame, away from this brute."

Elizabeth glared at Donovan, waiting for him to prove he meant those pretty words he just said. Waiting for him to prove this was not just an act for the benefit of his friend.

"Giles, assemble the servants." Donovan said. "I need to make an announcement."

"One more condition," Elizabeth decided to make the best of it while she had the chance. "I want Giles to be my butler, the head of the household staff instead of Tabby."

"Consider it done." Donovan boldly kissed her cheek before releasing her and stepping out of the pool. He clapped Giles on the shoulder. "You passed with flying colors, old boy."

"My lady?" Giles intoned, waiting for her to explain the stable master's odd behavior.

Not up to the task of explaining her husband's elaborate masquerade, she stepped out of the pool. Donovan took the blanket and wrapped it about her shoulders. Elizabeth shivered. Her legs felt boneless. It seemed the ground had been transformed to pitching seas. She swallowed the coppery taste in the back of her throat. A peculiar detachment was stealing over her.

She heard her husband cursing as the world was plunged into an inky darkness.

Chapter Twenty Three

"God-damn-it!" Donovan caught Elizabeth, preventing her head from slipping to the cobblestones. Sinking to his knees while holding her torso against him, he jerked off a glove with his teeth and placed two fingers in her mouth to prevent her from choking on her tongue.

"Find his lordship, quickly!" The middle aged footman shouted, causing Donovan to look up for a brief instant. The courtyard had been empty moments ago. Now a pack of wide eyed maids stood watching with a mixture of horror and fascination as their mistress convulsed and jerked like a fish on the docks beneath the effects of a full blown grand mal seizure.

"I'm right here." He insisted. His declaration went unheard over the footman's bellowing. He concentrated on the convulsing girl whose head was cradled on his knees. "I'm here, Lizzie. It's all right." He glanced about for Jack and was relieved to see the man emerge from the front door with Pearl hurrying after him. The pair brushed past the line of bewildered servants and knelt to assist him rather than join the fools gathered as if to watch a freak show.

"Don't just stand there like stupid cows." Giles shrieked. "Find the count. He's a doctor!" The maids scurried into the house to search for a man who did not exist.

"Pearl, tell Giles who I am." Donovan said, as the convulsions eased. Elizabeth became deathly still. "Lizzie." He pleaded. "Don't do this, Sweetheart, you need to stay awake."

"Let's get her inside." Jack suggested, touching Donovan's shoulder.

"Yes, my lord." A very florid Giles added, as Pearl nodded beside him. "Her ladyship will be more comfortable in a soft bed."

Once he had Elizabeth safely in his room, he began to remove her wet clothing.

"Shame on you, O'Rourke!" Elizabeth's maid slapped his hand away from her mistress. "Go find his lordship." She ordered in a Spanish accent softened by her Caribbean upbringing.

"I am his lordship." Donovan snapped, now thoroughly exasperated by the ruse.

Pearl entered the chamber with his physician's case. "What else can I do, my lord?"

"Oh!" Chloe sputtered, gazing at him with alarm. "*Por favor*, she did not say anything!"

"I instructed her not to." Donovan replied. Chloe helped him remove Elizabeth's wet clothing. A slice of fear went through him as he discovered bruising along his wife's hips and ribcage. Judging by the discoloration, they were several days old. Recalling her penchant for climbing ladders, he looked to the maid. "How did this happen? Did she fall recently?"

"I do not know, my lord." Chloe returned, but the look in her eyes unsettled him.

The sun lowered in the sky.

Elizabeth remained unconscious.

Donovan forgot Jack was downstairs until Pearl came to inform him the captain was leaving. He didn't want to leave Elizabeth's side, so he had his valet escort Jack up to his suite.

"All this time," Jack stood at the foot of the bed, "and she's not regained consciousness?"

Donovan nodded, resentment mingling with his fear as he sat beside his wife.

"What happened in the courtyard?"

"A brain seizure. I won't know how serious until she regains consciousness."

"I'll be back tomorrow." Jack promised, stepping close to grasp Donovan's shoulder.

"That's not necessary."

"Oh, it is." Jack's voice, like his, quickly dropped the friendly tone. "I promised Elizabeth I would see her through this and I intend to keep that promise."

"Damn it, Jack, you're overstepping your bounds."

"I don't care. I'll keep coming, until I'm assured she's not being mistreated, until I hear from her lips that she's willing to remain with you after the spiteful way you've treated her!"

"Did she ask your help in leaving me?"

"No, but she did say if she were in England, she'd have taken refuge with her grandfather by now." Jack returned, looking him square in the eye, "Which speaks volumes to me; the lady is obviously not happy as Mrs. Beaumont and has thought about leaving you."

Donovan rose from the chair with his fists clenched. "How convenient—for you."

"Don't you dare accuse me of foul play." Jack retorted. "I'm here as a concerned friend."

"Of course you are, Jack." Donovan was barely able to contain his urge to throttle the man. "She's a beautiful woman and it's a long voyage to England. You'd hardly allow a young lady of quality to make the journey alone. Be honest, you want her."

"No." Jack countered. "What I want is for Elizabeth to feel safe again after all that's happened to her. She does not feel safe living here, with you. She sought my help because she's frightened by your behavior. I don't give a damn what you think, I will not look the other way when a woman I care for deeply is being subjected to intolerable cruelty."

There it was. The truth. Donovan didn't say a word. He just kept glaring at the man.

Jack didn't attempt to deny his declaration of having feelings for Elizabeth. "Don't look at me like that. If the situation were reversed, if my wife sought your help because my behavior frightened her, you'd be right there, your hand at my throat, demanding I set things right."

"Get out of my house!"

Elizabeth opened her eyes. She gazed about with alarm. She was in a strange room. The candles were lit. It was evening. Her mind wasn't working properly. She couldn't remember this place. She gazed at the man sitting in a chair beside the bed. "Where am I?"

"You're in my room, at Ravencrest Estates." The dark haired man leaned close to scrutinize her with pale blue, anxious eyes. "Do you know who I am?"

"Of course!" She insisted, disturbed by his question and her uncertainty of the answer.

And then it came to her. Relieved, she loosened her death grip on the covers and smoothed them with her palms. He must not know of her queer mental lapses, the lost bits of time and her inability to recall where she was for a brief span when she emerged from the frightening episodes. "You are my husband."

"That's right, darlin'. What is my name?" He persisted.

Elizabeth swallowed the uneasy feeling in her throat. "Donovan."

The tension in his features lessened a little. "What is the last thing you remember?"

Everything was fuzzy. It was an effort to think. She tried to sit up.

"No." He cautioned, preventing her from rising. "You had a seizure this afternoon. You've been unconscious for nine hours. You need to rest, Lizzie."

A seizure? That was news. Epileptics had seizures. She wasn't an epileptic, was she?

"Can you remember where you were and what you were doing before you collapsed?"

Elizabeth rolled her lips. She tried to concentrate. She'd been at the fountain, with Peter. They discovered tadpoles. "You—you stepped into the fountain--you ruined your boots."

"I can afford another pair." Frowning, he lifted a candle from the nightstand and held it near her face.

"Look at me, let me see your eyes." He leaned down close to peer into her eyes. "Does your head hurt?"

"No---yes--a little. You stepped into the fountain; you said that you *love* me?"

"I do love you. I thought you knew that." He set the candle aside.

She didn't know. He never said it and lately, he'd been acting just the opposite.

"Count backwards, from ten. Please, dearest, it's important."

Elizabeth did so, and then she was asked to state her full name. Donovan nodded and asked her to tell him the date. She stared at him, unable to do so.

"How old are you?" He asked when she didn't answer the previous question.

"Sixteen—ah--eighteen? Where is Captain Rawlings?"

"The captain left." His eyes hardened and the tenderness left his voice as he sat up straight, pulling away from her. "He'll be back, come morning. Did you write to Jack and ask his help in leaving me?"

God in Heaven—what did the captain say to him?

"I never told him I wished to leave you!" She clutched his hand, desperate to make him believe her. "I was frightened; I asked him here to t-talk—I--Oooh---ssss!"

Pain shot through her skull. Her body felt as if it were all just one great bruise.

"Easy, lass, don't try to talk." Donovan eased her back onto the pillows. He pushed up the sleeve of her gown to check her pulse and cursed. The back of Elizabeth's wrist was turning bluish-crimson. Similar marks were forming at her elbow and on her left arm. He stood and lifted the covers. Sure enough, the backs of her legs and her hips were darkening ominously.

A sick dread settled in his gut. Jack had been insistent about making sure she was not being mistreated. If Jack convinced Lizzie to leave him, this could be the proof needed to petition the court for a divorce on the grounds of cruelty. And Donovan knew his carefully cultivated reputation as Count Rochembeau was enough to make any magistrate suspect him of the charges, regardless of his innocence.

He could not lose Elizabeth. Not like this, falsely accused of something he didn't do.

In her fragile mental state she might be manipulated by a cunning rogue desperate for money--someone with a gallant streak—someone who desperately needed to rescue a woman from a brutish captor to assuage his guilt for not saving his beloved. *Someone like Black Jack.*

Donovan tamped down the rising panic. He had to focus on the cause of Elizabeth's battered condition, not his fear of being falsely accused of vile crimes yet again.

Why did she have bruises on her ribs? They were older than the ones forming now.

"Honey," he asked, unable to keep the anxious warble from his voice. "Where did you get the bruises on your abdomen?"

Her hand moved protectively to her left side. It must still be tender, he realized. "Sleepwalking. I bump into things, and then I wake up. As I did the other night."

He recalled hearing a loud thump in her room and finding her lying on the floor. *Sleepwalking?* That was cause for concern. "Have you ever awakened outside your room?"

"No, but I do seem to wake up on the floor a great deal of late."

Donovan released his breath. He was relieved, and yet, disturbed by her confession. He patted her leg. "From now on you will sleep here, with me. We can't have you wandering about, stumbling into things or falling down the stairs." He added quickly, fearing she'd misinterpret his intentions and protest. She didn't. She remained quiet, subdued.

This wasn't like Lizzie. She always had some smart remark or argument to toss at him.

He watched her, concerned at her pliant behavior. Well, it had been a very trying day.

The bruises upset him. Sleepwalking might explain the older marks, but how did she come to be bruised from head to toe tonight? The new bruises weren't present when he undressed her this afternoon. Chloe could attest to that. It was as if an unseen force had assaulted her while she lay unconscious. That was preposterous—he was here the whole time.

With his heart pounding, Donovan mentally retraced the events of the day, searching for a logical explanation that would counter an invisible assailant and any suspicion cast on him for her battered condition. This seizure had been much more serious than the one she had on the ship. Her limbs had thrashed violently against the cobblestones. His main concern had been protecting her head ...and the bruises were curiously limited to her posterior.

That was it!

In a quiet, steady voice he explained it to Elizabeth, the hard cobblestones, the intense thrashing of her limbs. She meekly accepted his explanation without argument or accusation. That made the tightness in his chest ease a little more. And yet, he saw that she was frightened by his words, badly frightened, as anyone might be if told they'd slipped into convulsions.

He gave her a sedative for the pain she must be feeling and talked of inconsequential things as he waited for the medicine to take effect. He spoke of his Arabian stallion and of the foals due in the spring that had been sired by his stallion. He asked if she'd ever seen a foaling. Elizabeth shook her head. She didn't flinch at the slight movement as she had earlier.

Satisfied that her pain and her fear were receding, Donovan turned the conversation back to the matter of her leaving him. "I've taken care of everything you asked of me in the courtyard. The household knows I'm the count. Giles is your new butler, and I'm hiring a steward to take the job of Mr. O'Rourke. From now, on there shall be no more disguises or games between us. I meant what I said; I love you, and I'll do whatever I must to prove it."

"Donovan, I'm sorry . . . please, don't hate me . . ."

Donovan frowned. Women said the most peculiar things under the influence of Laudanum, a fellow medical student once confessed to him. He was finding it to be true.

"He said you'd despise me if . . . you knew what he did to me . . ."

His mind careened to an abrupt stop for a terrifying moment. And then a razor sharp fury replaced his earlier bemusement. He leaned over Elizabeth, his hands pressed flat to the mattress on either side of her shoulders. "Who said that?" Her excuse of sleepwalking no longer seemed plausible. "Who told you I'd despise you if I knew what he was doing to you? Has one of the footmen been trifling with you? Tell me. Was it Elias Jones? I fired him, but if he hurt you, by God, I'll make him pay!"

"No . . ." Her grasp on reality was shaky as the opiates coursed through her. "It was that awful captain—the one who kidnapped me. Please, don't hate me—I tried to fight—I bit him. I tried to make him stop!" The high voice cracked from strain, and then she was weeping softly.

"Oh, Lizzie, sweet Lizzie, what happened wasn't your fault." Donovan countered. He gathered her up in his arms, held her, and whispered sweet words to her until she fell asleep.

Determination settled upon him. He was not going to lose Elizabeth. Not to Jack. And not because of his own churlishness. Jack was right, he probably didn't deserve Elizabeth, but she belonged to him. He was not losing her, not without a fight.

Chapter Twenty Four

Elizabeth awakened to find Donovan hovering nearby. She thought it strange he was not out riding about his estate, as was his habit in the mornings. After making his rounds he usually spent the rest of his day cloistered in his laboratory or out in the stables.

His routine was not all that had changed. He wasn't dressed as O'Rourke or the malicious count. Today, he was the gentleman planter she knew from the voyage. A fine lawn shirt replaced the stable master's worn cotton. His face was clean shaven, his hair restrained in a neat queue, and he wore his signet ring again, proof he was indeed the master. A black silk vest shot with silver, black broadcloth breeches and gleaming top boots completed his costume.

"You asked me to set aside my disguises." He said, noting her surprise at his changed appearance. "I have done so as proof of my devotion." Holding his hands out, palms up, he asked, "Does my lady disapprove?"

"Oh, no! You are very elegant, sir."

Donovan bowed like an actor at the end of a grand performance. As he rose, he smiled at her and said, "Now, you must give me something in return, Madame. I want you to stay in bed today, in fact, for the remainder of the week." He walked to the foot of the bed and stood with his hands on his hips, observing her in his quiet, pensive way. "You're not well, Elizabeth." He chastened, as if expecting an argument.

She didn't have the energy or inclination to argue. She was tired of being at sixes and nines with this man all of the time. She was wrong to share their difficulties with the captain, she realized, as Donovan stood before her and she examined her situation in the light of a new day. Donovan should be furious with her. Instead, he was showing a great deal of forbearance, considering she'd maligned him to his friend and made a terrible scene on the front drive.

"I'll do whatever you wish, my lord. I'll be good from now on, I promise."

"You *are* good!" He chastened in a cheerful mien. "You're my good lass and don't you be thinking otherwise." Coming around the bed, he sat beside her and took her hand. "You are also ill, more than you realize. Yet, I'm told you work to the point of exhaustion, scrubbing along with the maids. I hired servants to do the work for you, not to try to keep up with you."

"Well, I did need to train them--"

"That is the housekeeper's responsibility, not yours." He cut off her excuse.

Elizabeth wanted to point out that the housekeeper was useless by lunch due to her ongoing affair with a rum bottle. The fury in his eyes reminded her that she was on thin ice with the man. His ire was justified. It was scandalous for a lady to be caught doing menial chores. Gossip spread quickly via the servants. If they lived in London tongues would be wagging about the eccentric countess who washed her own windows and hung her own curtains.

"Mark me, there will be no more climbing ladders, polishing furniture or moving it, for that matter." He lifted her hand and lightly kissed her knuckles. "From now on, I intend to make certain you don't lift anything heavier than a tea cup."

Chloe came with a breakfast tray. The aroma of hot chocolate and crisp, salty bacon filled the room. Donovan stood and moved to the veranda doors. He leaned against the portal, arms crossed about his chest, his back to the women as he gazed out at the sea.

Dear, sweet Lizzie. Fletcher made her believe she was an encumbrance to those about her. And her grandmother allowed her to be far too independent for a young lady. Donovan sighed. He had quite the task before him if he were tame his headstrong little mare.

Alas, they were not at leisure to work through their marital difficulties.

Jack was here demanding to see Elizabeth, and this time he brought armed reinforcements.

And so, they were at odds, both knights fighting for possession of the queen. He considered his options. Perhaps Jack's visit could be turned to his advantage.

With a plan quickly in place, Donovan went to stand at the foot of the bed, his arms still crossed about his chest. "Don't dally over your eggs and rashers, my sweet, we must get you ready to receive your visitor."

"Not the captain!" She said, taken aback by his statement.

"Yes. Rawlings is waiting in the salon as we speak."

"I can't see him. Tell him I'm sick."

"Come now, you keep insisting that you are not. Surely, you don't intend to hide behind that flimsy excuse now. I'll send the captain up directly." He stalked to the hall door.

"Please, my lord, if I must see him I prefer that you remain with me."

My Lord. Lizzie addressed him thus when she was intimidated. He turned to face her. She looked frightened. It almost gave him pause. Almost. He would not be deterred from his objective. He would learn what was going on between his friend and his wife before the day was out. He steeled himself against that sweet face and turned to sarcasm to deflect the impact of those beautiful, wounded eyes. "Rawlings is here to make certain you are being treated well in my keeping. That being the case, I can hardly stand over you without it appearing as if I am bullying you into answering in my favor, now can I?"

"Why would he think that?" She asked, appearing confused.

"Perhaps you gave him that impression yesterday, my dear."

He left, before he lost his resolve and gathered her in his arms like a besotted fool.

Donovan met Jack in the salon. After enduring more of the same arguments from last night, he instructed Giles to escort Jack up to see Lizzie. Once Jack was upstairs, he had Gus and Ambrose take position in the salon as a counter to Jack's two escorts. Thus fortified, he took the servant stairs to the second floor and entered the veranda through a vacant room. He crept to the open window.

Crouching against the wall, he listened to the pair on the other side of the window.

"---believes bed rest will make all the difference."

"Do you agree with him?' Jack asked.

"He is a doctor. Why wouldn't I?"

"He could be exaggerating your condition so that you won't leave him, Madame."

"How dare you make such a horrid accusation?" Elizabeth's voice echoed outrage. "And Captain, why is my husband convinced I want to leave him?"

"Yes, ah, I might have embellished a little. It's a tricky situation, Madame. If I take you from him without his consent he could have the law sent after me for kidnapping, regardless of whether you wanted to go or not. So, I'm blackmailing him, I'm using the fearful reputation he's cultivated with the locals against him. I've threatened to bring the authorities here if he doesn't comply with your wishes and allow you to leave freely—if that is your wish."

"How could you do such a wicked thing to him? He must feel very betrayed."

"I was worried about you after you sent me that note." Jack defended. "You did say that it was matter of grave importance requiring the utmost secrecy."

"For all you knew I could have been seeking your advice on a Christmas gift."

"You wouldn't send such a dire message to me if something weren't terribly wrong."

"That is very kind of you, captain." Elizabeth fairly purred. "Donovan thinks I'm a silly, empty-headed girl given to far too much imagination."

I do not! Donovan opened his mouth to refute such rubbish, but caught himself.

"He undoubtedly believes we're all idiots compared to that superior intellect."

"He was so sweet and attentive during the voyage. He changed as soon as we arrived here. He became moody and distant. I wish that kind man would come back, but I'm afraid that Donovan doesn't exist."

Lizzie! Donovan closed his eyes, shamed by her confession.

"He's been using disguises for years, Madame. I doubt he'll be able to give them up."

"But he promised me he would, last night and again today!"

"I have him boxed into a corner. He'll say or do anything to prevent outsiders from investigating his affairs." Jack countered. "I need you to be truthful, my lady, as I may not be able to return so easily after today. Are you being treated well? Has he hurt you?"

"Captain Rawlings!" Elizabeth chastened. "How could you imply such a thing?"

"Those bruises on your wrists are reason enough, my lady."

Donovan held his breath. Elizabeth could damn him or exonerate him in the next instant.

"Oh . . . He didn't do this, captain. It's from the seizure. He kept my head from hitting the cobblestones, but my limbs are terribly bruised from the convulsions. I feel as if I've been run over by a coach and four. See, even my elbows are swollen and bruised."

Jack's sharp intake of breath betrayed his outrage at the landscape Lizzie revealed to him.

The fist squeezing Donovan's heart loosened, allowing him to breathe a little easier. Lizzie was defending him, and not allowing Jack to influence her impressions as he'd feared.

"Yes." Jack hesitated. "I saw it happen. And it looks quite painful. But I remind you, Madame, yesterday you were vehement that I not speak to him on your behalf. You gave me to believe you feared he might punish you if I did so."

"I didn't mean physically! And I-I was afraid. I behaved foolishly. He's been so angry of late. I didn't know how he might react if you spoke to him on my behalf." Lizzie admitted, taking the blame herself, as was her habit. "He's been very sweet to me since then. I didn't mean to give you the idea I was in danger, sir."

"Any young lady would be frightened, living under these conditions." Jack responded with indulgence. "Donovan is adept at making others think he's on their side. He could be lulling you with false promises due to my presence. Once I'm gone, you'll be defenseless here."

Defenseless! Oh, that's rich. She's my wife, you idiot, not my enemy.

"Captain Rawlings," Elizabeth scolded. "Had I known you would come rushing in and attempt to persuade me to run away from my husband, I never would have sent that note."

"Why did you send it?"

"I was frightened by his behavior. I needed to know if he has any mental peculiarities. You assured me he does not. Did you lie when you assured me he isn't mad?"

Oh, that was quite big of you, Black Jack. Why didn't you just tell her I'm bloody well crazy? It would have suited your purposes and you could have whisked her away to your lair.

"No, but I've had a great deal of time to think about this since yesterday." Jack responded. "A man cannot fully know the workings of another man's mind. My dear lady, all I'm saying is that you needn't stay here out of loyalty to a man whom you've admitted frightens you. I could rent a modest house in Basseterre if you'd rather not make the long journey to England right away. I'm not as well situated as he is financially, but you could live in comfort under my protection. I care for you, very much, my dear Elizabeth. And I give you my solemn word that I would never expect anything from you in return."

You dirty, double-crossing bastard! Donovan held his breath, waiting for Elizabeth's response to the captain's scandalous offer.

"I-I-I-oh--oh." She was trying to speak, but in her agitation, she seemed unable to.

Donovan knew he should cut this off, for the sake of her health. First, he needed to hear her response to Jack's brazen offer of escape.

"Please try to understand." She whispered in a strained voice that was a strong portent of coming tears. "I encountered hell on that smuggler's ship. I couldn't have survived, not without Donovan's support. His great kindness is all that carried me through the darkest time of my life, captain. And now you're asking me to betray him—I cannot, I will not-- "

"I understand, you feel grateful to him for caring for you when you were at your weakest point. But, I don't intend to leave you trapped in another hell, one made of gratitude. I'm here for you, Elizabeth. I'm here to help you, in whatever capacity you require."

"No. You do not understand." Elizabeth returned with vehemence. "I love my husband. I could never leave him! I know I said yesterday that if we lived in England I *might have* gone to stay with my grandfather for a time--" She paused, sniffling as emotion overcame her.

Damn it, Jack. Take a hint. You did your gallant knight routine and she's refused you.

"If we lived in England—" Elizabeth went on after composing herself, "It would be a few day's journey by coach to my grandfather's estate and it would be an extended visit until Donovan decided he wished me to return. We are not in England, sir. I could never place myself at the mercy of rough sailors for the duration of a sea voyage again, not to mention that by doing something so reckless, I'd be destroying any chance of reconciliation. Donovan would never journey to England to ask me to come back to him. He'd cut his losses and divorce me."

Donovan strangled a pained gasp, impaled by her lack of confidence in his love for her.

"Thank you, for being concerned." She continued in voice heightened by strong agitation. "I've felt so alone here—and I never expected—oh, please--just go—"

Donovan heard footsteps, and then the door closing. He stood, pressing his forehead and his palms against the wall separating him from his beloved. He winced as soft sobs wafted through the open window. Pushing away from the wall, he turned with fists clenched, torn between the need to comfort Elizabeth and the desire to go after Rawlings.

The weeping intensified. He strode into the room and gathered her up into his arms.

"Why did you leave me alone with him? H-he—oh—it was awful!"

"You weren't alone. I was on the veranda the whole time. And please make note that should you ever leave me, I would cross hell to bring you back to me."

Elizabeth blanched, realizing he heard every word. "I'm sorry, my lord, I'm so sorry!"

"No!" He chastened. "I'm the one who should be sorry for making you unhappy, and I am, believe me, I am." Donovan hugged her, vowing to never allow her to suffer a moment's regret again for becoming his wife.

Once Lizzie was calm, he marched down to the salon. Jack was waiting for him.

"Well, are you going to call me out or not?" Jack asked with amusement.

"How dare you make an obscene offer to my wife. I should kill you."

"You heard the lady; *you* are her preferred poison."

Donovan gave the man his fist full in the face and then quickly brought one leg behind the captain's knees, disturbing his center of balance. Jack landed with a thud, flat on his back.

"No!" The captain held up a hand to his companions. "This is between him and me."

Rawlings rolled up from the floor. Donovan assumed a defensive stance as he waited for Rawlings to rush him. Jack did as he anticipated. He turned about, grasped Jack's arm and rolled the captain over his shoulder in a move he learned in the east. Jack's fall was interrupted by a low table. Table and vase shattered. Jack groaned, his hand went protectively to his backside.

"God's tooth!" One of Jack's men swore. "How'd he do that?"

Jack lurched to his feet. He offered Donovan a broad grin. "Oh, she's a fetching creature, to be sure." He shook his head, grinning hideously. "I didn't believe for a minute she'd accept an offer from an old salt like me. But I knew it would set your blood boiling. Makes the treasure seem that much more valuable when you think someone wants to take it from you, doesn't it?"

"You conniving squid's dick!" Donovan spat. "You set me up."

"Aye!" Jack snorted, thoroughly amused. "Let's not quibble about who set up whom. I knew you'd be hovering nearby, listening to our exchange. And just look at you!" Jack made an expansive sweep with his hand towards Donovan. "Frothing at the mouth like a rabid canine, ready to protect what's yours when twenty-four hours ago you weren't speaking to the poor girl. Damn it, you really don't deserve her."

Advancing upon him once more, the captain took another swing at Donovan.

Chapter Twenty Five

Donovan instructed her to remain in bed and relax.

Elizabeth couldn't relax. He said he'd be back in a few moments.

Surely he wouldn't hurt the captain. Rawlings was his longtime friend.

Oh, the poor captain. She threw off the covers and rose from the bed, pacing as she worried for Rawlings' well being. But--he asked her to become his—it was unthinkable!

"*I could provide for you to live comfortably under my protection.*" Her face burned as she recalled the illicit offer. How could she bear to face that man again?

She couldn't, she told herself as she limped about her husband's suite. She couldn't face the man again without wilting from humiliation.

And Donovan had heard everything. He overheard the indecent proposal, and there had been murder in her husband's eyes when he left.

Elizabeth raised a jittery hand to her strangled chest. She couldn't bear to see that man again, but she didn't wish him to be maimed or killed for his indiscretion, either. With Donovan's temper, the outcome could be none other.

Donovan sank down in the Queen Anne's chair in the salon, cradling his swelling cheek with a fresh piece of beef that was solicitously retrieved from the cellar by the new butler.

"Perhaps a drink would steady your nerves, my lord? I believe port is your preference."

He was coming to appreciate why Elizabeth found Giles appealing. The man was the epitome of decorous concern. "Yes. I would also have a word with you as the head of the household staff. I'm disappointed with the behavior of the maids in the courtyard yesterday."

The butler handed him the libation with a sour face. "No more so than myself, my lord."

"What would have happened if I had not been there to take care of Elizabeth?"

"I would have attended her, sir. When I was a lower footman in England, my employer's son suffered epilepsy. We were all given instruction in how to care for Master Percival. I shall instruct the staff to be more helpful in the future; unless you prefer to speak with them, sir?"

"No, you may deal with it." Donovan wanted to point out that his wife did not have epilepsy, the severity of her head injury merely brought on similar symptoms. It seemed a weak argument, even to him. Only time would determine if the seizures were transient, or if she was indeed cursed with the unfortunate illness. "Inform them I will not tolerate whispering about the incident. My lady does not remember it and I'll not have her hearing exaggerated accounts from the servants. It would frighten her unnecessarily."

"You may depend upon me, sir." The stolid servant bowed and withdrew.

Donovan held the cold steak against his cheek and sipped his port. He looked about the pristine salon that had been recently painted a deep, sunny yellow. Sunbeams streamed through the windows, banishing the prior gloom. Elizabeth was responsible for the pleasant changes. She exposed this old, neglected house to the healing rays of the sun, just as her presence in his life opened the cold, dark tomb that had been his heart.

And now, thanks to Jack's malicious meddling, his wife had the option of leaving him firmly planted in her mind. White hot anger suffused his blood once more. He set the steak aside and rose with determination. Duchamp wanted a position on land, did he?

Well, it appeared he had a job for the former king's assassin after all.

Elizabeth sank down at her husband's dressing table and stared into the looking glass. She sniffled and scrubbed at her watery eyes with the palms of her hands. Seeking distraction, she examined the items spread neatly before her. She loosened the cover of a tin of ointment that smelled of peppermint and lemon, sniffed it, and rubbed a small portion on the back of her hand. It brought a warm, soothing sensation on her skin. The black silk sheath Donovan wore when he pretended to be the count lay folded beside the ointment. She held it in front of her face and gazed at her reflection through the eyeholes.

The silk felt soft against her face. Cool and comforting. It smelled like Donovan, of spice and tobacco. She wouldn't mind his wearing it if he were charming instead of boorish beneath it. Elizabeth imagined him playing a highwayman for her amusement, stealing kisses from her and threatening to steal much more once he spirited her away to his lair.

She banished the fantasy with a weary sigh. Playful and Donovan didn't combine easily in her mind. Somber, hard, demanding, those were words that described him more accurately.

Dropping the mask, she opened a velvet case containing a pair of silver handled razors. She traced the glistening edge of one with a fingertip. *Would he forgive me if he knew?*

If there were to be a true reconciliation between them she must confess her duplicity and face the consequences. Perhaps--if she were careful to confess only the essentials to Donovan and avoid the particulars, she might escape unscathed. The bare truth remained that she was a maid. As his wife, that reality had to be breached at some point. There was no need for him to know the rest.

Elizabeth pressed a fist to her lips. Her chest burned and her throat ached. She had to be careful. Any chance of forgiveness would be lost if he knew what took place in that dark hold. He assumed she'd been raped. She did not correct his assumption. It was the same as lying, for it was within her power to alleviate his concern and she chose to remain silent.

"Oh you stupid, reckless girl!" She told her reflection.

How could she tell him? Her husband possessed some rather lofty ideas about honor. He might not be able to forgive her. He could divorce her. Then again, he might feel forced to keep her out of duty but never look kindly upon her again. The bleak prospect of enduring Donovan's contempt for the rest of her days was unbearable. She endured one man's smoldering hatred as a child, having little choice to do otherwise.

She would not endure it again as an adult. She'd run away.

Oh, but to where? She was in a foreign place, devoid of friends, family or monetary support. She'd be forced to accept the type of protection Captain Rawlings offered. She'd be at the mercy of feckless men who would promise no future beyond her present ability to please them. It was a frightening, desolate future. She couldn't bear being thrust so low, beneath the regard of all decent society forever. She covered her face with her hands as she imagined being forced to entertain the most revolting men and submit to disgusting acts to please them.

"Elizabeth?" Large, familiar hands circled her shoulders. "What is wrong?"

Mortified by the grim prospect before her and the cruel images conjured by her misery, Elizabeth lifted her head to stare at her sorry reflection in the mirror. Dark stains shadowed watery, swollen eyes. Her nose was red and her unbound hair was tangled from anxiously winding her fingers through it. "Nothing, sir." She swiped at her eyes and reached for the ivory brush with the intention of busying herself with it.

"Ah, my mistake." Donovan's sarcasm sliced through her as he snatched the brush from her before she could attempt to repair her appearance. "Where is your maid?"

"I cannot say. S-she often disappears at this t-time."

Donovan's brow furrowed, but he refrained from commenting. He didn't need to.

"You will not fire her!" Elizabeth challenged as she held his gaze in the mirror.

"I can, and I will." He replied, his eyes narrowing. "A lady's maid does not wander off without her mistress' permission. Her duty is to attend you at all times unless given leave to take an afternoon for herself."

Elizabeth made a noise in her throat, quelling her fury. She had little cause to champion Chloe when she herself had much to answer for. She sucked in her breath, resolving to be meek in her lord's presence and not quarrelsome, for once. "She's my only friend here."

The quiet fury in his features made her insides twist into an uncomfortable knot. She nibbled on her lower lip, aching to defend Chloe, to demand that she stay, yet, fearful that her own standing with the man behind her was severely weakened due to their continuing estrangement. She must be careful. Years with Fletcher had taught her the virtue of biding her time until the atmosphere proved favorable for bargaining with the devil. She had to calm herself and find a reasonable argument for keeping Chloe, avoid the temptation to rush into the fray, matching her fury with his and ultimately losing the battle in the resulting clash of wills.

She inhaled sharply, attempting to find calm amid the storm of frantic emotions churning within. *Stay calm, don't plead—don't beg—and for heaven's sake, don't cry!*

"What of Tabby?" He asked, in response to her statement about the scarcity of friends here. Donovan's voice was taut, as if he too, were struggling to contain his frustration. "My mother is very fond of her house woman at Belle Reve plantation. They had tea on the back porch every afternoon when I was a boy. Tabby hasn't been unpleasant to you, I hope?"

Elizabeth rolled her lips and studied her bruised wrist, avoiding the piercing blue eyes studying her in the looking glass as she refused to give the expected response. She tried to befriend the sour woman, but Tabby had remained frosty in her dealings with her mistress. Taking her cue from the master, Elizabeth assumed.

"I see." He murmured and did not press further. "Why are you not in bed? Did you forget our discussion earlier about resting?"

"No sir." *Oh, Bollocks.* she'd angered him already, and there was still such news to be delivered. "I got up to use the chair." She lied, gesturing to the privy chair in the corner.

He released a strangled sigh and his look told her he knew she wasn't telling the truth.

It was a habit she fell into when he was irritated, she realized. She lied easily--too easily--to appease him, a trait learned early on when dealing with a drunken stepfather who searched for any excuse to strike those about him. Donovan wasn't her stepfather. There was no need for quick lies to appease his ire. He deserved an honest wife—if he decided to keep her, that is.

"I was frightened, my lord." She amended in a subdued tone laced with respect. "You seemed angry when you left me. I imagined terrible things happening below the stairs." She lifted her gaze to meet his in the mirror, truly looking at him for the first time since he'd entered his chamber. The bright red swelling of his cheek caught her attention. "Oh—you're hurt!" She turned about to face him. "Did you fight with the captain?"

"We had a scuffle and he left." With austerity, he lifted her hand, turned it and kissed the center of her palm. A warmth moved up Elizabeth's arm and settled over her heart. She stared at him, astonished by his tenderness.

Donovan studied his wife's reflection as he stood behind her. It was not the portrait of a joyful bride reflecting back at him. She was too pale. The shadows beneath her eyes screamed exhaustion. She appeared broken, crushed by grief, weighted down with regret.

He cupped her slim shoulders and began massaging the rigid muscles. "You mustn't allow Jack's ill behavior to upset you. Had I known he would offend your tender sensibilities with his obscene ramblings, I would not have allowed the meeting."

"I didn't ask him to interfere." She spoke in a whisper, her voice stretched tight as she peeked cautiously at his reflection in the mirror before dropping her gaze again. "Honestly, I had no idea he would scheme against you, my lord."

"Hush, my sweet. You are not responsible for the delusions of a middle-aged man. We will speak no more of it." He insisted, as he took up the brush and began to work through her tangled tresses in an attempt to soothe her. She remained silent beneath his ministrations, her mind engaged in some formula as she pondered a world beyond her image in the glass.

"I've been thinking." He began, "I could rent a place in Basseterre. That way, whenever you're feeling the need for some diversion in town, you can stay in the city. Basseterre is not like London, but there are a few shops—"

She turned about to gaze up at him directly, her awe apparent. "You would do that? You would allow me to leave the island when I wish?"

"You're hardly my prisoner here, my dear." He managed in a bland tone that did not betray the agony piercing his heart. Perhaps she did wish to leave him after all.

With a perplexed look, she turned about and took to staring at the mirror as if she beheld something disturbing beyond the silvered glass.

Once he had the tangles under control, he set the brush aside and began plaiting the silky strands of burnished copper. As he hoped, the familiar routine seemed to calm her. He'd attended her thus on the ship when she'd been ill. It was a task he looked forward to each night as it was a form of intimacy between them. His task done, he secured the end of the braid with a ribbon. "There. Now back to bed with you, my sweet. You look like the last rose of summer. And if I'm not mistaken, I see a headache looming on the horizon."

"Everything hurts today."

"I don't doubt it, little one." Considering the bruises marring her tender body he was surprised she was able to get out of bed, as the act of moving must cause immense pain. He cupped her shoulders as he stood behind her and gazed at her reflection before them. "I believe a dose of Laudanum may be just the thing."

"Wait." She protested, placing a hand on his arm as he bent and began lifting her with the intention of carrying her back to the bed. "I have unpleasant news to tell you, sir. And when all is finished, you may yet be relieved that the captain is willing to take me off your hands forever."

Donovan's mind went still, his heart contracted in a painful knot as fear solidified.

Had his wife decided she did not wish to remain with him after all, thanks to Jack's unwarranted interference?

"Whatever it is, I'm sure you can tell me lying down."

Chapter Twenty Six

Elizabeth had it all worked out in her head, but as she looked at her husband's face, she couldn't make the words come forth. Donovan lifted her easily and carried her to the bed.

He paced to the end of the bed, granting her the polite distance she needed to proceed. He stood framed between the green curtained bed-posts, hands clasped behind his back and a stoic expression on his face as if bracing to receive bad news.

Well, it wasn't good news she had to tell him.

"Do you wish to leave me?" He asked when she remained silent for several moments.

"No!" Elizabeth couldn't understand this obsession he seemed to have about her leaving him. "I never told the captain that. *He* decided it was what I wanted, when nothing could be further from the truth."

Donovan closed his eyes and cleared his throat stridently, as if he had something lodged there. He leaned forward to brace his hands on the bed post. Opening his eyes, he met her startled gaze with a relieved smile. "What could possibly be wrong, my sweet?"

"No, stay back." She held up her hands. "What I have to confess is difficult, my lord. I need assurance you will do me no harm when all is finished."

His eyes widened. He opened his mouth to chide her, but seemed to think better of it. With a nod, he returned to the foot of the bed, arms crossed akimbo and waited.

There was no easy way to tell it, yet tell it she must. She loved this man, but love could not flourish alongside deceit. She hugged a pillow to her as malicious serpents twisted and writhed inside her belly and squeezed around her heart. Focusing on the canopy above, she forced the words out. "The smugglers didn't rape me, I'm still a maid. I know it was wicked of me not to tell you—I couldn't--I didn't know you back then and I-I was so . . . *afraid!*"

214

Rallying her courage, she let her eyes dip beneath the canopy to gauge his response.

Donovan was no longer there. He was coming towards her.

"No—no, you promised not to hurt me." She screeched, scuttling back against the headboard. She drew her knees against her chest and crossed her arms about her head in hope of warding off the worst of the blows.

None came. She shuddered and listened to the deafening sound of her heart.

"Elizabeth." Donovan knelt on the bed. "My sweet girl." That voice became velvet. He grasped her wrists, and uncrossed her arms. His hands slid over her wrists to take her hands in a firm grip. "Listen to me, listen carefully. What happened is not your fault."

Blood rushed through her temples. She willed herself to not tremble, to not give in to the panic clawing through her. It was no use, her limbs betrayed her, and surely he could hear her heart pounding out the weighty cadence of an executioner's drum.

Seconds marched into an uncertain eternity as they stared at one another.

"Come, love, what's this?" He cocked his head, appearing confounded. "After all we've come through together, how can you believe I would hurt you?"

"My stepfather—"

He dropped her hands and cradled her face in his palms. "I am not Fletcher, my love."

Elizabeth nodded and whimpered indistinctly.

"When I touch you, it will only be with love." Donovan pulled her closer. His arms enveloped her, forming a firm barricade against flight. He just held her, remaining quiet and resolute as she sat across his knees.

What was wrong with her? She never gave in to tears. Stupid, useless things. They were a sign of weakness. And yet, she couldn't seem to stop this abominable weeping.

Donovan went on making soft sounds that gradually became words as the haze of fear lifted from her. "So you see, darlin', there's no need to concoct fanciful tales."

He didn't believe her? "I'm not lying! I'm still a maid. Nothing happened on that ship—"

"Captain Sully told me he hurt you. He confessed everything before I killed him."

"*He lied!*" Elizabeth insisted, now well beyond panic. She struggled to be released, but he was not of mind to grant her desire. "He forbade his crew to touch me." She gave a shrill laugh. "He shot one of them—and h-he took me down to the hold. He *tried* to rape me—my purge came earlier that night—he was disgusted— nothing happened, I tell you; *nothing!*"

"Lizzie, don't do this." He insisted sternly. "It doesn't matter what happened."

"It's the truth. You're a doctor. Examine me. I wasn't raped— you must believe me."

"I said stop this." Donovan insisted, using a sharper tone. "You'll bring on another seizure. You must lie down and remain calm."

She had little choice. He was forcing her to lie on the bed even as he spoke.

Elizabeth moaned, the pain of her injuries coming alive as she sank back on the pillows.

Donovan cursed. He rose, disappeared behind the dressing screen but returned quickly, holding out a glass to her. The Laudanum he'd promised earlier when he believed she might be nursing a headache.

She was falling apart. She knew it, and so did he.

He was trying to help her in the only way he knew, with his strange potions and elixirs.

"Drink this. It will calm you. Then we'll talk. We'll reason it all out, together."

Elizabeth didn't want him to help her *reason it out*. She needed him to believe nothing happened to her on that ship. If she could convince him, perhaps she could believe it herself.

She was tired, so very tired. She wanted it all to go away; the nightmares, the guilt, the horror, and the shame. Elizabeth took the glass from him. She swallowed the bitter medicine, now well acquainted with the taste of numbed forgetfulness.

216

The poor girl trembled so Donovan feared she would slip into convulsions. He took the glass from her and set it on the table.

"Why won't you believe me?" She looked up at him with liquid anguish.

"You must not excite yourself so. You need to calm down."

"I need you to be-believe nothing happened to me on that ship!"

Her stammering belied her statement. Something was not right in this, but he couldn't make it out. He sat on the bed. Lizzie was reclining on her back. Knowing her luscious derriere was bruised, as were her posterior limbs, he guided her to curl onto her side to lessen her discomfort. She lay facing him, looking up at him with such misery he could barely stand it.

"I deceived you—hiccup—I-I know it was w-wicked. If you cannot f-forgive me—hiccup—I'll understand, I'll go away." Her fervor was waning as the sedative did its work.

"Let's have no more talk of leaving." He whispered as he moved his hand along her spine in steady manner. "I love you, regardless of what did or did not happen during your abduction."

He gazed out the veranda doors as he tried to puzzle it out. Why did she persist with this fractured tale? It wasn't like her to contrive fanciful stories or behave in such an emotional manner. His Lizzie had always been a serious, sensible young lady. She cried once during the voyage that he recalled; *once*—after surviving unimaginable horrors that would send an octogenarian in to hysterics. If anyone deserved a good cry it was Lizzie, yet each time the tears threatened, she stubbornly refused to give in to their healing catharsis.

Elizabeth did not cry. The fact slowly permeated his anxious mind.

Yet, she cried easily and frequently in recent days-- *that was cause for alarm.*

He expected tears and melancholy after her rescue. When the tears didn't come, he worried over their absence but concluded her head injury must be the reason. Her cognitive abilities had been severely compromised for weeks afterward, bringing him to deduce that she might not be able to fully recall or comprehend the events of her abduction.

As her mind healed, she could be experiencing a delayed melancholy. That, coupled with their estrangement and her new surroundings . . .

"Forgive me." Elizabeth's opiate laden voice jerked him back to the present. He pulled his gaze from the open veranda to the girl on the bed. "Please, I can't endure your anger . . ."

"Honey, I am not angry with you." The uneasiness that plagued him last night returned. Did she think he despised her for what happened? Only a cad would be so callous and unfeeling.

Christ, this was what Gareth tried to warn him about in the garden last week. *"Every time you cross paths, her heart cries out for a kind word from you, for love and acceptance—for forgiveness for what she perceives as her failing in your eyes."*

Gareth saw what he couldn't see. While he remained distant, Lizzie convinced herself it was because he despised her for having been abused by her captors.

"I don't deserve your kindness. Please, don't hate me." Lizzie pleaded last night.

And Jack had sized up the situation quickly; *"I'll not look the other way when a woman I care for is being subjected to intolerable cruelty."*

There it was, the true reason his longtime friend turned against him. The reason his uncle reproached him. They saw what he couldn't see. His wife was staggering beneath a load of guilt and shame that should never have been her portion.

His eyes burned. His throat closed up. Donovan turned away and held his head in his hands, unable to think or breathe as the full weight of his carelessness settled upon him.

"Why do I feel as if I'm being punished?" He bit into his knuckles as Lizzie's words yesterday flayed his conscience with fresh meaning. *"All you ever do is snarl at me . . . You act as if you can't stand me—as if you regret marrying me!"*

Christ, and in her state of mind, she would believe it was her own fault for it all.

He turned back to her, determined to remove the cruel barb lodged in her heart.

Lizzie was asleep. She was out cold and would be for hours, as he'd given her a strong dose of Laudanum.

Donovan paced the room aimlessly. He moved out onto the veranda as the afternoon stretched on without mercy. He stood at the balcony, his eye on turquoise seas beyond the estate.

The soft trill of delight caught his attention. He shifted his gaze to the gardens below. A woman's laughter was answered by a resonant baritone he knew well. He couldn't see the couple but it was apparent Gareth was entertaining some female in the secluded gardens. He watched, hoping for a glimpse of his uncle's mysterious companion.

A woman darted out from behind a marble statue, giggling as her lover gave pursuit. It was Chloe Ramirez, Elizabeth's maid. That explained her mysterious absences in the afternoon.

Gareth caught Chloe in his arms, although she didn't make it hard for him. Quite the opposite, she wanted to be caught. They engaged in an earthy kiss. Donovan hunched over the rail, his wrists crossed as he studied the pair below. Chloe was a servant, not just any servant, but Elizabeth's favorite. Perhaps he'd better have a talk with Gareth. Lizzie would never forgive him if her maid were taken advantage of by his uncle and he did nothing to dissuade the man.

Then again, a little romance could be just what his uncle needed. A woman to provide for and the promise of a family could be the making of Gareth. It might stir him a little and make him take an interest in the estate he himself garnered a living from.

Yes, Donovan thought, *Chloe could be just the tonic Gareth needed.*

How could he encourage the relationship without overtly appearing to be doing so? He could raise Chloe's status. As a paid companion instead of a maid, Chloe would be on a little more equal footing with Gareth, clearing the way for a proper courtship to blossom. Chloe's father, the youngest son of a noble Spanish family, had been the steward here some years ago. Her mother had been the man's slave mistress who died giving birth to Chloe. Juan Ramirez fairly doted on his child by all accounts. When the

Spaniard died, Donovan's grandfather callously sent the girl to the slave compound to live with her maternal grandmother instead of taking her in as his ward and notifying Ramirez' relatives in Spain of the child's existence, which would have been the honorable thing to do.

Alas, his grandfather was remembered for his peccadilloes, not for decency and kindness.

Turning away from the clandestine lovers, he went inside.

The sun moved lower in the sky. Lizzie slept. Donovan brooded.

Desperate for some task lest he go mad with waiting, he summoned the butler for a private interview. He began by informing the man of his decision regarding Chloe, and directed him to attend the necessary details. He asked Giles' advice on a suitable replacement for a lady's maid. Upon receiving it, he told the butler he must assume responsibility to train the new maid in the absence of a competent housekeeper. The butler struggled to hide his shock at such a bald assessment, obviously not accustomed to plain speaking from his American employer.

Donovan paused to rein in his anger. It had been a mistake trying to pass Tabby off as a housekeeper with his wife. She'd been his grandfather's live in mistress for twenty years. He allowed Tabby to remain after his grandfather's death as she was old with no family or means of support. She looked after the stable lads, did laundry, kept the old cook company, and ordered supplies from Basseterre. The arrangement worked for both; an old tart and a bachelor. He assumed the woman would treat his new wife with respect. Such had not been the case.

He shared his concerns regarding the 'housekeeper' with Giles, with the admonition that he expected the man to be his eyes and ears in that quarter and report any indiscretion on Tabby's part immediately.

The butler stood with hands clasped behind his back. He groaned like an old bulldog and then said, "I discovered something disturbing, sir, but as her ladyship is ill and you are distracted with her care, I thought it prudent to postpone my report until a more opportune time." He glanced at the form on the bed, and back at Donovan, his face a study in sorrow.

Seated next to the bed with his booted calf balanced across his knee, Donovan gave an exasperated hiss. "She's sedated. She can't hear a word. Out with it, man!"

"My lord, you are being slowly and efficiently robbed by that wretched woman."

"*What!*" Donovan thundered, dropping his foot to the floor. "Explain yourself."

Giles started. His gaze darted to the bed. Seeing the mistress was unmoved by the master's loud outburst, he ventured further in a low voice. "I thought it prudent to acquaint myself with the cost of maintaining the household, given my new position. I discovered the sums in the household expense ledgers have been fixed. It appears you have been feeding a full staff of servants here for the past four years, sir. I believe Miss Wilkes pocketed the difference and has managed to put away a tidy sum at your expense."

Half an hour later, Donovan sat at his desk in his laboratory. Giles stood to his right, directing him to the suspicious entries in the ledger. There it was, in Tabby's hand, the inflated supply bill from Basseterre for each month, the dry goods exaggerated beyond what was needed to feed the two gentleman, three servants and three stable boys residing on the estate before Donovan's marriage. He summoned Tabby and asked her to explain.

Her reply was fraught with a rancid bitterness she'd kept hidden over the years. "I played his twisted games of dominance and submission. He promised to make me his wife. I gave that man twenty years of my life. He didn't leave me a damned shilling—"

"Whatever promises my grandfather made to you in the throes of passion are of no concern to me. I repeat, why have you stolen money from me, Madame?"

"You're his heir. It's all the same to me." She responded tartly. "I should be mistress here, not that pathetic twit upstairs. She needs a keeper and a locked room if you ask me."

Donovan had never hit a woman in his life. He was dangerously close to it now. With Giles and Pearl beside him, he struggled to contain his fury with the shameless, ungrateful tart. "Giles, have Duchamp and O'Leary escort Miss Wilkes to her room to pack her things and then take her to Basseterre. And you,

Miss Wilkes, had best hope some pox ridden sailor will take you in, because you are no longer welcome under this roof."

Donovan returned to his suite. He resumed his vigil near the bed. The silence was maddening. He cursed himself for his eagerness in giving Lizzie Laudanum.

Drumming his fingers on his upraised knee, he went over the bizarre conversation with Lizzie before she fell asleep. Why was she desperate to make him believe she was untouched?

Why now? Her abuse was a long established fact between them.

There was one way to determine the truth, by examining her, as she suggested. Doing so when she was unconscious would prevent further upset when his findings countered her outlandish claim about being a virgin.

A short time later, Donovan sank into the chair again, greatly perplexed.

Lizzie was telling him the truth. Her maidenhead was still intact.

"*I shagged the wench!*" Captain Sully had insisted.

Elizabeth claimed her menstrual flow repulsed her attacker.

Her story could be true. The difficulty came as he considered her profound fear of intimacy. Her terror was not contrived. She had merely to look at his groin and a paralyzing fear claimed her features. That reaction was too severe for a maid unacquainted with male passion.

He gazed at his sleeping angel, dread gnawing at his insides as he tried to resolve her fear of intimacy with the physical evidence of her inexperience. He could not reconcile the two facts. Not without coming to a disturbing conclusion: something happened to this girl on that ship. Something that left no visible damage, yet something so perverse she felt guilt over it and feared the discovery of said act would damn her in his eyes forever.

Donovan sat forward in the chair and held his head in his hands, disturbed the cruel workings of his own mind as he considered the ways a man might pleasure himself with a maid and leave no evidence of his intrusion. "Oh, you sick son-of-a-bitch!"

Impulsively, he stood and was bending over his wife. "Elizabeth, wake up. I need to ask you something." His tone was brusque. He regretted it instantly.

She stirred at his insistence. Lethargic from the opiates, she gazed up at him with confusion. That was good, he reasoned. She'd never be able to confess the truth without its influence. And it might prevent her from remembering this conversation come morning.

"Captain Sully didn't interfere with you in the usual way, did he?" Donovan was careful to keep his tone light, and coaxing.

"N-n-no . . ."

"But he did hurt you. In a perverse, wretched manner, didn't he?" The slight dilation of her pupils confirmed his suspicions. "Tell me what he did to you."

"I can't. He said you'd despise me if you knew. He said you'd cast me aside in disgust."

"He lied to you." Donovan insisted. "I love you, Elizabeth. Nothing will change that. I promise. Tell me what that man did to you so I can help you through the pain."

Elizabeth's hands flew up to cover her mouth. She let out a tortured whimper.

He went cold with fury as she gazed up at him with unshed tears, the implication clear; the perverted swine had defiled her sweet mouth.

"My poor little girl!" Donovan embraced her as that whimper became a wail of anguish.

Chapter Twenty Seven

"Kieran, my boy! Still so glum? I have something to cheer you." Barnaby glided into the shop, wielding a newspaper triumphantly. He seemed pleased after the weekly guild meeting of shopkeepers and merchants. The meetings usually left the man in a sour mood.

Kieran set down the pestle. "What is it, a potential client for the Midnight Bell?"

"Something better." Barnaby danced a little jig around the shop, waving the folded paper in the air like wizard's wand. "It's a miracle, my boy."

Barnaby routinely scanned the obituaries for the best customers, the rich who would pay dearly to keep an angry relative from coming back to bother them with unfinished business. He read the death notices just as fastidiously as the society pages, as the old man liked to speculate on the scandals inferred in the bland reports of domestic occurrences.

"Someone died and left you his plantation?" Kieran was amused at the old man's antics.

"Not me. This concerns you. Look." He placed the paper on the counter. Sure enough, it was opened to the society page. "Read it aloud." The old man tapped the paper insistently. "Third one down, in the marriage column."

"Dr. Donovan O'Rourke Beaumont, Count Rochembeau, owner of Ravencrest Plantation recently returned from England with a bride. The new Countess du Rochembeau, formerly Miss Elizabeth O'Flaherty," Kieran paused, giving Barnaby a significant look.

"Read on!" Barnaby insisted. "It gets better."

"Formerly Miss Elizabeth O'Flaherty, is the *daughter* of the late Viscount Shawn O'Flaherty of County Galway, Ireland and Angela Wentworth-O'Flaherty-Fletcher of England, also deceased. The new Mrs. Beaumont is the maternal grand-daughter of James R. Wentworth, the ninth Earl of Greystowe. Master Michael

Fletcher, Lady Beaumont's younger brother, heir to the Wentworth title and fortune, resides with their grandfather, Lord Greystowe in England."

"Sit, lad." The old man coaxed, pulling him toward the stool.

"Fletcher said mama died in childbirth."

"He was hardly telling the truth, was he?" Barnaby shrugged out of his coat and crossed his arms about himself. "Apparently your mother lived long enough to have two children after you were sold on the docks."

Kieran stared at the paper while Barnaby paced about him with distraction.

Pausing in his pacing, the grey eyes fixed on him with excitement. "Kieran, my boy, do you realize what this means? You are the eldest grandson of Lord Greystowe. By the laws of primogeniture, you should be the next Earl of Greystowe, not Michael Fletcher."

Barnaby's arrogant presumption revealed another sobering implication. "Do you think this is why Captain Fletcher sold me as an indenture and had me shipped to the Indies?"

Barnaby gave a grave nod. "Once you were out of the way, all he had to do was produce a son with your mother, a son who would inherit Lord Greystowe's title and fortune in your place. Your sister would pose little threat to Fletcher's schemes. That is, until she was old enough to marry and produce a son that might threaten his claim." The apothecary made a sour face and gestured at the society page. "You know how these things become twisted when people have fortunes to bestow. Affections change. Promises settled upon one heir can be revoked in favor of a more promising one."

"You make it sound like a chess game; rooks blocking knights to steal the queen."

"Ah." Barnaby nodded, fingering his snowy goatee. "When money is involved, you'd be surprised at how often family interactions mimic the movements of a chessboard."

"I have to go to her. I have to see her." Kieran rose, as the sense of urgency he'd felt earlier returned.

"You should write to her first." Barnaby placed a hand on Kieran's arm to restrain him. "One does not simply sail across the bay to Ravencrest and knock on the front door. Our count does not welcome visitors. It's invitation only. Those who tried when he first came were driven off--at gunpoint."

"She's my sister. And she's suffering. I can't wait for an invitation to Ravencrest."

******

Elizabeth recalled little after the captain left. She recalled trying to tell Donovan the truth and then being given a strong sedative that made her sleep until morning.

She experienced a wondrous dream under the opiate's sway. Sheila would say she'd been visited by the fairy folk while she slept. She had been lying on a bed of soft moss in a dark forest. A dim light nearby allowed her to make out tree trunks laden with verdant foliage. She wasn't afraid to be in the forest alone at night. The Oak King was guarding her. Oddly, the ancient lord of the woodlands looked just like her husband. In the dream Donovan possessed arched brows, luminous eyes and quick, unnatural movements of one from the magical realm.

The dream was disjointed. One moment, she was floating on a feather, buoyed up on a breeze and the next she was falling from the sky, sinking into that incredibly soft, mossy bed. The Celtic god of the forests had worked some enchantment over her. At one point, he was weeping as he held her close and pledged his love to her.

Her insides grew warm as she recalled the tender-sweet dream. She wished she could go to sleep and return to that secret glen and be in the arms of her fairy lover who looked so much like Donovan. She rubbed the sleep from her eyes and with it the absurdity; men like Donovan didn't become spoony over a woman!

It was a hallucination, conjured by loneliness, longing and a heavy dose of Laudanum.

Presently, Elizabeth was reclining on several plump pillows in her husband's bed with a breakfast tray across her lap. Puck was beside her, purring, and busily grooming his face after enjoying his breakfast of chopped meat and a saucer of milk.

Chloe was sitting in the chair next to the bed, declaring her gratitude for being raised to the position of lady's companion. Elizabeth listened with bewildered apathy as she tried to banish the cobwebs in her head with a bracing cup of tea. Chloe's advancement was news to her. Apparently Donovan made the decision yesterday, while she was sleeping. It seemed a great deal happened while she was asleep these days. Elizabeth sipped her tea, hoping to make it out later.

"And that old Tabby cat has been dismissed!" Chloe informed her brightly.

"Tabby's been let go?" She asked, uncertain she'd heard correctly.

"It happened while we were all in the servant's hall last night, just finishing our dinner. Duchamp and O'Leary marched her out the back kitchen door, each holding an arm."

"Why?"

The doe eyes sharpened. "She was stealing from his lordship. Fudging the household accounts, for years, apparently! Giles wouldn't say a word, but I asked Mr. O'Donovan about it this morning—oh, he is such a handsome man." Chloe waved her hand about as she spoke with her usual animation. "We had breakfast in the dining room, just the two of us. Gareth said--"

Chloe placed a hand over her mouth and giggled as she looked askance at Elizabeth.

"*Mr. O'Donovan*," She corrected, "Said we must not use the breakfast room until you are recovered as you are responsible 'for its rescue from darkness, dust and neglect'. Oooh, that man has the soul of a poet!" She placed a hand on her breast dramatically, as if ready to swoon.

Elizabeth stretched, attempting to shake off this annoying languor. She usually didn't mind Chloe's chattiness. Today, it was just too much to keep up with the exuberant woman. She longed for silence with her tea. She yearned for her husband's quiet, soothing presence.

Where was Donovan? More importantly, what might his mood be after the upset she'd caused him with the captain? She searched the forest green canopy above, uncertain how her lord might be feeling toward her after such high dramatics. A queer impression made her do a quick review of the four solid oak bedposts festooned with luxuriant green curtains. Her fingers brushed the velvet coverlet that could easily be mistaken for a bed of moss.

Oh, Bollocks.! The bed bore an uncanny resemblance to the fairy bower in her dream. And her 'enchanted lover' looked too much like Donovan to be a coincidence— *and hadn't the lord of the woodlands been demanding to know her deepest, most disgusting secret?*

Sunshine was streaming in the open windows. A refreshing sea breeze wafted in from the veranda doors. The birds were singing. Everything appeared just as it should be, and yet, Elizabeth knew *everything* had changed in the past hours.

"Where is my lord?" She asked when Chloe paused in her nattering. "Did he seem angry? Did he tell you where he was going, or when he would return?" Her hand trembled. She set the teacup on the tray before she doused herself with the tepid liquid.

"I forgot to tell you, he made Mr. Duchamp the steward of the estates to replace Mr. O'Rourke. He was meeting with Duchamp at ten this morning. He said that he was going to speak to Alice after that. She is to be your new maid. I am so relieved, Madame. It would be a shame if Sally were given that position. She's lazy and a terrible gossip."

"Yes—but--did my lord seem unduly upset when you spoke to him?"

"Well, he was not our sunny O'Rourke, if that's what you mean. His lordship left strict orders that you must not become distressed and agitate your poor nerves. 'She needs rest and quiet', he said to me." Chloe mimicked the count's stern, deep voice. "He was most adamant about that. Oh, is this not the most wonderful of news, Madame?" Chloe clutched Elizabeth's hand, jubilant and irritatingly pleased.

Elizabeth blinked. What was so wonderful about her husband believing she was a pathetic twit needing to be coddled by the household staff?

"Is it not wonderful that I am to be your lady?" Chloe clarified, swinging their clasped hands as she gushed on with unspoiled delight. "I've been given a room on this floor instead of the servant's quarters, directly across from Mr. O'Donovan's room. It overlooks the back courtyard and the stables, but I don't mind. It's a lovely room. And I'm to have new gowns made, suitable for my position and am to be called *Miss Ramirez* by everyone. Papa would be pleased, he had hoped to take me to Cadiz once I was of an age and present me . . ."

Chloe kept blathering on about her father's family in Spain, oblivious to her lady's distress. Where was Donovan? She needed to feel his arms about her. She needed to hear his voice assuring her once more that he loved her and nothing could ever change his love, just as he promised so sweetly last night—in that peculiar . . . *dream*?

"Madame, you're shivering. Are you cold?" Chloe removed the uneaten tray from Elizabeth's lap and tugged the blankets up about her bosom. "What is wrong?"

"I'm afraid. What am I going to do?"

"You are safe in his lordship's room. The spirit will not attack you here."

"The spirit?" Elizabeth gasped, having forgotten about her mother's harassment in her distress over Donovan's absence. Mama's behavior was becoming more malevolent with each encounter. Perhaps Chloe was right; Mama wouldn't trouble her with Donovan nearby.

"Do not be frightened, Madame. I will make a charm of protection for you. I know plenty of spells for warding off evil spirits. My grandmother taught me--"

"What the devil is going on?" A voice boomed like cannon-fire from the opened veranda doors. "I left you with the admonition that my lady is not to be upset for any reason."

"My lord!" Chloe dropped Elizabeth's hand and backed away from the bed. "I-I tried to talk only of cheerful things. Still, she became upset. I do not know why. I think she is frightened by her illness, yes, is that not so, Madame?" Chloe's eyes were beggars, silently imploring Elizabeth to agree with her.

Elizabeth stared at the woman, not sure why Chloe should feel threatened by Donovan's appearance. And then it came to her; being overheard in a conversation about magic. Chloe didn't know that Donovan did not believe in magic or fear those who claimed to practice it.

"C-Chloe didn't upset me!" She stammered, attempting to deflect his ire from her friend. "I-I-I'm s-s-sorry—I-I-I" *Oh, Bollocks.! Why was it so difficult to form words?*

"Don't apologize, my sweet." Donovan's tone softened as he addressed her. "You've done nothing that warrants an apology."

Elizabeth nodded. His words held a deeper meaning than the woman between them could know. Her face burned. She didn't think she'd ever be able to look at him without turning scarlet.

"Chloe, you may go, for now." Donovan addressed the maid. "Come back in an hour."

Elizabeth studied her hands and choked on the pain rising in her throat. She didn't want to be alone with him. Not now. Whatever could she say? And there were those penetrating eyes to contend with, eyes that seemed to look right through her. *He knew.* He knew she was tainted.

"How are you today?" Donovan's strangely cheerful voice invaded her panic.

Elizabeth didn't answer. She kept looking at her lap. Puck stood, stretched, and came to stand on her legs. She stroked the tabby's back, desperate for distraction to avoid meeting that pale blue gaze. Puck turned about beneath her hand, raising his rump higher beneath her attentions and me-owing his pleasure.

The dark figure at the edge of her vision moved closer. Puck stiffened, and poised himself to investigate the huge bouquet of tropical flowers edging beneath Elizabeth's downcast gaze. "I found these outside my laboratory. They're Frangipani, a local bloom."

The kitten rose on tiptoes and sniffed reverently, as if the offering were meant for him.

The petals were a deep, vibrant pink. "They're beautiful. I'm sure Puck will enjoy shredding them." She whispered, her voice having deepened with pain. "I'm sorry about yesterday. I didn't mean to cause so much trouble, sir, I honestly didn't think the captain—"

Two long, lean fingers covered her lips. "Don't apologize. And don't call me sir. You know I despise such formality from you."

Thus corrected, she sat holding the flowers, wishing she could wilt into the mattress.

"Sweet Lizzie." Donovan sank down before her on the bed and bracketed her face with his big hands. "You remember last night, don't you? I hoped you wouldn't. Don't do this. Don't torment yourself over something you couldn't control." He paused, and when he spoke again, his voice warbled with emotion. "My precious girl, that man raped you—"

"No--I told you--*he didn't*. He didn't rape me. I'm still— a maid!" A flush of hot tears made her world blur. And thus she was spared the agony of looking into the pale, penetrating blue eyes of the man she loved, eyes that knew her most wretched secret.

"He raped you." Donovan insisted. "He forced himself on you against your will, the same as if he'd forced himself on you in the traditional manner."

"You weren't supposed to know!" She squeaked, as her throat clogged up with thick, hot, mortifying emotion. "No one was ever supposed to know."

"I needed to know. And you needed to tell me." Donovan pulled her against him. He hugged her fiercely. His hand guided her head to rest in the familiar nook beneath his chin. "We'll get through this, my love. I promise. We'll get through this, together."

Donovan steeled himself against the searing pain in his heart as her anguished cries filled the room. The tears were necessary to bring healing, just as one needed to lance a festering wound and allow the infected material to be released. He let go of her for a moment and piled the pillows against the headboard so he could recline sitting upright. He turned about, extending his legs, boots and all, on the bed and then drew his wounded goddess into his arms.

Gradually, her sobs ceased and she slept.

He closed his eyes for a moment, content to lay with his darling cradled in his arms.

An eerie presentiment jarred him. Donovan opened his eyes. A pale woman with long, dark hair stood next to his bed. She was peering down at him while he lay asleep. She wore a white gown and seemed so forlorn he immediately felt pity for her.

And then, her face transformed from fragile waif to harpy as malice filled soulless black eyes. Before he could utter a sound the woman disappeared like mist before his eyes.

It was a dream, he decided as his heart cantered past the gateposts of logic and reason. He'd hardly slept for two nights running. He'd simply dozed off without realizing it and had a nightmare. Donovan settled a sleeping Lizzie on the pillows, and rose with reluctance.

He wished he could just lie here with Lizzie in his arms for the rest of the day.

He could not rest, not until he confronted the charlatan awaiting him in the salon.

Chapter Twenty Eight

A tall, slender, flame haired man entered Donovan's laboratory behind the butler.

Giles gave his master a significant look before withdrawing and closing the door.

Donovan thought he'd steeled himself to meet with the impostor, but the moment he laid eyes on the fellow, the universe shifted beneath his feet.

The man possessed features Donovan knew by heart; high cheekbones, a perfect nose, a slender jaw and a stubborn set to his chin. Hair the color of sunset was shoulder length, tied back in a queue. Framed beneath arched auburn brows, the visitor's eyes were neither blue nor green but a curious mix of both-- like the woman lying upstairs in his bed. Donovan saw the tragic vulnerability he observed a thousand times in his wife's features. The expression was fleeting; quickly masked by pride and willfulness, more traits belonging to the woman he loved.

He understood Giles' bewilderment. If not for the span of years between them, this man could be Elizabeth's twin.

"Mr. O'Flaherty." Uncle Gareth walked across the room, extending his hand. "I'm Gareth O'Donovan, his lordship's relative." Gareth shot Donovan an uneasy glance, unsure if he should make known their blood ties to a stranger.

"This is my esteemed uncle." Donovan responded, wanting to clear away any uncertainty on that account. "Have a seat." He instructed with impatience. "I have little time. My wife is seriously ill and I don't wish to be away from her for long."

"I know. That's why I came." The man replied with a trace of impudence.

"You know?" Donovan frowned, the enchantment quickly losing its power. He opened his bank book. "That fact was not in the society page, Mr. O'Flaherty or whoever you are."

Gareth gave an exasperated sigh and sent Donovan a look of censure.

Well, he was exhausted, damn it! He should be upstairs with Elizabeth. He didn't wish to deal with a con man claiming to be her long dead brother. Sheila told him about the mysterious disappearance of her grandson when Lizzie was born. Donovan came to the same conclusion the old woman had; the boy was murdered long ago to secure Fletcher's son as the legitimate heir.

"No, it wasn't in the papers." Turquoise eyes flashed to a dangerous green, just like Elizabeth's when she was angry. "Nor was it in the papers that Lady Beaumont has an older brother of Irish descent. If you believe me to be an imposter, my lord, how would I possess knowledge of the existence of Kieran O'Flaherty?"

"You could have worked on the same plantation in your youth." It was Gareth voicing Donovan's thoughts aloud. "Knowing his history and possessing a similar coloring, you may have decided to see if you could pass yourself off as him."

"To what end? Viscount O'Flaherty lost everything when he was arrested. And how is it you know Kieran O'Flaherty was sold as an indenture?" The man fixed Gareth with accusation before leveling crisp emerald shards at Donovan. "If they knew what happened to me, why didn't they try to find me?"

It was a valid question. The pain the man's voice revealed much.

Still, Donovan was determined to be careful, to play his hand to the last card.

"No one knows for certain what happened to Viscount O'Flaherty's son." Donovan replied. "It may interest you to know the boy was declared legally dead fifteen years ago."

"When Captain Fletcher's son was born." The man gripped the arms of the chair, his manner grave. "I didn't come here for money, your lordship."

"So, if I wrote a bank note for two thousand pounds with the proviso that you never attempt to contact my wife, you wouldn't take it?"

"I would not." The face was unwavering as the man returned his challenge.

They eyed one another in silence, each one taking the other's measure.

"Money cannot replace the loss of family." The man responded hotly, bolting from his chair. "My father and my uncles were hanged when I was nine. I watched them die, along with my mother and my grandmother. We were evicted from the castle shortly thereafter, in the dead of winter." He paced about the room, his hands fisting at his sides. "Alone and without funds, in a strange land, my mother had no recourse but to remarry quickly. Captain Fletcher took us back to London. My mother died several months later in childbirth, so I was told. Fletcher sold me to white slavers the next morning, without waiting until Mama had a proper burial. Barnaby bought my indenture. I came to him as Kieran O'Flaherty when I was nine years of age."

The man stopped pacing. "Imagine my shock, my lord, as I pick up the weekly newspaper and discover I have a younger sister who is very much alive. And imagine my concern as I recall a tale I heard in the taverns last week, told and retold for the price of a drink by a pair recently fired from here. They speak of a twisted count who keeps his bride locked up like a prisoner in her own home. Imagine, my lord, finding out the sad heroine of such a sinister tale is none other than your own baby sister!"

"Elias and Henry." Donovan remarked. "I fired them for making lewd advances to my wife." He shot Gareth a significant look. Gareth nodded, supporting him in his word.

O'Flaherty observed the exchange between them.

"And as the head of Clan O'Flaherty it is my duty to make certain my sister is being treated well here--and if not, to remedy the situation." Emerald shards fixed Donovan with challenge. "I'm not afraid to call you out, sir. *The O'Flahertys always take care of their own!*"

Donovan's jaw dropped. Sheila muttered that same phrase many times in his hearing. He fully expected to be fleeced out of a few thousand pounds by a wily fellow with red hair and a fake Irish accent. He didn't expect his honor to be challenged by a thin, spindly creature who had obviously never handled a weapon in his life. Only a Chieftain's son, raised in the old world, would possess such a fierce loyalty to blood kin.

He stood and extended his hand. "I hope that won't be necessary, Mr. O'Flaherty."

Reluctantly, O'Flaherty took his hand. "My lord. Or should I say Mr. O'Rourke?"

"You're the apothecary's assistant in Basseterre." Donovan recalled, unable to restrain a grin. "We have much to discuss, but not now. My wife is ill. I must give her my full attentions."

"I understand." O'Flaherty responded after a moment, as if deciding Donovan was telling the truth. "I came to find out if my sister is well after the horrors she endured during her abduction. I already knew the rumors circulating in Basseterre about you are unfounded, sir."

The words shot through Donovan like a jolt of lightening. No one knew of Lizzie abduction. No one but himself and the crew of *The Pegasus*, and he'd paid them a fortune to keep silent to protect her reputation. Donovan looked down, inherently conscious of O'Flaherty's hand on his arm long after their handshake ended. No one touched him. Not without his knowledge and permission. And yet . . . this man had been touching him for several moments without both.

That was his first thought. The second realization came swiftly galloping over the first awareness: Lizzie saw things when touching others. Could a full blood brother possess that gift?

"Mr. O'Flaherty," Donovan said emphatically, extracting his wrist from the man's grasp. "You are welcome to remain as my guest for as long as you wish, but only with the promise that you will not attempt to see Elizabeth without my permission. She had a severe seizure two days ago. I cannot allow her to become agitated at present. In a few days she may be well enough to meet you. Today, it's out of the question. Can you agree to those terms?"

"Yes." O'Flaherty's surprise revealed that he did not expect to be treated so graciously by the notorious Count Rochembeau.

The last strands of sunlight melted into the western sea. The room was bathed in a soft orange glow. Donovan sat in the chair near the bed, drinking scotch and dining on ashes after the events of the past days. His booted legs were propped on the mattress, his ankles crossed. He'd sent Pearl to the cellar to fetch a bottle of his grandfather's prized Scotch, as he craved something stronger than port to steady his stretched nerves.

After meeting with O'Flaherty, Donovan returned to his suite to find his wife curled up with pain, clutching her abdomen. She claimed it was nothing and begged him to leave her to Chloe's care. He refused. Realizing he was not about to back down and slink away as she'd hoped, Elizabeth blushed and hid her face in the pillow as she confessed the nature of her strange affliction; severe menstrual pains. She admitted to having an irreverent cycle that stretched close to two months between purges, causing heavy bleeding and excruciating pain when it did arrive.

His physician's mind wandered down a more perilous path as he silently assessed her symptoms. His worst fear was internal bleeding due to the severe beating she'd endured from the smuggler. The intermittent chills and the coldness of her extremities contributed to his fear, along with the distressing abdominal pain and the frightening pallor of her skin. He'd tucked the blankets about her as he worried about what to do, at which point his boot inadvertently kicked over a porcelain chamber pot next to the bed containing bloody linens.

Relief flooded him as he bent to inspect the discarded linens. He rose, lifted the blanket and pressed his palm over the place she'd been cradling protectively. Donovan swore under his breath. He could feel the powerful contractions seizing her womb. They were intense, like one of his mares when they were about to deliver a foal. He'd heard of Dysmenorrhea, the medical term for painful menstruation. He read about it in a medical text years ago when he'd been a student. That was the extent of his knowledge, an abstract term that meant nothing to him--until today-- when he witnessed the agony the affliction was bringing to the woman he cared about.

At a loss as to what to do, he administered a mild dose of Laudanum to ease her suffering. He'd have to do some research, find or develop some herbal formula so she wouldn't suffer so every time. He rubbed his brow and propped his head in his hand as he admired the sleeping angel in his bed.

Lizzie's cat was slumbering at her side. The kitten perked up, stretching lazily on his tiptoes. Donovan patted his lap. The red tabby crossed the chasm between bed and chair using Donovan's crossed legs as a bridge. "You're quite the brick." He said, rubbing the tiger behind his ears and receiving a loud purr of gratitude. "Is there anyone you don't like? You make friends too easily. You should be more reserved. Not all humans are nice to fat kitties, you know."

Green eyes gazed up at him solemnly. Puck commented with a mournful meow, as if he understood precisely what Donovan had been saying.

A couple of glasses of scotch would do that to a fellow. A few more glasses and he'd understand what the cat was saying. He downed his drink in one swallow and poured another, welcoming the numbing effects as the fiery liquid coursed through his insides. Puck crawled on his shoulder and batted at the hair that came loosened from his queue. The kitten chewed on it for a while, alternately biting his hair and licking his earlobe before curling cozily against his neck. Donovan's eyelids became heavy. He should lie down beside his wife, but it required too much effort. Besides, the cat was comfortable, purring against his neck in a mesmerizing tone.

A low, feral growling startled Donovan from his inebriated doze.

He opened his eyes and his heart stopped. The hair on the back of his neck rose.

Puck was still on his shoulder, crouched and growling at the dark haired woman he'd seen in his dream this afternoon. She was bending over Elizabeth, whispering some insistent message in her ear.

The woman wasn't alive. Donovan knew it instinctively, just like the cat.

As he watched, the mysterious woman drew back the covers and slipped pale arms beneath his sleeping wife. Elizabeth was lifted above the bed . . . and then hurled across the room as if she were naught but a feather pillow.

The bone crunching thud of Lizzie's body hitting the floor was enough to stir him out of his stunned lethargy. He stood and grabbed the only weapon at his disposal, the empty bottle of scotch. "Get away from my wife." He warned, tossing the bottle at the pale woman in white.

The bottle went through the woman's body and shattered the dressing mirror across the room. The sound of tinkling glass gave solid evidence that he was not dreaming.

The pale woman grimaced at him. Her face became ugly and skeletal. She gave him a look of pure malice before disappearing into thin air, just as she had earlier today when he awakened from a startled doze to find her hovering near him.

Donovan rushed to Elizabeth's side.

"Donovan . . ." She murmured, hugging him in recognition through her drug induced daze. He carried her to the bed and settled the covers about her. He stood looking down at her as she returned to a serene slumber. He ran a hand through his loose hair, and turned toward the doorway, desperately searching for tangible proof that he was not losing his mind.

"*Poor child.*" The soft cooing came from behind him. He twisted on his heels and nearly shrieked his horror aloud. His dead grandmother was hovering over Elizabeth, stroking her hair with a transparent hand. "*I've tried to protect her. The woman is too powerful.*"

This was why people shouldn't drink! He thought with revived conviction. Donovan tried to swallow. His throat was bone dry. He didn't seem to have a drop of spit left in him.

"*The Englishwoman is cursed.*" His grandmother continued, looking directly at him.

Donovan took a step back and attempted to hear her words over the pounding hooves as his blood raced through his temples and thundered over his heart.

"*Powerful magic keeps peace from her, ancient magic wrought by your wife's ancestors.*"

"Elizabeth's English ancestors?" He asked, confused by Maureen's words.

"*No.*" His grandmother appeared directly in front of him, startling him. "*Your wife is a descendent of the ancient priesthood who ruled Ireland before the Christians. She's a child of nature. You cannot keep her confined inside. She'll wither like a flower kept in a dark room. Take her outdoors."* She floated toward the opened veranda doors. *"Let the healing energies of the earth restore her strength."*

Donovan nodded. "Why is this spirit bullying her? What does she want?"

There was no reply. Moonlight spilled through the balcony doors, illuminating the large, empty room with pale blue glow.

Chapter Twenty Nine

"*Ghosts*! Yes, I told you. There are ghosts at Ravencrest Estates. Everyone told you." Gareth finished when Donovan faltered in recounting the bizarre visitation.

Unable to close his eyes after the disturbing encounter, Donovan had lit all the candles in his suite, locked the door and paced about the room with uncertainty until the first strands of light appeared in the sky. All along, his logical mind screamed at him that he was being irrational; candlelight and a locked door were hardly a deterrent to spectral visitations.

When it was no longer night he had marched down the veranda to his uncle's room and pounded on the louvered balcony door.

Presently, they stood on the veranda, facing one another as dawn colored the grey skies.

Donovan scowled. Gareth's words rang true. Everyone, Tabby, Pearl and even Donovan's mother claimed to see both Marissa's and Maureen's ghosts and even the spirit of his grandfather on occasion.

He seemed to be the only one who could not see the spirits wandering about his home.

"I was drunk." Donovan countered, fearing the disintegration of logic and reason. "I drank half a bottle of scotch—it could be a hallucination brought on by—"

"*'There are more things in heaven and earth, Horatio, than are dreamt of in your philosophies.'*" Gareth quoted the bard he adored. "I suspect you've just discovered that truth."

"I do not believe in ghosts!"

"We can't *all* be hallucinating, Donovan." Gareth scoffed, crossing his arms about his chest. "We can't all be drunk or given to too much imagination!"

Donovan sucked his breath in with a hiss and struck the balustrade with his fist.

Sleepwalking, she said, and he believed the little vixen. Lizzie knew he'd never believe she was being bullied by a spirit. Not until he was confronted with it himself.

With them; two spirits in one night.

"Maureen is a good spirit." Gareth pointed out. "She may be trying to protect your wife. What does this malicious spirit want from her?"

"I don't know." Donovan tossed up a hand. "Maureen said Elizabeth's ancestors were magicians--sorcerers—some damned thing. As I said, I was drunk."

"There's a spirit catcher on Basseterre. I've heard he does wonders."

"Oh, I'm sure he does miracles, for the right price." Donovan retorted. "I'm not inviting a charlatan here to burn weeds, mutter incoherently and present me with an outrageous fee. I'll figure this out on my own. What about O'Flaherty?"

"He's an apothecary." Gareth shrugged. "What would he know about angry spirits?"

"I meant did he stay the night?"

"Yes." Gareth gazed oddly at him. "You invited him to stay, as I recall."

"Good. Keep him distracted until Ambrose returns from Basseterre with his report."

An hour later, Donovan summoned Miss Ramirez to his laboratory.

Seated behind his desk, he watched the woman's reaction to the preserved specimens adorning the shelves. As a rule he didn't allow strangers into his laboratory, particularly women, who tended to be squeamish. The one time he summoned Elizabeth here he'd had the more offensive specimens covered by a canvas to preserve her tender sensibilities.

The rest of humanity could run shrieking from him and good riddance.

Elizabeth was the one person he did not wish to repulse with his studies in anatomy.

Miss Ramirez started and gasped as she saw the grinning skull on his desk. "*El Diablo!*"

"Not the devil, one of his hirelings." Donovan replied. "I killed him and fed his body to the sharks. Sit, Miss Ramirez." He gestured to the chair.

She regarded him with horror, as if he would slit her throat if the mood took him.

Smiling, Donovan gestured again to the seat opposite his desk.

With reluctance, she sank into the chair. "Please, do not send me away." The woman blurted, near the point of tears. "I talk too much, it annoys my lady—I will try to be—"

Donovan raised his hand, indicating silence. "I did not summon you here to reprimand you. I need your assistance. How long has the ghost been haunting Elizabeth?"

"You know about the spirit, my lord?" Her eyes grew wide with alarm.

"She visited us last night. It threw Elizabeth to the floor, right in front of me."

"*Dios*! I did not think the spirit would attack her in your presence."

"What does she want?"

Chloe clutched the arms of the chair and pressed her lips together, as if the truth might fly from them unbidden. Her doe-like eyes begged him not to ask her to betray her lady.

Donovan maintained his impervious stare.

She crumbled. "I do not know, my lord!"

"Has Elizabeth said anything to you regarding the ghost? Who is it?"

"Her mother, my lord."

Donovan's heart chilled at the woman's words. "Her mother? What does she want?"

"I do not know, my lord. My lady does not speak of her mother at all. She talks about her grandmother often, but . . ." The woman paused. Her eyes took on a terrified cast as something slowly became apparent to her.

"Elizabeth is being harmed." He insisted in a severe tone. "If you have any insights, no matter how slight, now would be the time to share them, Chloe."

She stared at him, considering her predicament: angering the master, who paid her wages, versus reporting the truth to him about his lady. Her lower lip quivered, her eyes brimmed with rising tears.

Bloody Hell, Donovan cursed silently. That last thing he needed was another weepy female to deal with. Lizzie had been weeping off and on for days, and he fully expected that storm to worsen before it was over. He loved Lizzie, and dealing with her tears left his heart in shreds. He couldn't endure a bout of hysterical weeping from another woman—he'd rather die, by his own hand.

As he glowered impatiently at the servant, waiting for her to explode into an annoying torrent of tears, she straightened her spine, clasped her hands together tightly, and appeared to tuck her raging emotions neatly away beneath her colorful shawl for another day.

"At first," She sniffled, and went on in a throaty voice, "The spirit did not harm Madame. She appeared a few times to her at night and during the day she would toss items about my lady's room. Several times, we would find the wardrobe emptied all over the floor. After questioning me as to the reason for the mess, my lady realized it was the spirit doing this to get her attention. She said her mother was a having a—Oh!" She spun her hand in the air. "—acting like a child who does not get its way? I do not know the word, my lord."

"Having a tantrum?"

"Yes, that is the word my lady used. Every few days there would be an incident. Madame and I would pick up the mess and she cautioned me to keep silent. Lately, the spirit started attacking her. My lady has been pushed, slapped, shoved, and once she was locked in a closet."

"Yet, you did not come to me." Donovan chastened.

"My lady swore me to silence, my lord. And you are a man of science," She gestured around the room. "What could I have said to make you believe my tale?"

The woman did have a point. He would not have believed her—not before last night.

"Nothing like this happened on the ship. These attacks seem to have begun after our arrival here. What could have disturbed her mother's spirit since then?"

Her dark eyes moved about the room, from the stuffed raven to the owl and the lizard perched on the shelf behind him as if seeking the answers. "There is a magic charm in Madame's possession. She discovered it among her grandmother's things after we unpacked her trunks. My lady believes the charm is a protection against nightmares." The maid tugged her shawl about her. Her dark eyes widened. "But it is pure evil, my lord."

Donovan pondered her words. Maureen's ghost had said Elizabeth's ancestors were sorcerers. If senile Old Sheila had fashioned a malicious charm, it seemed prudent to remove it from Elizabeth. "Bring it to me." He instructed.

Twenty minutes later Chloe returned with the mysterious pouch.

"It is evil, Sir." She admonished. "I offered to make a new charm when she showed it to me, but Madame wouldn't allow it, sir. Destroy it. Let it be devoured by flames."

Donovan rolled his eyes, tired of the woman's penchant for the dramatic. "Say nothing of this to Elizabeth." He cautioned. With a curt wave, he sent her back to her mistress.

Once alone, Donovan withdrew a sheet of parchment from the drawer and dumped the contents of the pouch onto the paper. *Oh, it was evil, all right*; it reeked of mold and decay. He sniffed the odd coil of rope. It was encrusted with dirt and rotting plant litter. Intent upon his inspection, he stabbed the odd, bi-colored rope with the tip of a letter opener and lifted it from the moldy debris. He turned the specimen about on the knife edge.

The hair on the back of his nape prickled. The rope was made of human hair.

With an oath, he dropped the disgusting coil onto the paper and scraped away some of the dried, red-brown film between the twisted strands.

He lifted the blade to his nose: dried blood.

Human hair coated in blood.

Revolted, by the coiled hair and the implications behind it, Donovan folded the paper to contain the gruesome contents, shoved the packet into his desk drawer and turned the key.

Chapter Thirty

He was being so sweet, so attentive, so unfailingly tender, and it was killing Elizabeth.

She couldn't meet Donovan's eyes. She was afraid if she looked into those lovely pale depths and saw the tenderness inherent in his every word and touch, she'd start weeping, *again.*

So, she made deliberate attempts to avoid his gaze. She'd cried enough to fill an ocean in the past days. Now, she knew the reason she'd been so melancholy; her courses. She always became morose days before their onset. She would feel as if the world were crashing down around her. And then, days later, she would look back and be dismayed with herself for being so distraught over dust motes when everything was just as it had always been.

This time she'd made a horrific mess. She upset her husband and even involved his friend—all because she succumbed to a fit of the dismals due to her monthly cycle. As her perpetual misfortune would have it, she succumbed to the wretched pains of the first day while recovering from her seizure in Donovan's bed, and thus, kindled his appalling curiosity.

Most men would avoid a woman at such an uncomfortable time, not daring to trespass across the distinct feminine boundaries regarding the mysterious monthly occurrence.

Not him. As a scientist he was bold and inquisitive where other men would gladly take the coward's way and leave her to her maid's care. Granted, his medicine did help her through the worst of the pains--but she also had to endure and answer his many questions on the subject. Talking about it with a man, with *any* man, was humiliating.

Donovan's continual presence was unsettling. He hovered over her and treated her as if she were made of spun glass and would break easily in his hands if he weren't very careful.

He returned from his business affairs just before lunch, and sent Chloe on her way.

The change from constant chatter to silence was refreshing. Still, it was a heavy, tense silence that only reminded Elizabeth of her shame.

She sat quietly in the bed, resting, as her husband insisted, and listened to his enchanting voice as he read aloud to her from *A Midsummer Night's Dream.* He had asked her earlier in the week which of Shakespeare's plays she liked the best, and she replied "the one with the fairies." And so, to pass the time he started to read it aloud to her after lunch.

Elizabeth gazed about the room, her mind too fractured and splintered by all that had happened in recent days to really follow the story. She liked listening to his voice, however. It was calming, so deep and serene when he read to her like this. He had read to her a great deal while they were on voyage here. He had read the entire account of *Tom Jones* to her, and started to read Shakespeare's works during the long days. They made it through *As You Like It* and *Romeo and Juliette* and *Hamlet* by the time they arrived here.

It was good to have him so near again, as long as she didn't need to look directly at him. As her eyes moved about the room she noticed the broken mirror near the door. The glass had been swept up from the floor but jagged pieces hung loosely from the frame and the board behind it. There was writing on the exposed board that would support the unbroken glass.

Perplexed, she slid from the bed and moved across the room to investigate. She knelt before the broken looking glass and traced her fingers over the painted letters on the board. It was a craftsman's mark, painted under the mirror on the board behind, to identify the maker.

"Lizzie?" Donovan put the book down and rose from his chair beside the bed, just realizing she'd slipped away from him while he'd been reading. "What are you doing?" He was at her side in a trice, crouched on his haunches beside her and talking to her as if she were a little girl, a very beloved little girl. "Here, now. Don't fuss with this. You'll cut yourself. We'll order a new full length mirror to replace this one. Come, back to bed."

"She told me it was there." Elizabeth muttered, ignoring him as she finally realized what Marissa had been trying to show her last week. She turned to look at Donovan. "I have to go upstairs. I need the keys."

Donovan was peering at her with concern. "No dearest. You need to go back to bed."

"I know where it is!" She insisted, rising and moving behind the dressing screen to retrieve her robe. She slipped it on. Donovan followed her about the room with a frown. "She asked me to help her. She can't leave here unless I do. I have to help her." She looked into her husband's eyes for the first time in days as she spoke. "We need the keys, my lord."

Donovan merely stared at her, as if trying to judge whether she were delirious or lucid. "Who are you talking about?" He asked in a cautious tone.

"There are spirits in this house." She said quietly, knowing he wouldn't believe her.

"Yes." His response startled her. "And one has contacted you, asked something of you?"

Elizabeth was stunned. "You believe me?"

"I'll always believe you, Lizzie." His reply, while reassuring, was also disturbing. He sounded as if he were indulging a child's fantasy. Perhaps in his mind, he was.

Regardless, she had a duty to help Marissa find peace. She held out her hand. "We need the key to Marissa's room."

Moments later, Elizabeth and Donovan stood in the small, luxurious room hidden on the third floor. The box of Marissa's personal belongings was still on the bed where she'd left it last week. She'd been packing up everything, intending to give it to Gareth when she finished. Captain Rawlings' visit had interrupted her labors. She'd had the argument with Donovan, and the seizure, and hadn't been able to return here since.

Donovan looked uncomfortable in the room, as most people seemed to. There was a deep, pervasive sadness, as Marissa had taken her own life here. He stepped to the window and took to inspecting the rough marks along the frame where the men had pried away the iron bars that had made this a prison cell instead of a servant's room.

Elizabeth went behind the dressing screen and knelt at the shattered cheval glass mirror. She began picking away at the glass, piece by piece.

"Be careful." Donovan came around the screen, anxious to see what she was up to. He crouched beside her. "You'll cut yourself. Let me." He pushed her hands away from the slim wedges of glass and then gazed about the room. Spotting a discarded cleaning cloth left behind from her earlier visit, he snatched it up and used it to protect his fingers as he began to pull the glass wedges out of the mirror frame and set them on the floor, one by one.

After pulling several long, sharp shards away from the frame, they could see a folded parchment wedged up between the broken glass and the support board. Donovan pulled it out, and unfolded it.

He quickly scanned it and then gazed at her with awe. "Do you know what this is?"

"A promise." She replied. "Marissa was bound by guilt for leaving her baby to fend for himself after she died. She was the only one who knew of the existence of this promise. She hid it to keep his legacy safe until Gareth could claim it, but then weeks later, she killed herself."

"She took her own life?" Donovan seemed surprised by Elizabeth's claim. "We were told she died of Childbed Fever." He shook his head, gazing about the room with distaste. It was apparent he knew the reason for the lock outside the door and barred windows. "It makes sense. No one should be forced to live at the mercy of another's perverse whims."

Donovan looked at the paper again, apparently shocked by its existence. He gazed tenderly at her. "My sweet, clever girl. This is an amendment to my grandfathers' original will. It gives Gareth one-third ownership in the plantation. Two thirds is to be retained by my mother's offspring, namely myself and my descendants, but Gareth is to receive a generous income from the estate as this document acknowledges him as the natural son of Richard O'Donovan. My grandfather never told my mother about this. He didn't tell any of us."

"Do you intend to honor it?" She asked. She was not certain if this was good or bad, from his perspective. Donovan would be giving up part of his own income.

"Of course." He was quick to assure her. "Most of my wealth has come from sources outside this estate. I have my uncle's holdings, the wealth he managed to smuggle out of France before the Revolution, and I will inherit *Belle Reve* Plantation in the Carolinas when my mother is gone. Gareth deserves more than a paltry few hundred pounds every year as an allowance. The will my Grandfather left with us stated Gareth was to be allowed to reside here on the estate for the rest of his days and receive support from the family, like a poor relation. With this, he'll have a secure future. He would be a man of independent means, he could take a wife and support a family."

The days passed with an eerie tranquility. Elizabeth offered stiff competition for Puck in the number of naps she needed to get through the day. Much as it galled her, she knew Donovan was right; she was exhausted. The strain of the past months had taken its toll. She felt like a cleaning rag that had been used too vigorously and then tossed in the corner.

Chloe's prediction proved true. No longer alone in the night, her mother's spirit did not harass her, and there were no more disturbances in her room as the week progressed.

Donovan was sweet and attentive. Her mind could not fathom such pure, unswerving devotion. He was absent off and on during the day, just like on the voyage. He left her for short periods with Chloe while he conferred in his study with his new steward, Mr. Duchamp, or rode out with the man to inspect the estate.

At the end of the week, she sat cross-legged on the bed with her kitten nestled in the cradle made by her legs. She'd just emerged from a warm bath. Puck was purring contentedly and gazing up at her with drowsy eyes after having worried her damp, dangling braid as a kitten possessed. His ears tightened and his eyes grew perturbed at the voices and loud thumping noises in the hall. Male voices could be heard in her former room, along with the sound of heavy objects being hefted. Setting Puck aside,

Elizabeth rose and moved to the adjoining door. She opened the door just enough to peer inside. Two footmen were stepping into the hall while a third man remained with her husband.

"—he's outraged." Mr. Duchamp gave a sinister laugh. "Claims it's all a mistake, says he should be your guest, not your prisoner. You'd think he was royalty for all his braying."

"Keep him in chains." Donovan instructed, "I'll ride out to meet him in little while."

Duchamp spoke again and then left via the hallway door.

Relieved that the brooding fellow had left, as his presence always unsettled her so, Elizabeth pushed the door to her former room open. Dressed in black, save the white linen shirt with the sleeves casually rolled up to his elbows, Donovan stood rigid in profile in the center of the room, his hands on his hips, his mind absorbed in Duchamp's news. Violence swirled about him like a fine, dark mist. His mouth was tight with tension. The tender eyes had narrowed to a chilling ice blue as they probed the shadowed recess of the empty fireplace with malice.

He had been so sweet and attentive this past week, Elizabeth had forgotten Donovan's dark moods. They were rare, yet their intensity could be frightening. "Donovan?"

Lost in black thoughts, he started at the sound of her voice. A disguise of pleasantness dropped into place. "Lizzie, my sweet, you're awake." His hand lifted to welcome her to his side. Seeing her reluctance, he closed the gap between them and offered a limp smile.

"Is something troubling you, my lord?"

He wrapped an arm about her, drawing her close as she remained stiff at his touch. "Duchamp tells me the new indentures arrived from England. One is being particularly difficult. I need to deal with him. But first, why don't we open your presents, my sweet?" He cajoled in a buoyant tone, gesturing to the mysterious wooden crates stacked at the door.

Without waiting for her response, Donovan stepped away and took up the iron bar. He wrenched open the top box and gestured for her to come closer and examine the contents.

Books, dozens of them were stacked neatly inside the crate.

"All of this, for me?" She gazed up at him with astonishment.

A roguish grin worthy of Mr. O'Rourke tugged at his lips. "I sent Ambrose to Basseterre on business at the beginning of the week and while he was there I instructed him to have the bookseller box up anything that might be of interest to a young lady."

Never did Elizabeth imagine possessing so many books at once. She picked up the top book and let go a squeal of girlish delight. "Mrs. Radcliffe--it's been ages and this one is new!"

The title, *The Italian*, was in raised gilt letters on the cover. She caressed the letters with her fingertip, anticipating being held in wicked suspense for nights to come. Hugging the first book to her breast, she rummaged through the box, finding a complete set of Mrs. Radcliffe's works inside. "Donovan, you shouldn't have. You'll spoil me."

"It's time someone did." He grumbled, his anger roiling to the surface despite his attempt to conceal it. His arm snaked out to move her gently out of the way as he wedged open the lid of the second crate. He placed it on the floor and opened the last box.

Elizabeth knelt on the floor between the three crates, completely astonished by the offering. She took book after book out of the crate; *Gulliver's Travels* by Swift, *Amelia* by Fielding, selected works by Francis Burney, Mary Wollstonecraft, Wordsworth and Walpole. "How did you know I love to read?"

"You told me, when we were courting." He stepped back and set the crowbar against the wall. "You said once you thought it unfair only boys are allowed to go to university and confided to me one moonlit night during our walk that as a girl you often dreamed of dressing as a lad and going off to those sacred halls of learning to gain the education denied your sex."

"Oh dear. You weren't frightened off by such rash talk?" Most men would be.

"*Au contrare*, that was the moment I knew I was in love with you."

Chapter Thirty One

The portly man sitting in the ground of the prison compound was filthy.

Still, the hate-filled eyes were unmistakable.

"Captain Fletcher!" Donovan spat on the ground. "How thoughtful of you to join us at Ravencrest Plantation. I can personally guarantee your stay will be long and most unpleasant."

"You!" The middle-aged devil snarled, rising from the hard packed earth with difficulty, given his leg shackles. He raised a pair of dirty fists in defiance, the chains joining his wrists jangling with the movement. "Where's that Frenchie who married my girl? I demand to see Count Rochembeau. Mark me; he'll not like this shabby treatment of his relative!"

Donovan smiled. Jasper Winslow, the overseer, smiled. Gus O'Leary laughed out loud.

Ambrose grinned his malice and snapped the bull whip around Fletcher's legs, pulling him to the ground. "On your knees, *m'sieur cochon!*"

"Ambrose, don't insult the pigs." Donovan quipped. "Even they possess a higher moral character than this creature."

"O'Rourke." Fletcher grimaced with pain. "I remember you, sniffin' about my stepdaughter's skirts like a stray dog after a bitch in heat. When my son-in-law learns--"

"Shut yer pie 'ole!" Winslow cut in, snapping his whip near Fletcher's head without actually hitting him. He gestured to Donovan. "He is the count, you bloomin' idiot!"

"I met his lordship." Fletcher retorted. "He's ugly as sin. His face is scarred."

"Amazing what a silk scarf, an accent and a dark room will do." Donovan replied.

"Why, you dirty, conniving Irish Mick!" Fletcher rose and lunged at him.

Ambrose, Gus and Winslow quickly moved in to restrain the man.

"She put you up to this, didn't she? That ungrateful little slut—Oow—"

Before Donovan could respond, Ambrose had his whip coiled about the captain's throat. He held it taut with both hands as he stood behind his captive. He waited stoically for a signal from his employer to decide if the man would live or die in the next instant.

"I'll thank you not to talk about my wife in such low terms." At his signal, Ambrose released Fletcher and stepped back. Fletcher fell onto all fours at Donovan's feet, choking and gasping for breath. "In fact, I'd rather you not soil the air she breathes by speaking at all during your stay here. Pigs don't talk, they grunt." Donovan grabbed a thatch of greasy brown hair in his fist, jerking the man's head until he was forced to look up at him. "I can have your tongue cut out if you persist in these insults. I can, and I will."

There was no remorse in those eyes, no fear as he gazed up at his new master. "Oh." Fletcher cooed with pernicious venom. "The Irish dog is in love with his little whore!"

Donovan snatched the whip from Winslow's hand and slapped the coiled serpent across the man's torso repeatedly as Fletcher crouched on all fours and tried to protect his head with his chained hands. Donovan relished each jerk and grunt of pain as the dirty shirt became soaked with crimson.

Tossing the whip aside, he hauled Fletcher to his feet and shoved his raw back against the stone wall. Fletcher groaned. "I should kill you for what you did to her." Donovan snarled through clenched teeth, barely able to contain his rage. His hands closed around that grimy throat. "Another word about my wife and I'll strap you to my surgery table, bleed you, boil the flesh from your carcass and hang your bones next to those of your old friend, Dr. Linton."

At last, the hard, hate-filled eyes widened with horror.

"Oh, yes, we discovered your mole during the passage. His skeleton is in my laboratory, waiting to be strung together and put in a display case, a personal trophy you might say. I also have

Captain Sully's skull. I use it for a paper weight. Care to join you're old chums, Fletcher?"

"Y-y-you're mad!" Fletcher croaked.

"Perhaps." Donovan conceded, releasing his hold on the man and stepping back. Fletcher sank to the ground, coughing and wheezing. "Pray I am not. According to English law allowing the purchase of criminals for indentured servitude, your sorry ass belongs to me."

"I'm a free man!" Fletcher bellowed. His face was florid with renewed rage. "You kidnapped me and you have no right to keep me here."

"Men are kidnapped all the time, are they not?" Donovan held out his arms in an expansive gesture. "Some by their own government, forced to sail the world for King and Country. And nothing, short of a pirate, I'm told, can save them." Donovan turned on his heel to Gus. "Isn't that what happened to you, Mr. O'Leary?"

"Aye." Gus replied. "Pressed onto a naval vessel bound for Ceylon, I was, until pirates attacked the ship I was on and set me free. I'll be forever grateful to that pirate, sir."

Donovan gave O'Leary a gallant bow in acknowledgement of said gratitude before continuing his argument with his prisoner. "Why, I've even heard tales of little boys being ripped from the bosom of their families to become victims of the spiriting trade." He turned to Fletcher as he delivered his final riposte. "I recently met a man who survived that brutal fate. His name is Kieran O'Flaherty. Would you care to meet him, Captain Fletcher?"

"*I didn't*—" Fletcher began and stopped as Donovan removed the curved dagger from the sheath he had strapped to his thigh and stepped toward his prey.

"Oh, you did." Donovan countered, directing his men to move in with his weapon.

Gus, Ambrose and Winslow converged upon Fletcher, holding him fast. Donovan stepped forward, his blade aloft between his face and Fletcher's. Holding his victim's chin securely in one hand, he spat on the man's face and scraped his cheek with the blade, giving him a much needed shave as he spoke. "You kidnapped an earl's heir and sold him to white slavers eighteen years ago, a crime punishable by transportation, at the very least. Add to that the hiring of thugs to kidnap a countess—*my countess!*" Donovan's eyes widened at the last and his blade deftly sliced the man's cheek, drawing blood. "And I'm certain a hanging would be your future. That is, if you wish to pursue the legal avenues. Say the word, captain, and I can arrange to have you brought before the local magistrate before the day is out."

"No!" Fletcher's eyes betrayed his panic at the suggestion. "No—I—I—"

"Ah, I thought not." Donovan said with a wry grin. "Could be a bit tricky for you, what with stepchildren still alive and able to testify against you, despite your efforts to the contrary." He spat on his dagger and wiped the blood and stubble on Fletcher's soiled shirt.

"So, you brought me all this way to kill me, is that it?"

"No." Donovan slipped the dagger into the sheath strapped to his thigh. "*That* would be a kindness you don't deserve. As you recall, I paid off all your notes a few months back. In return, I'll have eighteen years hard labor for all the years you tormented my wife."

Fletcher's distress grew at the prospect of a lifetime of forced labor.

"Where do you want him kept," Winslow asked. "In the compound, with the others?"

"No. Chain him up with the pigs." Donovan replied. "He'll sleep with the pigs in the prison yard. He'll eat from their trough. During the day, he'll work the fields with the others, but keep him in leg irons. And no machete for this one or any tool he could use as a weapon. And no rum rations. He's the most dangerous when he's drunk."

Donovan rode along the winding roads as the sun lowered in the sky.

He couldn't stop thinking of all the things he longed to do to Fletcher now that he had the man in his power. His blood was seething and boiling in his veins, his mind whirling at all the wicked possibilities; he could use him for target practice or make him flush out the poisonous snakes hiding in the uncut cane. They lost at least one man every season to a venomous snake bite while cutting the stalks.

The one thing Donovan could not do was go home. Elizabeth's intuition would find him out. She'd be frightened by the violence seething in his soul. He'd spent the past days trying to surround her with calm. He couldn't go to her until he gained control of his turbulent emotions.

As the sun melted into the sea, he guided his mount down the path to the beach and allowed Zeus to cantor across the sands. They raced along the white sand, through the crashing waves toward the rocky promontory that reached into the ocean. When they reached the rocks Donovan turned his mount and galloped back down the shore.

By the time he'd repeated the invigorating race up and down the shoreline two more times Zeus' sides were heaving. Donovan dismounted and allowed the Arabian to sample the foliage growing along the embankment. He sat down on the sandy rise a few feet from the horse, braced his forearms across his bent knees and allowed the steady boom of the crashing surf to surround him as he attempted to calm his heart in the growing twilight.

He continued to struggle with his primitive emotions as he made long strides from the stables to the house. He ambled about his laboratory, searching for a distraction. His eye caught the report lying open on his desk, the investigation on O'Flaherty's background. He picked it up with renewed interest as he sank into the overstuffed chair behind his desk.

Twenty minutes later, Kieran O'Flaherty entered the laboratory at his summons. "Sit, Kieran." Donovan gestured to the seat opposite his desk. "Would you care for glass of port?"

"No sir." The sparse, tall redhead edged around the newly arrived crates of scientific equipment stacked near the door. Emerald eyes took in the specimens lining the walls with a mixture of awe and trepidation.

Donovan watched the man survey his collection of preserved animals, birds and reptiles with mild amusement. Scientific classification had been his hobby since childhood, much to his mother's chagrin, as he preferred to spend hours cloistered in his attic laboratory as a lad rather than in parlors under her enforced attempts to socialize him. His adult studies included human specimens. He had organs preserved in glass jars of salt brine and vinegar. A human brain was on the shelf behind him, compliments of the hangman in Basseterre. Donovan extracted it from a cadaver that came to him in exceptional condition, despite the typically destructive processes of execution.

"You wished to speak to me, sir?" O'Flaherty slid into the chair opposite his desk.

"Yes." He replied, pouring himself a glass of port and pausing to offer his guest a glass. Kieran declined his offer. "Are you sure? It's very smooth, well aged, from Portugal."

"I don't imbibe in spirits, my lord. It tends to muddy my perceptions."

Donovan sat back in his chair and extended his long legs beneath the desk. He cradled the goblet of ruby liquid between his fingers. "Ah, yes. You make your living using your peculiar *perceptions.*" He took a sip of the fine port and slumped lower in the chair, determined to be comfortable. "You are reputed as an adept in the metaphysical realm, according to my reports."

O'Flaherty swallowed convulsively. "Reports? You had me investigated?"

"Not all of us possess the gift of second sight. My agent merely questioned the locals to verify your claims." He took a sip of his drink, and watched Kieran's reaction. "My wife is very precious to me. I could never allow another man near her without scrutinizing his background, particularly not one who has the potential to engage her heart. A long lost brother is no trifling gift to present to such a fragile soul."

Nodding, O'Flaherty conceded Donovan's point, yet he was rankled, all the same. "Barnaby's position in the city is precarious. The wrong inquiries could cast suspicion—"

"--Yes, he could be driven out of town due to his dealings in sorcery and necromancy." Donovan finished with impatience. "And a bit of larceny, given his advertisement promising, let me see, how does that go? Ah, yes *discrete and efficient resolutions for those troubled by spirits—prices negotiable.*" He quoted the handbill in his file, lifting it to wave at his guest.

"It was never my choice to be involved in such practices. I was purchased for my peculiar gift as a child so Barnaby might use them for his purposes, namely, to make money."

"You are no longer a child." Donovan pointed out. "Your indenture must be paid by now. If not, I'll settle the account. Why do you stay if you disapprove of his dealings?"

Kieran shifted in his chair and cleared his throat. "He's the only family I've known for nearly twenty years."

"Did you ever consider contacting your maternal grandfather?"

"To what end?" Sharp green eyes met Donovan's. At last, that Fighting O'Flaherty spirit surfaced. "He disowned my mother for marrying my father against his wishes."

Donovan digested that tidbit quickly. "Did your father have contact with Wentworth?"

"Yes." Kieran hissed the word with pent up fury. He sat forward in the chair, his arms braced on his thighs, hands clenched together as if to try to contain the rage that radiated from within. "Mama was crushed by his refusal to reconcile with her. Father wrote the man more than once, attempting to heal the breach out of love for my mother. Wentworth refused to accept their marriage. He damned my father as an uncivilized pagan and my mother as an ungrateful child. So you see, even before my abduction, I had no expectation of eliciting Lord Greystowe's support or his affection."

Donovan lifted a cheroot to his lips and leaned close to the candle to light his tobacco. After pausing a moment to coax the cigar to ignite, he continued, "I met with Lord Greystowe after my wedding. He expressed deep regret at being a stranger to his grandchildren. When your mother died, Fletcher disappeared. Wentworth had agents searching for your siblings for years. That is hardly in keeping with a man who wishes to remain aloof from his grandchildren."

"My father would never forgive me if I went crawling to that cold English lord!"

"I've been to Ireland, O'Flaherty. I've seen the effects of British rule. My stable boys are casualties of that brutal system. Their parents died during an outbreak of Scarlet Fever. The boys were turned out of their tenant cottage, forced to pick pockets to survive. Johnny, the oldest, attempted to pick mine. Instead of handing him over to the authorities I offered him a job, a means to honestly provide for his brothers as my stable hand."

"The lad is hardly fourteen." O'Flaherty's look clearly questioned Donovan's sanity.

"Johnny is seventeen. Under my supervision, he looks after the stock. I brought the boys here three years ago. Danny was ten. Gavin wasn't yet seven. Gavin survived the fever that took their parents but he'll never be able to work as a laborer. With training, and my sponsorship, he could become a clerk in a law office. My point is that Gavin deserves more than being left to starve in the streets, Mr. O'Flaherty, yet starve he did, under British rule."

"You are a philanthropist, my lord." O'Flaherty remarked. "You collect the broken and discarded of society. You give them a sense of purpose and dignity."

Donovan stamped out his tobacco, disturbed by the man's bold assessment. No doubt, he was a great asset to his employer due to his intuitive abilities. "We were discussing you." He directed the conversation back to a comfortable path. "With your father dead and the O'Flaherty lands under British control, your tenants would be laboring under an English landlord, more than likely, an absentee one. If you were reinstated as your grandfather's legal heir you would be in position to purchase your ancestral home and regain your place as leader of the Clan O'Flaherty, and fulfill your father's legacy by being a fair and just landlord."

Kieran crossed his forearms, layering one over the other in front of his chest, a clearly defensive posture. "That's a very mercenary perspective, my lord."

"A pirate can do noble deeds. A priest can commit great evil. If you believe you are being noble by not claiming your rightful inheritance when you could be using Lord Greystowe's money and influence to help your father's people, you are entertaining folly. More to the point, you allow Fletcher to win by default. His son will inherit everything, just as he intended when he sold you into indentured servitude all those years ago."

Donovan straightened his posture, honing his last arrow. "Who knows what kind of earl Fletcher's son will be? I grant you he's young. Yet, he's had his father's influence all his life and now he will be guided by your maternal grandfather, a cold man who turned his back on his only child years ago over her choice in a husband, as you pointed out."

Kieran's face hardened. When he did manage to speak, it was in a tight staccato voice. "I didn't come here to seek your help in securing the Wentworth fortunes. I came to see my sister. After days of being detained as your unwilling 'guest' and entertained with constant frivolities by your kinsmen, I have yet to receive proof my sister is well. When will I be allowed to see her, my lord?"

Donovan took a leisurely sip of his port and regarded his brother-in-law calmly. "Tomorrow."

Chapter Thirty Two

Elizabeth placed a ribbon in her page and set aside *The Romance of the Forest*.

She was captivated by the heroine's ordeal; snatched from the safety of the convent by her nefarious father, locked in a room in an abandoned farmhouse for days, and then foisted upon strangers in a passing coach in the middle of the night--strangers running away from the law. The fugitives had just set up camp for the night in an abandoned Abbey deep in the forest. The heroine in the novel kept eyeing the eerie ruins with trepidation, but Elizabeth kept looking at the clock, distracted by her husband's prolonged absence.

She tugged the silk shawl about her shoulders and wandered out onto the porch. Puck trailed after her, his plaintive meows a reminder of his devotion. She picked him up, cradled him against her neck and was rewarded by his steady purring.

It was silly to fret over Donovan's absence, her mind admonished, yet her heart whispered a different song. Their closeness was so new, so fragile. She had to do something to keep his interest. She couldn't bear it if he retreated to callous indifference toward her again.

There seemed one option—seduction.

The trouble was, she had no idea how to go about seducing a man.

She paced to the corner of the veranda and wandered along the main porch abutting the front of the house. Donovan wanted her. His desire was unmistakable as they lay each night in the forgiving darkness. His organ would swell against her, but he merely held her. He didn't try to make love to her. His desire was not the problem. It was convincing him to act on it.

Elizabeth turned about as a noise startled her from behind.

Donovan came tromping down the porch toward her, looking quite perturbed into the bargain. "Where the devil have you been?"

"I might ask the same of you." She returned, resenting his demanding tone.

"I had a complication to deal with. Come inside. You know how I feel about you being outdoors alone." He took her hand and began leading her in the direction of their chamber as if she were an errant mare wandering from her paddock.

For pity's sake, I'm on the second floor! Elizabeth managed to still her tongue before she blurted her thoughts aloud. While his overprotective tendencies could be quite endearing at times, there were other times where she found it exceedingly exasperating, and stifling. He acted as if he expected someone to swoop in and steal her away from him at any moment if he weren't careful. He was being ridiculous, irrational. She wanted to tell him so.

Alas, her objective this night was not to argue with him but to encourage him to make love to her. She set Puck loose once they reached his suite, contemplating her next move. She didn't know how to be coy and seductive, having never studied the art as most girls her age would have before entering polite society.

"I see you found a book to occupy your time." He noted, glancing at the bed.

A rush of warmth bloomed in her chest as she remembered his gift, a veritable library. "Yes, a deliciously horrid Gothic tale by Mrs. Radcliffe."

"Ah, and what happens when the tale takes root in that fertile imagination?" Donovan gave her a rare teasing grin as he circled about her with his hands on his hips, adopting a playful mien. "Will my lady be starting at every sound tonight, disturbing her poor husband's sleep over melodramatic tripe?"

"No. I'll sleep safe and sound in my big, strong husband's arms."

"Oh, will you?"   Mirth illuminated his pale eyes as he stepped close.

"Yes, after he makes love to me, of course." She replied, smiling up at him.

Donovan regarded her with wariness. He stepped back a pace.

Had she offended him? Perhaps he believed ladies should not bring up the subject of sex with their spouses. Her mother would certainly believe so. Well bred ladies never spoke of such vulgar subjects, her mother would be quick to point out.

"Don't look at me with wounded eyes." He returned, "You've been ill. There is no need to rush the fences."

"*Rush the fences*? We've been married for three months."

He stood resolute before her, unyielding in his silence.

He was rejecting her, again? The hurt rose up, threatening to spill out onto her face in the form of tears. She blinked them back, resolved to avoid weeping at all costs. She'd wept enough in his presence for two lifetimes in the past week, she would not weep or even give the appearance of tears while asking him to bed her.

"Why do you push me away?" She asked after recovering her composure. Even so, she was not faking the squeak that crept into her voice.

"I'm not pushing you away, Lizzie. I'm waiting, just as I promised you I would."

"I only want to make things right between us." It was the truth. She wanted to make up for all the time she'd lied to him and kept him away. She wanted to make him happy.

Donovan's eyes softened. He dropped his arms, made as if to reach for her, and then seemed to change his mind about touching her. "Sweetheart, there is nothing wrong."

"Isn't there?" She shot back. "I've been your wife for three months and I'm still a maid!" It was galling, trying to get through to this man. Elizabeth wanted Donovan to love her as his wife. She wasn't living in dread of it any longer, or trying to connive her way around it. He should be pleased, damn the man. He should not be arguing the point with her!

"And this bothers you?" He waved his hands expansively as he spoke. "Not long ago, as I recall, my romantic overtures were rejected quite vehemently."

Elizabeth hissed her outrage. *How dare he bring that up! It was an embarrassment. And there was nothing romantic about the incident.* "Sod off, you arrogant coxcomb!"

"Ah, there's the spirited girl I fell in love with." Donovan quipped, laughing at her fury.

Elizabeth slapped her hand over her mouth. She'd slipped into using one of her stepfather's crude retorts, a lingering problem due to her head injury. She spoke her thoughts aloud when upset or made an impertinent or vulgar remark. And he---the impudent rogue—was always amused by her faux pas instead of outraged, as any proper gentleman would be.

Elizabeth wanted to scream at the man. He seemed to enjoy their verbal sparring and tended to encourage her to cross words with him. Did he find it invigorating? Amusing? Perhaps it was preferable to him after the torrent of tears he'd endured of late.

Again, she had to guide her mind away from their debate and back to her objective. "I was a ninny back then. I'm not afraid of you anymore, Donovan, that's what I'm trying to tell you. I'm not afraid, I-I'm ready—"

"Well, I'm not." He cut in before she could inform him of her change of heart.

His bold declaration left her with dampened enthusiasm. *Honestly! She was offering herself to the man again--and he was brushing her offer aside--again.*

He stood with his hands across his chest, reeking impatience. "I've had a hell of a day. I'm tired, I'm dirty. I need a bath and a drink."

Elizabeth had no reply. As she stared at him, incredulous, he moved across the room and jerked the bell pull.

Damn it. Donovan sat in the steaming tub behind the dressing screen. It wasn't a lie. He was tired, dirty, and furious.

He did not intend to touch her after just leaving her 'undead' brother--after coming close to beating her wretched stepfather into a bloody pulp at the indenture compound. He was full of rage and frustration—anger, hatred.

She was a maid and yet she had been traumatized by her encounter with the smugglers. It was a precarious situation, requiring him to be at his best so he could gently ease her past her fears. He would not risk frightening her again and perchance putting her off lovemaking forever. He'd come too far, worked too hard to regain her trust.

Donovan scrubbed his scalp and massaged the back of his head with his fingers.

He was not making love to her. Not tonight. Not when so much was at stake.

Elizabeth sat on the edge of the bed, her knees apart, her gown ruched up, exposing her legs in an inelegant pose. She couldn't believe the argument that had just taken place.

What man would refuse the very thing he'd been lusting after for months on end?

She could hear the splashing on the other side of the screen. Obviously, he felt the need to relax after his long day on the plantation.

A drink? He needed a drink. That was new. Something nasty must have happened while he was out today. Donovan wasn't the type to drink much. He told her so himself. She saw him drunk but once—and that turned ugly rather quickly.

The man had a trying day. Perhaps that was why he'd snapped at her; he had more important things on his mind at the moment than appeasing his lust.

That was new. Elizabeth assumed all men were like animals when it came to their sexual need, showing little more restraint than a dog determined to hump someone's leg to appease its instincts. She underestimated him. Donovan was a scientist. He thought too much. He thought out everything precisely before acting upon it. He was probably sitting in the tub this moment dissecting their conversation, trying to see some hidden meaning in her words.

"Oh, Bloody Hell!" Elizabeth whispered. How could she get him to consummate their vows so she could move past her fear of the unknown? Yes—in truth, she was afraid of the sordid business. She wasn't afraid of Donovan, but the idea of enduring all that pawing and mauling and humping was unsettling. Donovan didn't need to know that. Once the consummation part was over, she could stop being uneasy about it. Stop feeling guilty. The mystery would be gone and then she could devote herself to making him happy.

What more could she do to push him forward? She tried talking to the man, and that ended in an argument with both of them sulking at opposite ends of the room.

Elizabeth looked down at her bare feet and her exposed legs. Hmmm? Men liked to see a bit of flesh. An exposed ankle, she'd been told, could send a man into raptures.

Well, then, she'd give him something to look at, a bit more than ankles.

Chapter Thirty Three

Elizabeth held her breath, waiting. She was unclothed beneath the sheets.

Donovan had come around the privacy screen dressed in his robe. He had a goblet in his hand as he meandered about the room, appearing deep in reflection. He stopped at the veranda doors and stood with his back to her, examining the night sky.

She watched him, uncertain if he would climb into bed or go out on the veranda with the drink he needed so badly and brood over his day.

Well, he would come to bed at some point, no sense trying to push the situation. She was determined to just lay still and let him come to her.

It was half an hour before Donovan came to the bed. He lifted the covers, and she felt the bed dip as he climbed in.

"What is this?" His voice was not happy. As she opened her eyes she could see Donovan's disposition was not improved by his long soak or his drink.

"I was warm." She explained, receiving a grunt from him as he slid in next to her wearing his small pants as an imaginary shield over his masculine parts. It did not conceal them but rather emphasized the contours as the fabric fit snuggly over him even without arousal.

"Stubborn little mare." Donovan murmured in rebuke. Still, he did not reach out to snuff out the candle or turn his back on her. He simply stared, long and hard, taking in every inch of her flesh as if it were a strange new specimen he'd never examined before. Oh, he had examined her from head to toe on the ship, back when she'd been riddled with bruises and hardly enticing.

Elizabeth watched his face as his eyes lingered over her breasts, her belly, and then moved lower to the patch of deep red hair between her thighs. She glanced below the waistline of his

269

small pants. Yes, indeed. That part of him strained the thin fabric that held it in check.

Say something, anything. Elizabeth thought in sudden desperation, directing her command to herself and to him. It was awkward, his staring, this silence, this waiting.

His hand covered her hip, draping over it, tracing the curve in a slow, leisurely fashion.

"Elizabeth." He murmured, stroking her hip slowly, and tracing the outline of her thigh with a firm yet gentle hand. "Sweet Lizzie, you're so pale and so lovely."

She blushed. It was ridiculous to feel reticent when she'd deliberately stripped and crept naked into his bed, yet, Elizabeth felt the heat flood her neck and her face.

Donovan reached up to cradle her cheek. "Are you certain this is what you want?"

Elizabeth pulled her gaze from his taut abdomen. She looked into those pale, penetrating blue orbs that seemed to see into her soul. "Yes. I want you to love me as your wife."

His eyes narrowed. Like a wolf he could sense the frailty of her trust. "Lizzie, don't lie. I will wait for as long as you need me to. I promised you I would, and I intend to keep that promise. Are you certain you want this, *tonight?*"

"Yes." Her voice sounded so small, so uncertain, and she needed so much to convince him otherwise. "I trust you."

He frowned. His mouth was set in a firm, *grim* line, as if he would to dispute her claim.

Oh, Bollocks.! Were they going to start arguing again?

"When did *that* come about?" Donovan said with a roughened voice. "In the last hour?"

He did have a point. This man was not as easily fooled as she would believe.

"Yes, well . . . it's been coming on slowly, over the past week."

He gazed at her, intently, searching her eyes for the merest hint of deceit. Elizabeth steeled herself, willing herself not to falter and give away her apprehension. Her heart thundered in her chest. She prayed he could not hear its treacherous drumbeat. She licked her lips, waiting for him to stop staring at her with the intensity of an inquisitor questioning a witch.

Donovan noticed her slight capitulation. He followed her tongue across her lips with his eyes. "You trust me?"

She nodded.

"But you are still afraid, aren't you." It was not a question.

"Uncertain, a little uneasy, yes." She softened the verb, watered it down to be nearly as meaningless as possible. "It's only to be expected. I am still a maid."

His lips turned into a wan smile. "You are a courageous lass." His finger wound around a stray lock hanging near her ear. He brought it to his lips, kissing the coppery ringlet captured in his finger. "I prefer a lass with a bit of spirit." He whispered, and brushed a kiss across her lips. It was brief, chaste and oh, so enticing.

Donovan drew back, watching her, smiling a little more as he gauged her reaction. He released her hair, traced a path along her temple and then her chin with his forefinger. "You're a handful, you do realize that, don't you?" He chided, his eyes alight.

He leaned close, kissing her once more, tasting her lips briefly, retreating and then returning to linger and tease her lips again and again. It was like a dance. Come forward, embrace, step lightly, and then retreat. Elizabeth was tingling with anticipation.

Each brush of his lips was a little longer, a little more insistent.

She kissed him back, anxious to prove her enthusiasm. She missed this potent, beguiling side of him, missed the precious hours they spent kissing so in his cabin on *The Pegasus*. It seemed a lifetime ago, a romantic dream that she had began to fear never happened except in her imagination.

But this, no, this was real; this was the Donovan she fell in love with.

Donovan's light fingers traced the outside of her arm, down and then back up to circle her shoulder. Down to her elbow and then up, up the inside of her arm. She sighed, and leaned into him, welcoming his kiss, his touch.

His tongue traced her lips, teasing, taunting until she opened her mouth to welcome his bold exploration. He'd kissed her like this a few times on the ship, but when he had breached her defenses thus far successfully, he would end their kissing sessions.

Elizabeth wrapped her arm about his neck, hoping to hold him this time, to see where the kiss might lead if allowed to go further than the brief inspection of her mouth by his tongue.

He didn't pull away. His palm pressed over her breast, cupping her so gently it bordered on reverence. As his fingers moved lightly over her sensitive breast, it brought an answering burst of longing for him low in her belly. The more he caressed her breast, the more she seemed to want him to. Elizabeth could not contain a moan.

The noise startled him. He withdrew his hand and gazed at her with worried eyes. "If you wish me to stop—"

"No—no." She insisted. She didn't want him to leave her. This time, she wanted him to follow through and bring them to the end of it, bring her to a sense of . . . fullness, completion? She didn't know the words, only the need his touch evoked within her; the need to belong to him completely.

"Elizabeth." He said sternly. "If you need me to stop you've only to say so. I swear to you, nothing will happen tonight that you do not wish to."

She nodded, agreeing with him and placed her hand on his cheek. She leaned in and kissed him. She trusted this man.

"I love you." He whispered, placing his hand at the back of her head as he drew her in for another breathless kiss. She loved the feeling of being held tight against him and kissed with such passion it seemed their souls were colliding in the quest to become one.

Elizabeth was distantly aware of being guided back against the pillows so she was lying on her back. Donovan was curled on his side next to her. She traced the firm contours of his shoulders, reveling in the rugged power of his masculine form. He was hard, like marble, yet warm and smooth. She encountered the scars on his back, and caressed their ropey contours with devotion. They were not repulsive. The scars forged him into the tender man she loved.

His mouth left hers to trail warm kisses along her neck and then paused at her breast. She exhaled as he kissed the tip and gently took it into his mouth. She rubbed and stroked his rigid bicep, following the ropey contours of his forearm to his hand. He responded by clutching her hand and bringing it to his lips to plant a soft kiss in the center of her palm. "I love you, Lizzie."

"I love you." She responded, as the buoyant feeling soared inside her. Yes, she loved this gallant, irritating, beautiful, arrogant man. She wanted to erase the loneliness she sensed in him, absolve the guilt that haunted his soul.

The brush of his fingers along her hip made her squirm with anxiety. Donovan's face lifted from her breast. He was watching her again, gauging her reaction.

"It tickles." She told him, smiling to dispel the worry in his eyes. "I'm ticklish."

"Are you?" His devilish look warned her she'd regret the confession.

His head dipped, he kissed her other breast and blew softly on the nipple after moistening it with his tongue. It was unbelievably exquisite, the warm, moist air of his breath caressing her in a way she couldn't imagine. Donovan inched up to kiss her mouth, bringing a sweet sense of fulfillment, and at the same moment evoking an intolerable need.

The large, firm hand once more slid purposefully down her hip and along her outer thigh. This time, she didn't flinch. He caressed her knee with his fingertips, and traced a path along the inside of her thigh. Elizabeth stiffened, preparing for a rough invasion as she recalled the smugglers groping her as they surrounded her that night. *Coarse, cruel hands. Male laughter. Pinching fingers caused pain and sought her humiliation as they reveled in her terrified cries.*

"Easy love." Donovan whispered, bringing her back to him again. His hand glided firmly over her hip, back and forth, comforting in its heaviness. "It's me. Let me caress your delicate lotus petals. Let me give you pleasure. I won't hurt you. I swear it. It's all right, Lizzie."

She was panting. She'd panicked, frozen, fallen into that dark place again—and he knew precisely what was happening to her. *He knew.* And he was trying to help her past it.

"I'm fine." She whispered, eyeing him with conviction and praying he would believe her. She didn't want him to turn back.

"Ah, you're a fine lass." He returned in a silken voice. "A fine, courageous lass."

Elizabeth snuggled closer to him, trying to convey with her body the words she was too timid to speak.

And then she had an idea. "Am I allowed to touch you?" She honestly didn't know.

He seemed puzzled by her inquiry. "I'm yours. Touch me as you wish, Mrs. Beaumont."

Elizabeth skimmed light fingers over his abdomen and his hip just as he had caressed her. She caressed his leg, enjoying the firmness beneath her hand, the power in those well muscled thighs she'd admired so often in tight doeskin breeches. She tentatively stroked his taut bum, giggling as she did so, feeling naughty. She liked cupping that firm curve.

Donovan grinned at her girlish giggles. He patiently watched her trace his body in a leisurely exploration. The only part of him she avoided was the rigid mound straining to be freed of his breeches. She wasn't ready for that, not yet. She edged around it and caressed his ribbed abdomen and hard chest. Elizabeth was oddly calmed by the exercise.

Noting the change in her, Donovan leaned low to kiss her with infinite tenderness.

Elizabeth was further bolstered by the gentle caress of his lips, no longer demanding or searching, but sweetly caressing with unstinting devotion.

She wrapped her arms about his neck, inviting him to deepen the kiss. They melted together in a satisfying kiss that seemed to have no end. Donovan's hand moved along her hip, a soothing gesture of possession and comfort. She leaned against him, wanting to be closer, to understand the heady need each kiss and persistent caress wrought deep within her.

The moment came again; his hand on her inner thigh. This time, the tip of his finger brushed over her delicate folds. Elizabeth started slightly but clung to him instead of retreating from his touch as she willed herself to permit his intimate exploration.

Donovan whispered sweet words to her. He paused with his hand posed at her entrance, waiting for her to accept his intrusion into her feminine flesh. She showed her acceptance of his intent by kissing his neck, leaving soft, moist trails of devotion along his sun kissed skin.

His physician's hands were gentle as they explored her sensitive flesh. Elizabeth never imagined a man's caress could be so tender or so clever as to bring shudders of unbelievable delight as her body responded in a way her mind could not comprehend. She sagged against the pillows, surrendering to his bold caress and to the astonishing sensations he awakened in her untried body.

She felt buoyed up on a breeze, lost in the wondrous feeling of pure, unexpected bliss.

Yet, beneath the pleasure a savage need was growing inside her, a need for *more*.

He slid a finger inside her moist channel. And then she knew. Elizabeth understood. What she yearned for so urgently was Donovan. His intimate touch had awakened a primitive desire to take him inside of her. She'd been so concerned about meeting his needs, doing her duty by giving him the pleasure of her body she failed to consider there could be pleasure in surrender.

He withdrew his finger, but before she could offer protest at the loss, that light forefinger returned to a sensitive place within her slick *lotus petals*, as he'd dubbed her womanly flesh. The exquisite sensation made her writhe and gasp beneath his finger as she was lifted into another plateau of raw, unexpected yet wondrously sensual delight.

Elizabeth gasped and shuddered as pure waves of undulating pleasure washed over her again and again to crest at last with an explosive power that ultimately overwhelmed her.

She lay quietly, her eyes closed, just breathing for several seconds as she slowly floated back to the solid earth.

As she opened her eyes Donovan was watching her with a pleased smile.

She knew what he was thinking. She would not allow it. He was going to say that this was enough for one night. Before he could say it, she slipped her hand beneath the waistband of his inexpressibles. "Take them off. Before I get cold feet and change my mind." Even as she said it, her teeth were chattering. Not from cold. She was still recovering from the explosion of pleasure he'd wrought in her. Elizabeth tugged at his manhood, no longer feeling craven about it. She grasped him beneath the fabric, demanding him to emerge to fulfill the bargain begun.

Donovan peeled the fabric back, freeing himself from his bonds. Elizabeth swallowed, a moan rising in her throat. Seeing that rigid male organ displayed in full battle array, poised to invade her tender flesh was nearly her undoing. Donovan's big hand lifted her chin, averting her eyes from the display of potent male power and guiding her to gaze at his face. He moved and settled himself between her legs, hovering over her, his weight on his forearms, waiting.

"Are you certain?" It pained her that he still felt he needed to ask.

"Yes. I trust you, Donovan."

"It will hurt a little the first time, only for a moment, Sweetheart."

Elizabeth nodded. She knew that. She placed her arms about his waist, urging him to drop down to put his full weight on her instead of hovering above her. She wanted it over with, plain and simple. She wanted to belong to him in every way.

He lowered himself and she felt the inflexible granite spear poised at her entrance. He was big, so big. She took a breath, steeling herself for the expected pain.

Donovan kissed her, leisurely, tenderly. She closed her eyes, and focused on that kiss.

With one quick thrust, he was inside of her.

Oh, God! Elizabeth moaned and buried her face in his shoulder. She wanted to scream, but quelled the urge as that would surely upset him. It felt like she was being impaled.

"Breathe, just breathe, relax. You'll stretch and relax around me and then it won't hurt." He held perfectly still inside her, waiting for her to 'relax' as he said.

Relax? How does one do so with a pike shoved inside them?

She gasped, several times, trying to overcome the panic at being so wholly possessed. It took more than a second. It took more than a minute. Gradually, she felt her pierced flesh relax around his imposing shaft. As he promised, it stopped hurting so much. She felt very full, as if her flesh were stretched too tight having him there . . . and then it started to feel sort of nice.

Sensing the change as her body slowly accepted him, Donovan began to move. He withdrew slowly, almost completely, but not quite. And then he gracefully glided inside her again, filling her with himself.

The idea of Donovan being inside of her brought a curious feeling of awe and exaltation.

It was an unrivaled, inexpressible sensation to be stroked by him--from within.

Intimacy. She understood the mystery of that word now, and the inherent delight behind the term. Elizabeth hugged him and kissed his neck. He arched his shoulders up, his face seeking her lips, and then kissed her with an intensity that was delightfully overwhelming. Donovan captured her mouth and at the same time glided deep inside of her. After several such earthy thrusts, she instinctively lifted her hips, arching in an attempt to match his sensual movements. It was like a dance. He was being so careful, so gentle. She sensed his restraint and she loved him for it. It was still a little uncomfortable, but the pain was giving way to a more urgent rising pleasure.

He stopped kissing her so deeply, as his breathing made it difficult to keep their lips joined. His muted moans told her he was nearing his own explosion. As she concentrated wholly upon Donovan, on meeting his thrusts and giving him the pleasure of her body, a sudden onslaught of unexpected desire moved through Elizabeth. She was swept up with him on a crest of intense pleasure more forceful than the timid shivers she experienced during his earlier love play.

Donovan's body stiffened. She felt him shudder and heard his gasp of completion echoing her own. He remained still, hugging her as their skin sealed together in moist delight.

Pulling back slightly, he gazed into her eyes for a moment, and then kissed her. So gently, so sweetly, it made her toes curl.

When his delicious kiss ended, he murmured, "It will get better for you, my sweet girl, I promise."

Better? Elizabeth thought, with a purr of pleasure. Aside from the pain at his entry, she couldn't imagine this becoming any sweeter than it had been just now.

She is exquisite. Aphrodite. His own sweet Venus, lying naked in his arms.

Donovan was lying on his side, watching his sleeping bride. Her face was tilted toward him on the pillow. Her hair fanned out in vibrant waves of silky copper like a halo circling the head of an icon. *Damn.* What else could he say?

Blushing innocence beguiled the rogue. It sounded like a bad line from a romantic poem.

How many hours had he spent planning her seduction? How many nights had he lain awake imagining all the ways he wanted to make love to her? And all the arguments he thought to use to convince her he could be trusted to guide her past her fear of intimacy.

Donovan had been determined tonight that it was not going to happen.

And then . . . Lizzie happened. She seduced him.

Chapter Thirty Four

As soon as Elizabeth finished breakfast, Donovan insisted she get dressed.

He kept pushing her as she dallied over her wardrobe. He was insensitive to the fact that she was deliberating over her appearance on the occasion of being allowed to go downstairs again after a week of bed rest.

She lingered over the generous selection of dresses he'd provided as part of her trousseau, a thoughtful gesture on his part when they married as her family would never have been able to see her turned out properly as a countess. There were many beautiful silk evening gowns, and several light, elegant day dresses of muslin. All of them were in the newer Empire fashion, with high waistlines that came just beneath her bust and with full, billowing skirts. The heavier silks were more appropriate for special occasions like balls and formal dinners, but Elizabeth couldn't help admiring the rainbow of jeweled hues lining her wardrobe.

"Come now, it's been half an hour with you mooning over the contents of that closet." Donovan stood behind her. "Pick one or I'll be forced to conclude you enjoy your confinement and carry you back to bed for more lovemaking."

Elizabeth smiled. "Truly, sir, I would not mind the delay as much as you appear to."

"Don't temp me." He muttered. "Come, now I have everything arranged just so."

She narrowed the choices to two. The sprigged muslin with indigo stripes or the solid apricot muslin with ivory lace flounces at the sleeves and hem?

"That one." He made the decision for her, hastily grabbing the apricot gown from its hanger and holding it out for her. "It brings out your coloring to best advantage."

Half an hour later, Donovan guided her up the stone steps to the balcony near the gnarled old tree and the rock wall. A red silk canopy had been erected to form a shelter against the mid-day sun.

Golden tassels secured the curtains at each corner, forming a luxurious outside room with golden red walls on opposite ends. A chaise sat beneath the canopy, along with a small table and two chairs. A pitcher of lemonade and glasses were on the table, several pastries, and a crystal vase of exotic purple orchids.

"Where did you get this?" She remarked, awed by the opulent silk tent glowing red in the sunshine as Donovan backed up, and led her beneath it with both his hands clasping hers.

"In Ceylon. It was the fashion for Pashas to use them when picnicking with their favorite concubines, so they might woo them with complete privacy. The canopy will protect your fair skin from the sun. You loved being outside when we were courting. I have fond memories of us walking through fields hand in hand in the evenings. You wore your hair undone and you were lovelier than the most celebrated debutante in London."

"With chapped hands and a patched, outdated gown?" Elizabeth completed his idyllic picture. "You must have been bewitched by the fairy folk, Mr. O'Rourke!"

"I was beguiled by beauty devoid of guile or artifice." He countered, leaning close to capture a kiss. His lips were sweet yet possessive. He lingered, tasting her, nibbling at her lower lip with gentle teeth, teasing and leaving Elizabeth yearning for more after he released her and encouraged her to recline upon the silken chaise.

She sank back in a leisurely repose and listened to the birds singing nearby, the insects thrumming, and the breeze rustling the leaves of the tree behind them. The sound of waves crashing on the rocks beneath the cliff and the salt tang in the air was exhilarating. She inhaled the fragrant scent of musty earth mingled with the crisp sea air.

An iridescent blue butterfly lighted on Elizabeth's arm. The wings shimmered like miniature jewels. Another settled on her knee. A third blue blur hovered in front of her face. As if by magic, the tent was instantly swarming with blue butterflies as they danced about her in a swirling wave. Recalling her grandmother's stories, she closed her eyes and silently opened her heart to the earth spirits bidding her welcome here.

When Elizabeth opened her eyes, the insects were still swirling about her in a vortex of rising and cascading wings. The footmen were staring, open mouthed. Donovan, too, stood immobile, watching her. As a scientist, he would be fascinated by this unusual display of insect behavior. Elizabeth remained still as the creatures glided about her in silent wonder.

Finally, her charming ambassadors danced upward as one fluid body and swirled away.

"Thank you." She was touched by his thoughtful gift of a picnic in the gardens.

"This isn't your gift." Donovan replied. "O'Leary, go retrieve our guest."

Donovan pulled the chair close, sat down and took her hand, his manner becoming grave. "I have a surprise. It is also shocking." He paused, studying her for a moment. "You must prepare yourself, dearest."

Elizabeth was confounded by his solemnity. "You say it is wonderful, yet you're so stern. I am all amazement, my lord. And I am not made of spun glass. Please, do tell."

He paused, trying to find the right words. "Sheila told me of Kieran's disappearance when you and I were courting. I discovered recently that he is alive. He resides in Basseterre. He saw our wedding announcement in the paper, and he's come here, to meet you."

Elizabeth's mind tumbled through the years. She couldn't believe it. Mama mourned Kieran's death all her life, and Sheila, too. "But . . . how?"

"Fletcher sold him as an indenture on the London docks." Donovan explained, as she gazed at him with her mouth agape. He kneaded her hand as he explained Kieran's story.

The sound of gravel crunching on the cobbled stones heralded the approach of their visitor. A tall, slender man walked beside Gus along the garden path. His brown broadcloth suit was simple, befitting a merchant. Clean white stockings and buckled shoes provided a more civilized contrast to the military boots Donovan and his men went stomping about in.

She glanced furtively at the man's downcast face as he treaded the uneven cobblestones banked by tall weeds on either side of the narrow path. His face was clean shaven, his features refined, almost too delicate for a man. His coppery brows arched up slightly, and his lips were turned up in the mere hint of a smile. He possessed hair the same fiery shade as hers. He kept it restrained in a neat queue in a longer style still popular among older men and arrogant ones like her spouse, who didn't adhere to the dictates of fashion.

Enchanted; that would be the word to describe him. He possessed the majesty of a Faerie prince emerging from a hidden glen. She imagined him with a cloak of velvet green and a circlet of gold on his brow, a legend conjured from the forest mists in all of his glory.

"Good morning, Kieran." Donovan spoke and the image faded as reality replaced her idyllic vision. Her husband stepped forward and extended his hand.

"My lord." The man replied in a softened Irish burr.

The man transferred his sea green gaze to her. Elizabeth stared at him with awe.

"Lizzie," Donovan crouched beside her. "This is Kieran O'Flaherty. Kieran, I present my wife, Lady Elizabeth Beaumont, Countess du Rochembeau."

Kieran bowed before her. "I am honored, my lady."

The sound of wind rustling leaves in the nearby tree went unchallenged. It seemed the world was holding its breath, not merely Elizabeth, as she stared at her kinsmen with wonder.

She smiled at the ethereal stranger. "Mr. O'Flaherty."

How often she'd longed for him as a child. At eleven, she pretended he wasn't dead as they claimed--he was just away at school. Many of her friends had had older brothers away at Eton so it was easy to fashion a fantasy brother as an escape from the constant fear of living with Captain Fletcher. *One day*, she would tell herself, *Kieran will come home and I won't have to be strong anymore. I won't have to pretend I'm not afraid for Michael's benefit.*

But Kieran couldn't come home to hide with her in the closet, hold her hand and tell her not to be frightened. Kieran couldn't come home because he'd been sold by their stepfather, lied to about his mother's death, and sent halfway across the world at the tender age of nine.

"He hurt you." Elizabeth blurted out, as the pain of the brutal betrayal choked her throat.

"No, dear lady." He responded. "Don't weep for me. I was the fortunate one. I was sold to a man who treated me as a beloved son. You suffered the greater part of Fletcher's evil."

"You were treated well?" Her voice was reduced to a high-pitched squeak.

"Barnaby is a kindly old grandfather." The soft burr replied, as the image before her remained blurred behind a veil of tears. "I didn't know you existed. If I had, I would have come for you. I wouldn't have left you to deal with that bastard alone. "

Was it magic? This fantasy--this childhood game that had helped her survive the darkness?

"Please, my lady, do not cry."

"Come now, Elizabeth. This is no time for tears. Fletcher did not succeed in destroying either of you." Donovan's arm wound about her as he sat close.

"I'm sorry, my lord. I did not mean to make her cry." The Irishman apologized.

"Shhh," Donovan's big hand moved up and down Elizabeth's back in a comforting mien as her tears continued, despite her best efforts to vanquish them. "Lizzie, my sweet. You'll have plenty of time to become acquainted."

"Sh-sh—" she whimpered, "Sheila would be s-so r-re—" She hiccupped and sputtered. "Relieved." She gazed adoringly at her brother. "Sheila never stopped mourning you."

"Sit Kieran, please." Donovan intoned, when the gentleman remained poised before them with his head bowed. "Gus, pour some lemonade." He directed Elizabeth's guard.

Kieran did as Donovan bade, as did the sailor-cum-bodyguard he'd appointed to keep Elizabeth safe in his absence. The scraping of chair legs and clinking of glasses as the refreshments were served helped mask the sound of Elizabeth's frantic snuffling. Donovan pressed a handkerchief into her palm as Gus handed him a glass of lemonade.

Kieran nodded to the footman and then to Donovan as he took his offering. "My lady, may I ask what happened to our grandmother? I always worried what became of her, but as a boy thousands of miles from home I could do nothing but hope that fate had dealt with her kindly." He hesitated, as if it pained him to speak of it. "When did she actually die?"

"I told him what I knew." Donovan interjected, gazing at her with assurance as he knew quite well she had no memory of Sheila's death and he no knowledge to give.

Elizabeth shivered in the warm sunlight. A paisley shawl was placed over her shoulders. She looked up, surprised to see Chloe hovering behind her. Chloe smiled and pressed her shoulder. Elizabeth reached up to squeeze her friend's hand.

Fortified by Donovan's calming presence and Chloe's stalwart affection, Elizabeth spoke. "I don't recall how Sheila died. It was a few months ago, before my wedding." She looked to Donovan, uncertain. At his nod she continued. "I cannot remember the past two years of my life, with the exception of being abducted. Sheila was our nanny—more than that. She loved us. She used to tell me stories about Ireland, of Father, and of you."

Kieran nodded. "I have fond memories of following her about the garden, barefoot—she was always barefoot, and so I was, too, as a lad. She'd tell me about various plants growing around the castle grounds, and quiz me on their healing properties."

The afternoon passed in golden sunshine filtered through vibrant red hues as they sat beneath the canopy eating pastries, cold ham and cheeses. Kieran told Elizabeth what he remembered of their father.

Finally, Kieran set his plate aside and leaned forward, his elbows on his knees as he regarded her with somber eyes. "And what of our mother? His lordship told me she died three and half years ago. How did she die?"

Again, the chill came. Elizabeth tucked the shawl tighter about her neck. She looked her brother in the eyes and told him the same lie she'd been forced to tell the constable years ago. "It was late, past midnight. I heard a noise on the stairs. I slipped out of bed to investigate. Papa was out, as always, at his club. I thought perhaps he'd come home and tripped on the stairs. When I went to stand at the top of the stairs, I saw Mama lying at the bottom. She was so still. She was dead, but her eyes were open."

It hurt—the retelling, and the horrid memory of her mother's broken body lying so still at the bottom of the stairs. "She must have slipped and fallen. Sometimes she was woozy at night, because of the Laudanum she took. There was blood behind her head. Blood pooling on the floor, soaking into the floorboards. Her death was ruled an accident."

Donovan's arm wrapped about her waist as he leaned close. Chloe's hand circled her shoulder. Elizabeth cursed herself for her cowardice.

"And *you* found her? How horrifying it must have been for you." Kieran remarked.

"Yes, that's enough excitement for one day. If you will excuse us, Kieran, I'm taking Lizzie back to our room to rest." Donovan was rising already, noting the change in Elizabeth's demeanor and mistaking it for weariness instead of mortifying shame.

Weary would do. Yes. She was weary of keeping the secret, but after so many years, how to tell it? How to speak of it and not incur the abhorrence of these two men in the telling?

She lied to the authorities. She lied to Michael, and now to Kieran and Donovan as well.

She covered Fletcher's foul deed. She protected a murderer, allowed him to go free.

Was she not just as guilty as he?

Chapter Thirty Five

The next days were framed in bliss. Elizabeth felt secure in her role as Madame Beaumont. Donovan's devotion made it clear she was firmly entrenched in his heart.

Donovan made arrangements to meet with his steward each morning directly following the family breakfast in the newly opened breakfast room, giving Elizabeth time alone with her brother. She and Kieran strolled the gardens and discussed their peculiar Druidic heritage.

Elizabeth could not contain her amazement at finding Kieran was alive, just as she'd imagined as child. When she explained it to him he said it was the gift of second sight. She was a child and had never known him. Thus, unlike their grandmother, her vision was not blocked by extreme grief or the rationalizations adults use to disregard the supernatural. She knew he was alive yet very far away. As a child she lacked the ability to determine more. The power to form a metaphysical link with him would come years later, after Sheila's death.

Kieran told her how she had summoned him months ago, when she was in the smuggler hold. He shared his confusion at being pulled from his body like a fish yanked from the water on a hook, and thrust into hers so he experienced the horror of her abduction along with her.

That was disturbing. Elizabeth believed he spoke the truth, but it was beyond her ability to comprehend. "How could I do that? I don't remember doing any such thing."

"You wished me there, just like when you were a child." Kieran replied. "This time, you had Sheila's powers coupled with your own. You don't remember because it was instinctual, an act of self preservation during great distress. I doubt you even thought of doing it, you just did it. It's called Soul Travel. There are stories of the ancient ones traveling outside their bodies, but it's rare that one of us can summon another to them. You have extraordinary powers, Elizabeth."

They walked along in silence, as Elizabeth mulled over his praise. She wouldn't call the things she had seen and experienced extraordinary. She considered them a curse, not a gift.

"Have you had any visits from those behind the veil?" Kieran asked one day as they walked the cobbled path.

"Yes. There is resident ghost. She's appeared several times to me."

"Maureen O'Donovan." Kieran nodded. "I've met her. There are others, too. I sense their presence, but they remain as shadows, unwilling to reveal themselves."

Elizabeth hid her panic at his words. *Their mother?* Apparently, she had not appeared to Kieran. That was a relief. She'd been afraid to broach the subject. "Yes, I've sensed them as well. To be honest, Kieran, I don't wish to see them."

"I know." Her brother took her hand, a unique gesture of affection he'd not attempted before this. "I felt the same, growing up. I just wanted to be normal." He sighed, and looked quickly about them. "Your man, he's always following and watching us."

Elizabeth turned to where Kieran was looking. Through the bushes, several feet away stood her bodyguard. "Mr. O'Leary. Donovan assigned him to watch over me when he is absent. Gus is actually quite charming, compared to his companion." She rolled her eyes heavenward as she recalled Mr. Duchamp. "Donovan's afraid something bad will happen to me. I've tried reasoning with him but he clings to his irrational worries, so Gus follows me about all day."

Kieran made a face. "It's not irrational. Something horrible did happen to you. He feels guilty. He believes he should have been able to prevent it."

Elizabeth stopped walking. She let go of his hand and sucked in her lower lip.

It was a rebuke, although much gentler than she deserved.

She'd been so absorbed with her own suffering she'd failed to see how her abduction affected her husband. Kieran's simple observation clarified a great deal regarding her spouse's behavior.

Donovan was so fiercely protective of her, vigilant about her well being due to her head injury-- and no wonder, he blamed himself for it.

"Let's sit here." Kieran took her elbow and guided her to the stone bench at the edge of the gardens, overlooking the sea. "I can teach you a few exercises to keep the spirits from pestering you. It takes practice. You'll have to do them every day. Take my hand."

Elizabeth did as he said. Quietly, so Gus didn't overhear them, Kieran guided her through an exercise to establish a barrier against wandering spirits.

On another morning, he talked to her about 'walking the Veil between the Worlds', the term for visiting the Summerland, the Celtic place of the dead.

Once more, they sat on the stone bench overlooking the sea. They had their back to the gardens and appeared to be merely talking as they looked out at the sea. Taking her hand, Kieran guided her into the Veil. He chanted a few phrases in Gaelic. When Elizabeth opened her eyes, she was in a grey place, shrouded by fog. It was cold. She shivered, and wished she had a cloak to protect her skin from the cool dampness. She could see grey shapes moving about. She could hear whispers of conversation. Panic rising, she turned about, searching for Kieran in the eerie grey twilight, searching for someone, anyone she could recognize. Her heart pounded in her temples. The air, if one could call it that, was so thick, heavy, cloying. She saw only dark, shadowy figures moving about in the fog. "Kieran!" She shouted, fearing he abandoned her.

"I'm here." He squeezed her hand. She looked down and saw his hand clutching her own in the gloomy mists. And then the rest of him appeared. "Don't be afraid. They won't hurt you."

"Is this the Summerland? I thought it was supposed to be warm and pleasant here."

"No." Kieran replied. "This is the Veil between the Worlds. The spirits who have crossed over come here to try to talk to those they left behind. We can meet them here."

"I want to go back." She said, panicked by the constant swirling figures brushing past her and the cold, damp misty twilight of their surroundings. "Take me back, please."

"Just wait. They're happy to see you. You are the new seer. They want to meet you."

"Who are they?" She wanted to run. She wanted to get back to Ravencrest, to the sunshine, to the warmth, and to Donovan. She clutched Kieran's hand, frightened that if she let go of him, she would be stranded in this dark place forever.

"These are our people; the O'Flahertys and many other clans who looked to the Druids for guidance throughout the ages. You are their link to the physical world. They will not hurt you. As high priestess, you have the power to call them forth, to use their power and combine it with your own when the need arises. In ancient times, during battles, Druid priests stood near the battlefield, chanting and calling forth the power of the ancestors to help vanquish the enemy."

As he spoke, faces materialized from the swirling mists. Elizabeth studied each face as it hovered before her briefly, like courtesans bowing and passing before her. Men, women, young and old; Warriors, both men and the brave women who fought beside them in ages past.

"Elizabeth!" A familiar voice called from a great distance. Elizabeth gasped, and was suddenly hurtled through a freezing void of sooty, black mist.

She sank forward, her head in her lap, gasping and choking, as she let go of Kieran's hand. The world spun about her, but it was brilliant world of sunshine and warmth.

"Elizabeth!" Donovan was kneeling in front of her, his face livid. He looked as if he wanted to kill someone—and that someone was sitting next to her.

Kieran was gasping as well. He looked like he might choke to death on his own. He put his arm about her protectively and looked into that angry visage before them.

"What the hell is this?" Donovan demanded. "What are you doing to her?"

"It's fine—" Elizabeth gasped. The world was spinning erratically beneath her.

"We—" Kieran coughed. "I was showing her how to—how to—meditate—my lord—"

"Like hell you were." Donovan crouched in front of Elizabeth. He touched her cheek, and studied her face intently. "Lizzie, are you all right?" He stroked her arm and then slipped his arm about her shoulder protectively. He turned his face to Kieran, who was still recovering from their abrupt retrieval. "She was terrified."

"I'm just a little dizzy." In truth, she was relieved by Donovan's presence, relieved to be back in the sunshine instead of in the spiritual catacombs. "He's teaching me how to control my gift so I am not overcome by random visions like the one I had with Linton."

That brought Donovan's attention back to her. He gazed at her with sympathy.

"That was most unpleasant." She reminded him.

"Yes, it was." Kieran agreed beside her.

Elizabeth turned to her brother. He saw that, too?

This was becoming quite disturbing.

"I'll ask again, what were you doing to her?" Donovan insisted hours later, when he'd effectively removed Elizabeth from Kieran's presence. "Out with it, man."

O'Flaherty did not answer. He sat with his lips clamped tight. They were in Kieran's room, upstairs. It had taken all of Donovan's strength not to throttle him in the garden earlier. The horrified look on his wife's face was one he hoped to never see again.

Lizzie was in Donovan's suite, quite exhausted and pale. She kept insisting she was fine, but she had that haunted look in her eye that worried Donovan and made him furious with the man responsible. And she kept shivering, from fear, he gathered, as she hadn't a fever.

Donovan paced the room, his fists tight, his fury rising. "I told you she was frail. I told you she is recovering from a very serious illness. She'll claim she's fine, but people with severe head injuries don't realize anything is wrong with them. They don't feel any different."

He turned, glared at the man, and stalked closer. "Do you have any idea what might have happened out there if I hadn't arrived when I did? She could have succumbed to another grand mal seizure. She had a brutal one ten days ago, and then she slept as if she were dead for six hours after. I thought she would be dead by the end of that day. She cannot be upset or agitated. I told you—*Damn you*—I warned you. Now tell me what the hell you were doing to my wife."

O'Flaherty wilted in the face of his fury, a small recompense for the outrage in his heart, and the terror behind that outrage. He could not lose Elizabeth. He would do anything to protect her, even from her doltish, wizard of a brother.

The man sat forward in the chair, his arms about himself as if he suddenly wanted to be anywhere but here. Donovan half expected the man to disappear into thin air and good riddance.

"I didn't think of that, my lord." O'Flaherty murmured. His face had a fallen cast. "I'm sorry, I forgot about her seizures. I-I didn't think. I was just trying to teach her our ways."

At dinner that evening, Kieran announced he had to leave the next morning to return to his employer. Barnaby was old and depended on him for a great many things.

Elizabeth was saddened by his announcement. She was enjoying his company, for the most part—today's incident aside. And she'd hoped he'd stay on indefinitely. She looked to Donovan, hoping he'd raise a polite objection, but his features remained stony. She looked to Kieran again, hoping for an explanation, but her brother seemed to find the contents of his plate fascinating and did not meet her eyes for the rest of the meal.

Kieran departed the next morning. He promised to visit often and reminded Elizabeth he was just fifteen miles away, across the bay in Basseterre if she needed him. Donovan shook his hand and bade him a polite farewell. Elizabeth could not shake the impression that the men had quarreled after their interlude in the garden and Kieran had been asked to leave.

It bothered her, but she decided to let it go for now. Perhaps Donovan was justified in his concern. She had been frightened yesterday, much more than she cared to admit. Perhaps he was being silly or jealous of her time with Kieran. At any rate, she did not wish to argue with him about it. She'd let a few days go by, give his ire a chance to wane and then address the issue.

Later that same afternoon, Donovan's eyes were aglow with intrigue as he lifted her into the canopied curricle and climbed up beside her.

Lush jungle vegetation gave way to a sea of waving green as he guided their carriage along a low road skirting cane fields on the eastern edge of the island. The breeze was crisp and demanding on the windward side of the island, refreshing on such a hot day. Elizabeth clutched her hat to hold it fast. Even with the hairpin, it threatened to float away as the lively winds buffeted through the light straw weave.

They passed a windmill poised to catch the strong breezes coming off the sea. Rough scaffolding hugged the front of it. Squinting in the brilliant sunlight, Elizabeth could make out the figures on the top of the platform who worked busily to repair one of the damaged blades.

There were several low buildings nearby. An array of large copper vats with a series of pipes connecting them were being set up near the mill in preparation for the coming harvest.

After the juice was pressed from the cane stalks under the wind powered grinding stone, the series of troughs delivered the liquid to the copper vats. Once there, the juice was boiled until only fine granules remained. The granules had to be pressed into clay cones for shipment to England, where it would be further refined and then sold exclusively on the English market. It was short harvest season, a matter of weeks. It was a labor intensive process requiring every able man's efforts through the long days, Donovan explained as they moved past the mill.

The view of the sea was blocked by lush foliage on either side of the road as the landscape gave way to a thick jungle. Donovan brought the carriage up short at the end of an interior road. He secured the horses to a nearby tree, and then helped

Elizabeth down. As soon as her feet were on the ground, he kissed her thoroughly and then held her against him for several moments before releasing her and taking her hand to lead her up the trail.

The path was narrow, hemmed in by thick foliage on both sides and straggling branches.

"That's unusual." He remarked, examining branches and large leaves that had been snapped off along the trail to the interior jungle. "Someone else has been here not too long ago. I expected to have to hack our way through the brush."

It was then that Elizabeth noted he had a machete clasped in his free hand, and a brace of pistols beneath his vest. Couldn't the man relax for a moment and let down his guard?

He stopped at the crest of a steep incline, giving her a chance to catch her breath. As if having read her thoughts about his inability to relax and enjoy the day, he once more took her into his arms, although he didn't try to kiss her as she was nearly panting from the exertion. He just held her against him and gazed down at her with unveiled adoration. "It's not much farther, my sweet. I could carry you, if you like."

"No. Don't be ridiculous. This is what comes of making me stay in bed to rest all day. I used to go out walking in the woods all the time in England."

"Alone. It's not proper for woman of your station to do so now. Your grandmother allowed you far too much freedom as a girl."

She made a face at him. "Nothing happened to me in the woods."

"That doesn't change the fact that it could have." He returned. "Come."

He helped her down the steep embankment. They continued on the path for several moments. Elizabeth admired the lush foliage and the exotic thrills of birdsong as she allowed him to lead her deeper into the jungle.

A sudden movement ahead of them made her cry out. A snake meandered across the path before them. It was well over six feet long, just as Peter faithfully reported. Donovan stood still, the machete held out, watching the serpent with wariness. It lingered, lifting its head as it gazed at them for what seemed an eternity before slithering away into the safety of the jungle brush.

As she watched it, a cold fear surrounded her, a sense of foreboding.

"Come. He's gone, he'll find a fat rabbit or two and then sleep away the afternoon."

"No." Elizabeth gasped, that uneasy feeling only growing at his insistence that they continue deeper into the snake's lair. "Serpent's are messengers from the underworld." She said without thinking. "They are the harbingers of death."

"*Lizzie.*" He shook his head and gestured about them with the blade. "This area is populated by indigenous snakes; it doesn't make it an evil place. Snakes are useful. Like cats, they eat rodents. Come." He tugged at her hand.

After studying her grandmother's book, she knew a snake crossing her path was an omen that spirits from the underworld were near. Donovan didn't believe in the ways of their Celtic ancestors, and he obviously thought her silly for being uneasy.

They stopped at a translucent pool fed by a small waterfall at the opposite end. Lush vegetation and flowers hugged the rocks about the waterfall, and a fine mist of spray added to the mystique of the place. Moss covered rocks jutted out to the right, and the trilling of wild birds complemented the serene music of the flowing falls.

"This was one of my favorite places to loll away the afternoon as a boy." Donovan told her with a smile. "I came to visit my grandfather for a couple of months every spring. Gareth and I used to slide over the falls and let the current carry us to the opposite edge of the pool."

It was breathtaking, and yet Elizabeth could not dismiss the eerie sensation in the pit of her belly since encountering that enormous snake. She gazed about, trying to relax and enjoy the outing as Donovan intended. She gasped as she looked out at the jungle beyond the pool. Three figures were watching them from across the sparkling pool. They stood beside a mossy rock.

"What is it?" Donovan slipped his arm about her, drawing her close as he followed her startled gaze. "What frightens you so?"

"Those men, they're watching us."

He shoved her behind him. A cocked pistol was instantly in front of him. He squinted, holding the arm gripping his machete up to block the shimmer of sunlight from the falls. "I don't see them. They must have slipped back into the thick jungle growth."

"You can't see them?" She whispered frantically, peering around him. "Donovan, they're standing right there." She pointed. "Beside the waterfall, next to that big pointy stone."

He stared determinedly at the spot directly across the pool. When he turned to her, his face was stricken. "I don't see them. You said there were three men?"

Elizabeth held her tongue, remembering his rebuke regarding the snake.

"Lizzie, talk to me. Tell me what it is you see." His tone had changed, from disdain to alarm. He clutched her shoulders. "We've been looking for the three missing indentures for weeks. We assumed they found a way off the island somehow. If you see them now and I cannot, it can only mean one thing."

"You don't believe in 'ghosts and spirits and all that metaphysical' horse crap'. I heard you telling Pearl so on the ship."

"I've become a little more open minded about the spirit world since then." He placed his pistol back in his belt and took her hand. "Tell me what you see now. Are they speaking to you? What do they look like?"

"They're wearing dirty work clothes. They are barefoot, and they're wearing leg irons." She said. "They've been hurt. One looks as if his face was beaten in. His forehead is open." She made a face. She could see inside his skull, it was dark grey and shiny. "There's a very large gash." She brushed her own brow to indicate the spot.

The spirit closest to them beckoned for her to follow him. She walked around the pool, toward the three men waiting at the jagged, mossy stone. Donovan followed, keeping a hold of her arm. He had the machete gripped firmly in his sword hand.

The spirits glided ahead for several paces, and then melted into the ground behind a huge boulder adjacent to the waterfall. Elizabeth followed them to the spot, and crouched on the ground, letting her palm rest on the freshly disturbed earth.

She listened and then repeated to Donovan what the spirits told her.

"Mr. Crowley had been ill for days. The overseer accused him of lying to get out of work. He demanded Mr. Crowley get up out of his bunk and go outside to the lineup to go out to the fields. When he didn't the overseer hit him with his cudgel. He kept hitting him on the back and when Mr. Crowley still didn't get up, he whacked him on the forehead with it. When the two men sharing his hut returned from the fields they found him dead. The overseer denied their accusation, saying one of them had to be the killer, as he'd left the man alive that morning."

"Damn Winslow." Donovan swore. "I knew he had a brutal streak. I warned him many times to restrain himself. What happened to the other two?"

"Mr. Winslow ordered the two men tied to the posts in the prison yard. He sent the guards away. He whipped them without mercy, saying the punishment would go on until one of them confessed to killing Crowley. He was drunk. He beat them to death, and when he realized what he'd done, he dragged their bodies here and buried them."

"Lizzie." Donovan grasped her by the shoulders. "Sweetheart, let's get you back to the house. I'll come back with Ambrose and some of the guards from the compound to see what we can find." He helped her to her feet, and dragged his heel through the dirt where she had been squatting to mark it with a deep X.

The ride back to the estate was solemn. Both of them knew the only way to prove that what she claimed was to dig to find the bodies.

"You do believe me?" She prodded when they reached the stable yard.

Pulling the carriage to a halt, Donovan turned to her. "Lizzie, when you were very ill on the ship, you told Pearl things about his mother in India, you gave him accurate messages from the woman--and she's dead. You spoke to Captain Rawlings' deceased fiancée and gave Jack and I detailed information about how she died. You gave Jack a message from her. You couldn't have known any of that, Sweet Lizzie, not unless Miss Pemberly told you how she died."

"I don't remember it." Elizabeth said with bewilderment.

"You were right about Linton." He added. "And you found Marissa's hidden papers."

"And I was right about the snake."

Chapter Thirty Six

Giles was waiting for them at the back door, his face lit up with undisguised glee as he told them her grandfather and brother had just arrived and were awaiting them in the salon. Elizabeth could hardly believe his report as she rushed to the salon upon entering the house.

Donovan followed, looking vastly displeased at the idea of guests invading his home.

"Liz!" Michael met her at the door of the salon, lifting her in his arms and whirling her about with unfettered exuberance. "I say, you're light as a feather, doesn't his lordship feed you? I can wrap my arms about you twice."

"Only when I'm good and as you know I rarely am." She said, hugging him. "Oh, Michael, I thought I'd never see you again."

"Don't be a goose. There was only an ocean between us!" He laughed, hugging her just as tightly. "Grandfather was determined to spend Christmas with both of us this year." He turned, gesturing to the thin, elderly man observing them as he leaned on his cane.

"My dear child." The old man moved quickly across the tile flooring to embrace her. "I'm so relieved to see you, Elizabeth." He whispered, hugging her with more emotion then she'd ever thought the proud old man capable of. When she was a girl, he seemed so autocratic and imposing, sending everyone in the household, including their mother, scurrying nervously about to do his bidding. He seemed frail now. His skin was papery thin, his complexion pasty. Even his voice sounded withered and tired. She shot a glance in her husband's direction, longing to share her concerns with him.

Donovan had an impassive look on his face, a polite, well bred blank. His eyes locked briefly with hers, and his impatience was all too clear. He needed to attend this ghastly murder business.

She nodded her understanding to him, yet he lingered at the foot of the stairs.

"I situated Lord Greystowe in the blue room, my lady." Giles informed her, breaking the tension. "And Master Michael is in the green room, the one you appointed for him earlier."

"Thank you." She told the butler. "Grandfather, would you like to rest for a while?" She placed her hand on his arm, anxious to establish physical contact with him and discern the situation a little more. She sensed an undercurrent of anxiety in the old man. She couldn't discern anything beyond that. "I was just on my way upstairs for an afternoon nap. I can't seem to make it through the day without one. Shall we both go?"

"Yes. I'd fancy a bed that doesn't rock and sway. I've yet to get my land legs again. You there, young buck." Grandfather held out a bony hand to Donovan. "Help me up the stairs. We need to have a private word. I fear that we may need to make some drastic changes to our legal agreement." It was a command, not a request.

This was the grandfather Elizabeth remembered; the intimidating, autocratic earl.

"Giles will help you upstairs, Lord Greystowe. We'll have to postpone any talk of legal arrangements." Donovan informed him in an equally commanding tone. "I have urgent business on my estate." Her husband gestured to the butler to assist her grandfather and made his exit.

"I'll be right up to check on you." Elizabeth told her grandfather as Giles took the old man's arm and gestured smartly to the footmen standing near the front door to step quick and take the other arm. Elizabeth slipped into the parlor with Michael in tow. "What's going on?"

"All I know is that Grandfather and Donovan are both my legal guardians, Liz. Grandfather is the primary, but Donovan's to step in and take over in the event Grandfather dies before I reach my majority." He gazed about the room with a sour face. "He was mad as a hornet with Donovan for taking you away without allowing him a reunion. We spent two weeks in London trying to find a ship that would book us passage during hurricane season, he was that determined speak to Donovan. I think he means to leave me off here with you."

"No." Elizabeth soothed, rubbing his arm with affection.

"I'm a disappointment to him. He's always snapping at me. Claims he's seen stable boys with better manners. I'm not cut out to be a lord. I'm going to be an artist. Grandfather says it's beneath the family dignity to be painting whores all day and mingling with the wrong sort."

"Well, Michael, Grandfather does have a point. As his heir, you have obligations to fulfill. But, things may take an unexpected turn." She didn't wish to point out that their dour grandparent might be dead within a year, and with Kieran alive, Michael's expectations may have changed considerably. That was a conversation for another time.

So much for bliss, Elizabeth thought, having cherished what might be termed a rather late honeymoon over the past week. She hoped there was no fight in the offing between her grandfather and her husband. Donovan would emerge the victor in any battle of wills, but she didn't wish for the men to be at sixes and nines and spoil the holidays.

She turned to her brother, unable to keep herself from giving him yet another hug. "I've missed you. Is it really so bad living with Grandfather?"

Michael shrugged, and glanced about the room. "He's tolerable. Stiff in his starches, but we always knew that. He's not too bad of a fellow, once you get used to his brusque manner. Donovan's been good to you? He seems a different bloke than the one we met in England."

"He's tolerable." Elizabeth mimicked his speech. "Once you get used to his solemn, grave demeanor." Michael looked stricken. Elizabeth laughed. "Oh, he's not Mr. O'Rourke, Michael, if that's what you are expecting." She grinned at her brother. "He's American. Quite the opposite of Grandfather, completely unconventional but he's absolutely wonderful."

"He hardly said hello to me." Michael complained.

"He has urgent business to attend to. There may have been a murder on the island. He was just going to drop me home and gather some men to investigate when we were told you arrived." She stifled a yawn. "I really am all in. Will you forgive me if I follow grandfather's example and take a nap before dinner?"

Michael nodded. "Perhaps I'll take a walk out to the stables."

"If you need anything ask Giles for it, he's our butler. He'll make sure you are comfortable. Oh, Michael. I've missed you so much, and I have the most wonderful news to share with both you and grandfather."

Dinner that evening was a somber affair. Elizabeth looked about the dining room, pleased to see the table nearly full with the addition of Michael, the earl, and Michael's tutor, Mr. Marceau. Chloe and Uncle Gareth took their usual places at the table, completing the family circle. Donovan had not returned from his excursion into the jungle.

Grandfather kept looking at Uncle Gareth with disdain. Elizabeth endeavored to ignore his ill manners, and strove to make everyone comfortable. "So, Master Michael, do you approve of our stables?" She asked, teasing her brother a bit with her formal address.

"Oh, yes." He said between chews. "A fine stock. Johnny really seems to know his horseflesh. I talked with him for quite a while out there. We're to go riding tomorrow."

"Riding, with the groom?" Grandfather interjected, incredulous at the idea of his heir rubbing elbows with a servant. He made a face, and grunted his displeasure.

Elizabeth was pleased that Michael was making friends here already, and Johnny O'Reilly was a very nice young man. "Well, I'm certain you two will have much to talk about, as you were a stable boy, too, until a few months ago." She commented, smiling at her brother.

"Donovan's stallion is magnificent, an Arabian!" Michael enthused. "I'd give my eye teeth to have such a fine horse. It's a lord's mount, that one."

"Zeus. Yes. He's very spirited." Gareth put in. "Donovan has set him to stud with several mares. There will be five foals born in the spring. You might ask him if you could have one."

Lord Greystowe cleared his throat. "Such language, and with a lady present." He glowered imperviously at Gareth. "Breeding horses is not a proper subject for the dinner table."

"Yes, sir." Michael was quick to respond.

Gareth shrugged off the old man's rebuke with a smile and a toss of his serpent's mane as was his way. Elizabeth was fuming. Gareth was just being kind to her brother. The old man didn't need to make it sound as if his speech was a moral affront. Donovan talked about breeding all the time, at the dinner table and anywhere else he pleased. She hoped Donovan would not be the recipient of such open disdain.

"The gardener is supposed to arrive tomorrow." Chloe chimed in, changing the subject. "I have that list of herbs you wanted me to make of plants to cultivate for our recipes, my lady."

Elizabeth smiled at her companion. While confined to bed, she and Chloe made a list of herbs they needed based on their grandmother's potions. "I do hope he can rescue what remains of the gardens from the jungle."

"Who is this young woman?" Grandfather fixed his condescending gaze upon Chloe.

"Miss Ramirez is my companion. Chloe, I present my grandfather, James Wentworth, the ninth Earl of Greystowe." Elizabeth responded in what she hoped was a patient voice.

"Indeed." The earl huffed, dabbing his lips with his napkin. "Rather odd when a married lady needs a companion?" His icy gaze moved dismissively from Chloe to rest upon Elizabeth, expecting an explanation.

"It is isolated here," Gareth informed the man. "The count is often busy with estate affairs, so it is a very agreeable arrangement, my lord."

"Mr. Marceau," Elizabeth smiled down the table at their quiet guest, remembering that he had yet to join the conversation. "Is your room to your satisfaction?"

"*Oui,* my lady." The man appeared relieved that she had deigned to notice him.

"How was your journey here?" She persisted, trying to bring Michael's tutor out. If he spent six weeks confined in close quarters on ship with her irritable grandfather, she pitied him.

Mr. Marceau swallowed his mouthful of herbed pork and then regaled them with the horrors of the storm that had swept them nearly a hundred miles off course; the tail end of a hurricane. So their six week passage had turned out to be closer to eight.

Grandfather behaved himself for the rest of the meal, remaining silent and morose.

With Elizabeth's encouragement, the others talked and began to relax. Just as they were about to retreat to the salon, Donovan arrived. He was still wearing the clothes from his excursion, Elizabeth noted, casting a quick look in her grandfather's direction. This wasn't London. They did not stand on ceremony here. She waited for some rebuff to slip from the earl's lips, but only his eyes marked his host's rumpled attire as Donovan stood before them.

Donovan took his place at the head of the table next to Elizabeth, having insisted from the first she be seated to his right instead of at the opposite end of the table so that they could converse easily. Elizabeth found his relaxed manners adorable. He took her hand, lifted it his lips, kissed it, and then boldly held it captive on the table for all to see.

"My apologies for being late." Donovan told their guests. "I see you've finished dessert. Miss Ramirez, would you stand in as hostess for a short time? I'm sure you and my uncle can manage to entertain our guests in the salon. I'd like to have a private word with Elizabeth."

"As you wish, my lord." Chloe rose, as did the men, except Grandfather. He appeared outraged by the idea he should follow a paid servant into the drawing room.

"I'll be along shortly." Donovan said to the old man, noting his reluctance. "When I'm finished, you and I can retreat for that private chat you mentioned earlier, sir."

The old man stood up, doddering just a bit so that Michael was forced to support him at the elbow as he followed the others out of the room. With a nod from Elizabeth, the footman was quick to serve the master. Donovan inhaled several gulps of meat and potatoes as if he were starving, drank his wine in one tug, and then gave her a somber look.

"Was I correct? Or have I made a fool of you, my lord?"

He nodded, wiped his mouth with the napkin and set it aside. "We found their remains, with leg shackles still on them. I hung Winslow tonight." He paused, and she sensed the regret in him as he grasped the stem of his refilled goblet in his fist. She held her breath, hoping it did not break in his hand. He lifted it to his lips, took another generous sip, and continued.

"I hired that ape last year when my overseer dropped dead of a heart attack in the middle of the cane pressing. I was desperate. I knew Winslow had a cruel streak, but I had no choice, I needed him back then. Alas, I'm in need of a new overseer, with the cane harvest less than a fortnight away. Come here." Donovan tugged at her hand until she had to stand beside him. He pulled her onto his lap. "How are you getting on with your grandfather?"

"He's rude to Gareth, Chloe, Mr. Marceau, and anyone who isn't a titled lord or married to one. It's—oh--you've no idea how much I despise that kind of condescension and cruelty. People should not be treated badly for the mere circumstances of their birth. It's hardly something one can control."

Donovan was amused. "You have the beginnings of an enlightened mind, my dear."

Donovan sipped his brandy and listened to the old man natter on about inconsequential things for an eternity. The Earl was not being direct, Donovan thought with annoyance, noting the movement of the clock. He should be upstairs by now, making love to his wife.

When he ignored the earl's comments about this strange new practice of allowing the help to dine with their betters, Donovan assumed he meant Chloe and Michael's tutor, the old man changed direction. He brought up his concerns for Michael's future. Fletcher had been observed following the boy on several occasions in London. He feared the man was scheming to extract money from the lad, and decreed Michael must not go out alone. He must always be accompanied by a footman and Mr. Marceau. As a result, the boy voiced a deep resentment of his strictures and did his best to elude his escorts.

Wentworth then complained of Michael being a handful, and an embarrassment socially due to his lack of refinement and his father's influence.

Donovan reminded him that his grandchildren had been given an uncommon freedom in their adolescent years in exile, so it was natural for Michael to resent the implementation of rules when up until this time there had been few due to Fletcher's neglect. He experienced similar difficulties with Elizabeth, but he did not share them with the earl.

"My valet has reported, via servant's gossip, that Elizabeth was ill recently. Is this true?"

"It is. I must insist that you and Michael are not too demanding during your stay."

"Is she breeding already?"

"No." Donovan shifted his chair, debating the wisdom of telling the man what had happened to Elizabeth. Confiding in the earl might be best. It would save Elizabeth the humiliation of explaining if she had a confused episode or a seizure while the earl was here. If the old man knew of her frailty, he'd not be asking her impertinent questions and he'd be mindful not to weary her. Donovan poured them another drink and gave the man a brief, sanitized account of Elizabeth's abduction by Fletcher's cronies, and her resulting head injury.

The earl did not speak. His face had become grey as his hand pressed over his chest.

"Are you well, sir?" Donovan asked, setting down his glass and rising to go to the man.

"I believe so." The earl said, holding up a hand to dissuade him. "Why didn't you bring her to my home to recover instead of making the treacherous journey across the sea?"

"She was a month in bed. She slept almost continuously the first two weeks. It hardly mattered where the bed was, sir." Donovan countered easily. "As a physician I must point out that a long coach ride to your estate, a full day's journey in the best of conditions, with her injuries, would not have been wise. My vessel was already equipped for luxury accommodations for our voyage. It was no hardship for her, I assure you."

"Fletcher has had his eyes on my fortune from the first." The earl confided. "I'm convinced it is the reason behind my elder grandson's disappearance, but nothing could ever be proved."

Donovan pinched his brow. He'd forgotten about O'Flaherty. Judging by the earl's grey cast, it would have to wait until the old man was rested from the long voyage he'd endured under less than sterling conditions.

"He was Angela's first born." The earl went on to explain the circumstances of Kieran's disappearance when Donovan remained silent. "I tried to get my daughter to leave Fletcher many times over the years. I threatened to take the children away, although I never had the heart to do it. I told her I'd never see her again and did not see her for an entire year, the last year of her life." Again, the man's hand flew to his chest. "Something I'll regret for the rest of my days."

This time, Donovan did go to his side. He took the earl's wrist. His pulse was racing. "Take deep breaths, relax." He pulled the footstool over and lifted the man's legs to rest upon it. "Have you had a doctor examine you?"

"Yes, several. They all say the same thing, I'm old." He waved Donovan's hand away. "Surely, you'll not deny an old man the chance to be acquainted with his granddaughter before he cocks up his toes?"

"You are welcome in my home provided you keep in mind that your granddaughter's health is fragile and she must not be distressed by demanding guests."

The earl nodded. His eyes glazed with moisture. "You are a godsend, young man. You saved my family from ruination. If not for you, my grandchildren would be starving and I would die without finding them and reclaiming them. You may call me James, son."

Chapter Thirty Seven

Lizzie sat before her dressing mirror. Her maid was brushing out her long, luscious hair.

Donovan was watching. It was a habit he'd fallen into, watching his wife each morning.

He no longer felt the need to rush away early in the morning to escape the swollen desire he always awoke with. He no longer needed to run from his lust or his bride. Now, his main goal was trying to entice her away from her family in order to enjoy a few precious moments alone.

He couldn't get enough of his wife. Two weeks had passed since their first coupling, and they'd managed a running tally of two to three times a day. He smiled. Lizzie was very accommodating when it came to soothing his desire. More than accommodating, she seemed to have acquired a taste for his flesh as well. Lizzie met him in the stables just yesterday when he sent her a note. She came to him quickly, and then came for him, twice, in the tack room. Once against the wall, and once bent over a saddle with him taking her from behind.

"What are you grinning so deviously about this morning?" Lizzie asked.

Her maid had left the room. "I was remembering yesterday, in the tack room."

Lizzie blushed and looked away. It made him feel wicked. And horny. His cock surged to life in response to her maidenly blushes and her scanty attire. She was wearing only silk stockings, garters, and a silk dressing robe.

She busied herself by arranging the glass bottles of feminine potions in front of the mirror. "We shouldn't have done it there. What if one the stable boys came in to the tack room?" She looked up at his reflection in the mirror. "Little Gavin, even my brother, Michael? We should not be doing it outside our chambers, don't you think?"

Oh, fuck and damn. He was sick of her family. The same day he booted the older brother off the island, and had hopes of having her to himself for a much deserved honeymoon, the younger brother showed up with the cantankerous old earl in tow. He wanted Lizzie to himself. He wanted to make love to her in the garden or the billiard room, right on the billiard table if the mood took him. And he wanted her at this moment.

"As a newly married couple," Donovan began, careful to temper his words to hide his resentment. "We should not be inundated by family and forced to restrain our affections in our own home. If it upsets someone when they enter a room without knocking first, shame on them, not me. There's a reason people don't visit newlyweds for months after their nuptials, not until the couple extends a proper invite that they are receiving visitors. At least, that is how it is done in proper Charleston society." He couldn't help adding the last, having heard more than he cared to about proper society with the earl in residence. Damn. He was ranting. And she was frowning.

Lizzie rose, giving him a tormenting view of one full breast before quickly adjusting her dressing robe. She came to him and placed her hand on his chest in a soothing mien. "I know you dislike having people about. You needn't be jealous, dearest. I'm always happy to escape with you. When you sent me that note summoning me to the stables yesterday, I was relieved." The hand on his chest was no longer soothing. It was slapping him in her agitation. "I love Michael, I do, but he's always talking of some incident I cannot recall, and then he niggles me to death because I cannot remember it. And Grandfather looks down his nose at--"

Donovan took her face in his hands. He kissed her and the thumping hand on his chest stilled. He undid the fastening of her robe. The fabric opened, displaying her luscious body.

"You scoundrel." She chastened, pulling back. "How long has it been, an hour?"

"Two." He laughed, infinitely pleased as he glanced down at those pert breasts. She was divine. Part of him noted that she could do to add a little more flesh to her bones. He'd like his wife to be a little rounder, a little more pampered. "It won't take long." He whispered, desperate to be inside her as his hands slipped beneath her robe to outline her shapely hips.

"What if I want it to take a long time?" She asked saucily, placing her hands on her hips. "Are you in such a hurry, my lord?"

"No, Ma'am." He said in an exaggerated Charleston drawl. Donovan pulled her into his arms and kissed her again, this time from the depths of his soul. His hands skimmed over her hips beneath her robe, and then upward as he lifted her at the waist. "Put your legs around me."

She did so, wrapping her long legs about his hips and her arms about his neck. Donovan's hands moved to cup her round bottom as he carried Elizabeth to the dressing table. He set her on it and stood between her open thighs. She looked uncertain. Before she could protest, he kissed her again, soft, subtle nibbles against her lips, distracting her until he could bring her to his level of desire. His fingers found that soft, moist cleft between her thighs and he plied his own magic, bringing her to arousal with knowing strokes.

"You're wicked." She whispered against his lips with obvious pleasure at the assertion.

Donovan looked down and feared he was about to become undone as he watched her arch against his fingers, her legs spread for him as she leaned back on the table and allowed him full access to her delicate lotus petals. He glanced in the mirror behind her. He looked ravenous, dangerous. No wonder she was afraid of him when he was aroused in their earlier days.

He returned his gaze to his lovely bride, convinced all his future happiness lay within this delightful woman. He leaned in to kiss her, devouring her mouth with his tongue. She started to purr, soft, demure little moans, letting him know she was starting to ascend the planes of bliss.

"Release me." He directed hoarsely. Elizabeth unfastened the placket of his breeches. As he sprang free, she palmed his swollen cock without reluctance--another hurdle breached in recent days as she explored his body with innocent curiosity during their lovemaking. "Lizzie, my sweet Lizzie."

She tugged him, leading his rigid sword toward her soft, silken sheath. As she gazed into his eyes her look was so sensual he feared he was about to end this erotic interlude prematurely. He closed his eyes, gathered his self control, and plunged inside her.

Lizzie gasped at the intrusion. He guided her thighs about his hips, tilted her back and plunged deeper into her hot silken core. He braced one hand on the wall as he pushed them closer and closer toward the gates of paradise. She arched up, boldly meeting each thrust, joining him as her delicate sighs transformed into desperate moans of sweet, primal pleasure. She tightened around his granite spear, pulsing and squeezing him as she achieved release, assuring that his completion followed close on the heels of her own.

Donovan gave one final deep thrust as his world exploded into pure exhilaration and triumph. He heard a dense crack beneath them as if from a great distance and Lizzie clutched at him. The table she was perched on dipped. He gazed down. A front leg had given way, bending at an odd angle toward the wall. The table was cockeyed, and Lizzie was in danger of sliding off.

He swore aloud, more from the bereft feeling his hand experienced upon leaving the lush, round moon of his wife's bum rather than the destruction of furniture. Lizzie laughed against his neck. Her legs dropped from around his torso, but she hugged his thighs with her own. Her arms were still about his neck. She eased her head back from his shoulder and gazed up at him. Her eyes had that far away, dreamy look that brought pride and pleasure deep within him. They remained still with him standing between her opened thighs, his cock still inside her, though now spent. They were content to remain joined, clinging to each other and steadying their breathing.

The gasp to their left caught them off guard. Alice, Lizzie's maid, stood inside the doorway, a gown draped over her arm and her mouth hanging nearly to her knees. "Mum--oh--sir--I--I--pressed yer gown like ye asked---I--I--" She lifted the garment draped arm as if to add proof to her claim. Her face resembled a volcano about to erupt. She hurried the nearest chair, draped her mistress's freshly pressed gown over it and fled the room.

Donovan chuckled and pulled out of Lizzie. Damn, he hadn't had this much fun flummoxing servants since he was nineteen and lived with his uncle in France. It was a game among the younger nobles at the French court, getting drunk and then tupping the maid, or a pair of them in the palace. And getting caught tupping one was even more the rage among his jaded companions. As a green lad from the colonies, he'd had to work hard to keep up. He grimaced as he tucked himself inside his breeches. "Will she recover or will you need a new maid by lunch?"

Lizzie giggled. Her sweet face twisted into a delightful smile. "I'm certain she knows we do this as she changes the sheets and draws my bath each morning. Still, I am rather fond of her."

He nodded, pleased by the knowledge that he could still shock a maid now and then, even as he neared thirty. "I'll give her a raise. Is there anything I might do for you, Ma'am?"

Lizzie's hand moved from his neck to smooth a stray wisp of hair from his brow. She had a mischievous gleam in her eyes. "Yes. Tonight, I'd like you to wear the silk mask to bed."

Donovan grinned. She was becoming quite the accomplished seductress.

Elizabeth waited until Donovan left for the stables before checking on Kieran. Giles, her butler, was proving to be worth his weight in gold. He'd sent the letters to her brother in Basseterre and brought Kieran's replies to her every day for the past week without anyone knowing, including her spouse. Giles would pocket the letters from him and deliver them to Elizabeth when she was alone. Kieran wrote long letters to her, mostly answers to her questions about magic and their gifts, giving her instruction on some aspect of their heritage.

Today, the supply wagon was scheduled to arrive with fresh produce from Basseterre. She decided it was best if Kieran arrived on the supply wagon while Donovan was distracted to prevent any unpleasantness between the two men before she was able to present Kieran to Grandfather. Donovan was easy to distract these days. She'd sent Alice to the kitchens to inform Giles that his lordship would be occupied for the next twenty to thirty minutes. During that time, Giles was to escort her brother into her private parlor, the library.

Kieran rose when Elizabeth entered the room. She embraced him warmly.

"Are you ready?" She asked, gazing up at him with excitement.

"No." He made a face. "I doubt I'll ever be ready to meet The Earl of Greystowe."

"Donovan is out of the house." She told him, rubbing his forearm in comfort. "I wanted to do this with him away for as you well know he tends to over-react where I'm concerned."

"He is your spouse and the owner of this island estate." Kieran released an exasperated sigh at her description. "We've neither of us little in the physical realm to trump that high card."

"We have Grandfather." She informed him. "No one denies Lord Greystowe anything. Earl trumps count every time."

Kieran tossed his coppery head. "You're quite the strategist. How did that come about?"

"Growing up with a military man, and a grandmother who behaved as if we were at war with him. Donovan will accept this after it's finished. I will not have him interfering because he thinks I'm too fragile to deal with anything more strenuous than pouring tea." She paced before the mantle as she spoke and wiped her moistening palms on her skirts. "We should have a couple hours before his return. By the way, he never did tell me why he sent you away."

Kieran turned from her and studied a small shepherdess figurine on the mantel. He picked it up and turned it about in his hand, as if he'd never beheld anything so dainty before. He was nervous, too. She could sense the tension in him. He set the piece back where it belonged, but did not face her as he rested his elbows on the mantel and spoke to the mantel wall. "It was over our astral journey. He said you looked terribly frightened and he feared your eyes were going to roll back in your head any moment and you would have another seizure."

"Bollocks!" Elizabeth spat the word as she went to stand by his side. She moved the shepherdess so it was situated in front of the gilded music box instead of beside it. *That was rich. Donovan had been making her eyes roll back a couple of times a day, for a different reason.*

"Another habit learned from our infamous stepfather?" Kieran's amusement at her unladylike expletive only made Elizabeth feel more wretched.

"Yes." She breathed, angry with herself. "It seems a hard knock on the head gives one difficulties controlling one's speech, particularly when vexed. Well, let's get on with this, shall we? Before my beloved dragon returns from inspecting the cane fields."

Elizabeth summoned Grandfather and Michael to the library. She sat on the chaise, her hands clasped tightly on her lap, her belly roiling with serpents. Part of her wished she hadn't decided to do this behind Donovan's back, but if she waited until he deemed it the proper time she'd be in her dotage before her brothers were introduced and Kieran was restored to the family.

Kieran was hidden behind an open bookcase. He could hear them and peer at them from between the shelves. Grandfather was sitting in the chair near the marble fireplace, facing her chaise. His autocratic nature was difficult to deal with in the best of times, and at this moment she hadn't the patience to deal with Grandfather's arrogance.

Michael sat beside Elizabeth on the chaise. He was his usual cheerful self, and his presence was a boon. He was actually smirking, quite pleased with himself over something.

Now that the moment was upon her, Elizabeth faltered. She clasped and re-clasped her hands, smoothed her skirt, adjusted her hair, and released heavy breaths as she mulled over the proper opening for such an important announcement.

"So then," Michael put his hand over her fidgeting ones to calm them. "Your butler said you had something to tell us, in private. Out with it, when am I going to become an uncle?"

Elizabeth turned to gape her brother, completely aghast by his statement. Of all the things to conclude from a simple summons?

"Michael." Grandfather hissed. "We do not speak of delicate matters with the ladies."

"Tosh!" Michael responded, squeezing her hand and grinning. "This is my sister."

"I'm not breeding." Elizabeth stammered, certain her face was as pink as the hibiscus flowers Donovan had given her yesterday.

"Why else would you be summoning us to your private parlor for a family chat?" Michael countered, appearing crestfallen by her news.

"Manners, young man." Grandfather stomped his cane on the floor. "You do not speak over a lady in her own drawing room. Do go on, my Dear Elizabeth."

My Dear Elizabeth? Touched by this rare display of tenderness, Elizabeth spoke the words that had previously become tangled in her throat.

"I called you here because I have recently met someone who was lost to this family for many years, and through my marriage to Donovan, he has been reclaimed. Kieran, our elder brother," She took Michael's hand. "And your eldest grandson," She looked to Grandfather, "Is still alive. He lives here, in the port city of Basseterre. Kieran?" She glanced at her brother's outline behind the books. "Come. Join us."

"I say--" Grandfather began, and then seemed to choke on his words. He coughed, and reached up with white, gnarled fingers to loosen his cravat. "This is--this is highly irregular."

Kieran slowly walked round the shelving with his hands behind his back. He stood before them, silent, uncertain. He was very handsome in his best linen shirt tied at the neck with a gentleman's cravat. Elizabeth suggested the cravat, and had lent him one of Donovan's as he did not own one. He wore newly purchased buff colored breeches and a slate blue linen vest which complimented his tousled auburn hair and deep turquoise blue eyes.

Elizabeth rose and quickly went to him. She snaked her arm through his elbow, and stood before their imposing elder. "Kieran and I met two weeks ago. Donovan met Kieran some time before that. I was waiting for the proper time to intro-"

"*Proper?*" Grandfather spat the word as if it were phlegm. "Don't speak to me of proper, young lady. Your husband should be presenting this news to me--not some thin slip of a girl barely out of short dresses--there are formalities to be adhered to--his identity verified--"

Good Lord! She was presenting him with his lost grandson and he would go on about etiquette and formalities and legal nonesuch?

"Enough." She was determined not to let James Wentworth's arrogance and staunch adherence to formality ruin this reunion. Her mother always quoted an endless litany of rules to her about etiquette and societal expectations. Now she knew where it all came from. Elizabeth was at once thankful for Donovan's relaxed social expectations as an American. "Donovan has verified everything Kieran has told us, Grandfather, so do not presume for a moment to be too high in the instep to welcome a member of our family back into the fold."

Kieran stiffened beside her. Grandfather did likewise. The old man was furiously chewing his upper lip, as if he were trying very hard not to say that no one addressed him thus.

There was a rustling to their left as they stood arm in arm. Michael rose and came to stand before them. Sweet Michael, he looked as if he might cry. His big, soulful blue eyes, so much like mama's, were glazed with moisture. "Liz," he croaked. "Please, don't take offense. You're a diamond as sisters go, but I've always longed for a brother."

Even now, Michael could joke, with tears brimming in his eyes.

"You are a brat." She teased, thankful for Michael's innate ability to find the humor in any situation. "Of all the times I saved your bum!"

"Yes, but Liz, you were just a girl. Someone should have been saving yours."

Elizabeth opened her free arm to her little brother. Michael came and wrapped his arm about her. "She's a fright when she gets mad." He told Kieran, grinning. "When I was ten, the neighbor boys were bullying me. I came home once with a bloodied nose, and didn't my sister go marching out the back kitchen door to the curb, grabs the biggest bully by the collar, and says 'leave my brother alone or I'll kill you.' Danny and his chums never bothered me again. They were that scared of her, sir."

"I doubt it was fear that kept him from bothering you, Michael." Elizabeth mused, surprised by the forgotten memory surfacing. "After that, he professed to be in love with me."

Kieran was laughing and smiling. He released Elizabeth and offered his hand to Michael. "Hello Michael, I'm pleased to make your acquaintance."

As the brothers shook hands Elizabeth went to kneel at her grandfather's side. His face was very grey. "Grandfather, are you well? Should I ring for a footman?"

"No, dear child. This is most irregular, yet better than I could have ever hoped."

After everyone sat down, Kieran related to them how he had been sold on the docks by his stepfather and told his mother had died the night before. Kieran and Michael were very different. Kieran was serious and thoughtful where Michael was cheerful and lighthearted. Kieran answered questions about his life in the Indies, about Mr. Barnaby purchasing his indenture and treating him as a son. He was to inherit the apothecary shop, he told them with pride.

"And of what consequence is that to me?" Grandfather came alive with indignation. "You have no need to boast of being the sole proprietor of an apothecary shop, young man."

Kieran was startled by Grandfather's outburst. He looked at Elizabeth with uncertainty. She rolled her eyes heavenward. She did warn her brother that their grandfather held a rather exalted view of his station and of the Aristocracy.

As the trio remained silent before his haughty outburst, the earl went on to explain. "You'll be heir to my title and to my estate in England very shortly. In fact, if his lordship has already taken pains to verify your identity, I'll have the count's solicitor draw up papers immediately to make it official. There will be no more working as bondsman for you. "

No one said a word. Elizabeth looked to Michael, her heart going out to him. He was being told with no delicacy or concern for his feelings that he was being replaced as heir.

As usual, Michael put on a bold front. "The eldest always inherits the title. It's the English way. Now I can go to France and study art."

"No, you won't." Kieran put in. "Most of Europe is at war with France, or will be soon."

"Oh, I like that." Michael made a face. "Half an hour in and already bossing me about."

At that moment, Donovan entered the library. He took one look at the quartet gathered near the fireplace and his hands flew to his hips in his typical commanding stance. "What is this?" His question was directed to Elizabeth. "I can't leave you alone for an hour? We decided to wait until things settled a bit here before bringing Kieran out."

"You decided. I wanted my brothers to meet. So I took care of it."

The silence from the three other men in the room was oppressive. They all seemed to take a fastidious interest in the furnishings as they waited for the lord of the manor to scold his lady.

Elizabeth did not flinch. She glared at Donovan with no apologies.

Donovan sighed, his exasperation evident as he held her defiant gaze. "You should have listened to me, Elizabeth. Now, if you will all leave us, I wish to have a few words with Lord Greystowe."

Kieran and Michael rose. They looked askance at Elizabeth, then Grandfather. When neither interceded, they shuffled out of the room without daring to look at Donovan.

"Elizabeth." Donovan insisted. "You *will* respect your grandfather's wish for privacy."

She looked to Grandfather, hoping he'd ask her to stay, but she knew he would not. He would never interfere in a matter of another man's domestic disputes. She wanted to say something. She wanted to lash out at Donovan for being so high handed in front of her grandfather. Wasn't it just like him, to come into the room and transform a perfectly sunny moment into darkness, suspicion and gloom? This was her family. Yet, he was dismissing her as if she were an impudent child, reinforcing Grandfather's arrogant beliefs and humiliating her.

She turned to leave before she said something she would regret later.

As she reached the door, Donovan's hand circled her wrist. "Lizzie, wait." His voice was no longer commanding. "I asked you to leave because I need to examine him, privately." He turned her about to face him. "I'm not angry with you."

"What a relief!" Elizabeth quipped. "I can't say the same. This is my family, Donovan. My brothers. You've no right to interfere."

Donovan looked down at the floor and then away, grimacing. He glanced over at the man in the chair by the fireplace before turning his gaze back to Elizabeth. He cupped her cheek with his big hand. "I'm not angry with you for defying me by bringing Kieran here and presenting him to your grandfather without preparing the old man for the shock of it first. I understand your feelings, honey, believe me, I do."

He paused, searching her eyes desperately before adding, "But please understand this; your grandfather is dying."

Chapter Thirty Eight

"I don't think he meant it would be today, Liz." Michael assured her as the trio gathered in the sunny yellow salon at the front of the house. "Think of Old Sheila. We always said she'd never survive another winter, and yet survive she did, year after year, if you recall."

Elizabeth didn't remember. She didn't recall many things Michael nattered on about. She meandered about the confines of the large salon, her arms about herself. She should have known. Why hadn't she sensed it when she touched Grandfather? She touched him many times in the past week and she had no idea. She turned to Kieran. "Did you sense it?"

"No, but I did not touch him. Even so," Kieran shrugged, and looked askance at Michael before continuing. "It doesn't work with everyone, particularly blood kin."

Elizabeth tilted her head, considering his words. "What about spouses?" She didn't understand why she could not read Donovan as she could others.

"That, too. I've heard." He replied, eyeing her and then their brother, clearly uncomfortable discussing their gift. "It's a form of protection for the seer." He stepped casually toward Elizabeth where she stood near the window. "Imagine being able to know everything your husband thinks and feels every time you touch him. It would be overwhelming. It's the same with children and other blood kin. A safety mechanism within the gift." He touched her arm, and she felt the familiar tingling as he did so. She felt his anxiety, his uncertainty. "You and I are different. Magnets." He said emphatically, giving her a knowing smile.

"Care to explain? *Magnets*?" Michael asked with a wave of his hand, watching them from across the room. "I know, I'm not an *O'Flaherty*, but I am your brother, too, Liz."

Elizabeth didn't need the gift of the seer to tell her Michael was feeling left out and more than a little jealous of Kieran's closeness. "Do you recall Sheila claiming she could see and sense things about people, hidden things?"

Michael nodded. "Scared me to the devil when I was little, all that mystical mumbo jumbo and talk of seeing spirits everywhere."

"It's hereditary." Elizabeth informed him with impatience. "Sheila died and now I have her gift, as does he." She gestured to Kieran. "We're cursed with being able to see other people's secrets, their desires, their sins, all their flaws--"

A flush of raw, pent up fury washed over her. She moved to the doorway and stood with her back to her brothers for a moment, trying to contain the emotions flooding her. She turned to them. "It's a damned shamed it doesn't work with the people we actually care about!"

Donovan searched for her everywhere in the house, to no avail. As he gazed out at the gardens from the second floor window, he had an idea of where she might have gone.

Sure enough, when he reached the stone terrace he found Elizabeth sitting beyond it in the grass outcropping beneath the gnarled old tree. She was sitting cross-legged, shredding blades of grass between her fingers as she stared violently out at the sea.

She looked so forlorn he didn't have the heart to chide her for her excursion outdoors alone. Donovan maneuvered past the crumbling wall, making a mental note to have it fixed. Carefully, with arms balanced and his steps precise, he went to where she was sitting so precariously on the sloping grass mound overlooking the sea. He sat behind her and placed a light hand on her arm.

"Why didn't you tell me?" She asked, anger seeping into her voice.

"I should have." Donovan conceded. "Your grandfather made me promise not to."

"How long does he have?"

"It's hard to predict." He admitted. "A few months at most. He came here to die, Elizabeth. The voyage was difficult. He endured the hardship because he wanted Michael to be safe with us when he died so there would be no chance of your stepfather interfering in the months it would take for us to arrive in England after news of your grandfather's death reached us here. James made me Michael's legal guardian from this point forward. That was before he knew about Kieran. I'm sorry, Lizzie."

"Where are my brothers?" Her voice was wet. He could tell she wanted to cry, but refused to allow herself to do so. That was his Lizzie, defiant to the last.

"I left them in the salon. They were getting to know each other."

"And Grandfather?"

"Upstairs, in bed. It was a severe shock for him." He rubbed his hand along her spine.

Donovan was of two minds on the subject now that it was over and done. He intended to wait for a few weeks, allow Wentworth time to recover from his arduous journey as much as possible before springing the news on him. Elizabeth had the blindness and invincibility of youth on her side as she rushed boldly into the fray. She didn't stop to consider the old man's age or health, any more than Donovan would have at her age. Given Wentworth's precarious condition, had they waited the old man might have died without knowing his eldest grandson was still alive.

"I recommend limited visits from the three of you in the coming days. Half hour increments, no more."

She nodded, and sniffled. "I just wanted them to meet."

"I know." Donovan wrapped his arms around her. He pulled her back to lean against his frame. They sat together like spoons with his long legs bracketing her hips as she reclined in the shelter of his arms. The only sound was the wind and the waves as they crashed over the rocks below. He didn't like her sitting on this small outcropping. The thick grass provided some traction, but even so, if it were wet or her shoe slipped, she could fall to her death on the jagged rocks. "We should go in. The lads will want to know you're alright."

"Oh, Donovan!" She cried out, "It doesn't work."

He pressed his cheek to hers from behind. "What doesn't work, my love?"

"My gift. Kieran says it doesn't always work with immediate blood kin. I didn't know. I didn't know Grandfather was so ill." She wilted in his arms, turning toward him for comfort. She wept bitterly, for her grandfather, and because she was angry with herself for not being able to see the outcome of her impetuous scheme.

It was past midnight, two days after O'Flaherty returned from Basseterre.

As the candles burned low in the salon, the only sound was the steady thwacking of the cards as Michael shuffled and dealt the next hand.

Gareth picked up the cards the lad dealt and studied them before making his opening bid.

Marceau, the boy's tutor, had a definite tell, his lips warped into a twisted grimace.

Michael showed no outward sign as to the contents of his hand. The boy was a natural when it came to cards, yet he confided to Gareth that he's never played them until the voyage here as his sister frowned on it. Michael asked him not to let his sister know of their nocturnal activities, so they waited until Elizabeth retired each night before breaking out the card deck in the salon. O'Flaherty turned down the invitation of cards for the past few nights, but Gareth didn't mind overmuch. That one was far too serious for his liking, a bit of a spook.

"I pass." Marceau informed them, setting his cards face down on the table.

"Five." Michael opened the bid.

"Ah, confident, are we?" Gareth teased, pleased to see a smile break through the melancholy that seemed to envelope the lad of late. "Lead out."

Michael led the first hand and won.

Gareth managed to steal the second from him, lowering the boy's chances of winning his bid, unless the boy had some very good cards tucked away. He was about to lead out the next play, when a noise on the stairs distracted him. It was too late for servants to be traipsing about. Someone was mumbling at the top of the stairs. He'd spent a great deal of time listening in the shadows as a boy. As a result, Gareth had developed a good ear.

"Lead out, or are you afraid you can't meet the challenge!" Michael teased.

"Shhh!" Gareth hissed, setting his cards aside and lifting a hand.

"No—stop it--" A high pitched, girlish voice insisted from the stairs.

Gareth was on his feet and out the door instantly. Michael and Marceau were at his heels. He stopped dead at the foot of the stairs in the foyer. Elizabeth was teetering on the top step. Dressed in her night rail, barefoot, with a distant expression on her face, he realized she was sleepwalking. Donovan had mentioned it a couple of times.

She didn't notice the men at the foot of the stairs as she spoke to someone in her dream. "I'll tell them the truth, you did it. I saw you—"

"She's dreaming." Michael said. "Elizabeth--"

"No." Gareth commanded, grabbing the boy's arm. "You'll startle her, she'll fall."

A white mist appeared, hovering on the stairs before them. The mist moved, floating up the stairs. A female shape materialized. A dark haired woman paused at mid flight. Her angelic face became distorted and skeletal, and then she disappeared.

The hackles on Gareth's neck rose. The woman reappeared behind Elizabeth at the top of the stairs. The devious eyes tipped him off as the spirit glowered at him from behind her victim.

"No!" He shrieked, vaulting up the steps to Elizabeth. The quick blur of ivory limbs coupled with the alarmed shouts of the men behind him spurred Gareth on.

Sudden horror on Elizabeth's face told him she'd awakened in the fall.

Halfway up the stairs he dropped to his knees and grabbed the railing with one hand and pressed his other palm to the wall to form a barrier to stop her perilous descent. Her body jerked to a stop in mid flight. She'd managed to grasp a vertical rail.

Elizabeth's bare heel slammed into his shoulder. The knee of her other leg clouted his head.

He heard a snapping noise, followed by a cry of pain.

Elizabeth was a crumpled, moaning form four steps above him. Her arm was caught at an odd angle between the stair railings.

"Liz, are you trying to kill yourself?" Michael tromped up the stairs toward them.

"Wait." Gareth cautioned, putting an arm out in front of the youth to prevent his passing. "Go into the salon and get a pillow, now Michael. Bring a pillow to cradle your sister's wrist."

The lad didn't argue. Gareth crept up the few stairs to Elizabeth on his hands and knees, trying to remain calm in the face of what he expected to become full blown hysterics from the girl before him. "Easy, now, my dear. Uncle Gareth is here."

Her response was a muted whimper. She was staring at her mangled arm, transfixed by the sight of her hand bending back at a bizarre angle. It wasn't a view one could become accustomed to, except mayhap for a physician. *A doctor—Yes--Donovan!*

"Marceau—get the count." Gareth instructed.

The tutor hurried up the steps. He stopped near Gareth, turning his wide girth sideways to maneuver around Gareth and Elizabeth. His boots echoed like thunder as he tromped down the hall to the master chamber.

"My lady?" The feminine voice intruded. Gareth glanced up to see his *petite-amour* at the top of the stairs, clad in a cotton bed-gown with her dark hair forming a luxurious mantle over her snowy gown. She glided down the stairs on nude graceful feet and sat behind Elizabeth on the step above her. Relief came at her presence. He wasn't any good at comforting hysterical females. Chloe was Elizabeth's friend; she'd know how to comfort her.

"What have you done to your arm, my lady?" Chloe asked in her exotic Caribbean voice.

Elizabeth looked up, unable to explain why she was crouched on the stairs in the middle of the night with her arm wrenched between the rails. "I don't know."

Light footfalls were heard above them once more. "What happened?" Kieran appeared shirtless at the top of the stairs. He jaunted down to the step she was crouched on. His dismay as he took in her mangled limb added to the panic she'd been trying to hold in check.

"It appears I'm stuck." Elizabeth replied. She meant it to be humorous, something Michael would say to ease the tension if he were in a situation like this. It didn't sound half as smart as it would have if Michael said it.

"I can see that." Kieran replied. He sat down next to her on the step and leaned close, trying to get a closer look at her distorted limb.

Voices came from above, a cacophony of servants chattering excitedly as they emerged from the third floor in various stages of undress. Had she screamed? She didn't remember it.

"Here we are." Michael vaulted up the stairs with the cushion Gareth requested.

Gareth was kneeling on the step below her while Chloe sat behind her on the stair above. Kieran sat next to her with his arm about her shoulder. Carefully, the three of them maneuvered Elizabeth's mangled wrist from the rail and lowered it to the cushioned support Gareth held.

A loud clatter of military boots ricocheted off the walls as someone came down the hallway at a run. *Military boots.* How she hated that gut wrenching sound. Fletcher's boots echoed on the bare plank servant's stairs when he chased her, screaming promises to deliver fresh pain whenever he caught her. Elizabeth dropped her head to her knees and covered it with her good arm as she fought the bitter memories of life in the Mayfair Townhouse.

"I'm here, darlin'." Donovan's hand draped over her neck. Elizabeth lifted her head from her knees, relieved by his steadying presence as he took Kieran's place beside her. He'd pulled on his breeches in his haste, arriving at her side with his torso bared, the pitted scars unveiled for all to see. And he was *barefoot*? Did she image that awful noise of Papa's boots on the stairs?

She looked up at the throng gathered above. The sound came from the second floor hall. Mr. Marceau moved forward as she watched and paused at the top of the stairs, his meaty hand on the banister and one Hessian boot poised to descend and lend her further assistance.

"*Elizabeth*!" That flesh chilling voice sliced through her.

She turned to look at the bottom of the stairs. Mama stood there, glaring up at her and pointing to the black and white tile floor beneath her dainty shoes.

"No—go away--leave me alone!" Elizabeth shrieked.

"Shhh! You were dreaming, love." Donovan's arms grew firm around her as he pulled her against his scarred chest. "Shock." He whispered to those beside him.

In defiance of his logic, Mama's ghost remained a solid form at the bottom of the stairs.

"What is your purpose here?" Kieran inquired, startling everyone with his brusque commanding tone. "Leave this house. You have no business here."

Gareth, Chloe, Donovan and Michael turned to gape at Kieran. He ignored their baffled looks as he glowered at their mother. His anger melted into horror as he continued to stare at the bottom of the staircase.

Elizabeth turned to see what he found so disturbing. She screamed.

Blood slowly rose from the crack between the tiles, pooling before a pair of satin feet. Mama's face was grey and her blue lips were formed into an accusing snarl. She kept pointing ominously to the pool of blood blooming at her feet.

"No." Elizabeth buried her face in Donovan's neck.

"*El Diablo*!" Chloe's voice quivered behind Elizabeth.

She lifted her head from Donovan's chest. Chloe was staring at the bottom of the stairs.

Gareth turned and looked down and then gasped, as if he, too, could see the pool of dark crimson shimmering in the low candlelight at Mama's feet.

"Stop it." Kieran shouted. "Stop trying to scare her. Leave this place."

Donovan frowned at Kieran. "What the devil is going on?"

"Blood. Don't you see it?" Gareth gestured to the pool at the bottom of the stairs.

"No." Donovan snapped, refusing to look where Gareth indicated. He cupped Elizabeth's cheek, directing her gaze away from the ghost to look at his face. The anxiety she saw there was mirrored in his voice. "She isn't bleeding. I can set this. It takes six weeks for bone to heal—"

"--*You cannot see the blood?*" Chloe's high screech interrupted Donovan's determined mumbling. "On the floor, my lord, below us!" She pointed to the bottom of the stairs.

"No." Donovan's panicked eyes darted to the crimson pool below and then he fixed his gaze determinedly on Elizabeth's face. "You're going to be fine, Love, I promise."

"Get out of here!" Kieran went rushing down the stairs, his right arm outstretched and his hand splayed in a commanding gesture as he started speaking in a language Elizabeth hadn't heard for some time: Gaelic.

Mama's ghost glared up at them and then melted away like a misty mirage.

The blood reverted and slipped slowly into the crack in the tiles as they all watched.

Oh God, the blood . . . there was so much blood.

Elizabeth shook her head and clamped her jaw tight over her teeth, containing the scream rising in her throat. She'd scrubbed and scrubbed the parquet floor in Mayfair until her hands were chapped and raw. Still, the stain remained; a permanent reminder of her betrayal.

"Lizzie, listen to me." It was Donovan reaching into her panic to wrestle her free of its cloying hold. "There is no blood. Your bone didn't break through skin."

Elizabeth stared at him, desperation rising to choke her. Had she said it aloud?

"I say, would somebody tell me what is going on?" Michael asked.

Donovan answered without taking his eyes from Elizabeth's. "Your sister was sleepwalking. She fell down the stairs and broke her arm. Now, we've the devil to pay, as I have to set the bone back into place. Kieran," His tone became severe as he addressed her elder brother. "I want Mr. Barnaby here, immediately."

327

"Agreed. Barnaby will know exactly what to do. I can be at the docks in a trice."

"No. You aren't leaving, Kieran. I need you here." The fear in Donovan's tone was unmistakable. Elizabeth realized he knew what was happening and he was terrified, just like the rest of them.

"Gareth," Donovan directed, "Have Ambrose and Gus sail to Basseterre to bring Mr. Barnaby here. Tell them to kidnap him if need be, but I want him here by dawn."

Chapter Thirty Nine

Elizabeth was being escorted, en masse, to Donovan's room.

They moved rapidly down the hallway, as each candle sconce they passed wavered ominously from the rush of people and cast odd shadows on the walls.

Donovan carried her with Gareth keeping step with him, holding the pillow that cradled her twisted limb. Chloe, Michael, Kieran and several servants followed them.

Donovan set her gently on the bed and barked orders at the troop behind him. Warm blankets, a fire, two twenty inch boards, leather bindings and Laudanum. He wanted them last week, judging by his sharp command.

Pearl, Giles, Alice, Sally, and Chloe spun about, bumping into each other as they moved to obtain the requested items. The room emptied quickly as they hurried to obey.

"I don't understand." Michael was standing close to the bed, peering down at her with worry. "Liz, what is everyone blathering on about? *Blood and spirits*? You fell and broke your arm. It's the same one you broke when you were ten, your left. Remember? Mama had to send for the doctor to set your arm after one of Papa's tirades."

Fletcher broke her wrist. And Mama made her lie to the doctor when he came. Elizabeth forgot the incident. Is that why Mama led her to the stairs, not to kill her but to remind her of the violence in their home? The awful throbbing in her limb grew worse.

"Michael, out." Donovan turned from his discussion with Kieran and Gareth. "I've a nasty job ahead splinting your sister's arm. I can't have you crying or fainting. Off with you."

"No." Elizabeth hardly realized she'd spoken, but the three men across the room gazed at her as if she'd just done the impossible. Donovan and the others were standing near the veranda doors conferring about what needed to be done.

"Michael should not be in here, darlin'." Donovan approached the bed. "I'll give you something for the pain before we set the bone, but he shouldn't see this."

"I'm not a child." Michael chimed in. "He's allowed to stay." He pointed to Kieran.

"Michael." She understood his resentment at being sent away when he was upset and frightened. She offered him her uninjured hand and when he took it, she tugged at him to sit on the bed. "I'll need you to hold my hand through the worst of it."

Michael eased carefully beside her, clutching her hand. He laced their elbows together and their fingers, just like in the old days when they stood against Fletcher.

Mama would surely kill her one day, or she'd be exposed for the coward she was.

How would they all feel about her when they knew?

A tortured moan emerged from her lips. She didn't kill her mother, but she'd covered up the crime and that was just as bad.

Someone pushed a blanket over them, shoving it tight against her neck. She was so cold, and shivering. Ice surrounded her. Her heart ached, but her feet, her hands, even her nose felt the frigid January winds coming off the Thames. Her teeth were chattering.

A cup was pushed against her lips. She drank it greedily.

It was done. Elizabeth wasn't screaming anymore. The bone was set. Donovan sipped the scotch his uncle placed in his hand as soon as he stepped away from the bed. He stood near the veranda doors, bathed in sweat, heart pounding as he watched his wife and her brother sleep.

Christ, they look like children. Orphans clutching each other's hand as they slept as if all they had in the world was each other.

Donovan swirled the last of the scotch in his glass and tossed it down the back of his throat. The stinging was comforting. He managed to distance himself from Elizabeth's cries as he realigned her wrist bone. Gareth and Kieran held her arm still while he managed to bind the damned splints with leather straps Pearl had fetched from the stable tack room.

As soon as it was done, he turned away so she wouldn't see his tears. And Gareth wisely shoved the glass of scotch into his trembling hand. The three of them watched over the pair in the bed, and didn't speak again until Elizabeth and Michael were asleep.

"What does your mother want from her?" Gareth asked.

Kieran O'Flaherty's eyes were wide, his lips bloodless. "That *creature* was not our mother." The scalding pain in Kieran's voice made Donovan wince. Kieran's eyes swung to the pair on the bed and then to Donovan. "She wouldn't do that—not the sweet woman who held me as a babe and sang me lullabies."

Gareth touched Kieran's shoulder as the words cut deeply between them.

A mother's ghost returning to harm her own child? It was unthinkable.

Donovan saw the woman at the bottom of the stairs. He tried to avoid those malevolent eyes. He saw the phantom blood. Saw it sink into the tiles like a mirage. Even so, he did not want to admit he had seen the bizarre manifestation. It defied logic.

"Kieran!" An aged gentleman with grey hair tumbling about in disarray came striding through the open hallway door. The man was at O'Flaherty's side immediately.

"Barnaby—she tried to kill Elizabeth." Kieran choked. His voice was tremulous.

Mr. Barnaby looked to Donovan. "Someone tried to kill Mrs. Beaumont?"

"A spirit. Our mother!" Kieran blustered, not trusting Donovan or Gareth to explain.

"Shhh!" Miss Ramirez vaulted up from her chair where she'd been keeping a silent vigil over the pair on the bed. "Do not disturb my mistress."

Gareth nodded toward the veranda and tugged at Kieran's elbow. Barnaby took Kieran by the arm and they escorted the Irishman out onto the porch. Donovan followed them. It was daybreak. The golden sun was warming the cold grey skies.

After several precise questions from the elder spirit catcher and rambling answers from his apprentice, Donovan inserted himself into the conversation, explaining the progression of events Kieran knew nothing about.

"So, it began after your arrival." Barnaby summarized. "Hmmm. Something awakened the spirit recently, my lord."

"Tell him about the pouch, my lord." Miss Ramirez insisted as she joined the men on the porch, tugging her shawl about her shoulders against the chill morning air.

Donovan gestured for her to proceed.

Miss Ramirez explained how Elizabeth discovered the ancient book and the charms made by her grandmother when they were unpacking her trunks shortly after her arrival. Chloe said her mistress assumed the charm would ward off nightmares and she placed it under her pillow, and the haunting began shortly afterward.

"The spirit was awakened by the charm when Madame began using it." Barnaby concluded. "Charms can lie dormant until sympathetic magic, such as Madame's yearning for home and family revived the charm as she touched it and used it. This in turn gives the spirit linked to the charm more power." He let the words trail off, leaving them bewildered as he descended to mouthing obscure mutterings.

"I took it away from Elizabeth." Donovan confessed. "I locked it in the drawer in my laboratory three weeks ago and the attacks stopped. Until tonight."

"Uh-huh. Mmm? Indeed." The old wizard fondled his chin and stared haplessly into space, as if pondering the ramifications of Donovan's statement. "The spirit wants something from your wife, sir. As time passes and my lady does not do what the spirit wants her to, the spirit is becoming angrier, and hence, the attacks are becoming more violent."

"What can we do to protect Elizabeth?" Gareth asked.

"Place a circle of salt around the bed." Kieran said with conviction, glancing about at the gathering as he spoke. "Salt repels spirits the same as the vinegar bowls we place under furniture to keep insects from invading our beds and our dinner tables. Spirits can be kept out of a room with a boundary of salt."

"A temporary fix." Barnaby raised his finger in protest. The old man put his upraised finger to his lips momentarily, appearing deep in thought, and then asked, "Each time Madame was attacked, was there a lull of inactivity afterward?"

Everyone looked at everyone else with uncertainty.

"Yes." Miss Ramirez spoke up. "Each attack happened a few days apart."

"That is typical." Mr. Barnaby nodded as he looked about the gathering. "When a spirit uses energy to cause a physical manifestation, it weakens them." Barnaby placed a hand on Donovan's shoulder. "The good news, my lord, is the spirit will not have the strength to attack your wife for several days. And it gives Kieran and me time to figure out how to stop it."

Chapter Forty

Cloistered upstairs in his guest room, Kieran was pouring over the O'Flaherty Book of Secrets that Miss Ramirez had given him. Barnaby paced the room with restlessness.

The room was luxurious. Kieran did not recall being surrounded by such splendor in his lifetime. His father's castle had been ancient stone, rather cold as he recalled, and the furnishings echoed a sparse medieval flavor. Here at Ravencrest the furnishings might be several decades old, but they were the finest, evidence of the unrivaled prosperity of the sugar lords. The four poster bed would house three people comfortably, with room to spare for a dog or two at the foot. Lush red brocade silk hung from the tall louvered windows and heavy mahogany furniture brought from England at mid-century filled the elegant suite.

Situated at the back of the house, the room overlooked the gardens and stables. It did not have access to the pillared veranda that swept across the front of the plantation house, bracketing the rooms of the immediate family. Still, the room Kieran had been assigned was larger than necessary to house one person. As the remaining guest rooms on the second floor were inhabited by Grandfather, Michael, and Kieran himself, he had offered to share his room with Barnaby as the recent influx of guests left little choice for his mentor aside from sharing a room with Michael's tutor, in the attic. Kieran preferred his mentor to be given the same luxury as himself as they endeavored to resolve the haunting.

While Kieran studied the book, Barnaby paced and kept rearranging scraps of paper on the bed in an attempt to make sense of the events of the haunting. The old man had written out each incident on a separate scrap of paper and each new fact gleaned through their interviews with the witnesses. He kept puzzling over them, trying to piece together some clue as the reason for the haunting. Kieran had been scanning through the journal for two days, trying to find an entry recorded within it that would verify

Donovan's tale of a curse his grandmother's ghost insisted had been placed upon their English mother by an O'Flaherty.

Barnaby had interviewed Elizabeth and Michael regarding their mother's death. Michael told them everything he knew, which was nothing. He'd been told what happened the morning after by his sister. Elizabeth remained circumspect regarding the haunting, Barnaby noted. They were uncertain if it were a reluctance to speak about an event that had obviously been disturbing for her—or something else that made her edge carefully around every question they posed.

"Here is something." Kieran remarked, rising from the table to stand beside the bed where Barnaby was pondering his web of clues. "The entry is June 12th, 1795, on the night before mother's funeral. It says here Granny Sheila created two spells."

"Hmmm, wrought when in extreme anguish." The old wizard commented, tugging thoughtfully at his beard. "A dangerous form of magic, indeed."

"The first spell she recorded was to summon a redeemer to take Elizabeth and Michael into his protection. Sheila used fresh rose petals, dried heather, one of Elizabeth's baby teeth, a lock of her hair---and a tin knight of Michael's. A knight. That's clever, don't you think?"

Barnaby shrugged his indifference and rubbed his aching brow with his thumb.

"The knight. Not only does it link Michael with the spell as the item belonged to him, but think Barnaby, a knight signifies many things; honor, integrity, duty, romance, chivalry . . ."

"Posh. You are lending too much significance in the choice of catalyst, my boy. Perhaps the woman simply grabbed what was readily accessible."

"This spell is very specific." Kieran insisted. "Listen to the wording, it is very precise: *Send a Dark Hero, faithful and true; with hair black as midnight, and eyes bonny blue. Send a Dark Hero, one we can trust; with a will forged in iron, yet, tempered and just. Send Elizabeth a champion with the soul of a Celt, with a heart full of love, a sword on his belt. Bring a Dark Knight*" He paused, giving the old man a significant look before continuing.

"To fulfill all her desires. With a soul that's been purified; through blood and through fire.'"

The old man tossed up a hand in dismissal. "The count has blue eyes, many people do."

"It's not his eye color that concerned my grandmother. She wrote *Send Elizabeth a champion!'"* Kieran couldn't contain his excitement. "A champion is a knight, a trained warrior capable of defending the weak. And a knight's first duty is to protect the weak, namely women and children. It's no coincidence Sheila put a knight figure in that charm bag."

Barnaby didn't comment, but his look was one of impatience.

Kieran glanced down to where he'd marked his place with his finger, reading the line again. *"Send Elizabeth a champion with the soul of a Celt?* Donovan O'Rourke. His mother named him after her parents' clans. And in Gaelic Donovan means *Dark One.* Strange coincidence, wouldn't you say, when Sheila was summoning a dark hero? *Bring a Dark Knight to fulfill all of her desires, with a soul that's been purified through blood and through fire?* That is how he was tortured. I saw it that first time I touched him. Every word of this spell fits the count precisely."

Barnaby moved about the room, fingering his goatee, his habit whenever he was puzzling over something. "Your grandmother was obviously adept in spell casting. But finding this spell does nothing to aid our present dilemma." The old man rubbed his eyes and glanced wearily at the papers arranged on the bed. "We have to figure out what it is the spirit wants before she returns and tries to murder Lady Elizabeth again."

Kieran's excitement died with that chilling reminder.

Elizabeth was in danger. The count vowed he would not sleep until he knew his wife was safe from her mother's vengeful spirit. That was three nights past. If the man's surly temperament was any indication, he was keeping that punishing vow.

Kieran returned to the table and sat down. He turned the page and began scanning the next spell, the one Granny Sheila completed directly following his mother's burial.

"Here's a spell listing the ingredients in that pouch." He pointed to the offending charm before him on the table. "Sheila took rosemary, a lock of father's hair, mother's and mine. She braided them together. She cut open her hand and let her blood drip over the braid. She invoked the power of three, bound by blood."

"Ah, blood is a powerful medium." Barnaby agreed. "What was the spell's purpose?"

Reading on, Kieran's heart sank. "Oh, Granny Sheila, what have you done?"

"Let him sleep, the poor man." Barnaby said, when they entered the laboratory to find their host hunched over the desk with his head on his arms, sleeping soundly.

Barnaby gazed about the count's private lair with wonder. The wooden workbench in the center held a curious array of glass jars, vials and globes. There were iron pincers, saws, scalpels and other devices of the medical trade. A microscope was perched on a table near the wide, tall windows. Jars lined the shelves, holding pickled organs of the human body. Stuffed creatures perched on shelves, frozen as if by some magic incantation and waiting to pounce on an intruder should the right words be spoken.

In contrast to Barnaby's fascination, Kieran disliked this room immensely. It held the aura of death in it.

"Perhaps you'd like to visit your sister." Barnaby suggested, noting his unease. "The count allowed her to go downstairs today. I believe she's in the salon."

"No." Kieran whispered, glancing at the sleeping count. "The quicker we reverse this spell, the sooner he can go back to sleeping at night instead of here. It looks uncomfortable."

A jerking movement across the room signaled that their host was waking.

"Milord." Barnaby made a creaky bow to the man who remained in a perpetually irritated state since the night Elizabeth was attacked. "We found a way to appease the ghost, thanks to your foresight in allowing us to peruse this journal."

"Speak, man." As his head lifted from his forearms, the austere blue eyes flashed his fury. "Or do you require money to loosen your tongue?"

"No, sir. Yes, sir---I mean, of course not my lord." Barnaby blustered.

The master of Ravencrest released a long, weary breath and thrust his fingers through his disheveled hair. "I didn't mean to be so sharp, Mr. Barnaby. Have a seat."

Barnaby took the chair opposite the desk. Kiernan stood behind his mentor as the old man explained the curse they discovered, ending with "Lady Elizabeth is the key. We need her assistance to undo the curse."

"Is this going to be upsetting to her?" The count's tone grew predatory once more.

"Milord, there is no other way. My lady has to confess what occurred on the night her mother died to someone with the power to seek justice on behalf of her mother." Barnaby gestured to their host. "Put simply, it means that by telling you or her grandfather what happened her part of the curse should end, provided that the party she tells will set the wheels of justice in motion to avenge Mrs. Fletcher's murdered soul."

"*Murdered!*" Count Rochembeau stood slowly and leaned purposefully over the desk. His crisp blue eyes fixed upon Barnaby. "My wife had nothing to do with her mother's death. Should you try to convince me or anyone else otherwise, you'll be facing me at twenty paces."

"We aren't implying she's responsible." Kieran countered. "Elizabeth is being attacked because she knows the truth about what happened." He paused, choking on the words he would deliver next. "Granny Sheila cursed Elizabeth along with our mother."

"Not intentionally, my boy." Barnaby turned in his seat to place a comforting hand on Kieran's arm. "Your grandmother was upset. She didn't stop to consider the consequences of what she was doing or how it would affect your sister." Barnaby placed the opened book on the desk. He turned it and pushed the page opened to the curse toward the count, encouraging him to read it for himself.

The count read the page before him, and his scowl deepened.

"There are two things we know of a certainty." Barnaby went on in the confident, steady voice he used to calm hysterical clients. "Mrs. Fletcher's death was no accident. And someone witnessed her murder. That someone, my lord, is your wife."

They were gathered in the cheery yellow salon; Elizabeth, Chloe, Uncle Gareth, Michael, his tutor, and even Grandfather Wentworth. Her grandfather had been carried downstairs in a chair by two footmen. As the house was in a morose mood after the incident on the stairs, Elizabeth decided she might arouse some levity amongst her guests by decorating the downstairs rooms for the Christmas holiday. Since the family seemed determined to hover protectively over her, Elizabeth informed them they must all help her with the task. As she was their hostess, none dared oppose her edict.

It turned out better than she expected. Everyone began sharing Christmas memories as they worked and the atmosphere became cheerful instead of grim as it had been previously. Elizabeth and Chloe were fashioning garlands from grape vines and tropical flowers that Chloe and the maids collected from the garden earlier. Elizabeth was painting sugar paste over the green leaves with her good hand, trying to mimic frost, while Chloe tied the flowers to the greenery. Michael was cutting red silk fabric into strips. The maids fashioned them into bows and attached them to the green garlands they created. Grandfather strung some red berries on heavy thread with more patience then Elizabeth thought possible for a haughty, self important earl. His fingers were stained red, but he did not utter a complaint.

Uncle Gareth and Mr. Marceau had their heads together in the far corner. They were compiling a schedule of entertainments for Christmas Eve. Even Gus O'Leary, Elizabeth's somber bodyguard, had been enlisted to help twist wire loops at intervals in the garlands the women made so they could be hung over the mantels of every room and the staircase banister.

Elizabeth wished Donovan were here to share the festive mood, yet she knew she must accept his strong aversion to social gatherings. Being shoulder deep in unexpected guests and forced to endure them throughout dinner and the evening hours was trial enough for him. Given his abominable mood of late she could not expect him to spend the entire day with her relations.

Her elder brother had become reclusive as well. Kieran disappeared directly after breakfast each morning with Mr. Barnaby in tow and they did not appear again until dinner. Elizabeth wondered why Kieran seemed so determined to avoid the family. Was it grandfather or Michael that he wished to avoid? Well, he would continue to feel an outcast in the family for as long as he chose to absent himself from their company. The only way to overcome his uneasiness with Grandfather and Michael was actually spend time with them.

Dismissing Kieran and his ill behavior, she hummed a Christmas carol as she painted the leaves with one hand. Elizabeth was looking forward to truly celebrating the holiday this year, with all the trimmings, all the festivity and food that had been denied her in years past. This year, she was celebrating with her new family and her husband for the first time, and she was not going to allow anyone's pouty demeanor to spoil it for her.

"Where shall we hang this, my lady?" Chloe asked, giggling.

Elizabeth considered the ball of leaves and berries tied together with a red silk cord. It was a kissing ball, made of some local plant she didn't recognize instead of mistletoe. "Do you think you have enough berries, Chloe?"

Her friend giggled impishly. The woman put together the kissing bough with mostly berries and few leaves, just enough to accent the heavy concentration of red berries.

"Are you planning on kissing the entire household staff and then the stable boys? You're only allowed to kiss someone once, according to tradition."

"Oh, tish-tosh!" Chloe returned, giving Donovan's uncle a hungry look. "I do not hold to your strict English traditions, my lady. I'll share the berries with you." She said with a gleam in her eye. "But I do not believe your man needs any encouragement to steal a kiss."

At that, they both giggled. Donovan was hopelessly unconventional. He kissed Elizabeth whenever he pleased, no matter who might be nearby.

"Have a care, Chloe, it works both ways." Elizabeth cautioned, "A man can entice a woman under the mistletoe. As you're the only single woman here, you may be tricked into kissing men you'd rather not." She leaned closer, whispering, "Like Mr. Marceau!"

Chloe gasped in mock horror, and they giggled some more.

"In that case, I'll recite the rule of one kiss per customer."

Pearl entered their salon and gazed about with amazement for several moments before delivering the message that his lordship required Lady Elizabeth's presence in the laboratory.

She rose and dipped her good hand in the bowl of water to rinse the sugar paste from it. Chloe stood and patted Elizabeth's hand dry for her with her apron. Pearl, always full of childlike wonder, asked what they were doing. Chloe enthusiastically began to explain their labors to the Indian and by the time Elizabeth left, Pearl had taken her place at the table.

"Mind if I tag along?" Michael was quick to make his escape. "I've cut dozens of strips from the fabric since luncheon. See, I've a dent in my finger from the scissors." He said, showing her the affliction. "I'll just have a brisk ride about the island and leave you love birds to your afternoon tryst."

"I should be so lucky." Elizabeth muttered as she paused at the oak door that formed a barricade to her husband's sanctuary. She couldn't escape the feeling of being summoned like a child to receive a scolding, as happened on her first day here. Donovan had been so moody and withdrawn of late. "Michael, I think it might be better if you go in with me, if you don't mind?"

"Been a bad girl, have we?" Her brother smirked. "Right then, I expect I owe you for the times you interrupted Papa when he was thrashing me. You were my hero. You would waltz into the study while everyone else was cowering behind closed doors, make some outrageous remark to the old boar and then he'd forget me and chase you up to the attic."

"And then I ditched him." Elizabeth put in. "He was easy to confuse when drunk."

"I hope this whipping boy bit won't become a habit. I do bruise easily." Michael quipped, feigning a helpless, wounded expression. Behind the teasing, she sensed a real fear in her brother. Donovan was now his official legal guardian so it was only logical her brother would be uneasy, considering Donovan's ability to intimidate most mortals when he was vexed.

"Donovan isn't like Papa." She paused with her hand on the knob. "Oh, he can be intimidating." She admitted, "He'll expect you to give him an accounting of yourself for what you've done if you cross him, but he just talks, Michael. There is no reason to fear him."

"Been through this a few times, have we, sis?" Michael's eyes gleamed with laughter. "I've got to see this. Doesn't he even toss a few curse words at you?"

"Of course not, he's a gentleman." She laughed as they entered the laboratory.

Donovan and the other men rose at her entrance. At the severe look on her husband's face her uneasiness returned. "Pearl said you wanted to see me?"

"Yes, darlin'." Donovan was quick to come around the desk to embrace her as if they'd been parted for a very long time, not mere hours.

Elizabeth welcomed his possessive embrace. She had become accustomed to his displays of affection in front of others. As a solitary man, Donovan did not care what anyone thought of his behavior. Even Grandfather seemed to sense that her spouse was not a man to be trifled with and refrained from directing any withering remarks toward his host. Unfortunately, the rest of the family was not so privileged as to be spared censure by the elderly tyrant.

Donovan led her to his chair behind his desk. "Michael, this is a private matter. Run along. We'll see you at dinner."

Michael appeared hurt by Donovan's curt dismissal. He eyed Kieran and Mr. Barnaby with resentment. "I'll just be off to the stables." He mumbled, closing the door.

Donovan gestured for her to sit in his chair behind the desk. She did so. He stood behind it, leaning over with his forearms dangling above her head, reminding her of a hawk perched on a nest protecting its young. Something nasty was in the offing. Mr. Barnaby, who was always a very pleasant fellow, looked exceedingly grave. Kieran, too, gazed at them with a severity.

Elizabeth's mind sprang into action, immediately fashioning an escape. She could plead a headache and retreat to her room. She considered the idea. The large hand caressing her temple settled the matter. She would not resort to lying to this man who loved her so fiercely. Donovan worried constantly over her health and she'd given him enough anxiety on that account without needing to fake a complaint and alarm him further.

No one spoke. The two men kept looking at her, as if waiting for a signal to proceed.

"Your brother and Mr. Barnaby have been investigating the haunting at my request. They've discovered something and wish to discuss it with us, my sweet." Donovan took charge of the situation. With that, he nodded his permission for the inquisition to begin.

Chapter Forty One

"My lady, your husband was kind enough to lend us this book so that we might attempt to learn why your mother's ghost has been trying to communicate with you." Mr. Barnaby held up The O'Flaherty Book of Secrets.

Elizabeth gasped, and turned to look at her husband. "You took that from my room, without asking me?" She didn't know if she was more hurt or angry at the intrusion. "That is a private journal. It belongs to my family."

"I'm trying to save your life." Donovan replied in a tone that did not welcome further debate. "I deemed it necessary to allow your brother, who is also of O'Flaherty descent, to study it for some clue as to why this is happening to you. Go on Mr. Barnaby."

Mr. Barnaby spoke in a confident, moderated tone of one accustomed to dealing with a subject most people found distressing. "Your grandmother O'Flaherty fashioned a curse that affects both you and your mother."

"That's impossible." Elizabeth argued, unable to keep the surge of emotion from her voice. "Sheila was my flesh and blood. She would never do anything to hurt me!"

"Not intentionally." The old man raised a hand in protest to her argument. "When your grandmother fashioned this spell, I doubt she had any idea it would bring direct harm to you. Yet its power is evident in your life today, just the same."

"If I may?" Mr. Barnaby asked her spouse. At Donovan's nod, he began reading the curse aloud. "*Angela Wentworth-O'Flaherty-Fletcher, your soul shall never rest, your grave will lack peace until justice is accomplished, until the wrong done to my family is avenged. You kept silent as a grave, unwilling to speak or act for those without a voice. You denied them justice through your cowardice, thus, justice shall be denied your murdered soul. By the power of three, bound by blood; my blood, Shawn's blood, and Kieran's blood—O'Flaherty blood; you'll wander this earth a restless spirit until those who know the truth are willing to speak for you and set the wheel of justice turning to avenge your murdered soul."*

Elizabeth was silent as the reality of Sheila's spell washed over her.

She never dreamed her grandmother could be capable of such unrelenting cruelty.

The betrayal brought a bitter taste to her mouth. She gripped the arm of the chair with rigid fingers. She wanted to scream, to throw something, to break something. Granny Sheila knew the years of suffering Mama endured at Fletcher's hand, yet she blamed Mama for the wrongs done to her own family and cursed the poor woman for it? Good heavens, was she senile after all?

Elizabeth could not contain the agony tearing through her throat. She gasped out her pain. She released the arm of the chair and sat forward, her head in her good hand. Poor Mama! Before the haunting, Elizabeth considered her mother to be a pathetic victim; weak, afraid of her own shadow, unable to stand up to the man who made her life hell. Elizabeth saw her as Sheila had, with only contempt, not mercy or understanding.

After being married to a man she didn't know, seeing how dependent a woman was made to be on her spouse, Elizabeth began to better understand her mother's perspective. Society was not charitable toward women. According to the law they were at the mercy of a male relative or the man they married. Mama was fortunate in that she had a powerful father, whom she might have been able to gain help from in securing a divorce--had she lived. Fletcher killed her before she could take that bold step.

And then, to be cursed in death so she could never find the peace she deserved--all because Sheila didn't think Mama dealt with Father's death or Fletcher's abusive nature in the manner Sheila wished her to. It was utterly cruel. Vindictive. Unforgivable. Elizabeth struggled to contain her tears. She would not cry in front of them. She wouldn't!

Donovan's hand was on her shoulder. He moved around the chair, and was crouched on his haunches beside her. She lifted her head to face the men before her.

No one spoke. Everyone was looking at her, waiting for her to respond.

"I am very sorry, my lady." The old man pushed his spectacles up. "This is what comes when magic is used in a rash moment of anger. The person doesn't stop to consider how the working will affect those connected to the person they've cursed. Lady Elizabeth, in order for us to help your mother find peace, you must tell us the secret you've been keeping all these years."

There it was, laid bare in front of her. Elizabeth remained silent, not daring to speak.

"According to this, we know your mother was murdered, my lady." It was the old man speaking as they all continued to study her. "You were there that night. You've been frightened, as anyone would be to witness such a ghastly crime at a tender age, but you must speak, Madame. You must tell us who killed your mother and how, so she will have no further cause to oppress you. It's the only way to free both of you from this curse."

"Don't be afraid, Lizzie." Donovan's hand stroked along her arm to settle on her shoulder. "You can tell me."

She focused on him, on his beloved face. "He said no one would believe me over him."

"I believe you, Elizabeth." His hand moved to cup her cheek. "Fletcher told you that, didn't he? He wanted you to think no one would believe you if you told the truth about what happened that night. It was the only way he could keep you silent."

She nodded, unable to speak as the pain constricted her throat.

He took her hand and squeezed it. "Your mother didn't fall down the stairs, did she?"

"No." Her voice transformed into a crude croak. She closed her eyes, took in a great gulp of air and clutched his big hand, seeking the strength he offered her.

"What happened that night?" Donovan persisted, his arm coming about her back as he leaned in to draw her close. "Tell us-- no--tell me, Lizzie. I'll believe you. I swear it."

"They were arguing." She whispered in a rough, pain deepened voice. "About Sheila." Elizabeth sniffled and swallowed the pain. "He wanted Mama to send Sheila away, literally to toss her out into the street. Mama refused. She threatened to divorce him. She said she could enlist the help of grandfather to procure a

346

divorce. That made him angry. He grabbed her by the hair and dragged her to the top of the stairs. He said, 'Useless bitch, you can't divorce me if you're dead.' And then he pushed her."

A sharp outcry from across the desk startled her. Kieran was sitting in the chair Barnaby had vacated. Kieran clutched his throat as if he were in pain. He was in pain, she realized. They were magnets, the two of them. He could feel her pain resonating within him, and it was magnified by his own at hearing of his mother's murder. Mr. Barnaby stood over him, trying to console him.

"Where were you, dearest?" Donovan asked gently, drawing her to focus her attention upon him. "Where were you when all of this was happening?"

Elizabeth gazed into pools of soft azure blue as the sound of her jagged breathing became the only sound in the room. Seeing her distress, Donovan pulled her against him. His warm hand cradled the back of her head, guiding it to rest on his shoulder, effectively turning her gaze away from their guests. He held her like that for several moments while she attempted to regain her composure. The scent of his tobacco wafted about her, and the clean, masculine smell of his skin.

At last, she recovered her courage. "I was hiding behind a curtain in the hallway outside Mama's room. I saw him drag her down the hall. I saw him push her down the stairs. I rushed out to confront him. He grabbed me and started choking me with his hand at my throat. I thought he was going to kill me, too."

"Yes. I'm sure you did." Donovan crooned. "You must have been terrified." He was nuzzling her hair at the top of her head with his lips as he spoke. "But you're my brave lass, aren't you. What happened next? Did he say anything to you?"

She nodded into his shoulder. The fabric of his vest was wet from her tears. "He said if I told anyone what I saw he'd tell the authorities I pushed her down the stairs. He said they'd hang me at Tyburn, and Sheila with me. He said he would tell them she was a witch and that she made me turn on my own mother. He instructed me to wait twenty minutes, and then summon the constable. I was to tell them Mama fell due to her Laudanum addiction, and I found her lying there at the bottom of the stairs. I was to say Papa wasn't home when it happened, he was at his club and then ask them to send word to him there about the accident."

"Cunning." Mr. Barnaby commented. "He made it appear as if he wasn't home when the incident occurred."

"Like a fox." Donovan agreed. "My poor Lizzie. He left you to deal with the authorities, and Michael. It was you who had to tell Michael about your mother's death."

Elizabeth wiped her cheeks with the back of her hand, and sniffled as more rose and threatened to dampen them further. "I told Michael she was with the angels. I didn't know what else to say." Donovan hugged her, trying to absorb some of her pain. His chin rested on her head and his strong hands moved comfortingly along her spine.

"There now, I have you. I have you, Darlin'." Donovan was crouched on his heels in front of her, supporting her weight as she leaned into him.

"Michael must never know." Elizabeth whispered hoarsely.

No one responded, no one said a word. They just kept staring at her.

"Please, it was Michael's father who killed our mother. No child should have to live with the knowledge that his father killed his mother. It would be a terrible burden for him."

"Yes." Donovan soothed. "The truth will remain here, between us. Agreed?" He turned to the two across the desk, waiting for their response.

"Of course." Barnaby said, gazing at Elizabeth with empathy. "A girl of fourteen should not have to deal with her mother's death alone, without adults to turn to. You are a courageous young woman, my lady. A singular young woman."

"Captain Fletcher will be punished." Donovan looked about the room as he spoke, as if expecting Mama to appear. "I will see to it personally. And now, Mrs. Fletcher should have no further cause to attack Elizabeth, isn't that right, Barnaby?"

"I believe so." The old man sounded less than certain. "Is that the whole of it, my lady?"

"Yes." She replied breathlessly. "Sheila never told me about the curse or what the charm bag was created for. I didn't know Sheila cursed Mama after her death."

"The charm." Mr. Barnaby exclaimed, slapping his forehead. "We will burn it, Kieran and I. Destroying the charm, coupled with your confession should dissolve the link between you and your mother's ghost, my lady."

"Thank you, Mr. Barnaby." Donovan rose and extended his hand. "I hope this will be the end of it. I'd like you to stay on for a few days, to be certain."

Chapter Forty Two

Two days had passed since the haunting had been resolved. There had been no further activity in the paranormal realm. Barnaby and Kieran were confident that Mrs. Fletcher's ghost had been released and had found peace at last.

Still, Kieran felt a dire sense of foreboding.

It was late afternoon. He was sitting beside his grandfather's bed. Lord Greystowe had been talking to him, and then paused, too tired to carry on his discourse about the responsibilities Kieran would assume in taking over the estate and becoming a member of the House of Lords.

Kieran suggested the earl rest and promised to visit him after dinner. He waited, not sure what to do. Should he send for Donovan?

Grandfather's valet was watching over his charge with a devotion that was touching, considering the earl's haughtiness. The valet held the old man's wrist in the way Donovan instructed. He nodded that all was well and resumed his post near the bed.

Kieran stood at the foot of the bed, watching grandfather as he nodded off. The old man wasn't as fearsome as Kieran expected. He'd heard about the imposing Earl of Greystowe from his father. But now twenty years later, the man seemed feeble rather than ferocious. Kieran was feeling things he didn't wish to for his grandsire; pity, concern and God forbid--*affection*.

He had no desire to become an English earl. But Donovan had challenged him when he'd laid out the miserable conditions he witnessed in Ireland recently. As the tenth Earl of Greystowe, Kieran would take his grandfather's seat in the House of Lords, and have some say in the governmental policies regarding his people in Ireland. He didn't aspire to become an English lord, but if it meant he could buy back his father's estates and fulfill his destiny as the clan chieftain, so be it.

Kieran's gut churned. Something horrible was in the offing.

He left his grandfather to the servant's care and went downstairs.

As he moved through the house, the feeling of impending disaster thickened and solidified in him. His first instinct was to find his sister.

He searched for her in the usual places, first the sunny yellow salon, then on to the kitchens. Not finding her there, he checked the count's laboratory, and finally the library.

"Kieran?" Elizabeth looked up from the book she was reading. "You feel it, too, don't you?" She set the book aside at his entrance. "Something is happening."

"We must stay together." He said, glancing at his sister's personal guard. Kieran was relieved by the two pistols on O'Leary's belt and the dagger strapped to his thigh. Even so, he had the feeling it wouldn't be enough; nothing could avert the evil about to descend upon them.

Elizabeth came to stand beside him. Kieran placed an arm about his sister, wanting to reassure her. He held the guard's questioning gaze. O'Leary, although silent whenever the countess was talking with her guests, heard much of the conversation around him.

With a nod toward Kieran, the man stalked to the window and peered through the louvered slats at the estate grounds. He shrugged, giving Kieran the clear message that all appeared well. "Looks to be a thunderstorm rolling in from the west, Mr. O'Flaherty. 'Tis not unusual this time of year. It makes the atmosphere feel tense, my lady." The guard explained.

As if in answer to O'Leary's comment, thunder rumbled above their heads.

Taking Elizabeth's hand, Kieran led her to the chaise and sat down beside her. "I think we should stay here and *concentrate*."

Elizabeth clutched at her brother's hand, relieved by his presence. She had been enjoying solitude for a sparse few hours in the late afternoon as her house guests were all otherwise occupied. She had felt inexplicably frightened and she could not understand why. She wished Donovan were here. He was busy with the cane harvest, and although he insisted she was more important than his business affairs, it would be silly to draw him away from the mill over a mere feeling she could not even justify.

"Close your eyes." Kieran instructed, holding her good hand. "Try to clear your mind. Don't force an impression, just stand at the shores and let the impression come to you, like a wave rolling in from the sea."

It was easier said than done. Elizabeth took steadying breaths in order to calm herself and focus instead of letting her thoughts race haplessly about like spooked horses.

"Michael!" They said as one, and gazed at each other with horror.

Michael was on all fours on the ground.

His head was ringing, and he saw the proverbial stars behind his eyes.

A dark shadow loomed over him from behind.

He'd been out riding all afternoon. He stopped along the road and crept into the bushes to piss. He'd been minding his affairs when something hit him on the back of the head, knocking him to his knees with blinding pain. He'd been ready to sum it up to an errant coconut hurled at him from one of the mischievous monkeys on the island, but the stench reminded him of a larger animal that had rolled in pig shit recently. There were wild boars on the island.

His eyes focused on the shadow before him, the only clue as to the entity behind him.

Michael's gut slithered and sank.

It wasn't an animal behind him. He saw the clear outlined shadow of a man.

His assessment proved true as a leather strap was cinched around his neck.

"Michael is in danger." Elizabeth stood and rushed to her guard. "Michael was out riding. Something must have happened, Gus. You must go look for him."

"I cannot leave you, my lady, until the master returns. If you'll wait here, I'll go speak to Giles." The guard replied in a soothing mien. "We'll send the footmen and the stable lad, Johnny, out to look for him. I'm sure he'll turn up, my lady." Looking to Kieran, the guard's tone became terse and commanding. "Stay with her until I return."

Kieran nodded. The guard left to find the butler. He placed a consoling arm about his sister. "He could have just fallen from his horse."

Elizabeth frowned at him. He patted her hand, realizing he wasn't fooling her.

Thirty minutes passed.

Forty five minutes ticked by.

Finally, the minute hand of the ornate clock on the mantle signaled the passage of a full hour since the guard had left them alone.

"He's been gone a long time." Kieran remarked, staring at the door. He stood and stepped away from his sister. This was strange. It shouldn't take this long to give orders to the butler. O'Leary wouldn't leave Elizabeth for a moment longer than was necessary. Kieran peered out into the hall. There was no sound of servants chattering. No sound whatsoever for a busy, bustling household full to the brim with servants and guests.

Kieran closed the library door and went to the fireplace to retrieve a poker, feeling like a boy with a wooden sword. He wished his brother-in-law were here. Donovan was a former pirate, a seasoned warrior. Kieran was an apothecary.

"I'm going with you." Elizabeth said decisively. She was not the type to sit by and allow others to act when there was trouble brewing. "Oh, why did he have to go out riding alone?"

"It's an island." Kieran remarked. "As long as he didn't go into the interior jungle, he'll be easy enough to find."

They moved to the door and hurried down the long corridor. There were no noises coming from the kitchen. No clattering of dishes or the continual chopping and clanging of pans that evidenced the cook was ruling over his tiny kingdom. There was no chatter of footmen or maids echoing from the downstairs rooms, as would be the case if they were absorbed in their duties. Elizabeth stopped in the billiard room to close the window casements as the skies opened up for a late afternoon downpour. In the absence of servants, Kieran helped her close all the windows as they moved through the progression of lower rooms.

In the foyer outside the salon, just before the main staircase they encountered Mr. O'Leary's body. Thunder cracked above and shook the rafters as Kieran knelt beside the man and felt his throat. "He's alive. Someone knocked him out." He said, indicating the shattered remnants of a large vase and tangled flowers on the floor near the guard's head. What he didn't tell his sister was that O'Leary's pistols were missing from the man's belt.

He rose, clutching the handle of the brass poker firmly in his fist. He listened. The rain pummeled the house, adding to the sick feeling of isolation growing in his abdomen. He heard muted weeping. He tilted his head, trying to locate the sound. The doors to the salon were closed.

Elizabeth was staring at the closed doors, coming to the same conclusion as he.

"*Wait.*" Kieran grabbed her elbow to prevent her from going to the salon.

At that precise moment, the front door burst open. Donovan came charging through it, his hair plastered to his head, his linen shirt drenched from the sudden tropical shower. He had a machete clutched in his fist. "Lizzie!" He breathed. His free arm wrapped about her.

He kissed her hair. While she was turned away, hugging her lord despite his sodden condition, Donovan's eyes sought Kieran's over her shoulder. "An indenture escaped in the fields. I believe he's headed here." He stepped away from Elizabeth and gestured for Kieran to come near him, out of his wife's hearing.

Kieran indicated O'Leary's unconscious body behind them, at the entrance to the hallway. "There were two pistols on his belt before. They're gone, my lord." He whispered.

Donovan nodded curtly, absorbing the information.

Elizabeth stepped close to the whispering men, unwilling to be separated from her husband now that he was present.

Donovan stopped whispering at her approach.

"Michael is missing. Gus sent the footmen to search for him." She informed him. "And something odd is happening in there." She pointed out the closed salon doors. They were never closed, not since she had become mistress here.

Donovan put a finger to his lips. He crept noiselessly to the door and tried the knob. The doors were locked. Donovan knocked. A door was unlocked and opened a few inches.

He held up his hand, gesturing for Elizabeth and Kieran to stay where they were. He stepped forward carefully and poked his head inside.

"You twisted whore's son!"

Elizabeth's heart chilled. She knew that voice. It was the embodiment of every childhood fear she possessed.

Fletcher was here?

As the heavens rumbled above, the door panel in front of Donovan exploded. His body jerked. He shoved her back as he scrambled away from the door.

"Donovan!" Elizabeth shrieked. His sleeve was quickly turning crimson.

"I'm fine." He told her through clenched teeth, his face a grimace of pain. "The ball grazed my bicep." He sat on the stairs and held his right arm up, bending the elbow. She sat next to him and peered at the slit where the bullet tore his shirt with worry. There was no hole in his flesh, just a long, ugly gash.

"I want you to go up to my room and lock the door. Kieran, go with her. I have reinforcements coming from the mill." As Donovan spoke he tore his shirt sleeve away, revealing a waterfall of blood flowing down his arm from the gash. He rolled the fabric quickly, wrapped the strip about his wound with one hand and tied it, using his teeth to tighten the knot.

He'd done this before, Elizabeth realized. He didn't look the least bit dismayed by his wound. "Why is my stepfather here?"

"Go upstairs, Lizzie. Let me deal with this."

"No. I will not hide in the closet. My brother is with him, isn't he?"

Donovan did not respond. He merely looked at her and then at Kieran before nodding.

"Our brother is in there?" Kieran snapped. The fury rising in Kieran's eyes told her that he was not going upstairs to hide, either.

Before Donovan could stop him Kieran turned and vaulted to the doors.

"Kieran, wait!" Donovan shouted. Elizabeth echoed his plea.

The door opened as he reached it. Kieran stood face to face with Sally, the downstairs maid. The poor woman looked terrified. She asked in a high, panicked voice. "He wants to know if he hit his lordship?"

Kieran turned to Donovan. Donovan nodded and gestured to his arm.

"Yes." Sally relayed the message to the man inside. "There's an awful lot of blood."

Demented laughter came from within. "Get back inside, wench, or this boy will bleed."

The door closed. This time, it did not lock. Whether Sally left it so intentionally or merely forgot to lock it again, Elizabeth did not know.

She rose from where she had been seated on the stairs, intending to rush into the salon with Kieran to help Michael. Donovan's big hand shackled her unbound wrist.

His eyes held a fury mirroring her own. "You are not going near that monster."

"My brother is in there, you great ape! Get out of my way." She jerked and twisted her good wrist in his hand in an attempt to shake free. Donovan held her firmly.

"Stop this." He hissed, seizing her by the shoulders. He shook her slightly, as if trying to bring her to her senses. "There is nothing you can do but become a target and I will not allow it."

Elizabeth kicked him in the shin with her soft slipper. Seeing it had little effect, she stomped on his foot. He didn't budge, he just glared at her.

"Michael is in need of rescuing at the moment, not me." She returned tartly.

"He wants Lady Elizabeth to come in." Sally said, interrupting their argument as her head peeped out the door again to convey Fletcher's wishes. "He says he'll shoot one of us if she doesn't give him an audience."

Outrage crossed Donovan's features. "Who's in there?"

"All of us." Sally murmured in a rushed whisper. "Giles and we three maids. The footmen and Pearl were sent out to search for Master Michael, my lord. After they left, Michael came home with that one holding a gun to his 'ead. They went in there and rang the bell. They kept ringing, one of us would answer it, and then, well . . ." Sally made a wild gesture with her hand, "By the end we was all in there with 'im."

"Stay calm." Donovan told the maid. "We'll get you out of this. How is Michael?"

Looking to Elizabeth, the maid swallowed hard. "He's bleedin', mum. Roughed up bad, he was, before they made it here."

Seizing the opportunity, Kieran pushed past Sally as she reported the situation to Donovan.

Fletcher bellowed. Sally stepped back inside and closed the door. This time she locked it.

"No!" Elizabeth jerked forward, but was held fast by Donovan's arms about her waist. Another deafening crack and another ball came hurtling through the door, this time splintering the wood panel, leaving a hole the size of an apple. There was no cry of pain from within.

"That's two." Donovan said, setting Elizabeth aside. "Good work, Kieran."

Elizabeth didn't understand what he could possibly mean by that blithe comment. What good could come of Kieran walking straight toward death? She stared at Donovan with confusion, awaiting an explanation.

He gestured to O'Leary's unconscious form. "He had two pistols in his belt. Fletcher has used the two shots. The reloading pouch is still on Gus' belt."

Amazed by how calmly her husband was able to size up the situation, she gulped and nodded. Perhaps it was best to listen to him and not go boldly rushing into the fray.

"And whatever tools he managed to scavenge during his escape." Donovan continued to explain. He placed her directly behind him as he spoke. He took her good hand and curled her fingers around his belt. "Stay right here, behind me. Hold on to my belt. Don't let go. Either you swear to stay right beside me or I'll take you upstairs right now and tie you to the bed post."

Elizabeth nodded. She didn't doubt the veracity of his threat.

He picked up the machete on the stair, advanced toward the door and knocked sharply.

Sally unlocked the door as instructed from within. She looked about to cry.

The three downstairs maids stood in a row near the doors. Kieran stood in the center of the room, several paces ahead of Donovan. Her brother remained still, watching some spectacle at the far end of the large room.

Donovan glided slowly into the salon with Elizabeth following. She tried to edge about to stand beside him, but his bleeding arm snaked around her, pushing her back behind him.

"Fletcher, let the boys go and I promise I won't kill you." Donovan said in a cool, commanding voice that would make a pirate tremble. "Let the maids go, now."

"Oh, my lady!" Sally whimpered, touching Elizabeth's arm as they passed the maids.

Elizabeth let go of Donovan's belt just long enough to gesture to Sally to slip through the open door. The woman didn't need further prompting. The other maids followed Sally's retreat. When she looked to the butler, and nodded at him to do the same, Giles refused to flee.

"I didn't give anyone permission to leave!" Fletcher barked after them.

Elizabeth cringed, waiting for another shot to come from across the room. Donovan was a large target as he advanced into the room, but as he predicted, none came.

"Let them go." Kieran insisted, aligning with Donovan as he advanced, keeping step with him. Together, they formed a shield in front of her. "They're just boys."

Them--there were two boys in Fletcher's control?

Elizabeth rose on her tiptoes and whispered in Donovan's ear. "What is happening?"

Donovan leaned left, allowing her to peer briefly between Kieran and himself.

Captain Fletcher sat in a Queen Anne chair in the center of the room. The rest of the seating arrangement had been tipped over and tossed near the wall, giving him an open space so none could approach him without his seeing them.

Not one boy, but two sat as bound captives on the floor beside him.

Michael was on Fletcher's right and Gavin, the youngest stable boy, was on the other side. Both had leather lead reins cinched tight about their necks and biting into their flesh. Fletcher held the reins in one fist, like a coachman sitting high in the carriage holding a pair of matched horses before him. Both boys had their hands bound behind their backs.

Michael's jacket was drenched crimson as blood oozed down the back of his neck. His right eye was swollen shut. His nose was bleeding. He kept licking his upper lip, trying to stem the steady trickle of blood from his nostrils that flowed over his lips and into his mouth. Little Gavin was crouched forward on the floor. His cheek was bleeding from a fresh cut. He whimpered, making soft, muted cries of desperation.

Fletcher's free hand held Mr. O'Leary's blood soaked dagger. He waved it in front of Gavin's face, and the boy cried with earnest.

That was all Elizabeth could see. Donovan blocked her view by straightening quickly.

"And just who the bloody hell might you be?" Fletcher asked.

"Kieran O'Flaherty of the Clan O'Flaherty." Her elder brother said with pride.

"They assured me a boy your age wouldn't last a year as an indenture." Fletcher spat. "I should have killed you myself. And your sister, too. Hired thugs never see it through properly."

Kieran released a sigh of pent up fury. "Tell me, do you *ever* take on anyone over the age of fifteen? Aside from women?"

"Don't taunt him." She pleaded. Kieran didn't realize how vindictive the man could be.

"Well, Kieran O'Flaherty of the Clan O'Flaherty, how do you suppose I was able to marry your Mama? Someone had to make her a widow first, didn't they?"

Kieran swore as Fletcher's arrow met its mark. "*You* sent the soldiers that night?"

"I didn't send them, boy. *I brought them*. I was the captain of the light brigade. I brought down the house of O'Flaherty, even got a medal for it. Where's that bitch your mother tried to pass off as my own? I'll have my say with the redheaded slut or this one will bleed a little more."

Elizabeth couldn't see, but as Gavin's muted weeping intensified to desperate cries, she knew precisely what Fletcher meant; he intended to use the dagger on Gavin's flesh again.

"Stop this senseless cruelty. Let him go." Elizabeth insisted, stepping out from behind Donovan. Donovan's arm snaked out as he thrust her behind him again.

"Donovan, look out!" Kieran shouted.

The machete in Donovan's right hand clattered to the floor. "Ssss—missed her, you bastard."

Elizabeth screamed. The dagger Fletcher flung at her had sunk into Donovan's arm below the shoulder, precisely where her throat had been before he reached out and pulled her behind him. Grimacing, he reached up with his free hand and removed the dagger from its fleshly sheath.

"Gavin won't bleed anymore for his amusement, my love, nor will you." Turning to her, Donovan grabbed her by the waist and pulled her with him to crouch behind the sofa.

Chapter Forty Three

Elizabeth screamed. The increasing bloom of crimson on Donovan's shirt sleeve was horrifying. He held his hand over the wound, but blood continued to flow over his fingers.

"That's a good girl." He said, "Scream for me. It's more convincing." Looking to Kieran and Giles, he gestured for them to come behind the sofa." The men did as he instructed. They huddled together behind the barricade, no longer targets for their adversary to pick off.

Elizabeth could not stop staring at Donovan's wounds. His right upper arm had been grazed by a bullet, and now he'd been stabbed in the left. He was bleeding, giving orders, trying to be noble and save them all.

"Elizabeth, get your scrawny arse over here." Fletcher's cruel voice reminded her that they were not alone in the room. "Do it now or the boy dies."

She tried to move, but that bloody hand circled her broken arm above the elbow, holding her fast. "I don't think so." Donovan's voice hissed in her ear.

Kieran inched his head up from the barricade that his brother-in-law has so wisely maneuvered them behind. He swore aloud. "No, God, no!" He stood, appalled. Fletcher was choking the little boy, literally strangling the child with the leather strap about his neck. The boy's face was turning blue as he struggled for air that was so cruelly being denied him. Tears flowed from the poor little mite's eyes as he tried to beg for mercy that would never come from his captor.

"I'll stop, if she comes over. I'll let the boy go free."

Elizabeth's head jerked up from behind the sofa. "Stop, Papa, please, I'll do what you ask--stop hurting Gavin--please--"

"No." Kieran shouted. He would not allow his sister to go near that man ever again. His fists became gnarled balls of fury. Fletcher had killed so many of his kin; mother, father, his uncles and nearly his sister and himself. It had to stop--but how? The men couldn't approach Fletcher without it costing another life, either Michael's or the boy's. It seemed he'd allow only Elizabeth to come close to him, and she was not capable of besting him in the *physical realm*.

"Don't tarry. I'm out of patience." Fletcher's hand eased the tension on the leather strap, and the child dropped forward on the floor, coughing, gagging, and weeping profusely. The bastard looked at Kieran, then, staring directly at him as he spoke. "We used this trick in Ireland. Strangle one of the cottager's children in front of him to get information from him. We'd choke them a little and then let them up for air, again and again, for as long as it took. It was effective in getting your clan to give up your uncles. Occasionally, the brats died on us. No matter, we did find the rebels, didn't we?" The man grinned, revealing his pleasure in torturing innocents.

Kieran vowed that before this day was over, Captain Fletcher was going to die. Donovan had been a fool to think he could bring the man here as his prisoner and control him. Fletcher was too dangerous to be contained by anything less than thick prison walls. It was like keeping a wild tiger on a leash; eventually the tiger would break the bonds and turn on you. And that was precisely what was happening to them now. The tiger was loose, and he wanted revenge for being captured and bound. He wanted blood. Elizabeth's blood, most of all.

As he stared at his sworn enemy with rising hatred, a noise startled him. Kieran looked behind him. Elizabeth and Donovan were wrestling on the floor at his feet. She was trying to be free of his grip, to go to Fletcher in the hope of freeing Michael and the child. Blood from Donovan's hand was smearing everywhere, along Elizabeth's arm, over her neck, her cheek and her dress as she tried to be free of his grasp and Donovan refused to release her.

The frantic weeping of that little boy sliced through Kieran's heart.

He had to do something, but what? He looked to Michael, who sat there, stunned, unmoving, not trying to free himself or help the younger boy beside him. "Damn it, Michael, snap out of it. Be a man, for once in your life--stop cowering, stand up to that cruel bastard!"

Kieran flinched at the words flowing from his mouth. But Michael was the closest to Fletcher. And although a youth, he was no scrawny specimen. He had some muscle, and if Fletcher were distracted with tormenting the other boy, Michael might be able to overpower him long enough for the other men to come across the room to his aid.

Was the lad stunned from the bump on the head?

"Michael! Damn it. Fight back. Don't give in. Don't let him win."

Donovan had his hands full, literally, trying to subdue his wife. The butler, Giles, watched them, looking with uncertainly to him for direction. "Get Fletcher a drink." Donovan instructed in a tight whisper. "A brandy, anything--get him a drink, now--it will buy us time."

Giles rose from his crouched position and darted across the room to the sideboard. Donovan heard the clink of glassware and liquid being poured.

"Here you are, Captain. My lady said you might enjoy this while you wait."

Despite the harrowing circumstance, Donovan had to smile. Giles was unshakable. He delivered the line with such aplomb, he deserved a medal.

"What's taking the chit so long?" Fletcher asked the butler.

"Well, sir. Her husband, my lord the count, ah, fell on my lady after you stabbed him. And as you know, he's a large man. I believe you wounded him quite badly, Sir." Giles continued. "She's trying to prevent him from bleeding to death at the moment."

Lizzie had stopped fighting him. She sat very still, listening to Giles and Fletcher.

Cruel laughter filled the room. Fletcher was amused by Giles' story.

Lizzie flinched. Donovan watched the terror rise in her eyes as Fletcher laughed.

"Sweetheart, it's going to be all right." He told her, "I promise--"

"--Shhh! Be quiet." Elizabeth scolded. "I can't hear them." She tilted her head. Her limbs quivered. Her eyes had a queer cast. Donovan feared she was about to have another seizure.

"Lizzie, relax. Just breathe." Donovan cupped the back of her head. "We'll handle this. Kieran and I will stop him. And help is on the way."

Reinforcements should be arriving any moment--*but where the hell were they?*

The blood. So much blood.

Elizabeth couldn't think. Her mind was frozen with panic.

It was happening so fast.

Donovan was bleeding. Michael was bleeding. Little Gavin was bleeding.

Oh, God, there was so much blood!

She gazed at Donovan's shirt, and at her hand, now smeared crimson from his blood.

Fletcher was a monster. He kept killing and killing, with no remorse. He just admitted to killing her father and uncles. He'd shot and stabbed her husband, and he was now gleefully hanging the stable boy!

What do I do? What do I do? There has to be something I can do to end this?

She gasped and shook. She couldn't breathe. She couldn't think past the horror.

But she had to think. She had to do something.

She had to stop Gavin's death. But Donovan wouldn't let her go to her stepfather.

The frantic cries across the room crushed her heart. She was crying, too, sniffling like a child when she should be out there challenging that bastard, making him come after her instead of Michael, making him so mad he'd forget Michael and Gavin and go after her, like in the old days. She could always out run him. Well, most of the time.

Donovan wouldn't let her go. He was strong. He outweighed her by several stones.

Oh, God--that poor little boy. Elizabeth longed to put her hands over her ears to shut out his pitiful cries. He needed comfort. He needed a mama to hold him and comfort him.

And then she heard it. A soft, crooning Irish burr. *A mother* was there beside him, trying to soothe that frightened little boy. Maureen's ghost was attracted to crying children. Elizabeth could hear her trying to comfort the boy, but poor little Gavin couldn't hear a word she said.

Donovan was speaking to her. "Shhh--be quiet! I can't hear them." She scolded.

She tilted her head, listening to the tumult around her.

She listened to Maureen trying to soothe the little boy.

She heard Gavin's frantic, terrified weeping.

She could hear Fletcher's laughter as the butler told him her love was mortally injured.

She heard Donovan conferring with Giles now in low whispers as the butler returned to their barrier behind the sofa. Donovan stopped speaking. He took to watching her with concern.

Elizabeth shivered as her elder brother taunted Michael. Poor Michael was beyond their reach. Michael was trapped in his own terror, like a rabbit, unable to respond even to save himself. As a girl she would always step in, challenge Fletcher by saying something outrageous and draw his ire away from her sweet little brother, who didn't deserve the beatings.

And over the calamity and tumult around her, she could hear Maureen's gentle voice.

"Maureen?" Elizabeth said the name aloud. "Maureen, please, help us."

She inched up on her heels and twisted her head to peer over the sofa back. Donovan's hand tightened around her upper arm, a stern reminder that she could not leave his side. Maureen was crouched beside Gavin, trying fruitlessly to hug the child with her transparent arms and soothe his fears.

"Maureen?" She whispered again. "Find out what Fletcher still has for weapons."

Maureen's dark, ghostly head lifted from her weeping charge. She floated behind Fletcher's back, and then turned a worried face to Elizabeth. *"He has another pistol."*

"Kieran." Elizabeth reached up to tug desperately at her brother's hand, urging him to get down behind the barricade. At the moment she tried to warn him, Fletcher reached behind him. "H-he--" Damn, what a time to stutter! "He h-has a g-ga--gun."

"Oh, do shut up, O'Flaherty!" Her stepfather bellowed over her warning. The awful smell of sulfur filled the air as the loud report of the pistol firing was overshadowed by the heavens rumbling the rafters. "I was saving this for your sister, but hell, why not? You're the heir."

Kieran dropped to his knees. He held his chest.

Oh, God. Blood, more blood?

Elizabeth's eyes grew dim. She clutched her temples, fearing she was about to faint. Donovan's bloody hand moved from its punishing grip on her upper arm to Kieran's chest as he took to investigating the wound. "Giles, your shirt." He commanded and received the hastily removed fabric quickly. Donovan wadded it and stuffed it against Kieran's ghastly wound. "It hit the left clavical bone. A few inches lower and you would be finished." He told Kieran. "Still, we need to slow the bleeding until I can remove the ball and cauterize the wound."

Blood, everywhere. So much blood. Kieran, Michael, Donovan, Mama . . .

Elizabeth crumpled. She held her head in her hands, fearing she was about to retch as the bitter taste of copper filled her mouth. She was panting, frantic, about to lose control and start screaming. Good God in Heaven--how she wanted to scream--needed to scream. Would this senseless killing ever stop?

"Oh God, so much blood--so much blood." She murmured, over and over as her body shivered and shook and her heart threatened to explode from all the violence surrounding her.

"Elizabeth, *the blood.*" Kieran shouted. He was sitting up, with help from Giles behind him. His hand reached out for hers. Was he squeamish, too? Did he feel ill when he saw blood?

She shook her head, unable to fathom his determined look or his pleading. She sat quiet and still as Donovan had instructed her to do. She hugged her knees with her good arm. She was going to be still for once and wait for Donovan to get them out of this. She was going to sit right here with her teeth chattering, her eyes burning, gasping for each breath, and wait for the carnage to end. Wait for someone else to take charge and save Michael for a change.

"The blood." Kieran said again, rising slightly and scuttling awkwardly toward her. Donovan was between them. Kieran's bloody hand came towards her. She flinched and ducked, trying to escape the grisly grasp. "Use it." Kieran insisted. "Use the blood to call forth the ancestors. You can do this. Use our blood and the power of three!"

Kieran touched her. She felt strength flowing from Kieran's soiled fingers on her arm. "Cast the circle, secure the guardians, open The Veil and bring them here--it's the only way."

The Veil Between the Worlds? The dark, gloomy place where spirits lingered?

Kieran wanted her to raise the dead, for what purpose? To confront Fletcher?

"*Yes. You are their bridge between the worlds. Call them forth.*" Elizabeth started at the voice so close to her. Maureen was beside her. The ghost had left Gavin's side. Unable to reach him, she came to help Elizabeth. "*The blood calls us. Take up the blade, draw your blood, cast the circle. Use your blood mingled with the other priest's to open the gates.*"

Blood. Elizabeth swallowed. She hated the smell of blood. It made her sick, the sight of it made her remember Mama's blood on the floor on that awful night.

Kieran let go of her knee. His eyes rolled back in his head. He wilted before them. Donovan cursed, and bent over him, muttering something about shock with loss of blood. Donovan was trying to save her brother's life. Trying to staunch the flow of blood from yet another victim, another family member fallen by

Fletcher's blood lust. As Donovan turned away from her to focus on Kieran, Kieran's eyes opened. He looked at her, his blood drenched hand reaching for hers, his turquoise eyes insisting she return to the one place that frightened her beyond words.

She eased up on her heels again and peered at Fletcher over the sofa top. He was almost done with his drink. Donovan was clever. Papa was a slave to the drink.

Fletcher noticed her looking at him over the sofa top. Those murderous brown eyes met hers. "Now that this brat's caught his breath shall we see if he's ready for another gibbet dance?"

"No!" She cried, rising, and Donovan responded by grasping her shoulder and pulling her back down. There was no way she could go to Fletcher. And Gavin would die because of it.

"Don't look at him." Donovan instructed harshly. "Don't listen to his rambling. He's trying to bait you, Elizabeth."

"He's going to kill Gavin." She told him, and clutched his soiled shirt. "He's going to kill that child unless I stop him."

"You are not going to stop him, Elizabeth. He's going to kill you if you go to him."

A noise from the hallway drew their attention to the splintered door. Ambrose stood there with several men behind him. "My lord." He intoned. He lifted a long black cylinder and aimed it at Fletcher. "The road is awash from heavy rains. Sorry we were late."

The steward's gun fired.

Gavin shrieked. Elizabeth screamed. Donovan swore.

Giles muttered a Catholic prayer.

In those horrifying seconds when Ambrose lifted the musket and pulled the trigger, Fletcher had jerked Gavin up and placed the child in front of him to shield himself from the ball.

And Michael lurched up in front of Fletcher and shoved Gavin out of the way.

She was going to faint, in the very least.

Elizabeth watched her little brother crumple with agony contorting his features.

She watched as Fletcher grabbed him, open mouthed, as shocked as the rest by Michael's action. He clasped Michael's body to him, drew the lad across his lap.

She was going to faint, in the very least.
She needed to faint, now.
If not, she didn't think she'd ever stop screaming.

Chapter Forty Four

Donovan stood. He stared, open mouthed as he watched the lad crumple in pain. He cried out. His oath was swallowed by the sounds of his wife's hysterical screaming.

Michael would have fallen to the floor in his agony but Fletcher grabbed him and pulled him onto his lap, cradling him across his knees in a maniacal antithesis of the Pieta sculpture. There was no tenderness or grief in this macabre tableau, only evil.

The clicking sound at the door told him Ambrose was reloading, determined to take down the villain at any cost. Donovan held out his hand. "Hold your fire."

Fletcher looked over at him, noting him for the first time. "Not dead? Bad Irishman."

"I'm not so easy to kill." Donovan said as he sank down and huddled close to Lizzie. "It's almost over, love. Michael was hit in the upper thigh, maybe his hip as far as I can tell. There is a possibility the ball could be deflected by the hip bone. If I can get to him quickly he'll be all right. Shhh, love. Can you hear me?"

His heart was in shreds. Lizzie was in shock, he was sure of it, distraught beyond reason as any girl her age would be in the face of such wanton carnage against her family. He rumpled her hair. "Hold on, sweetie. I'm going to end this." He snatched up the machete once more.

"The blood. There's so much blood." She kept murmuring. She was staring straight ahead, at nothing. Giles was tending to Kieran, keeping the shirt pressed tight to Kieran's wound to staunch the bleeding as Donovan instructed him to do.

"I have to help Michael." Elizabeth mumbled. "I have to go out there."

"No. I'll go this time." Donovan told her. He took her cold hand, wondering if she could hear him. "If anyone is going to play the hero, it's going to be me, not my wife."

Releasing her hand, Donovan stood. "Fletcher, it's over. Your son has been shot. Surrender and I might be able to save him."

The canny military captain looked up from Michael's pain filled face. "I've still got a hostage, don't I? Two, if you count the weeping pile of Irish shit on the floor." He nodded at Gavin's cowering form at his feet.

The meaning of Fetcher's words took a moment for Donovan to absorb.

"You would use your wounded son as a hostage? You insane bastard! He's going to bleed to death within the hour."

"The blood, Elizabeth. Use it to call forth the ancestors. Use your power."

Kieran's voice echoed in her mind. She pulled herself out of her lethargy. He was lying on the floor beside her, awake and looking hopefully at her.

"Cast the circle. I will help you. We can do it; together. Don't be afraid." He was actually speaking, she realized, it wasn't her mind playing tricks on her.

Kieran wrangled about to move closer to her, grimacing with agony as he did so. Giles was kneeling behind him. At her brother's insistence, the butler helped Kieran into a sitting position against the back of the sofa so he was sitting upright beside her. Kieran reached behind Elizabeth and withdrew the dagger that had fallen beneath the sofa after Donovan removed it from his shoulder. He held it up between them and gazed at Elizabeth with knowing eyes.

Donovan was standing above them. He was trying to talk Fletcher into giving up.

"I can't." Elizabeth shook her head. She held up her bound arm. "You must hold the knife. Hold it firm." Lifting her good hand, she dragged the fleshy heel of her hand across the razor sharp blade; not a deep cut, just enough to draw blood. She made a fist, milking the flow of blood until her hand was coated with it.

She then removed the wadded cloth from Kieran's wound and squeezed at the gory hole in his shoulder, making him gasp in pain.

"Here now!" Giles protested. "What's this--"

"Family business." Kieran ground out through clenched teeth. "Leave the countess be!"

His rebuke silenced the servant. As Giles watched, Kieran took Elizabeth's blood soaked hand and rubbed her wound against his, mingling their blood.

Elizabeth wiped her hand on the blade and then took the knife from him.

"By the power of three, bound by blood; my blood, your blood, O'Flaherty blood!" Kieran chanted aloud, looking intently at her. "Cast the circle first. Call forth the ancient guardians to guard the boundaries. You must contain the spirits within the circle."

"What about him?" She gestured to Donovan above them, attempting to beguile Fletcher with reason when physical force failed. She wouldn't get far without Donovan stopping her.

"Leave it to me." Kieran whispered as he leaned into her so Giles couldn't hear. With that, he sank to the floor on his side and started moaning. Donovan quickly crouched beside him to discern the cause of this strange new symptom. Kieran clutched his wounded shoulder and screamed as if he were on fire, giving Elizabeth shivers. Donovan started tearing Kieran's shirt away and took to inspecting his wound with concern, giving Giles curt directions to assist him.

While the two men tried to contain his thrashing body, Kieran turned his face to her and in the sparse second their eyes met he mouthed one word. "Go."

Elizabeth slipped off her shoes and moved around the sofa in her stocking feet. She understood now, bare feet helped the priestess connect with the earth and draw up the powerful energies within it into her body, enabling her to cast the circle and perform magic.

She held the dagger straight out before her as she approached Fletcher.

"Ach, you mean to come after me with that knife, little girl?" Fletcher scoffed. He still held Michael on his lap, unconscious, propped in front of Fletcher's torso so the men could not fire at him without hitting Michael. "It'll take more than a scrawny girl to bring me down."

Elizabeth ignored Fletcher. Donovan was right to tell her not to listen to him. He was a master at intimidation. He knew just what to say to hurt a person, and he used that talent to strike an emotional blow on his enemies. She kept her right arm extended in front of her and held the dagger in a horizontal line. She walked in a circle around his chair, keeping well out of his reach.

"Here is the boundary of the circle of stones. Naught but love shall enter it, naught but love shall emerge from within. Charge this with your power, ancient ones . . ." She repeated the chant in Gaelic until she completed the circle by returning to the starting point. Once there, she sealed the sacred circle and called the guardians by rote, as Sheila taught her years ago.

She could only hope Donovan didn't drag her away before she opened the Veil and released the power of the ancients. Kieran couldn't hold him off indefinitely with his false groaning. And there were Donovan's men at the door. Elizabeth turned, realizing Ambrose or one of the others might decide to come after her with the notion that they were helping her spouse by protecting her, and thus prevent her from working her magic.

"Maureen! Secure the doors." She commanded. The twin doors to the salon slammed shut and the lock clicked. Maureen's spirit materialized before them. She nodded for Elizabeth to proceed.

"Lizzie?" Donovan shot up from behind the couch, the machete in his upraised hand. "Come here. Come back to me."

Kieran's coppery head rose from the back of the sofa. He pulled himself up and hung over the sofa by one arm, looking pale and exasperated. He lunged forward and clutched his arms about Donovan's waist. "Stay out of this. Elizabeth must fulfill her destiny. Don't make me summon a Fetch to restrain you. They're obnoxious and very hard to control."

If not for the dire circumstances they found themselves in, Kieran's remark might be humorous. As threats went, it wasn't much. Donovan had no idea what her brother was talking about, and would assume a Fetch was an imaginary creature Kieran made up to scare him.

"Trust me." She said, turning to glance at Donovan. "As I trust you."

She shivered violently. Cold enveloped her body. She felt as if she'd just been plunged into an icy sea. A queer feeling swept through her, the bizarre feeling of being *inhabited*.

When she spoke it was not of her own accord. "Trust us, Lad. We will not harm the seer."

Donovan choked back a shriek. His wife just spoke to him with a man's voice.

And her eyes were . . . strange. Shimmering, glowing in a most unnatural fashion.

Kieran was hanging on him like a leech and chanting in Gaelic. A very heavy leech, Donovan thought, as he felt the Irishman's weight pulling on his hips and torso.

Damn. It was impossible for that skinny Irishman to weigh so much.

What was that revolting smell? Rotten eggs, sulfur, and vomit? Donovan scrunched up his nose, gagging from the sudden stench rising from O'Flaherty.

He tried to move. He could not. He couldn't make his legs budge. He twisted his upper body, but he could not move his feet away from where he was standing. Something was restraining him and it was not Kieran O'Flaherty. He felt hot, noxious breath on his neck. It was real, because it was moving his hair with each intake and outtake of breath.

"*Do not interfere. Let her summon the ancients. The judgment is overdue.*"

Donovan turned his head toward the throaty feminine voice to his right. As he feared, his dead grandmother was standing next to him, talking to him--*again*. When had the twin pillars of logic and reason shattered in his mind? This wasn't real, she wasn't real. She couldn't be. Yet, his mama's long deceased mother was here, speaking to him. He looked down at O'Flaherty hanging upon his waist and felt as if the gravitation pull of the earth was holding him in place. He was trapped, a useless statue still clutching the machete in his sword hand.

He looked desperately to his wife, fearing for her life if Fletcher released Michael and grabbed her. She held the dagger aloft. She had her eyes closed, and was chanting in the language of her ancestors. The room was becoming thick and oppressive. The hair on his arms was lifting, as were the hairs on the back of his neck. It was the same feeling he had on the voyage, when Miss Pemberly's ghost appeared in his cabin to harass Elizabeth---only this time, the heavy, oppressive atmosphere was much more intense.

He watched Lizzie fearfully, and then looked to the men at the door, hoping for help.

What? The door was closed? How did that happen? He heard Ambrose shouting and the men banging on it. He saw Ambrose peeking in the small hole made by the ball Fletcher fired at him earlier. Ambrose was trying to see what was going on.

As Elizabeth chanted, a curious black mist began to swirl and wend gracefully about her body. "By the power of three, my blood, Kieran's blood, O'Flaherty blood . . ." She spoke now in English and her voice was her own. Her hand was bleeding, he noted, as the scarlet jewel of bright translucent fluid sluiced down her upraised forearm.

He didn't understand what was happening.

But make no mistake, whatever it might be Elizabeth was at the heart of it.

Elizabeth was between the worlds. She stood inside the Veil, yet she was also still in the salon. She could see it beyond the protective circle she created. It appeared as if a sheer curtain of black lingered between her and the room at large. She could see Michael clearly, propped on Fletcher's lap. He seemed to be unconscious. He was bleeding from his hip, bleeding all over Fletcher as the man held him upright across his lap, a fleshly shield against the men gathered to conquer him. Looking at Michael's crimson soaked thigh she realized she had a second triad of power to call upon that would strengthen first triad.

"By the power of three, bound by blood; my blood, Kieran's blood, Michael's blood--*Wentworth blood*, I call forth the spirits beyond the Veil. I ask you as the seer and high priestess of Clan O'Flaherty to come to me and assist me in this time of great crisis. I call you to witness these rites and to judge the violent soul before me. I call those of O'Flaherty blood and those of Wentworth blood . . . as I will it, come to me, come to my aid and set us all free."

The Veil was opened, she could feel it leaking into the sacred circle she'd created to contain the spirits. The black mists grew heavier as they swirled around her. She felt the cold, damp, cloying air of that place Kieran had taken her to two weeks ago filling the room. She did not know what or who would emerge at her summons. She could only sense that something was coming, more souls were slipping through the Veil, filling the circle, coming at her summons.

Coldness swept through her. She could see her breath. She was no longer alone before Captain Fletcher. She felt them hovering behind her, waiting for her to direct them.

Fletcher's face became grey. His eyes were the size of shillings and his mouth was agape with horror. Good! It was time this wretched fiend tasted the fear he inflicted so often on others. Elizabeth swallowed the sudden gorge that rose in her throat. It was an acid bitterness. She felt as if she might become violently ill. She stiffened, fearing Donovan's admonition were about to come true; she was going to have a seizure, a nasty one, in full view of her stepfather, when she was trying to use magic to conquer him. It would be utter humiliation.

Kieran released his hold on Donovan. The Fetch had him secured and would keep him restrained until Kieran dissolved the spell. He needed to go to Elizabeth. He could feel her strength wavering. She was overwhelmed by so many spirits crowding about her. She was powerful, but still a novice in the art of necromancy. Supernatural power, undirected, uncontrolled, could be lethal to both the practitioner and to those within close range of the circle should it collapse and release the souls of the dead into the world of the living. Kieran was weakened from loss of blood. He'd have to crawl to get across the room to his sister. And it was draining his meager energies keeping the Fetch here so Donovan would not interfere.

Kieran watched and listened, adding his will and his power to Elizabeth's.

The circle Elizabeth cast was no longer invisible to the human eye. The outline was obvious; a swirling, transparent, smoky black mist contained within a curious bubble in the center of the room, much like a smoking pipe under a glass bowl. The Veil was leaking into the circle. His sister was bringing the souls of the dead to confront Fletcher.

"Captain Fletcher, we meet again." Their father, Shawn O'Flaherty, spoke through Elizabeth's vocal chords for a second time. "You have much to answer for among my people."

Fletcher seemed paralyzed with fear as he gazed at Elizabeth, who was not Elizabeth just now but their father, speaking through her so that the condemned could hear the proceedings of his own tribunal. Fletcher was about to be judged by the dead; specifically those he had killed.

The noise to his left distracted Kieran. The men were hacking away at the salon doors with an axe, trying, like men of any age, to storm the castle and save the day.

Or so they believed, in the physical realm. In the spirit realm, interference by mortal men could cause many deaths. The spirits were churned up, lusting for blood, and if Donovan's men interfered, they would die, plain and simple.

"Stop them." Kieran said, directing his command to his brother-in-law. "Tell them to be still and wait for your signal to advance."

Donovan, the stalwart warrior in the physical realm, looked at Kieran with panicked eyes. "What have you done? Why can't I move? We must protect Lizzie. Let me go to her."

"Do it. Give the order." Kieran insisted, tired of having to deal with the uninitiated when so much was at stake. "I will release you if you do as I say." He added, knowing he must release the man soon anyway as his ability to control the Fetch was waning.

"Duchamp, wait. Do not enter until I give the word." Donovan commanded.

Kieran nodded and summoned the last of his strength to chant the releasing spell.

Donovan stumbled as the Fetch let go of him. He righted himself. His sides heaved, and he leaned forward on the sofa, breathing heavily. "What the hell did you do to me?"

"I summoned an elemental to restrain you. Elizabeth needs help. I can't go to her. You--" Kieran paused, feeling as if he might pass out. He clutched the sofa, struggling to remain upright.

Noting his waning strength Donovan gestured for his butler to assist Kieran. "Put him on the sofa. You can sit down, can't you, while my wife opens the floodgates of hell?"

"Yes." Kieran held his blood slickened shoulder and allowed the two men to bring him around to the front of the sofa. They assisted him in reclining on it. "It is not hell." He corrected as Donovan pulled the saturated wad of shirt away from Kieran's wound and replaced it with a discarded shawl one of the ladies had left on the sofa. "It is the Celtic place of the dead. Not evil, a sacred place where souls wait to converse with the seer. You must go to her, but first listen."

Donovan nodded, white faced, no longer the arrogant warrior. He was a man of logic, and at this moment he must be frighteningly aware that he was well out of his depth.

"You cannot cross the circle's boundary, not with anger or violence in your heart. Only love can enter, pure love. And only love can emerge. That is a protection spell to keep the angry souls from breaking free and wreaking havoc on the world. Believe me, tracking malicious souls of the dead released from the Veil and returning them there is no easy task."

"What should I do when I reach her?" Donovan asked.

"Trust her. And remember your love for her. That will be your shield. Step into the circle slowly. You'll feel a pull. It's like stepping through a waterfall. And focus on love, only love." Kieran shivered and licked his lips. He was incredibly thirsty. "How long does Michael have?"

"Not long unless I can stop the bleeding." Donovan rose from Kieran's side, clutching the machete in his fist. "May I take this, in case I get close enough to strike Fletcher? I'm not one to go in unarmed, spirits or dark magic beside the point. Fletcher is near my wife and he's armed."

"Yes, but you must focus all your energy on love, not vengeance in order to penetrate the circle's boundary." Kieran insisted, wearied by the question. "Don't distract her--*with anything*--that is imperative. She must finish this. She needs your strength. She needs support from those who love her to be able to complete her task. Go, help her, give her the strength of your love. *Naught but love shall enter in, and naught but love shall emerge from within.*" Kieran repeated.

Donovan bowed his head. He took a deep breath, and stepped toward the circle.

Elizabeth felt herself weakening. She was going to swoon. It took so much strength to keep the circle charged, control the spirits and remain aware of everything going on around her. Added to that, a spirit had slipped inside her body, seeking to use her energy to speak to the accused. *Please*, she pleaded, trying to reach the entity, *Let me go. I can't do this with you here.*

"*My precious child, you've made me and your grandmother very proud.*" The male voice replied to her inside her head. "*All will be well, my little one. All will be well, I promise.*"

The sweetness that filled Elizabeth as her true father spoke to her was a soothing balm to her frantic, frenzied soul. His voice was like a waterfall flowing gently inside of her, a waterfall of warmth, tenderness and absolute, perfect love.

It was a timeless moment of perfection and completion that Elizabeth did not wish to end.

"Ah, my brave lad, you've come." Her father's spirit used Elizabeth's vocal chords to speak aloud. "Hold my girl. Hold her while I step away so she doesn't collapse from the shock."

Elizabeth started as solid human arms surrounded her. Donovan slipped his arms under hers and about her waist from

379

behind. As he did so she felt a sudden jerk within, as if something were moving and sloshing about inside her. And then that something very abruptly stepped through her body and stood in front of her.

She felt like a cast off garment being tossed to the floor.

Donovan's arms supported her as she wilted. She leaned back against him from within the circle of his arms. "Oh, Dear." She gasped, staring at the apparition who had stepped out of her body. Shawn O'Flaherty resembled an older version of her brother, more bulky and solid.

Two other spirits stood beside him. She recognized them instantly, although she had never met the gentlemen. They were her uncles, Rory and Pierce O'Flaherty.

"Name one of the lads after me." Her father told Elizabeth and then he and his brothers stepped into the crowded throng of spirits and disappeared among their grey shifting forms.

"Donovan?" She whispered, gaining strength from his mere name. She leaned back, against his solid form. "How can you be here?"

"Kieran sensed you needed help. He sent me across the boundary."

Elizabeth shivered violently. Her teeth chattered.

She hissed as the icy cold air sliced through her again. The abrupt cold was painful.

Someone was coming. She felt the spirit emerge from the other side of the Veil.

Immediately, there was a stirring amid the gathered souls. They stood still, recognizing the presence of a soul whose arrival was much anticipated and was essential to the outcome.

"I'm so sorry, my dear child." The female spirit whispered with deep regret before moving to stand between her and her cowering stepfather. *"I'm so sorry I hurt you."*

Elizabeth gasped. Her eyes filled with tears at her mother's words.

"William." Her mother spoke audibly in a light, sweet feminine timbre Elizabeth recalled from when Mama was alive. *"Why are you hurting my children?"* The spirit of Angela Fletcher stepped forward gracefully, inch by dainty inch. Her form

wavered, fading and then re-emerging in a jerky, inconstant manner. *"You will stop this. Now."*

"Go away!" Fletcher shrieked, clutching Michael's unconscious form against him as if his son were a talisman against the enraged spirit. "You're dead--Angela--you can't be here!"

Angela's ghost materialized into a solid form. She stood before Fletcher dressed in her burial gown. *"Yes, William. I am dead; because you killed me."* She tilted her head, one way then the other, as if puzzled, trying to understand. *"Why do you seek to kill my children? Why is my baby bleeding? What have you done to my sweet little Michael?"*

"I--I--" Fletcher blustered, his face contorting into an ugly mask of terror. "I didn't shoot him, woman--they did!" He pointed toward the doors where Mr. Duchamp had fired at him. "Here-- take him then, your precious little boy. Take him and be gone, I say." He shoved Michael's limp body to the floor and rose clumsily. He backed away, taking refuge behind his chair, as if that would shield him from Angela's steady, predatory approach.

Elizabeth wanted to go to Michael's crumpled form on the floor, but she could not. Donovan held her tight against him.

"Easy, my darlin' lass." Sheila spoke. Elizabeth turned her head. Sheila stood beside them, a solid form, just like her mother. She placed her cold hand on Elizabeth's arm.

"But Michael--he's hurt." Elizabeth pleaded, with both Donovan and Sheila.

"Ach, he'll live to give you much trouble in years to come." Sheila countered. *"Let her confront him. This is her moment. Her one chance to stop cowering and being a victim, her opportunity to initiate the justice she craves. The ancients have decided she must instigate the judgment, and he. . ."* Sheila's snowy white head tilted toward Donovan, *"He must finish it."*

"Angela--What are you talking about, my love?" Fletcher shook his head, denying her accusation, his eyes wide with pure terror as he tried to speak to her in loving tones Elizabeth had never heard him use when her mother was alive. "They shot him-- they shot your boy!" He gestured wildly beyond Elizabeth and Donovan, to the closed doors. "Go haunt them, not me."

He was shaking. Elizabeth noted the shivering of his limbs with satisfaction. Yes, he deserved to be frightened for what he had done; to Mama, Sheila, Father, Kieran, the Uncles and likely countless more. And now Michael, his own flesh, was bleeding due to his maliciousness.

But Mama was only a spirit. And a timid one, just as she'd been in life. Elizabeth doubted her mother would have the temerity to do anything more than glare fiercely at Captain Fletcher.

"You murdered me." Angela Fletcher accused. *"You murdered me, and you raised my children in fear instead of love. You broke their tender spirits. You bruised their bodies and poisoned their souls. You killed Shawn, my one true love. You sold my son to strangers. You tried to kill my daughter, time and time again. Sheila warned me. I didn't believe her. I believed you."*

Mama's pale hand rose. She pointed at him, leveling yet another accusation in the wake of so many others. *"You are a pernicious evil that must be banished from the earth."*

Before Elizabeth could blink, her mother's spirit had moved to hover before Fletcher's graying face. She snarled with malevolence. Her face became skeletal, frightening to behold.

Captain Fletcher screamed like a terrified child.

He kept on screaming when Mama took his face in her suddenly claw-like hands.

And then the screaming stopped. He gazed up at her with shock mingled with horror. He coughed and gagged. Blood oozed from his mouth.

Elizabeth cringed, and started to turn away. Sheila stopped her from turning into Donovan's protective embrace.

"No, child. It is the duty of the priestess to bear witness when judgment is dispensed on behalf of her people." Sheila's cold, solid hand touched Elizabeth's cheek, cupping it lovingly. *"Watch, record it in the Book. It is your duty as it was once mine."*

Elizabeth did as her grandmother bade. She watched Mama confront the man who abused her in life, the man who would murder her children, steal her inheritance and then spit on her as she lay gasping her last breath. Fletcher was turning blue, gasping for breath and no wonder.

Mama's hand was reaching inside of his chest. It was a transparent, ghostly hand.

"*Now, Lad. You must finish what she has begun.*" Sheila commanded, quickly wrapping her arms about Elizabeth. "*Donovan O'Rourke Beaumont, living Descendent of the Clans O'Rourke and O'Donovan! You are the chosen vessel of the ancients to secure justice on behalf of the innocent. You are chosen to be their sword of vengeance in this matter.*" Sheila spoke the decree of the Ancient Dead and the Druid priests and priestesses of ages.

Donovan remained immobile as they watched Mama's hand disappear inside Fletcher's chest. She was squeezing his heart, crushing it. Fletcher coughed, gasped and clutched helplessly at his chest. Fletcher's eyes bulged and his face was a mask of blue-grey horror.

"*Finish it!*" Sheila shrieked, raising the hackles on Elizabeth's neck as her image turned blue and she spoke in the frightful voice of the Banshee. "*Now. Dispense the Justice of the Ancients. Use the blade.*"

Donovan sprang forward, leaving Elizabeth trapped in Sheila's icy embrace. He lifted the machete clutched in his fist and swung the heavy steel blade in a wide, level arc.

There was a wet, fluid whooshing sound as Captain Fletcher's head flew up from his body, bouncing and turning slightly in a ruby spray of blood before hitting the floor.

Chapter Forty Five

Fletcher was dead. Elizabeth stared at the filthy bare feet of her tormentor.

His body lay sprawled on the floor several feet in front of her. He always wore boots.

And the sound of them on the stairs, in the halls, was the stuff of her worst nightmares.

"Close the Veil." Kieran shouted. "Send them back, quickly."

Elizabeth bent double. She dropped to the floor on three limbs and vomited the contents of her stomach onto the carpet. The scent of so much blood was revolting. Fletcher smelled like he'd bathed in pig manure. She gagged, and retched.

"Lizzie." Donovan prompted, touching her ankle. She looked in the direction of his hand. He was bent over Michael's body, but gazing desperately at her. "Send those things back. Get them out of here. You're the only one who can do it. I have move Michael and Kieran to my surgery room."

She wiped her mouth with the edge of her shawl-sling and steeled herself for the task ahead. There was nothing left to bring up. Her stomach was empty. Elizabeth rose and stood in the center of the circle. She raised the dagger. Chanting in Gaelic, she commanded the spirits to return to the Veil. Within the span of minutes the grey mists dissolved. Seeing no loitering spirits, she walked the boundary, retracting the sacred circle by pulling the energy back into the dagger and through it, into herself, as she had seen Sheila do thousands of times before.

It was done. She dropped the dagger. She stood with one hand in a sling, the other dangling at her side, coated with her blood. Kieran rose and staggered slowly towards her. She met his unsteady strides. They embraced with one arm as both of them had one free to use. Kieran's arm was bound and wrapped tight in Chloe's shawl.

"You did it." Kieran sighed and kissed her hair. "My brave little sister."

The room was suddenly swarming with men; Ambrose and his guards, Gareth, Barnaby, and Pearl. Even poor Gus O'Leary, who staggered in holding a cloth to his head. As two footmen helped him to an overturned chair another righted it so Gus could sit down.

Elizabeth and Kieran stood in their midst, clutching each other, unwilling to let go and face their curious audience. Everyone was looking at them with shock, wonder or horror.

Donovan was shouting orders, as always, as the man in charge of the world--his world, at any rate. Elizabeth wanted to lie down, to sleep, for days on end. But Michael was injured, and Kieran. Donovan, too, but one would never know it by the veracity of his voice as he instructed his men to remove Fletcher's body and bring a pallet to carry Michael to the surgery on.

"My boy." Barnaby intruded, genuinely worried about Kieran as any father would be upon seeing his son bleeding so. "I was with your grandfather upstairs. I sensed something, but I couldn't get past the count's men in the hall."

Pearl and Chloe were comforting little Gavin. Chloe sat on the floor and held the boy on her lap. She was speaking softly to him as Pearl checked the child for injuries. Johnny O'Reilly appeared in the doorway and seeing his little brother among the wounded, he ran across the long room and dropped to his knees to hug Gavin close.

"Lizzie." Donovan was at her side, pulling her away from Kieran's embrace and into his own "I could think only of getting to you. When I heard he escaped I came straight here."

His words had the effect of a harsh slap. "What?" Elizabeth cried out harshly, overcome with emotions. "How could you hear he escaped? *From where*? Where was Fletcher that he could escape and come *here*?" She demanded, knowing the answer.

Donovan's countenance became a study of shame and regret. He looked down for a moment, as if to avoid her gaze, and then, thinking better of it, he raised his eyes to meet hers. "I had him kidnapped after your rescue. I learned from Captain Sully that Fletcher hired the smugglers to abduct you. I wanted revenge. I wanted him to pay for what he did to you. So I made him my indenture. But I underestimated his--"

"*You* brought the devil to us!" Elizabeth shrieked. Everyone in the room froze and watched them. "*You brought the devil here.*" She slapped him across the face and pushed at him. He didn't budge. She hit his solid torso with her balled fist, and then pounded his chest, over and over. "I trusted you, do you hear me? I trusted you--how could you bring him here?"

Donovan didn't move. He didn't restrain her. Ambrose stepped close with an imposing frown, but the others merely watched as she vented her fury. She kept hitting Donovan and screaming at him, releasing all her terror. "How could you! You brought the devil to us! *You* did this--you did this to us--and Michael will die--"

"No, he won't." Donovan grabbed her fist at last, cupping it with his meaty hand. "Michael will live."

That did it. Elizabeth crumpled against him with frantic, terrified sobs.

Donovan caught her to him, hugging her and soothing her as she cried against his blood spattered shirt. "Shhh. Yes, you're angry with me. It's all right. It's over, my love. It's all over. Fletcher is dead. He can't hurt anyone anymore."

Elizabeth nestled against him, seeking the assurance only he could give.

"Actually, my lord. That's not necessarily true." Mr. Barnaby informed them as he stood with his arm about Kieran. "We must act quickly, Kieran, and seal his spirit in the grave so he cannot come back to reek havoc from the spirit world."

Kieran wavered. He staggered forward, looking as if he might drop to the floor.

Donovan released Elizabeth and went to catch her brother as he slumped forward. "Kieran is going to the surgery. He has a lead ball in his shoulder. Ambrose, Pearl, take him, please." The men stepped in to take Kieran from Donovan. They carried him out the door and turned in the hall toward the east wing where Donovan's laboratory was located.

"Barnaby, I believe you'll find Miss Ramirez to be a worthy assistant for your magical endeavors. Her grandmother was the

Voodoo priestess here on the island. Miss Ramirez, if you would be so kind." Donovan turned and took Chloe's hand, helping her to rise from the floor where she had been sitting with little Gavin before Johnny took him in his arms. Leading her by the hand to Barnaby, he continued. "If you're going to bury the sot, my men will assist you." He pointed to the three guards from the indenture compound, gesturing for them to follow Barnaby and Chloe's instructions.

Elizabeth watched as her capable husband took charge of the chaos around them, directing each person to a task and seeing that all the wounded were being cared for. She loved that man. He was, and would always be her hero.

Donovan crouched to check on little Gavin. Johnny was holding the boy. Gavin clutched his older brother about the neck as if he would never let go. Donovan spoke a few soft words to the boy and stroked his back reassuringly. "Bring him to the surgery." He told Johnny.

Donovan returned to Elizabeth, his face heavy with regret. "Forgive me, my love. I must leave you to your maid's care." He cupped her cheek, and brushed his thumb lovingly across her face. "I have to go pull a lead ball out of your little brother's arse."

Elizabeth's work was over. Donovan's had just begun.

He wished he'd kept Miss Ramirez and Mr. Barnaby close, as both were well versed in the healing arts and could assist him with his patients. Thankfully, his valet was present. Pearl had patched Donovan up time and again during their adventures on the Indian Ocean.

Donovan would have jumped right into the fray, starting with Kieran, but Pearl stopped him. Gareth and the stocky butler helped restrain Donovan so Pearl could examine his wounds.

"My lord." The gentle Indian argued as he held Donovan's grazed upper arm in his slim brown hands. "If you falter from your own injuries while performing surgery on these men, your dear lady's brothers, they will be without a competent physician's care."

Unable to refute the Indian's logic, Donovan submitted to his ministrations with impatience. Pearl cleaned the gash, bandaged it, and then inspected Donovan's stab wound.

The force of Fletcher's throw was hindered by his seated position and the distance of ten feet to throw the blade. Fletcher's need to hold on to his two captives with his other hand further contributed to the ineffectiveness of the knife wound penetrating deep enough to cause lasting harm. Had it been a powerful thrust close up, Donovan might be the one needing surgery at the moment or a mortician. But Fletcher was aiming for Lizzie. Had the man succeeded in hitting her in the throat where she stood second's before, Lizzie would have been killed. Donovan's battle carved hide provided a suitable shield against the sharp missile aimed at more vulnerable flesh.

He ruminated over his patients while Pearl washed his puncture wound and applied a generous paste of Golden Seal to it. Kieran concerned Donovan the most; his blood loss and the fact that he was presently complaining of his arm going numb. Donovan had to remove the ball but if it hit the sub-clavian artery, Kieran's wound would be difficult if not impossible to repair.

Michael, despite the profusion of blood seeping down his leg, was the most fortunate. When Michael stood and shoved Gavin out of the way, the ball aimed at Fletcher's chest hit Michael in the right buttock. It was a painful wound. No one could deny it. The boy wouldn't be able to sit without a cushion under his bum for a long time. Yet, with the large areas of muscle and fat padding the human buttocks, Michael should not suffer permanent damage.

Giles, Ambrose, and two footmen were hovering nearby. Pearl had moved to Donovan's cabinet to remove his surgical kit. "Did you order water from the kitchen?" Donovan asked, having learned in the orient that instruments purified by being dipped in scalding water before a procedure resulted in less incidence of infection in patients as wounds healed.

"Yes, my lord. Fritz brought it now. Which brother will you begin with?"

"Kieran." He replied decisively. "You may begin cleaning the wound." As he spoke, Donovan noted the short cook hurrying in with a steaming bucket of hot water. "Where were you when all this was happening?"

"*Moi?*" The man's moustache quivered and wiggled, like a grotesque catapillar above his lower lip. "Hiding in the pantry, *M'sieur.*" The wiry man admitted without shame. "I have no stomach for violence and blood. But I make *magnifique* pastries and *chocolat* every morning for *la comtesse.* Is why you keep me here, eh? Make the missus fat and happy, and when the mistress is happy, soon we will have little mouths to feed, *Oui?*"

Donovan waved the impudent cook away and turned his attention to his patients.

Two days later Donovan awoke alone in the bed. He'd slept later than usual, but Lizzie was not one to leave their suite before him. He found his wife in Michael's room.

Michael was lying on his side, facing Lizzie. She sat in the chair next to his bed, holding his hand. Michael was in pain. Kieran was standing behind her, his right arm resting on the back of Lizzie's chair, his left arm in a sling due to his wounded shoulder. The Irishman gazed with a fierce protectiveness at his two younger siblings.

They were silent; the three stunned survivors of a devastating domestic war that spanned nearly two decades.

Lizzie was unharmed physically, aside the wrist she'd broken a week earlier. Emotionally, it was different matter. He expected it would be some time before this last encounter with Fletcher was behind her.

As long as Michael's face was swollen and bruised, so would her heart be. The lad had taken the brunt of Fletcher's fury. He had a concussion from the blow he took to the back of his head when Fletcher initially subdued him on the jungle road. Added to that dangerous injury, Michael had a black eye, a broken nose, burn marks on his neck from the leather strap Fletcher used to garrote him, and he'd been shot in the bum. Loss of blood and emotional devastation added weakness to the lad's condition.

Donovan watched the trio, unwilling to intrude. He wanted to be with Lizzie, but he knew he mustn't be greedy about his time with her given the circumstances.

"Good Morning, my lord." Mr. Barnaby stepped into the room, looking for Kieran, he suspected. "I was hoping I might be able to talk with you regarding Lord Greystowe's condition?"

Donovan raised a brow at the man. Lord Greystowe's heart was giving out. There was naught to be done. Not even the noble Foxglove plant could help, Donovan concluded, as had several physicians in England. James Wentworth was going to die in matter of months.

"He intends to return to England soon with my boy, there." Barnaby gestured to Kieran.

"Does he?" Donovan responded. "And pray what brought about that foolish idea?"

"I was talking to him about his condition, sir." Barnaby admitted. "I may have a potion that could help strengthen his heart, giving him a little more time. You see, there is this bark that comes from South America. The natives there used it with the aged to even out the pulse."

That was refreshing news. Barnaby had been an apothecary for several decades. If the old man had a potion that could make the surly Lord Greystowe strong enough to leave his home and sail back to his own, Donovan was vastly in favor of it.

"Well." Donovan sighed, eyeing his wife, whose attention was fixed upon her brothers.

"It appears I'm free at the moment. Perhaps you'd care to join me in my laboratory."

"I'd love to." Mr. Barnaby said with the excitement of a child about to enter a toy shop.

Once Michael was asleep again, Elizabeth left him under the watchful eye of Mr. Marceau, his tutor. She liked the man. He seemed to have developed a genuine fondness for her brother. He was a pleasant, jovial fellow when out of Lord Greystowe's grim shadow, as different from the dour, stern tutors she and Michael endured as children as day was from night. Donovan appointed the man, and that explained a great deal.

She smiled at the tutor as Kieran escorted her out of the room. She had yet another reason to be grateful to her husband. He wisely chose a man to teach Michael who would do so by being his friend instead of his disciplinarian.

"Where are you off to now?" Kieran asked, following her as she moved down the hallway to the main staircase. "You should rest upstairs. You're still recovering from the stress of the other day. And the baby needs rest, Elizabeth. That's quite a shock we put him through."

"I promised to visit little Gavin." Elizabeth replied, ignoring his caution. Only Kieran knew of her pregnancy. She hadn't even noticed, not yet. But when she'd asked him what he meant when he'd chanted so precisely '*By the power of three, bound by blood; my blood, your blood, O'Flaherty blood*' during their skirmish with Fletcher as it was only the two of them to add their blood to the blade, he'd informed her she was with child.

"Walk with me, Kieran." She wanted to tell him something important while they were alone.

As they entered the garden and meandered slowly toward the stables, Kieran invited Elizabeth to sit with him on a stone bench. The Mastiffs came bounding after them, yapping and barking, frightening away the birds in the nearby bushes.

"I don't understand it." Kieran told her as Elizabeth stroked the massive heads. "How could Fletcher have gotten past these two?"

"Donovan told me; when Johnny O'Reilly went with the men to search for Michael, he instructed his brothers to go upstairs to their quarters above the stables and to stay there until he came back because of the incoming storm. Well, they did so, but Danny took the dogs upstairs with them. Danny loves them so. After the men left, Michael returned with Fletcher holding a gun on him. When he rang the bell at the back gate Gavin went to go unlock it, thinking Donovan had returned from the mill."

Kieran pondered her answer. "So, the dogs were upstairs, with Danny, and little Gavin was at the mercy of Fletcher. Damn that man. Has Gavin talked yet? Is he going to be able to talk after what that bastard put him through?"

"I don't know." Elizabeth admitted. "Donovan isn't certain if his vocal chords are damaged, or if he's just not speaking because of the fright he received." She pushed Ares' nose away from the basket of scones and strawberry jam she'd picked up in the kitchen to take to the boys. "That's one reason I wanted to visit him this morning."

They sat in silence. Elizabeth searched for the right words as she prepared to tell her brother of her decision. "Kieran, I need to tell you something. You won't like it."

That pulled his attention from the distant horizon. "You're evicting me again."

"No, of course not. It's this gift." She sighed, and licked her lips. "I don't want it. I don't want to be the seer anymore, or the priestess of Clan O'Flaherty."

"It's not something you can give back." Kieran pointed out. "It's hereditary. You'll have the gift of seeing all your life, regardless of whether you want it or not."

Elizabeth scrunched up her face. She'd been thinking of how to say this to him all night long. She hadn't talked to Donovan about it, but she knew what he would say if she did, and that solidified her decision. "It may be hereditary, but it isn't practical. Not in this time, Kieran."

"It's a timeless gift." He began, warming to his own argument.

"No, it is not." She countered. "It's an outdated tool. This isn't the 13th century anymore. We're not tribes and clans. Ireland is part of the modern world, ruled by England."

"He's talking you out of it, isn't he!" Kieran looked away with anger. "I know, it's all logic to him, cut and dried. You'd think after all that's happened he'd respect the gift and--"

"No, dear brother." Elizabeth transferred the basket handle to hang over her bound hand. She touched Kieran's hand with her free one. "Don't blame Donovan. He knows nothing of my decision, although his penchant for logic may have helped me to see reason. He slept last night while I worked this out for myself. Listen to me, please? Just listen to what I have to say."

Kieran gave a toss of his head, intimating his reluctant agreement to let her speak unhindered. He laced his fingers with hers, and stared down at the cobbled stones.

"My home is here, with Donovan. I can't be the hereditary seer and priestess of Clan O'Flaherty if I live thousands of miles away from our people. And I cannot ask Donovan to leave his plantation and move to Ireland. The gift is useless here, with me. I might still have visions, and see things in the people here, but I'm not moving to Ireland and I'm not going to be of any use to the clan living here. So, you'll have to take the O'Flaherty Book of Secrets into your keeping. It's the historical record of our clan; births, marriages, deaths, wars, and alliances spanning centuries. You must take over the charge of it and find someone to take my place when you go back to Ireland."

Kieran was silent. He kept staring at the ground, his face set. His lips formed a thin line. He removed his hand from hers, and cupped the elbow of his arm jutting out of the sling.

"Sheila wasn't an O'Flaherty by birth." Elizabeth went on. "She married the Clan Chieftain in 1740. She was an O'Malley, a descendant of the pirate queen, Grace O'Malley." Elizabeth paused, smiling at the idea of a woman pirate besting the English Queen centuries ago. "Yet, Sheila became the seer because she was married to the Chieftain. And, for the last eighteen years, she wasn't really the seer at all. Sheila was our nanny, *in England*, so the clan has been without a seer for a long time. So you see, the gift may be hereditary, and it may flow through the blood of us and our descendants, but it is still outmoded, a relic of another time."

Elizabeth paused. She didn't know how Kieran was reacting to her words. She waited.

"I don't know if I'll ever go back to Ireland." He said after several moments. "As the heir, I have a great deal of responsibility that will keep me in England."

"You'll go." She assured him. "You'll go to Ireland, and you'll reclaim your birthright. And when you do, you'll find an Irish lass to share your life with. She'll be the next seer . . . or perhaps it will be your daughter who takes my place."

Kieran shook his head, dismissing her words. "I'll take the book, if you want. But I'm not moving to Ireland. I'll be taking grandfather's seat in the House of Lords after he passes, and managing his estate at Greystowe Hall."

Elizabeth smiled. He would go to Ireland. She'd seen it, as if it had already come to pass. Perhaps he wouldn't go fulfill his destiny as a great Irish leader right away, but one day, Kieran O'Flaherty would return to reclaim his heritage and the lands stolen from their family.

Epilogue

One week after Captain Fletcher's violent intrusion upon the residents of Ravencrest Plantation, Christmas Day of 1798 was upon them.

It was the first time in fifty years that the old plantation house experienced a true Christmas. The new mistress had made certain bright greenery was festooned upon every horizontal surface of the first floor and that sweetmeats adorned every side table in the salon.

Elizabeth reveled in her new role as Countess Rochembeau. Although her title was of French origin, she was determined to celebrate Christmas in the English tradition, *sans snow*. She assembled the family and the servants together in the salon. A large table held a veritable feast Old Fritz had worked diligently on for days before. Elizabeth presented each staff member with a small gift for helping her bring the old manor house back to life.

Traditional wassail punch was served to the staff by the male members of the family and their guests, namely by Donovan, Gareth, Kieran, Mr. Marceau and Mr. Barnaby. Kieran stood at the table and used his one good arm to ladle the punch while the other men held the cups for him and served the gathering of servants for the promised toast. Michael was forced to sit on his cushion and watch the proceedings. Grandfather sat beside him on the sofa. The old earl watched the mingling of staff and servants with quiet disapproval.

After Elizabeth thanked the servants for their hard work, toasts were made for the coming year. With Giles help, she had hired a small company of players from Basseterre to provide music so they could dance and make merry at a true Christmas party. The furniture had been moved to the edges of the salon to make room for dancing.

Captain Jack Rawlings and his nephew, Peter had been invited to the party. Peter had made quick friends with Gavin and Danny, the stable lads. The trio hovered over the food table, sneaking sweetmeats and petit fours, but in truth, no one was paying them any mind as they stuffed their faces and watched the adults cavort about the parlor in pursuit of their own sweets.

Chloe's kissing ball, made mostly of berries, had become a sensation. Captain Rawlings stole more than one kiss from her. She didn't seem to mind his persistence, much to Uncle Gareth's chagrin. Mr. Duchamp and Mr. O'Leary gave the captain stiff competition as both men had dusted off their somber exteriors to don an unexpected charm as they lined up to dance with the beautiful Miss Ramirez and whirl her under the implied mistletoe.

Donovan even danced once with the dark beauty, as a matter of honor, since he was her employer, but both he and Chloe stoically avoided the mistletoe. Aside from Uncle Gareth, Captain Rawlings was the only man brave enough to ask Elizabeth for a dance, as he was Donovan's long time friend.

Donovan took Elizabeth by surprise as he smiled throughout the evening and dragged her out to the dance floor enthusiastically several times to partner him in the simple country dances. Elizabeth had no idea the man liked to dance. She expected just the opposite, as he hated being around people so and shunned social gatherings.

Donovan was happy to encourage his bride's generosity. The new staff had helped Elizabeth make the empty old plantation house into a true home. More than that, many had befriended her when she was lonely.

He whirled Elizabeth about the brightly lit salon as the musicians played another English country dance. When planning the party, Elizabeth had wisely decided on keeping the music unpretentious so the servants would not feel out of place. She was giving the party for them, to thank them in the tradition of the old days when the master and mistress of the household would put on a feast in honor of the servants one day out of the year.

Elizabeth was brilliant in the candlelight. She was wearing a green silk gown that complimented her unusual coloring. Her face was flushed, her red hair glimmering, and her sweet lips were plump and ripe, just ready to be kissed. Donovan guided her toward the conspicuous red ball hanging in the doorway, intent upon plucking yet another of the berries from the sphere to add to his pocketful. Miss Ramirez shouldn't expect to have all the kisses this night. The maids, he noticed, even brazen Sally, were being rather priggish about the kissing ball. When strategically placed beneath it, they all turned their heads, offering their partners a cheek to peck. Perhaps they were concerned about their reputations, as they were in the company of the family they served. He imagined that if the same women were at a party in the village, they'd be much more robust in their responses to the men seeking their affections.

Donovan had much to celebrate this day. His home had become more than a cold, shadowy refuge from the outside world. It had become a warm, sunny, welcoming place, thanks to the woman in his arms.

And as for his many guests, Donovan had faith that in the coming months the numbers would shrink considerably. Michael would stay on with them for a time, as Lord Greystowe had made Donovan Michael's guardian. As would Mr. Marceau, the lad's tutor. But, Donovan expected Michael would go to school abroad within the year.

Lord Greystowe seemed to be rallying his strength due to Mr. Barnaby's special heart tonic. His color returned and he seemed less tired. It was a bit too early to determine if it would be a steady improvement. Yet, the old earl was considering sailing to England when the cane harvest was over, and *The Pegasus* would make its annual journey to England with sugar cones in its hold. Donovan had been tactfully promoting the idea by promising the earl luxury accommodations on his Galleon should he wish to go through with his plans.

Yes, soon he would be alone with his darling bride, he mused, as he maneuvered Elizabeth under the hanging berry sphere.

"So, my lord." She teased, giving him a dimpled smile. "How many berries are in your pocket? I've lost count."

"Six." Donovan grinned back. He leaned in to capture her lips in a sensual kiss. He intended to add many more. He wanted a memento of this Christmas, their first as man and wife.

Lizzie seemed to have lost her earlier reluctance about kissing him in public. Her kisses this evening progressed in passion each time he whirled her to the enchanted spot that had become the most popular area of the room for the dancing couples. Alas, she'd had several glasses of wine and the wassail punch--not that he was counting, mind you.

With a little persuasion, he could spirit her away for a secret tryst in the garden.

First, he had to give her the gift he'd smuggled into the house earlier in the week.

"Let's go to the library. It's quiet in there, and you can rest for a few moments."

Elizabeth gave him an exasperated sigh. "My lord. We discussed this, remember? We cannot keep sneaking off to empty rooms and . . ." She paused, blushing profusely.

Yes, she discussed his propensity to sweep her away and have his way with her at odd times, quite often, as he recalled. Donovan ignored her lectures, as any red blooded man worth his salt would do, and just kept kissing her until she succumbed to the rising desire. And they hadn't been discovered in an embarrassing pose, not once.

"But I have a surprise to give you, my dear." He countered, grinning down at her.

She scoffed with mock annoyance. "Truly, sir? I'd hardly call your intentions a surprise any longer."

He shook his head in denial of her implication, amazed at the path her mind moved so easily down. "I'm not teasing, love. There was a package delivered the other day, from England. It took four men and a boy to move it."

That captured her attention. The wide look of pleasure and outright surprise on her sweet face was worth several fortunes. Donovan's pleasure had a bitter tang as he recalled her recent poverty while living in exile with Fletcher. The thought came that this lovely young woman hadn't been given presents by anyone, not for a very long time.

"Well, let's have a look, shall we?" He took her by the arm, urging her to accompany him to the solitude of the library so he could present her with the gift he knew she would adore.

Elizabeth closed her eyes as Donovan instructed. She couldn't imagine what would be so large that four men would need to carry it here.

Surely not more books! Perhaps a statue or furniture?

"Are you ready?" Donovan asked, holding her hands and guiding her slowly across the carpeted library to the corner, near the window. "I ordered it when we were in England. There, open your eyes."

She did so, slowly, and her eyes had to adjust to the low candlelight. There was one candelabra lit in the room, holding five candles. And it was perched on the gleaming mahogany top of a Broadwood Grand Piano. "Oh--Donovan--you shouldn't have!"

"You are displeased?" He teased. The high pitch in her voice told him just the opposite.

"It's beautiful." She turned to him with tears. "Mama had a Broadwood Grand at our home in Mayfair. Fletcher sold it to cover his debts. You have no idea what this means to me."

"Perhaps you could show me." Donovan moved to the door to secure the lock.

In the salon, the guests were deep in their revelry when a diminutive blonde woman dressed in rich traveling clothes entered the room. She watched for several moments, growing perplexed and frightened by the activities going on about her.

As the gathering continued drinking, feasting, dancing and making merry, the woman began to shriek. "*Oh, Lord*! He's done it, Rose. He's truly gone through with it!" She turned to her female escort, while the black man at the door struggled with her many trunks. "He's died by his own hand and no one bothered to send word to me." Her companion hugged her and tried to comfort her as she took to weeping. "They've sold the place. Oh, Rose, where is my son?"

"Madame?" Giles came to his senses. He put down his near empty glass of brandy he'd been savoring as it had been offered from the master's hand moments before the count had taken his bride down the hall to present her with her new piano. "Who is your son? Don't weep, dear lady, we'll find him. *I'll find him.*" Giles put in boldly, casting an appreciative eye at the regal beauty with sapphire blue eyes. She couldn't be a day older than forty, in his estimation.

"Who are you?" Her eyes narrowed as she examined him from her companion's arms.

"I'm the butler. Lady Elizabeth had me promoted, you see." Giles explained.

"*Lady Elizabeth!*" The blond woman returned with venom. "Just who the devil is she? And who are these people cluttering up my mother's salon? I demand to speak to the woman. I demand to know what you've done with my son's body. Where is he buried?"

"Alicia!" Gareth had just returned to the salon. "My dear sister, calm yourself." He hugged the dainty woman. "Your son is not dead. *Au Contraire*--Lady Elizabeth pulled him back from the edge of the grave."

The End

About the Author

Lily Silver lives in the Northwoods of Wisconsin, on the shores of Green Bay. She resides in a lovely old Victorian house with her husband, their German Shepherd and three charming cats, one who is named 'Puck', from *A Midsummer Night's Dream*. She loves to read and write historical romances and has degrees in both History and in Humanistic Studies with an emphasis in Ancient and Medieval Research. She loves to hear from readers so please send an email to her if you enjoyed this book.

Contact Lily Online:

http://lilysilver.webs.com

My Blog:

http://romancinghistorylove.blogspot.com

Books by Lily Silver

Some Enchanted Waltz: A Time Travel Romance
Available in June 2012 on Amazon
While working her shift at a radio station, a lightning storm sends Tara O'Neill back to Ireland of 1798. Tara is severely injured from the lightning strike and suffers a loss of memory. She is taken into the protection of one of the rebel leaders. Viscount Dillon, a handsome rogue, convinces Tara she is his betrothed. As her memory returns she must prevent the man she loves from becoming a casualty in the failed Rebellion of 1798.

Bright Scoundrel, Book Two of the *Reluctant Heroes Series*.
Available October 2012 on Amazon
Kieran O'Flaherty, Elizabeth's older brother in *Dark Hero*, has made a mess of things since moving to England. The scandal sheets and caricaturists regularly decry his name. He has become infamous among the Ton as a dangerous, womanizing Rake. Kieran returns to the Ireland he left as a child hoping to find his place in the world after failing to successfully navigate the intricate labyrinth of London society. His attempts to reclaim his ancestral home are fraught with obstacles. His most challenging task is convincing the Irish Beauty who steals his heart that he is not the heartless scoundrel the London news sheets make him out to be.
Coming in early 2013:

Gallant Rogue, Book Three of the *Reluctant Heroes Series*
Captain Jack Rawlings is given a mission by his longtime friend, Donovan Beaumont, (Dark Hero). Jack is to escort the beautiful Miss Ramirez to Spain, to protect her during the long voyage from the West Indies and deliver her safely into the bosom of her family. As her guard, Jack isn't so certain he can protect her from himself.